Tethered to Wanting

Constance Huddleston Anderson

Abednigo Hogge Press

In memory of my husband
Roger Ernest Anderson

In memory of my daughter
Ursula Anderson Smith

CONTENTS

i

ACKNOWLEDGMENTS

I am deeply indebted to my dear friends in the Highland Writers' Group who listened patiently and tirelessly to multiple readings of each chapter.

Thank you to Ann Babcock whose knowledge of literature is unsurpassed and whose ability to find instantly a misplaced comma or a dangling participle is hard-wired. Thank you to Kathy Oliver Brown, friend and poet, who so generously took the time to offer her friendship, cleverness, poems, suggestions, and inspiration.

I am immensely grateful to Dr. Dawn Field, an extraordinary woman at Oxford, who taught me how to structure a novel; how to paint a story using a broad brush and as many colors as I wanted; and how to move to the next idea while the paint on the previous one was drying. She also taught me to stand back and look at "the whole" of things more objectively and from a long distance. She is a woman with an amazing breadth of vision and an unforgettable depth of knowledge.

Thank you to Suse Field whose wisdom and suggestions were invaluable in making the manuscript blossom and who planted many ideas and influenced this book significantly.

Thank you to Leasha Fulton for her support and unconditional caring. I am most thankful for her gentle concern for my well-being during the writing of this book.

I am enormously grateful to June Henley Haney, my dear friend since we were twelve years old, for always believing in me and believing that I would someday finish this book about our beloved Tennessee. I am grateful for her intelligence and crucial insights, for our many conversations over the years about our lives, our dreams, our loves, our joys and our struggles. She dared to travel to Morley Mountain with me and she dared to discuss the matters that are central to this book. Her support, encouragement, and endurance through all these years and during the writing of this manuscript have made all the difference.

I am grateful to Paul Klein, a master of tenacity, who never gave up on me or the manuscript and who offered encouragement through each phase to make it better while at the same time urging me "to know when the blooming thing was finished."

My thanks to Wilma Evans Koel, one of the best storytellers I know, for her enthusiasm about this book and for keeping stories of Tennessee alive.

Thank you to Amy Baird Middleton, an immensely talented woman, who read from my manuscript as she worked on her own manuscript and illustrations and who taught me to take small steps that would eventually take me to the places I wanted to go.

Thank you to Carolyn Hevener Pohowsky who taught me the art of perspective, logical approaches to solving even the biggest problem, and how not to sweat the small stuff. Her smarts and support have proved invaluable.

I would like to thank D.B. "Doc" Rushing, a fellow Tennessean, who knows the name of every road and highway in Tennessee and who knows so many amazing, little-known facts about Tennessee history and the Tennessee landscape.

Thank you to Ishtar Stallings for reading portions of the manuscript, for encouragement, and for teaching me the simple pleasure in finding a beautiful oak leaf in September to last on my stairs until the next September.

I am forever indebted to Shirley Weissenborn, an awe-inspiring writer and passionate storyteller, who took this wondrous journey with me from beginning to end. Without her, this book would not exist. She read "the seed" of this story's beginning. She listened and read often from the warmth of Florida while we missed her from the snows of Virginia's Highlands. She offered support and brilliant advice, while creating many indelible memories.

In your longing for your giant self lies your goodness: and that longing is in all of you. But in some of you that longing is a torrent rushing with might to the sea, carrying the secrets of the hillsides and the songs of the forest.

~ Kahlil Gibran

Burden of Summons

The three of us crouched motionlessly in the kneehole of the old mahogany desk in the storage room next to the kitchen. Maudie and Ruby Grace drew up their knees, pressing them against their chins. Wedged between them, I could hardly let go of a breath.

We heard his footsteps in the kitchen and knew only a tall man had such a long stride between his steps. Maudie and Ruby Grace shushed me, although I wasn't making any noise. The sound of his footsteps stopped, and we knew he had paused at the back door.

Maudie and Ruby Grace had closed their eyes, clenched them tightly as if not seeing would keep him from us. "Or maybe they were praying," I thought, "praying our mother had gotten out of the house, and he would not find us."

We sat under the desk, refusing to move long after we could no longer hear the sound of his steps. For endless minutes we sat there, crouched in the tiny, airless space. Silent. Stunned. Not looking at one another, not believing he was gone. Believing he had discovered us and was just waiting on the back porch for us to reappear.

With my face pressed hard into my drawn-up knees, I felt my locked hands soaked with perspiration. My fear changed to anger. Nothing made sense. We, not our mother, were the ones who were scared senseless of him. Mother drew back from him one minute and provoked him the next minute, always leaving us to live in terror of his rage when he couldn't find her or when he started to think he was losing control of her.

It was late and especially quiet in the house that night. My 12-year-old brother, Robert Joseph, and nine-year-old sister, Elda Kate, were already in their beds asleep.

What started as a peaceful night had turned into an event that resembled a dream with no escape. I was working on a letter to the editor of *the Maynard Bald Press* voicing my opposition to strip mining around Egan and the absurdity of a proposal to "reclaim" centuries-old trees. Ruby Grace was busy, covering buttons with tweed fabric to match a newly sewn coat, and our cousin, Maudie, who came to live with us a few months before Elda Kate's birth, was trying to tease her hair into an outrageous "do," similar to the big hair that cost Ova Gay two full cans of Aqua Net.

My father came home and found Mother gone, and plainly, because of her absence without his knowing, the night was ending with the three of us cowering under a desk like three house mice.

At first, we thought he would calm down when Mother walked in, just fifteen minutes after he arrived. When she refused to tell him where she'd been, saying "Joe, you don't need to know where I am and what I'm doing every minute of the day," we knew it was time to leave the room. We listened from the other side of the wall in the next room and heard the screen door slam. I hoped the kids couldn't hear. Their rooms were on the far end of the house. "Good, he's leaving," I thought. Two minutes later, we heard the screen door again. Mother cried, "No, Joe, don't." Already, the three of us were crying. I bolted into the kitchen. Maudie and Ruby Grace were behind me. There we saw Daddy holding a piece of broken neon glass to her right temple.

"You're much too pretty, Helen," he said, slowly, lightly pulling the jagged glass across her cheek, "such a pretty mouth." Mother's body stiffened trying not to move her head. But her shaking was uncontrollable. A thin line of tiny beads of blood formed under her right cheek and near the corner of her mouth. She shook harder. Then, he let go and pushed her toward the door. "Go on, get out," he said, "get out of my sight." Mother eased toward the door as if letting her go was a tease, and that he would jerk her back. "She can make it to Mrs. Pruitt's to call someone," I thought.

Daddy hadn't noticed that Maudie, Ruby Grace, and I had disappeared into the storage room. He wasn't sure if we had run next door to Mrs. Pruitt's. He called my name.

I knew it was true—what was whispered about my father around Maynard Bald when no one thought I could hear. My father had always had the reputation of being a mean man. He worked hard to uphold that image and even took pride in it.

It was under the mahogany desk on August 29,

1962, that I made up my mind; on that night reason kicked in. I had to find a way to get out of these mountains, away from this place and this insane family. But, before my escape, I had to find a way to keep my father from killing my mother. Even though I hoped it was not true—what they said about my father, I knew something unthinkable was about to happen. I could feel it—a feeling as present as my own heartbeat.

But first, a plan had to be set into motion to keep Mother alive. "Coming up with a plan that will work won't be easy," Maudie and Ruby Grace warned in unison, looking at me and casting two deciding votes that the solution would fall to me. Deep down, all three of us knew, that for a problem as serious as dealing with a man like my father, we would have to discuss it with my mother's mama, Grandmother Evers, who would then talk it over with her five boys. They would know what to do, and they weren't afraid of my father or anyone, for that matter.

"Lunda Rose," he called out.

Ruby Grace and Maudie stiffened like corpses, their eyes and lips squeezed tightly, as if they, if touched, would explode like punctured balloons. I pressed harder into my knees trying not to exhale, not to bellow, letting go of unrecognizable sounds.

"Why's he calling my name?" I thought, as I covered my ears and curled my body even tighter into the kneehole of the desk. Ruby Grace and Maudie were older, but he always turned to me with his questions, which usually turned to interrogation. I had just turned fifteen in early August, but it had been this way since before Elda Kate was born: my older sister and live-in cousin baling out and leaving me in the line of fire. He chose me to question because Maudie and Ruby Grace avoided him. Maudie purposely stayed away from the house most of the time with a part-time job and a boyfriend. Ruby Grace had made her escape, a clean break, last December when she married David Martinelli. And now, for Heaven's sake, she was back in Maynard Bald and stayed at our house more than her own. When they were here, they stayed in the room they shared at the far east end of the house, coming out only when they knew they wouldn't cross paths with Daddy.

"You're the only one of us he likes anyway," Ruby Grace snapped.

"That isn't true," I argued. "He doesn't like anyone, and he only talks to me because I'm at home most of the time, since I can't drive, and he figures I will know everybody's whereabouts and their business, who called, and who came by. Of course, the one he's really interested in is Mother. He questions me because he knows I'm too scared to lie for her. The only other times he talks to me are when I show an interest in his neon signs or in watching him draw pictures."

Again, we heard his long steps fade from the kitchen and the back porch. We remained in the kneehole of the mahogany desk for another hour, feeling the air around our ears reclaim its place as it does after a tornado cell passes.

For the rest of the night, Ruby Grace and I sat in the front room near the big window staring at one another. We would see the headlights if Daddy returned. Maudie slept on the couch and looked more like she was in a coma than sleeping.

Despite their differences and alternating periods of

provocation and making amends, Mother and Daddy would sometimes go for months, once even a full year, of seeming to be perfectly fine. Most of the time they gave the impression of deeply loving one another, of being unable to live without the other. During the times when we managed to live in the same house for more than a few months, their fondness for one another led us to believe that peace between them could be lasting. There was never a warning of when or why my father would come home, start breaking up the furniture, or jerking the phone cord out of the jack. Once he even unscrewed the receivers of the telephones, removed the transmitters, and put them in his pocket, so if Mother called, we could hear her, but she couldn't hear us. I was sure he thought that after she heard the receiver being lifted, and after "hello, hello, Lunda Rose, are you there," there would be some tell-tale sound in the background that would tell him where she was. Or without thinking, she might even say it herself, not knowing that he was listening on the extension. Of course he'd thought this over, knowing she would not stay away from us, especially the two younger ones, for long periods, although Maudie, Ruby Grace, and I were perfectly capable of looking after them. That, after all, was the deciding factor for having Maudie come to live with us. At first, she was supposed to help mother when she was pregnant and after Elda Kate's birth. But now, almost ten years later, it was clear Maudie was here to stay.

Following varied and usually short stretches of peace between them, and, for no apparent reason, at least to us, the chaos would start again—the threats, the arguments, the battles, the fear, the crying, the

leaving. For several months after Elda Kate's
my father seemed calmer; we thought that p
between them might be permanent; that this might be
the golden period we'd all hoped for. But then, the
arguments and fights started again. Lately, my father's
rage and unpredictability had crossed the boundaries
of sound judgment and sanity. When one of us would
ask Mother why he was mad, she would shrug it off.
Once she slipped and said that he didn't like her
spying on him or meddling in his business.

His absences were longer, and all three of us,
Maudie, Ruby Grace, and I, slept every night wearing
our clothes, dressed to quickly escape his rampaging
or to run to the neighbors for help.

That night the three of us huddled in the room
Maudie and Ruby Grace shared, where we wouldn't
be heard making our plan. In case Mother or Daddy
came in without us hearing, Maudie turned on her
radio and instructed me to stand outside the bedroom
door listening to see if she and Ruby Grace could be
heard from the other side of the wall.

The three of us decided that night in the secrecy of
Maudie's and Ruby Grace's room that the uncles
must be told, and they must be told the whole truth.
Mother could not know of our plan for she surely
would not allow it; saying that if her brothers came,
someone would get hurt.

*　　*　　*

Only two things could scramble my mother's five
brothers down from Morley Mountain: a summons
from their mother or a plea, no matter how minor,
from any one of their three sisters. In fact, all it really

took for these women to call the uncles together was a single word.

We were never quite sure how word reached them, since the only phone in Morley was at the very back of the Bottoms Store, our name for the company store owned by the Morley Coal Company. When a call came in, news of it and what was said to Mr. Merlin Messer, the only person allowed to answer the phone, flashed across the Bottoms and through Morley, reaching even those on the far side of the train tunnel and across the mountains in Anthras, Tackett Creek, Cotula, Habersham, or Egan, in under twelve minutes. Bad news or a help-needed call could ring through the hollows in less than ten minutes, depending on the bleakness of the situation.

We also decided that night that a mere call to the uncles would not do. They would never talk on the telephone at the Bottoms Store. They seldom talked at all, much less into a telephone. And if the uncles came to Mother, she would cry and plead with them not to hurt my father. She would lie and swear that she was fine and in no danger whatsoever, knowing full well, that on this very night, he had threatened to shoot her and anyone she might call for help.

No. This conversation had to take place face-to-face. Eye contact. One of us would be required to travel 32 miles to Morley to tell our grandmother and the uncles of the situation. Maudie and Ruby Grace said I should be the one to go. Of the three of us, I had spent the most time there and was most at ease with the uncles and them with me, and Mother wouldn't be suspicious if I asked to go. I was sure it was Maudie's idea to elect me to be the one. She had bossed me around since she came to live with us after her mother, Elease, died. Neither Maudie nor Ruby Grace ever seemed to be as scared or concerned as I was about the state of this mess. I figured it was because they were older and could leave at any time. I knew, however, that they were not concerned for themselves, but for Mother.

It was taking longer than we expected to work out all the details of our plan. We emptied our purses onto Ruby Grace's bed. Among the three of us, we had enough money for me to take the 7:45 a.m. Greyhound bus that left from the Cumberland Diner and Coffee Shop bound for Jellico and stopped only briefly at the Morley turnoff to discharge or take on passengers. It would be daylight when I arrived at the Morley junction, and there was still the long walk to the Bottoms, which was perfectly safe. Ruby Grace wouldn't hear of it, shaking her head, clenching her eyes closed and contorting her face trying to come up with other ideas.

We decided to call Mr. Merlin Messer at the Bottoms Store to have him send a message to Grandmother Evers. The message should say: SEND ONE OF THE UNCLES TO MAYNARD BALD TO COLLECT NIECE, LUNDA ROSE. 10:00 a.m., TUESDAY. IMPORTANT BUT NOT AN EMERGENCY.

Not one of the uncles had ever owned a car. The five of them shared a 1949 Studebaker pickup truck with wood rails surrounding the bed. Weir had bought it for nearly nothing from a junkyard on Highway 25W near the Kentucky line. Most of the time it sat in the barn at Grandmother's house, and when on rare occasions it was needed, it never started. All five of the uncles would end up surrounding it like bullies in a brawl, circling it, studying it, cursing it, kicking its grill, lifting its hood, looking sideways at one another, each expecting that by some miracle, one of the others would be able to jolt its dead battery.

Three days after the argument, neither Mother nor Daddy had returned. I waited on the front porch for the sound of Weir's truck, hoping he'd arrive and we'd be off without Mother or Daddy showing up or neighbors noticing. Soon I saw the truck crest the hill. When Weir stopped in front of the house, he shut the engine off, but I knew he would stay in the truck. As I walked toward the pickup, he stared straight ahead and didn't speak. When I opened the passenger door, Weir didn't turn to look at me nor did he say a single word. He cranked the engine; we were moving before I closed the door.

When we'd traveled less than a quarter mile, I felt the silence lay heavily across us, and I wondered how I would survive for 32 miles. But, riding in total silence would give me a chance to think about how I would tell Grandmother. I looked at Weir's profile and thought about how much he looked like my mother—black hair with a hint of auburn and sharp, angular features. I wondered if he suspected that something was wrong. He'd never been summoned to Maynard Bald before. Inside my head, I rehearsed just coming right out with it, "Weir, I'm worried about my mother." Then I imagined he might wreck the truck, so I didn't say it.

By the time we turned onto Jellico Highway, I was already thinking about the three days since the argument. I wanted to come right out with it, to blurt out to him, "I'm afraid he's going to kill her. How long before he's dragging a jagged piece of neon glass across her face? How long before he kills her?"

No. I had to tell Grandmother first. And she would tell the uncles. She knew what to say to them and how to say it. She knew how to keep the five of them reined in.

*   *   *

The elevation at Maynard Bald, Tennessee, was high enough for the propagation of red spruce and Frazier firs, a minimum of 3,500 feet, but our ascent to the higher mountains and our arrival at Morley gave way to a separate world from Maynard Bald, a different place, one set apart from my life. I'd been to Morley many times growing up, but this time, 32 miles seemed a galaxy away. Part of me felt like I belonged here. I didn't feel afraid. But another part of me wanted to escape.

Even with the coal mine nearby, Morley's very difference was its beauty. We turned at the train trestle and in front of us a hollow opened with woods as green as emeralds, with tall black gum trees, and the scent of cucumber magnolias. Chestnut stumps, big enough for a square dance, were evidence of a past when chestnut trees made up a quarter of the old forest. The rich nuts were the big draw when farmers turned their pigs lose in the woods in September. Pawpaws (called custard apples here) grew up as a veil of underwoods along the creek bank and poked their spread-out leaves toward the ends of their branches to collect any secondhand sunlight that might break through. Witch hazel bushes and mountain laurel lined the narrow dirt road just wide enough for one car.

Weir hadn't spoken a word since he'd picked me up. I knew if we met a car, once we turned at the trestle, he would have to back up a considerable distance to find an opening in the trees or a smoothed, shallow ravine to let the other car pass. A giant overhanging rock ledge of Tennessee limestone had stranded a goat on the mountain, and, at the bottom, rooting pigs had torn bare spots between the ancient white oaks. Barking dogs ran after the wheels of the Studebaker. And, as I turned to look through the back window, vaguely through the black cloud of kicked-up coal dust, I saw a little girl—bare-footed and red-headed, wading in the creek and hopping from rock to rock. She was wearing a blue, rag-tatty dress, and she waved to us until I could no longer see her. "She looked like Josey Magoffin's little girl," I said turning toward Weir. He said nothing.

I closed my eyes as I sat in the truck waiting, while Weir moved a branch off the road. Someone had stopped behind us, and now they were talking. Weir propped his foot on the rear bumper, and I knew this would take a while. I couldn't stop thinking of the little girl in the blue dress, seeing myself in her. "I cannot be her," I thought, "she will never leave Morley. What she has ahead of her is a life of coal dust and scrip vouchers. No. Not me."

My mind returned willingly to the plan I'd envisioned in those hours under the mahogany desk: to leave this place and this family, to have choices, options. Miss Prudence Lorrineis told me I could do anything. "Anything at all," she'd say, "it's up to you. What is it that you want more than anything, Lunda Rose? If you don't know what your choices are, what your options are, then you don't have any."

I had studied on her question for a long time. "Well, what is it that you want after you get out of here?" Miss Lorrineis asked again months later, the same question Garrett Cumbow asked me years ago, when it was too hot to do anything but be still or lie on the ground under the persimmon tree and tell stories or dream.

"I'm going to write a book," I told him, "that is, after I get beyond McCloud Mountain and beyond that and beyond that. I am going farther than the Mississippi River."

"You'll never leave Maynard Bald. None of us will ever leave," he said, propping himself against the alligator-hide trunk of the persimmon tree and in the same breath boasting, "it's impossible for a girl to suck on a green persimmon and then whistle." I argued that if it could be done, I was the girl to do it, knowing that the mouth-assaulting, face-puckering little fruit was put on this earth to teach patience. I told Garrett Cumbow if I saw for myself that he could suck a green persimmon and whistle, I was certain I could do it. I thought of the anger I felt that day under the persimmon tree before I yanked up my quilt, tilted my head back, and marched home, all the while protesting, "Yes, I will leave." It was the same anger that swelled in me three nights ago under the desk.

Garrett Cumbow's dares didn't last beyond a green persimmon though. Once they turned golden orange and were soft and plump with sugar, all dares were off, and we were lured to the tree like it bore candy.

Weir slid back into the truck. I began to think of Mother again and worry. "What if Daddy came home while I was at Morley?" I thought. "What if? What if?" I wondered how Mother's life would have been different if she'd stayed here. Maybe Daddy had only borrowed her from Morley, and the mountains, and her family, knowing all the time he wouldn't allow them to reclaim her or even share her.

Many times I'd heard both my grandmothers and my mother call these mountains *the Great Forest*. That's what it was called by those who claimed to have a drop of Cherokee blood running through their veins. That's what it was called, too, by those who lifted their guns with both hands or sprawled their bodies spread-eagle across their porches when the forest was threatened by the Tennessee Valley Authority. And by those who lay on the spots of the forest cleared by bulldozers and dynamite to forge a highway across and sometimes through the mountains. "Something borrowed," Grandmother said, "if we don't kill it."

Driving through the Bottoms, we spotted in a lower meadow, a flock of wild turkeys that moved slowly across the ground like a breathing veil of fog. White oaks, yellow poplars, and a few mammoth white pines towered above the Bottoms Store and the rows of tiny shotgun houses owned by the coal company. Masses of rhododendrons grew on banks too eroded for mature trees.

Train tracks wrapped around the mountains like ribbons around a Christmas package. The winding ribbons of tracks through the Narrows between High Cliff and Morley and between Habersham and Duff were said to be the most treacherous swaths of tracks east of the Mississippi River. A yellowed newspaper article cut from a 1944 *Corbin News Journal* was still tacked to the wall behind the cash counter at the

Bottoms Store with the headline, TRAIN JUMPS TRACKS IN TENNESSEE MOUNTAINS KILLING HUNDREDS OF SOLDIERS. The people around Morley who could remember it still talked about the rescue attempt not only by the miners, who were the first to get to the wreckage, but also by those who came from every town in east Tennessee, east Kentucky, and southwest Virginia. The steep cliffs and shortage of roads meant that the rescue parties had to walk in and carry the survivors up the mountain on stretchers, sometimes handing the stretchers up hand-to-hand. The Martinelli brothers, who owned a rock and cement company in Maynard Bald, sent every piece of equipment and every man they had to help with the rescue, but it still took hours to carry the injured and the dead out of the mountains.

I had not expected the feelings of sadness that swept over me when I saw this place again. It was as if I was seeing it for the first time. And I realized it wasn't this place that brought the feelings of sadness, but rather, the thought of my mother's unhappiness. I was certain she had mistook her need to escape to the outside world for a need to escape Morley.

Grandmother Evers' house was near the crest of the mountain. Weir's house was in the hollow below the trestle and Morley Tunnel, and nearby, beyond the narrow rills of the mine, lined against the oaks, were those of the other uncles—Hoboch Lewis, Pinder, Caudill, and Purcell. Looking down at Weir's house and the other uncles' tiny clapboard houses, I wondered if Mother's conviction that she had sidestepped the legacy of this place and this life was a lie. "A mistake," I thought, "the mistake of failing to correctly identify the root of unhappiness." I knew a place didn't define a person. Mother knew it too. But now she talked about Morley like a beloved, long-ago friend who had betrayed her somehow. And yet the thought of that friend and what they had shared rested just underneath the paper-thin layer of pain. I didn't feel relief thinking about Mother leaving Morley and her family to marry my father. Leaving Morley just put her closer to the sucking vortex. Nothing more. And perhaps the thought and fear of it was akin to the friend's betrayal, reinforcing the fear of losing something, of missing something, or having something taken from you.

When Weir and I arrived late in the afternoon, the other uncles were out of the mine and congregated on Grandmother's porch. Their wives and six of my cousins were there. They were happy to see me, but how would I ever have known if the uncles were happy to see me? Not one of them said it. It couldn't be read in their faces. Only Grandmother hugged me. Seeing the uncles together and with Grandmother, I realized that she talked for them, as if she knew exactly what they wanted to say.

It became clear as I sat on the porch observing the uncles with their wives and Grandmother that they were different: not just their lack of talk, but not one of them asked for or accepted anything from another person, not even one another; they may have borrowed, but they never took; borrowers, but not takers. All of them were listeners, not talkers. Also, the uncles were fiercely protective of the women in the family, and not only their own wives and daughters and sisters and nieces, but every female in Morley. Grandmother said, "It's the way of the mountains."

Weir was the oldest of the brothers and the most complicated, considered in the mining camp as a man you could rely on to find a solution to any problem that arose in his own family or his brothers' families or any problem that confronted any person in Morley. Whiskey and silence worked well in keeping everyone, the coal mine, and this life at a tolerable distance. He had five sons, all of whom had tried to leave Morley at some time, but had ended up coming back to work in the mine. Grandmother said it was really because they were unhappy away from their people.

Weir's wife, Florence Nell, was the only one who stayed behind that night after the uncles and their wives left to go to their houses. In Grandmother's kitchen, they both leaned in as I prepared to tell Grandmother my reason for coming. I took a deep breath. They waited, bent closer to me as if they expected   me   to   whisper. "I'm afraid my daddy is going to kill Mother," I blurted out. Both were struck silent when I said it. I could tell that Mother hadn't told either of them. Grandmother sat with her arms crossed and rocked her body back and forth against the chair. She seemed to have stopped listening after that was said. When I told of the horror of the argument, that he had cut her face, and that Mother nor Daddy had been home since, she stared off, speechless; then, she put her arm around me and said confidently, "Now don't you worry none about this. It'll be seen to." Florence Nell shook her head up and down in agreement.

Finally, Grandmother asked only three questions, as if, after they were answered, she would have heard all she needed to hear.

"What was your mother's state when she left?"

"Her face was bleeding," I told her, "probably enough to leave a scar, but not enough to need stitches. I don't know. I don't know how she got away. The next day I asked Mrs. Pruitt, but she knew nothing of the argument."

"Do you have any notion of where she went? Any idea at all? Do you think she walked?"

"I don't know," I told her, "she had to have walked. Who could have driven her?"

"Who is with Robert Joseph and Elda Kate?"

"My other grandmother, Lillie Dabney," I told her, "but Maudie and Ruby Grace were there when the fight started. After they saw that Lillie Dabney intended to stay, they both left to go to Ruby Grace's house. Guess they didn't want to be there when Daddy came back."

A heaviness fell over the rest of the evening. Florence Nell lingered long into the night, telling stories, trying to ease the tension. Grandmother rocked. I knew that Florence Nell wouldn't tell Weir, but would wait for Grandmother to tell him when the others were told.

We sat in the front room that night half listening as Florence Nell told stories that Grandmother and I had heard over and over. It didn't matter. We wanted the distraction. She was as stoic and bulldogged as Weir. She was born and reared at Stinking Creek, a tiny hamlet near Clinch Mountain, where in 1780 (the coldest winter ever recorded in diaries and journals of mountain settlers), animals came to the creek bed and died there causing an unbearable stench once spring came.

We listened again to her story of how being raised

at Stinking Creek gave her the advantage of knowing how to live on next to nothing. She was a woods gardener and could persuade anything taken from the forest's edge or depth to grow: black walnut trees, honey locusts, persimmon trees, Westfield Seek-No-Further apples, butternuts, Carolina buckthorns, and wild cherries. She told of digging sapling sorrel trees to plant along the wood edge to call in the bees to its lily-of-the-valley flowers, and how she collected the pods of the stump bean tree to roast and brew instead of saving to buy coffee from the Bottoms Store. "Oh, I knew the pods didn't have a bit of caffeine in them, but I could pretend," she laughed. She told of how, in the fall, she burned places along the edges of the open patches and along the creek valleys and stream banks to encourage blackberries and wild strawberries, and how she gathered sheepnose apples to give away to everyone she knew for putting up in mayonnaise jars. "One winter, when the temperature dropped below zero for nine straight days and nights, Mrs. Tidwell fed her children nothing except fried sheepnose apples and bread until scrip to use at the Bottoms Store came from the mining clerk."

Aunt Florence Nell harvested just enough ginseng root, taking only every fourth plant, to make a medicinal potion or tea; she collected only one wild-turkey egg from nests with three or more eggs. Like Weir and the other brothers, she considered herself a borrower, taking from the mountain woods only the plants and trees that could be taken without disturbance or destruction.

Florence Nell's stories stretched into the night. As I sat listening, slumped in the huge chair, I couldn't help thinking about our arrival and seeing

Grandmother with all five of her sons and their wives. I had never talked directly to the uncles, not in conversation. It wasn't allowed. An unspoken rule. Thinking back, for men who seldom talked to anyone, they must have talked among themselves, and anytime a problem arose within one of their families, especially concerning their children or their wives, or if any problem came up at the mine, five minds behaved as one to call in a solution.

After Weir came Caudill, who asked me a question once during a summer visit, but only after I'd been at Morley for a solid week. We were sitting on Grandmother's porch, and he looked directly at me, something that had never happened before, and asked me a question. That, too, had never happened before: directing a question to me. The archaic texture of his speech sounded foreign and beautiful. Lilting at the end of his question like I imagined an Irishman would sound. Musical. I was sitting in the swing, drawing in a homemade book that Grandmother had pasted and sewn together with fishing string to keep me outside and busy. I had used a precious, full page to draw the row of houses below and the mountain behind them and the oaks, thick in the woods stretching up the mountain.

Caudill's broad face was in front of me, and his black hair shot out from his head and face in steel-like, coiling wires that resembled bed springs. His question was, "That what you see in your mind's eye or your true eye?" I was so shocked that he had spoken directly to me, not to Grandmother to ask me later when he wasn't around, but directly to me. Face to face. Eye contact. He looked eager, but confused, surprised that words came out. Maybe it was the image of the houses that made him speak to me that day. I couldn't answer.

It didn't matter that the uncles seldom spoke. They communicated among themselves the things that were important. Tomorrow Grandmother would tell them of my mother's dilemma, and they would fix it. The fear, though. How could they fix fear? They had warned my mother countless times about my daddy, but she refused to come back to Morley to live. She came back only to see her mother, brothers, and sisters. Said she'd die before she'd live another minute in black woods surrounded by people coughing up blood and always feeling the sadness of wanting something. Tethered to wanting, stricken by an insatiable longing, and the hopeless, undeniable truth that their longing may never be quelled.

As scary as the uncles were, there was something mysteriously safe in their presence. They were large men, tall, with full beards and black hair that glistened with just a sheen of auburn when the light was right. Hoboch Lewis was almost blind, so he wore round, wire-rimmed glasses so thick that, if anyone beside him looked through them, the view was as distorted as an image in a house of mirrors.

All the uncles carried guns, handguns on their persons at all times except into the mine. The coal company didn't allow pistols or any other firearms inside the mine or within 100 yards of the mine entrance. This was especially important during labor disputes and on paydays, which occurred weekly to discourage the squandering of two weeks' rather than one week's food money on whiskey. The county was dry. But the miners didn't have any problems in finding ways to get to the Kentucky or Virginia state lines to get whiskey.

My daddy, too, carried a pistol with him all the time; even when he slept, it was on the floor within an arm's reach next to him. Carried it stuck in the back waistband of his trousers unless he was driving. Each time before getting into the car, I remember seeing him slide his gun under the front seat.

I awoke to the sound of the mine horn at 6:00 a.m. Still slouched in the big chair, I felt as if I'd had no sleep at all. Florence Nell's voice still played in my head. Grandmother said she'd left around 3:00 a.m. to sleep a few hours before making breakfast and seeing Weir off by 5:45 a.m. His and his brothers' shifts would end at 3:30 p.m., and they'd be scrubbed clean and finished with supper by 5:30 p.m..

As the day passed, I could tell Grandmother was worried. She didn't talk much, and when she did, it was only surface chatter to appease me. I wondered when she would tell the uncles about my mother's dilemma. I waited on the porch for her to get glasses of water for us. Waiting for her, I tried to recall a single word ever exchanged between any of the uncles and my father. A collective loathing of my father had been enthusiastically shared since Mother and Daddy married at Morley in 1941. Grandmother had to make the uncles attend the wedding, and, although they behaved, she was sure that the only reason they didn't threaten or hurt Daddy on that day, when they were all present, was because Grandmother had warned them, and, it would not have gone unnoticed.

I thought of the stories mother's sister, Aunt Sudie, told when we were alone, stories of how every member of the Evers family tried to talk Mother out of marrying Joe Halverston, but she threatened to run away with him if they tried to stop her. "I will leave these wretched mountains, and you will never find me, never," she protested. They figured since the Halverstons were from Maynard Bald, 32 miles away was better than losing her completely.

Sudie only recently started to talk to me about my parents. Our conversations consisted mostly of her questions to quiz me to get information. After she found out I was sleeping in my clothes, she thought I was old enough to talk about such matters, saying Mother wouldn't tell her anything about her problems.

Once, just a few months ago when Sudie came to Maynard Bald and was driving me to the store, she told me about Mother's and Daddy's wedding, and seeing how the stories delighted me, she kept telling me more and more: how Morley didn't have a church or even a preacher in those days, so the Justice of the Peace was asked to perform the ceremony on the porch. The wedding was in late May, and Mother's oldest sister, Surrie, sought every wild hyacinth (they called them indigo-squills) within a two-mile distance to line the porch and steps with milk cans filled with arm loads of the blue flowers. They stored the roots of the squills in the cellar to cook in place of potatoes, a practice handed down from my great grandmother when the woods and damp hollows were still full of wild hyacinths and a time before people turned their hogs out.

Sudie said that before the wedding, Grandmother had sworn the uncles to acceptable behavior: no overt threats, no covert threats, no intimidation of any sort, no guns, no hunting dogs, no whiskey. "Not one of you will embarrass your sister," she had warned.

Tethered to Wanting

*   *   *

It was just before 4:00 p.m. I waited on the porch for Grandmother to return with our drinks, but, instead of bringing drinks, she emerged from the kitchen, carrying a large kettle and a metal water dipper.

Standing on the south end of the porch, where the planks had not yet rotted, she lifted the pot over her head and feverishly banged it with the ladle, summoning her boys. Her strokes rang out a distress call as identifiable and alarming as the horn at the mine opening.

One by one the uncles came running. And their wives: Florence Nell, Esther Ruth, Della, Lorrine, and Lettie flew out of their houses. Any child within earshot of the kettle strikes ran alongside the others. Breathless, they gathered around the porch. Once each saw that none of the buildings was on fire, they waited. Waited for Grandmother to announce the nature of the emergency.

Caudill got there first and moved in close to the porch, out of breath, bent over with his hands on his hips to gather himself. Pinder stood straight next to him, then Purcell, Weir, and Hoboch Lewis gathered next to them, their faces and hands still coal-smutted from the day in the mine. Each looked up, fixing eyes on Grandmother standing three feet above them on the stone-supported porch. Each adult set of eyes panned the crowd to account for children, as this was the signal also when a child was hurt or lost.

When Grandmother saw that all five of her sons were there, she drew in a deep breath, hesitated for just an instant, turned herself toward the brothers, and said just one word, "Helen," my mother's name. The uncles stood silent for a moment, and, without any talk among them, all five followed Grandmother into the house. Everyone else including the uncles' wives and children walked back to their houses.

I sat on the rock steps for a few minutes, then walked to a part of the woods familiar to me since I was a little girl. I stood there for a long while among the giant white oaks and hickories. There was a certain dignity, a nobleness that existed among these trees. When I played here years ago, I felt they closed in around me providing protection from the outside world.

I thought about the gobbler, a dastard that chased me into the woods—the most hated, spineless, ill-tempered animal on earth. I was little, and he stood just tall enough to look at me square. He would run toward me, flog me, spur at me, and charge with his elbow and wing extended.

I could see the black pond where Robert Joseph and I had waded so many years ago. Once, on a rare occasion when Daddy had come with us to Morley, he warned us not to go near the pond, but we couldn't resist the over-turned, rotting boat at the edge. We shed our shoes and waded into the black water to our waists to turn the boat over. Robert Joseph started squealing, clutching at his groin. He stripped off his underwear to see that black leeches had attached themselves to every inch of him from his feet to his waist, adhering to him like a live cloak. We both panicked. And as we pulled them off, he cried, "Daddy will kill us." Thinking back on it, I knew now that, even then, we were more afraid of our father than of the leeches.

I thought of my mother. "Where was she? Where was she hiding?" A red-tailed hawk flew over delivering its piercing call. It had been an hour since Grandmother had summoned the uncles. "How much was she telling them? Would she tell them the whole truth?"

I returned to the porch. The meeting had lasted over two hours now. I could hear the low timbre of her speech, as distinctively hers, as if she had a language all to herself.

The deadbolt sounded. The uncles filed out, each one's eyes meeting mine as they left the porch. Eye contact. A first. It was as if they were acknowledging my presence there for the first time. They walked back to the Bottoms together.

*   *   *

That night I couldn't sleep, or even get into bed for that matter. I sat numbed in the ugly mohair chair in Grandmother's living room, my body drawn up as tightly as a circus contortionist. I wrapped myself in a quilt, pulling it up to my mouth as if it could shield me somehow from what I had done. "What had I done?" I thought, going over it in my head. "Sentenced my daddy?" I knew how the uncles felt about my mother. She was their baby sister. She was special, beautiful, vulnerable. Their favorite. Perhaps because she was most like their mother. Perfect. A perfect woman who deserved a beautiful life, a life where she could wear white dresses and read books all day.

"How could I balance it? How could I choose?" I knew what the uncles would do to protect my mother. They hated him even before they knew about his threats. He wasn't one of *them*. He wasn't from the mountains. He was a Halverston. I knew that without their protection, Daddy would kill her eventually. It wouldn't happen right away, but it would happen. A see-saw. A choice too hard to make. Mother? Father? I pulled the quilt tighter around my head so Grandmother wouldn't hear. I cried until nothing was left inside me. What had I done? What had I done when given the burden of summons? Maudie and Ruby Grace had given *me* the burden of telling Grandmother—a load too heavy. And she had summoned her boys.

I stayed inside the next day. After packing my bag, I waited for the sound of the 3:30 p.m. horn at the mine. At 4:00 p.m. I saw Weir opening the barn door to get the truck. I thought he might talk to me, ask me questions, but he didn't. He knew the purpose of this trip. Weir, the other uncles, and Grandmother were of the Evers' single mind—when an Evers, especially a female, was in trouble, it must be seen to. And without any hullabaloo or crying.

Grandmother walked with me to the truck. While Weir slid his pistol under the seat, she pulled a small package from under her arm. It was wrapped in newspaper and tied with twine. "I asked Merlin Messer if he could get me a little roll of white butcher paper," she said, "made myself a pattern and finally got all the sheets torn to the same size. Folded the 15-inch papers once and stitched them together with a centipede binding of black cotton thread. I thought you needed a book of paper for your drawing and for writing your stories." It was at that moment I understood that the golden time—the time we were all waiting for—would never come. There would never be a time when my parents would live together peacefully, lovingly. It was akin to waiting for the persimmons to ripen, for the precise time they became laden with sugar, their skins a golden orange. Just hours later, they would be brown, rotten.

As we were leaving, unexpected feelings gathered inside me, making my throat swell with dryness, closing off any chance of normal speech, even though it wouldn't be needed.

I was changed. And there was no going back. I was lighter. Older. Not a traitor. No. I'd safely held over nine years of secrets, spilled my guts of nine years of fear, and now someone had smacked the ladle for me. They would not tell Mother I came, nor that they knew of her situation. They would wait for her to tell them.

Then, as we reached the Bottoms, passing the white oaks and the company houses, passing the Bottoms Store with its rotten boards, an unnerving calmness flooded over me. In the leaden silence inside the truck, I kept thinking, wondering if there was an escape from Morley and this life for my mother or for me? You never forget the smell of magnolia pods rotting on the damp floor of the woods nor the sounds of hogs running loose, rooting in the dead leaves.

As we crossed the wooden bridge over the creek, the same little barefoot girl with the dirty dress waved to us, smiling as she stepped from rock to rock. I waved back. "I was leaving," I thought, "and she never will." She went on waving, and the coal dust disturbed by our tires rained down on her like tiny black diamonds.

Yearning for More than a Whole Dress

In April, it had been eight months since the fight when both Mother and Daddy left. My father's mother had stayed with us the entire time, only returning to her house when she needed something and when we were at school.

I sat at the big, east window and thought about the ache pulsating inside me, an ache I'd felt as long as I could remember. At first the constant gnawing was hardly noticeable, and I was barely aware of the chronic condition until I started to think about the symptoms, how they appeared holding hands, strung together like cut-out paper dolls, each arm supporting the next one. Fear held onto dread. Dread held hands with worry. Anger held onto sadness. All strung together, paper-thin sculptures holding each other up. Supporting. Colluding. Each keeping one another not only alive, but thriving.

These maladies and miseries had plagued the

Halverstons, my father's side of the family, across generations—the family's hand-me-downs that were never talked about. I used to think that every family must be cursed with at least a few problems, but as I got older, I began to think the Halverstons were, by no fault of their own, just an entire family of crazy people. Finally, I realized these weren't curses at all, but *traits*. All this time I'd thought Cousin Maudie was intentionally mean and only to me, when, in truth, she simply couldn't help it; she was mean to everyone. Aunt Winnifred's hysteria, when she didn't get her way, was a trait—maybe one she was born with or maybe she was self-taught in nurturing it. It didn't matter how these traits came about. What mattered was that these unwanted traits were as much a part of our family as gray eyes and east-Tennessee accents.

It all started long before my great grandfather, Ira Odell Halverston, came to Maynard Bald from Virginia by way of the Cumberland Gap around the same time the Louisville and Nashville and the Clinchfield Railroads opened up the back country. Ira brought with him a special combination of ingredients for making what he called *heavy absinthe*: wormwood, sweet fennel, hyssop, lemon balm, green anise, and one other secret ingredient that he refused to divulge. His sons and grandsons figured out a way to propagate the foul-smelling wormwood shrub brought to the mountains by Ira. Grandmother maintained the secret ingredient was probably a certain strength of white mule, but that was only her opinion, since the stories of how the Halverstons arrived in east Tennessee, how they made their money, which maladies and questionable peculiarities afflicted each one, and tales of their blood

connections varied depending on which member of
the family was telling the story.

Like his father, my grandfather, William Oscar
(everyone called him W.O.) Halverston, never
acknowledged that absinthe or any other spirit had
anything to do with the Halverstons' livelihood.

He claimed that his first recorded ancestor to walk
on American soil was John Halverston, who came to
this country from Radcliff, Middlesex, England, in
1713, and settled in Norfolk, Virginia, where he died
in 1735. His successors spread out through other
parts of Virginia and Kentucky making their way to
Pocahontas County, Virginia (now West Virginia),
eventually making their way from Pocahontas County
and the Blackwater area of Virginia to the mountains
of east Tennessee (Maynard Bald and Jacksboro) by
way of Kentucky.

One thing you could always count on regardless of
where we came from, the state or house in which we
lived, or the genetic lineage of our family, was that a
crisis, apart from my personal crisis of not knowing
the sensation of full, always existed. For a relatively
small family, there was never enough of anything:
food, attention, acknowledgment, words, place; the
only things we had too many of were secrets.

If someone had broken me open when I was
fourteen, all they would have found would have been
a bottomless hole, an abyss that folded in on itself. At
least that was how I felt. And later when I thought of
the events and the course of things when I was even
younger, at impressionable stages, when the self was
forming, supposedly getting filled up, little by little
with each year of life; my matter, my entire length, the
essence of what living fills you up with, consisted of

longing—a transcendent longing so powerful that it threatened to take me over.

Of all the elements that eventually become parts of us and shape us into adults, fear was the most robust of the conniving, hand-holding culprits. I had learned to be afraid. Fear was the symptom that jarred all the others into full momentum. I longed to be without it, to spend just one glorious day without a sensation so biting that it caused me to jerk myself awake from dreams that I couldn't even recall. "How difficult could it be to purge the little squatter?" I thought, "after all, a person isn't just born with a bunch of hoarded-up, fully-grown fear. Something has to make her that way."

My father's mother, Lillie Dabney Halverston, always thought of me as her personal charge, making me her mission, and declaring right off that she would not permit me to sit by idly and let life pass me by, nor would she allow any Halverston to inflict their craziness on me.

"It is beyond my control that Lunda Rose is genetically predisposed by default to some of the less-than-desirable Halverston traits," she said once, pointing out my know-it-all attitude, bossiness, my uncensored, unfiltered, run-away tongue, and my inability to control every thought and impulse that popped into my brain. "She can't do anything about being born into this family," she announced, "but none of you will impose your thinking or your ways on her."

*   *   *

I wondered when my father would come home

again, swooping down on our world with the easy stealth of a searching raptor, rattling every one of us, freezing us in place like a pack of cowering mice too stunned to run for cover.

It was at the east window that I sat to daydream and to calm myself. It provided a clear view of the road to the top of the mountain. It also gave way to morning light that this time of year striped the floor and danced across the walls like little ballerinas wearing chartreuse net skirts.

The sloth of the willow, Lillie Dabney called it—those days in late April and early May when sleeping buds buried deep in the willow, still swaddled in a sheath of chartreuse, struggled to break loose and spread across the mountain like wispy green lace.

"Souls get lost in the gray of winter," she'd say, "lose their way, wander off like thoughtless children." She'd sometimes sit staring through the east window for hours—waiting: for darkness to swallow up the mountains and woods; for chartreuse skirts; for morning light; for longer days.

The east window had been my favorite place in the house since we'd moved in over two years ago. Ruby Grace and I calculated that it had been about 27 months. This was the longest we had lived in the same house, except *the Petticourt house* on Depot Road, where we lived for 29 months. Ruby Grace and I had made a game of naming our houses and trying to remember how long we were there. We called this one, *the Longmire house*, after the owner.

It was an old house with dark wood floors and mantles. The windows were of wavy glass and surrounded with dark wood trim. Grandmother called the east window, *the Janus window*, a big Gothic-shaped, wall-piercing hole that happened to have a glass in it and a frame around it. Above it, a fearsome, two-headed wood carving of Janus, God of Beginnings, stood watch over the room. "He can be your very own Janus, Sweets," she'd said, "looking back and looking forward. Imagine the big window as a gate. I suppose a window is a gate—looking in, looking out, depending on which side of the gate you're standing."

The carved faces troubled me at first, but I eventually started to take a strange comfort in their presence and silence, much like the solace that came with the indelible color of gray that colored sadness and coal dust, the same hue that ushered dusk light and the mist that rose from the mountains just before dark.

From the big window I could see Cumberland Mountain clearly up the road to the top of the ridge where the road parted naked trees. "I would see his car coming," I thought, "I'd know he was coming before I heard his long-spaced footsteps on the front porch."

It had been eight months since Daddy had broken up what measly few pieces of furniture we had left and threatened to shoot my mother and all five of her brothers. He warned her that he would shoot anyone she called for help. This would not be the time he killed her, though, because he couldn't find her. Her brothers would make sure of it. The only reason they had tolerated him all these years was because Mother would cry and plead, begging them not to hurt him. It was undisputed at Morley and within our family that the Evers' and the Halverstons' general contempt for one another would never change.

Yearning for More than a Whole Dress

The mines had hardened Mother's brothers; they were men with lives of double-jacking, crawling through tipples, and dead canaries; men who weren't afraid of death, but could be terrified of the slightest suggestion of discussion or conversation, which for them meant stringing more than three words together. Confronted with having to talk, even the common greetings of passersby: "How are you? Nice out today, isn't it?" were phrases that stretched their boundaries of comfort. Silence was the sole trait the men in both families had in common.

I was the oldest at home in April, 1963, and I had not forgiven Ruby Grace for marrying a year and a half earlier, leaving us , making a clean escape first to the flatlands near Chattanooga, then to Elcomb, Kentucky, with her new husband, David Martinelli, the boy she'd dreamed of claiming from the only Italian family in Maynard Bald. Now, she had returned to Maynard Bald, and I'd begun work on my forgiveness. Maudie had taken off to Baltimore with Toad Dobson.

Robert Joseph and Elda Kate were young and assumed all mothers and fathers were like ours. Unpredictable. Careless. Thoughtless. Unless the telephone or pieces of furniture were flying through the house or unless someone was bleeding, neither Robert Joseph nor Elda Kate showed the least bit of interest in helping me contend with our mother and father or our mucked-up lives.

I still slept in my clothes every night; it was a habit I'd taken up just in case the sheriff came or in the event Daddy came home and jerked the phone from the wall or cut the cord causing me to have to knock on Mrs. Pruitt's door.

I lay in bed at night and worried, maybe this would be the time my mother didn't come back; coming back would be an escape into the infernal nether world. I could see her dancing barefoot in her new wrap-around dress with soft pink and pale yellow flowers on a field of cream. I imagined her crocheted handkerchiefs and tubes of pigeon-blood-red lipstick and the distant look, as if she kept a deep, awful secret that none of us should ever know.

"Secrets wear you down, wear you out," she said once, letting go of a deep sigh and reclaiming that hollow, distant look that draped her face with the paleness of longing.

"Isn't it just beautiful?" I remembered her saying. *Gentle colors*, she called them, the soft pink and pale yellow flowers on a field of cream. Swirling like a little girl, she held up the hem of her dress in both hands. Swirling like the tiny pink and yellow velvet moths that beat themselves against the screen door. Swirling. Her arms waving gracefully as if the colors and flowers moved her body along. Swirling. Humming.

This was the longest Mother had stayed away from us. Grandmother had a way of knowing things, as if she possessed a special power. She sensed any commotion that occurred at our house. And dealing with Lillie Dabney Halverston was like trying to round up a swarm of angry bees using only one hand and a tiny lasso.

She was the one who could quiet my father. I wondered if it was from my father that she knew about any disturbance at our house—that she knew to come. All the intolerance, anger, and hostility he turned loose on the world around him missed her completely, as if she was the only one who had not wronged him in some way. Grandmother's voice could settle him. She knew which words to choose, which subject and tone to use, and a way of making whatever it was in him, whatever irritant or catalyst that grazed him, seem tolerable.

She had arrived in the sheriff's car a few hours after Daddy left the morning after the argument. It was daylight, and Pearlie Hille Butters, the busiest tongue in town, a Louisiana Redbone, stood in the shadows, back from her window, watching Grandmother get out of Sheriff Rose's car. Grandmother didn't drive. She seldom even rode in a car, saying they were dangerous contraptions contrived for lazy people. Sheriff Rosemund Motts would drop anything he was doing to drive her to our house, to Shelby's Grocery when she needed snuff, or to the Jacksboro Cemetery where she went every Saturday and Wednesday to stand next to Little William's grave where she delivered soliloquies that required hours of pacing. William Irish Halverston was her son who died of colitis when he was eight, only two years before my father was born.

Sheriff Rose would wait patiently in his car. Sometimes he napped. He would never hurry her. She'd known him since the day he was born and reminded him, each time she tried to coerce him into bending the law in some way, that she'd boxed his ears plenty in his life, and she wouldn't hesitate to do it again.

There were only a few places that were too far to walk in her clunky white shoes that sloped to the outside making her look as if her feet were sliding over the sides. Grandmother saw some sort of hay-wired virtue in the pain of walking in her cracked leather shoes that cruelly wrapped around her feet like vises. Her walks were even more virtuous if they were at sprint-speed and in the time of the year when the sun baked the ground to the hardness of bricks. She had been known to walk even to the Jacksboro Cemetery about five miles from Maynard Bald.

She slid across the back seat where she insisted riding even though Sheriff Rose told her over and over again that people would gossip saying they had seen Lillie Dabney Halverston hauled off to jail. She was determined, however, to sit in the back seat of the sheriff's car with a metal grill between her and the sheriff. "The reason I refuse to ride in the front seat," she explained, "is that I don't want people thinking Rosemund is shirking his job by driving me places in the patrol car."

She sat straight in the back seat, her body stiff, perched like a queen with one ankle crossed precisely over the other, the strap of her black, vinyl pocketbook laced over her forearm with the pocketbook resting on her lap. She slept the same way, never turning back the covers, stretched out on her back, ankles crossed, her arm laced through the strap of her pocketbook. Every night she slept on a smoothed, perfectly-made bed, never rumpling the sheets or counterpane, and wearing her white, lop-sided shoes and her white, starched-stiff dress.

I watched her from the window as she raised herself slowly from the patrol car. She was a slight woman—thin with shoulder blades that tried to poke through her back. It seemed all the bitterness she'd hoarded over the years had eaten away at her, picking her clean and leaving just a scrawny skeleton with thin, moth-white skin stretched across the bones that held her up. I doubted she'd ever had a bit of extra flesh that could be gathered into a pinch. She balanced Little William's death and Grandfather's abandonment on the yoke across her shoulders the way she balanced the black vinyl that teetered on her lap.

Sometimes when I watched her from a distance, she looked the way I imagined a turtle without a shell. Exposed. Bare. Unprotected. But my grandmother was wrapped in an invisible shell. I knew it was there. So did everyone around her. We just couldn't see it.

Her black, vinyl pocketbook swung from her arm as she leaned through the car window in an easy, deliberate motion to say something to Sheriff Rose. With one hand on her hip, she shook a crooked finger at him, and he immediately took on the look of a little boy, looking down as if studying something on the seat next to him. He nodded to her. I was relieved that he didn't come into the house and ask a string of questions about why I wasn't at school. He'd start asking questions about Mother and Daddy that I wasn't prepared to answer. He would surely ask how the furniture got broken. We had not moved the pieces or cleaned up the mess. Ruby Grace said, "Leave it. Leave even the table legs. Daddy should take a good look at what he needs to replace. Mother needs to see it too."

Grandmother knew when things were not right. She had not stopped asking questions or talking since she arrived, ignoring Elda Kate and Robert Joseph. She ignored that my focus was on trying to fry eggs and serve up anything that would keep them quiet for a while. She continued to ask questions without noticing that I hadn't spoken a word or that Maudie and Ruby Grace had retreated to the room they shared before Ruby Grace married.

Preoccupied with the current crisis, I tried to listen, to focus on what she was saying and answer her questions, but it was hard to pay attention when all I could fix in my mind was the top of the ridge, watching for his black Cadillac to come ripping over it. At least it was black when I last saw it. Lately, it seemed to be a different color almost every week.

Lillie Dabney Halverston was as uncomfortable with silence as the Evers uncles were with conversation. She wasn't like Grandmother Evers in any way, and engaging in the act of talking was the trait that most set them apart. Lillie Dabney never stopped talking. That was expected since the Halverstons' side of the family was the exact opposite of the Evers' side. Even though Lillie Dabney was a Halverston only by marriage, she went on talking that day as if she had a full audience for a public speech—the same way she talked at Little William's grave. Sometimes she made up her dithyrambs. *Ditties*, she called them—her little songs and chants and riddles with hidden meanings and careening, illusive lessons that, all my life, I'd had to run after to grab onto. Her private language of ditties, proverbs, and quotations was like a stream of continuous, sweet, lulling songs. High-wire nets. Tightly woven puzzles that I'd heard all my life and grown used to and most of which I'd come to understand.

"Did you know that humans are the only animals that know they will die?" she said, trying to distract me.

"An offering," I thought, "here comes a story she's made up—a ditty." She amazed me. "A gift?

Why did she feel compelled to impart such information at this particular time?" I wondered. I figured that in some convoluted way, this was meant to bring me some sweet-scented solace. A thought to lick up. A soothing distraction. The same alms that came with viper's bugloss honey and pralines.

I heard her singing in the kitchen. Occasionally, I turned to see her standing at the door looking at me. She smiled and tried to find a ditty to ease me. Settle me. Mrs. Pruitt said she had not had a single tooth in her mouth since her mid-twenties.

Lillie Dabney was a Cherokee, and she never let it go unknown. She was clever, discerning, and those who had known her since childhood said she had never stepped one foot inside a school or a church except years ago when her children were young, she was known to pick random days to arrive unannounced and uninvited at their school where she sat against the back walls of their classrooms scrutinizing all lessons, books, and presentations made by their teachers. The old men at Shelby's Grocery called her *the Cherokee without a tooth and without a birthday*. She claimed there was no record of her birth since she was delivered by a midwife at a place so far back in the mountains that the only ways to get there was on foot or on a sure-footed horse. "And even if there had been a record," she said, "it would have burned in 1926 when the Jacksboro Courthouse burned to the ground."

"Cherokees have no need for birth certificates," she grinned, confidently and proudly showing her pink gums.

She read everything: every book she could persuade Hallie Luttrell to order for the Maynard Bald

Free Library; every book she could borrow from friends and neighbors; and every book she could afford to have Sheriff Rose bring from Knoxville or Lexington. Shelves were reserved only for books. The last twenty years of *the Maynard Bald Press* and *the Knoxville News Sentinel* formed three-feet-high stacks that lined the walls of her bedroom. She said she might want to read them later, but we knew she had read every word in every newspaper. The truth was she couldn't throw away any piece of paper she'd ever touched. The most amazing thing though, was that she could retrieve, in an instant, an article or a newspaper of a particular date or about a specific subject from her stacks.

Her mother had passed down to her the things she knew about the Cherokees. She often chanted Cherokee words and phrases and told stories told to her by her mother about the Cherokees. *Necessary* she called them. "Stories are like pralines," she said, "as necessary as air. Cherokee means *multitude*. Remember that. It's important. Words give you power. They winnow out what's deep inside you and allow you to beat the air with your wings like a male ruffed grouse. Listen. Learn from the front wall," she'd say, touching my hair, sweeping it back from my face. Hopeful.

She admitted reading anything written by a Southerner. She admitted reading *old literature*. That's what she called the classics. And although I knew she read the works of American writers who were not Southerners, she never confessed to it. She claimed that more attention should be given to women writers and to any writer coming out of Vanderbilt. And that Faulkner was overrated.

"Vanderbilt is giving up some heavy-weights," she

warned, shaking a leathery, knobby finger as if she knew a state secret. "Those are writers that shake you hard. You'll see."

"Spend your time reading only things of significance," she warned. "Do not waste your time reading any printed word that is not valuable and worthy of every minute it takes you to read it. If when you've finished a book, a single phrase or sentence from it comes into your head the next day, or if you are a smarter person or a better person the next day, then you've spent your time well. Books are not for your entertainment; nor for idle indulgence. They are for your mind." And when she was sure no one was watching, she immersed herself in sublime indulgence pulled from a wrinkled bag worn soft from handling. She smiled. The pink of her gums showed.

I took note of every book I saw her reading, especially those that she tried to hide. Those written by non-Southerners were hidden under her bed. Some were rolled in brown paper bags and stuffed in her valise. Some were wrapped in newspapers and hidden in the bottom of her chifforobe behind her cache of Bruton snuffboxes that were rolled in crumpled butcher paper and, for added protection, stuffed into brown store bags.

The list grew longer: Welty, Porter, Williams, O'Connor; and if she felt at all confessional, she reluctantly owned up to Bronte, Darwin, Cervantes, Goethe, Steinbeck, Irving, or Dickens. Lately, she was reading Harper Lee's book and declared that she'd been right all along about Southern writers.

Once, lying under the big bed with a flashlight, I read the first 37 pages of *Catcher in the Rye* that I found wrapped in brown butcher paper and tied with twine.

Grandmother came in, opened the bureau drawer, plundered through her handkerchiefs where she hid snuff paddles, mother-of-pearl buttons, and a tiny, folded paper of coriander seeds. She closed the door halfway as she left the room. She knew I was there. Sweating. Holding my breath. There was too much fuss made over it. Why my grandmother was reading it was a mystery. However, a book wrapped in brown paper and string was not one that would be a candidate for discussion. That was unfortunate as Grandmother and I discussed every book both of us had read. Every book, at least, that we admitted reading.

Grandmother knew about men. She considered herself an authority on the subject of the male temperament. She frequently warned any female who would listen that "a woman must hear more than a man's sweet words before any notion at all of matrimony can dance in her heart. The most important things to be considered when you're thinking of marrying a man are: his reverence for his mother and his sisters; his manners at the supper table; his actions while in a drunken state; whether he's a mean drunk or a stupid drunk, as a mean drunk is as poisonous as a cottonmouth," she said with steadfast conviction. "Also, a woman must assess a man's reins on a vulgar tongue when in the presence of a lady; his handling of anger and jealousy; whether he's a stayer or a leaver; and his temperament when in the throes of misery, pain, fear, or a cold."

She reluctantly admitted that she did not know everything about my grandfather, whom she divorced a hundred years ago after he abandoned her. And she admitted that she didn't know quite everything about any one of her three sons, if you count Little William. When any part of her treatise on men came into question, she affirmed directly and with certainty that my grandfather and her sons, especially my father, Joseph, and Uncle Ogan were exceptions.

"Your daddy is different," she said. "I knew it from the day he was born. He was born on Christmas Day and that alone made him different. From the very first time I looked at his face, I knew. He was born angry and that never changed. He was always restless and unsettled. He always liked being alone, and as a little boy, he never seemed to like other children."

A distinct look came over her face when she talked about my father. An easiness and a certain softness came to her voice; a warmth to her face. For me, it was impossible to think of my father being born or to think of him as a baby or a little boy. Playing. Running. Crying. I was certain that he had never cried. Never.

When I was little, I didn't notice how my grandmother and my mother made excuses and apologies for him; offered up elaborate explanations for his behavior; and readily explained to anyone with enough courage to knock on our door, that he was working and couldn't be disturbed. They apologized; sometimes they told flat-out lies. All children and dogs were scared senseless of him, and so were most adults; even the sheriff; cats, too—especially cats. Cats ran from him, as if they sensed somehow that he hated them.

My friends would hide in the woods and watch our house for hours to see who was at home for fear of encountering him when they knocked on the door.

When my father was around, he kept to himself and moved through the house like a vapor, an apparition. When he was forced into the real world and faced with the fact that he shared the planet with other people, he seemed to nurture a certain intolerance of the world around him, as if he held the universe in contempt. He was estranged and unavailable. Most of the time, the loathsome world outside his head didn't seem to matter or even exist.

Mother said that when she met Daddy, she knew he was a little wild and peculiar in his ways, but she thought he would change. She hoped. Even though I was sure her own mother had lectured her on the impossibility of changing another person, Mother confessed that deep down she wondered if she longed for his changes or her own.

My father never sat at the supper table with us; not even for holidays or birthdays; not even for his own birthday on Christmas Day, when Grandmother baked her special Tennessee apple stack cake with eight giant layers of dried Black Twig apples covered with white icing that set as hard as concrete. He ate alone in the front room. Sometimes, so as not to disturb him when he was working on a neon sign, Mother or Grandmother would prepare his supper on a tray and leave it beside the door of his make-shift workshop located in a dilapidated building behind the house. We crept around him, measured his moods, read the veins that pulsed in his temple. We listened and watched for a single sign that the planets had aligned themselves perfectly, signaling him to acknowledge any one of us.

Mother confided once, when we were alone in her bedroom and almost without realizing it, "When I met your daddy, there was something exciting in his difference. He drew me into his magic and his promises of taking me to a place without coal mines, a place that resembled the make-believe world inside his head, a place where he could practice the art of glass and neon. Glass words of pretty colors," she said, staring off, sighing. "It's true. He made the most beautiful neon signs and glass sculpture, too—shaping the glass perfectly—curved glass words, neon swans with necks like emerging vines, and glass calla lilies with contoured edges as smooth and flawless as watered silk. Your daddy created beauty, and with the same masterful, gentle hand, he destroyed it; snatched it away like a hungry dog protecting his food; shattered it like the neon glass when it falls into the flame."

He didn't spend much time at home. When he was at home, he spent most of his time in the building behind the house where the long tubes of neon glass lined the walls waiting to be magically melted into words. On hot days, when the huge doors were open, I watched him from the back porch. I could see the rubber tube in his mouth, the fire of the burners near his head as he leaned in, the glow of the hot glass, and the sweat on his face. He moved his long fingers quickly, but gently, rolling the glass through the flame, changing it, molding it, controlling it when it tried to escape into the fire.

Sometimes when he was gone, I snuck into the building just to look at the neon letters, carefully running my fingers across an S or an O. Those in cursive were the most beautiful, like growing vines: continuous, no sharp turns.

All five of Mother's brothers and her daddy

warned her that marrying Joseph Walter Halverston would sentence her to a more miserable and torturous existence than the coal mines.

Lillie Dabney's attempts to agitate my mother and to confirm the futility of her hopes of somehow changing my father, were to say that she saw no reason to tamper with a temperament as complex, steadfast, and disagreeable as his. "He is just misunderstood," she'd say.

I sat in the kitchen and listened to Grandmother as I had every night for almost eight months. She seldom said anything positive about my mother, and I began to think she would be perfectly happy if Mother never came home.

Her stories of my father were endless, and I listened to every detail in hope of understanding him. She said that since the day he was born, he had had an unusual agitation and impatience in him. She said he was an artist; that he usually had an idea of some kind forming in his mind; and it was difficult for him to focus on the things that didn't interest him.

All of us, except my mother, fell into that category: things that didn't interest him. I was never sure of what drew him to my mother, but I was sure it was not love or even fondness that bound him to her. It was something else; something hidden from us. He was present with such remoteness and distance, that he was an *absent presence*. Sometimes when I looked at him, it was like trying to make out details through a gossamer curtain; knowing he was there, but not quite able to see his features or his definition, but rather, only able to make out a shapeless form with an intrinsic core of aloneness.

One night in early April as I sat in the kitchen

trying to write a paper on *Silas Marner* for my English class, Grandmother appeared in the doorway to see if I was listening as she talked from the next room or if I'd fallen asleep. She grinned only a half-grin and talked about a little brown bird she'd found dead by the steps outside. "I am ashamed," she said, "that I feel a little less sad for that little brown bird than I would have had it been red. Maybe it's because in some way it seems to matter less because we notice it less."

"What are you talking about?" I whispered, afraid to hear the answer; afraid to ask loudly enough to be heard. "Unbelievable. You're worried about a little dead bird? Daddy could walk in here at any time. Mother could be dead, and we'd never know. He could spend the rest of his life at Brushy Mountain State Penitentiary. Little Southeast Asian villages could be blown to Uranus. And you're worried about a little dead bird?"

I had trouble staying awake even with the steady cadence of her voice in the next room. The ditties were muffled and far away. It was dusk and unusually cold for April. There was enough light left in the eastern sky over the mountain to see the smoke rising straight up from the houses the way it does on cold, clear, windless days. My head tilted and jerked as I gave in to letting my eyes close. I could barely hear her voice, thin, watered-down, muffled by the heaviness of sleep.

The long silence between his footsteps brought me out of sleep and to my feet. Grandmother said as she stood up, "It must be Rosemund coming to see if I want him to drive me home."

I knew his gait. Only a tall man with legs as long as

stilts had that much distance and silence between his steps.

"Shush, shushhhh. It's not Rosemund," I said leaning on the table, feeling the uselessness of my legs, wanting, hoping for a single word to float on my breath and resonate to become a sound.

He did not speak as he crossed the front room, walked through the middle room, and moved toward the kitchen. Grandmother talked at a nervous, fevered speed and seemed thrilled with his very presence. She offered him coffee, and he nodded impolitely without a word.

"Sit here, Joe," she said, pulling a straight-back chair away from the table.

He stretched his long legs under the table as he leaned back and lit a cigarette. The wet paper stuck on his lip. As magically as a stage act, Grandmother pulled a large red ashtray from the cabinet and set it on the table. Still, he didn't say one word.

I stood in the doorway watching him, watching Grandmother flutter around him like an injured bird. Finally, after pouring his coffee, she landed on the chair on the other side of the table still talking at a headlong, hair-triggered velocity in an attempt to temper his muteness and calm the bulging vein at his temple.

For the first time, looking at my father's face, I understood it was not the light or the dangling bulb or the dingy walls that colored the room, but his presence did something strange to the light. People change the light in a room: the way it's refracted, the way it rests on a surface in a particular way, the intensity, the shadows.

In that moment he looked gray. Shrouded in his

absence with no definition, he didn't seem very real. Grandmother looked at him the way a child looks at someone trying to read his face, wanting desperately to see some sign or at least a cue. Searching. The light in the room changed.

"Where is she?" he asked, looking at me.

"I don't know, Daddy, I swear."

"You do know," he yelled as his fist came down in an explosion on the table shattering the cup and the ashtray, sending hot coffee and broken red glass shooting through the kitchen like shrapnel.

"I swear, I don't know, Daddy. Please."

"She doesn't know, Joe. Leave her alone," Grandmother pleaded.

"She knows," he said. "She knows," he shook his head, "I've told your mother a hundred times that there isn't a place on earth where I won't be able to find her."

He slowly pushed his chair away from the table, stood up, and in an easy, deliberate posture, walked to his and Mother's bedroom at the back of the house.

Grandmother raised her index finger to her lips motioning for me to be silent. There were sounds of rummaging and sounds of wire clothes hangers scratching the metal closet bar. The sounds stopped.

Grandmother and I stood motionless at the bedroom door watching him as he moved purposely around the room. He did not look at us or say anything. We watched as he took three of Mother's dresses from the closet, slid them off the wire hangers, and carefully laid them across the counterpane. He used a pair of sewing scissors taken from the top drawer of the bureau to cut each dress precisely up the middle: the pretty lavender one with the loose capped sleeves, the beautiful wrap-around the color of pink and yellow velvet moths on a field of cream, and the pale blue sundress with polka dots the color of willow buds.

We watched as he slowly, carefully took every dress from the closet, smoothed each one perfectly against the counterpane, and cut them one-by-one through the center, being especially careful not to cut the counterpane. Finally, the closet was empty. The bed was covered with pretty dress halves of every gentle and soft color. We heard the familiar sound of his car engine as he drove away.

*　　*　　*

Eight months had passed without any news of Mother: not a phone call; not a letter; not a word from the uncles. Nothing. Lying in bed at night I imagined that she was hiding in the woods, watching the house, watching us, watching him. I pictured her standing in the woods like a sentry guarding a pass. Sometimes I stood at the edge of the woods and called to her, hoping she'd call back, "I'm here, Sweets. I've always been here. I'm here."

She never called back, and, when I screamed into the woods, there was no hollow echo to tease that she might be there. The dense, plump trees swallowed up my sounds like a hungry beast.

There was no news of Daddy either. Grandmother stayed at our house all the time now, not returning to her own house for any reason. She seldom talked about him. That distinct warmness and the expectation in her voice were gone. She stopped pretending that everything was fine. Or normal. Or hopeful. Or was.

She stood at the east window for hours. Waiting. At dusk I could see her silhouette against the glass. After dark, she'd sit at the table and stare into the crass darkness. Stranded there. She stopped reading. Even the books pulled from brown butcher paper were of no interest to her. Most nights the only light in the house was from moonlight.

One morning a few weeks after Daddy cut the dresses, I awoke to what sounded like a hammer striking a board. I found her standing on a chair in front of the east window pounding four-inch nails through a scrap of wood and into one of the carved faces of Janus. With every word she slammed the hammer.

"I! Am! Sick! To! Death! Of! Him! Looking! Back!" she shrieked, out of breath. "We! My! Sweets! Are! Looking! Only! Forward!" she blurted, swinging the hammer furiously, then throwing it to the floor.

*   *   *

By mid May, the mountain laurel and flame azaleas were swollen with plump buds, and it was warm enough on sunny days to wear only a cardigan over my blouse. Sheriff Rose volunteered to drive Grandmother and me to an award ceremony at school where I was to receive a prize for a series of drawings and watercolors of moths. The sheriff sat next to her in the front row of the auditorium. When Mr. Morton called my name, she smiled proudly, displaying a mouth of pink gums, and the same contented look spread across her face—the fervent, pink-tinted expression she used to have when she talked about my father.

As the days grew warmer, Grandmother and I took long walks through the woods. She found a beautiful tree in the woods near our house. It was a large birch with crooked roots that stood like giant, arched, stilt legs that held the trunk above the ground and formed two, six-foot-tall archways. On warm, sunny Saturdays, we made sandwiches for picnics and lay on our backs under the arched legs of the tree. She said it was formed when a giant chestnut trunk had fallen years ago and birch roots had grown up around it, hugging and squeezing it. When the chestnut trunk disintegrated, the birch's legs kept growing, forming arched, skeletal buttresses that became towering entrances to a make-believe place.

"The tree is like the faces of Janus above the east window," she said, "turning his eyes and ears full circle; not away from the mountains or away from fear, but toward new beginnings; toward the place where the road parts the naked trees.

The anger came like rapid fire, overwhelming me, leaving me limp and piled up on the bedroom floor. Those were the moments I hated him. Endless moments of profound sadness and paralyzing grief followed, marching through my bedroom in tandem and at a respectful, mournful pace; saluting. Then came the relentless bursts of engulfment and consumption by anger as absolute as death.

His thievery was shapeless, insidious. Barely discernible. A monster unseen. All those years wasted in fear: fifteen years for me; twenty-two for my mother; forty for his mother.

Now, gone. A careless leaver. Like a murderous, feeding goshawk leaving only feathers floating in a small space of air as if nothing at all happened. Puffffff! Floating feathers. Ear-splitting silence. I searched the sky for a glimpse of the culprit as if he'd linger in sight, holding his prey in his talons. I knew before looking up that he was miles away.

The flood of anger, guilt, and grief came routinely in the beginning. And yearning. Immeasurable yearning. Unremitting hunger. "Hunger for what?" I asked. I was imprisoned by the same pull of longing as my mother—bound by a pull as forceful as a sucking eddy—a maelstrom that draws you in and presses down as heavily as leaden dirt. Usually in front of the bedroom mirror. And always, the little swirl of soft feathers on the bedroom floor.

I was alone. No mother. No father. Orphaned. It was during this time that I came to face the ever-present gnashing of certain truths: that there was a remote possibility that I did belong to this obscenely mad family; and along with that shocking realization (or perhaps admission) came the awareness of the unnerving notion of their abandonment. These things were true; as dreadfully, unmistakably real as coming to view the very things I rejected, ran from, denied, not as impediments, but rather, as the catalysts that would carve me like whittled cane.

How would I have known that the very things I feared and at times even held in contempt: a hopelessly damaged family, an eccentric, near-insane father, and the seemingly most isolated town in the hinterlands of Tennessee would be the things that changed me, that catapulted me to the outside world, to adulthood, to reality, to myself.

Sometimes in the evenings when the indelible colors of gray shrouded the woods, I listened; not to the sounds of a house irreparably, hopelessly, terminally damaged; but to the perfect, beautiful silence of the mountains at dusk; to the sweet muteness of Janus; to the still, deep, empty darkness of the mines. I stood at the edge, but not too close. I did not call out.

Tender of the Rue

It was a mistake. This was not my family. I tried to think through the whole situation; to look around me; to both sides of me. But regardless of how I viewed it, the picture was always the same—my parents were *missing.*

It was May, 1963. I was relieved that the school year would end in just a few days. I thought of something I'd learned years ago in Mr. Neville's science class, and I was certain it was a horrible error. This was much more serious and complex than a mistaken zygote or the union of two renegade, incompatible gametes. This was a problem that required a proactive approach: evidence, facts. I had to find proof that I did not belong to this family of strangers—interlopers as foreign and unknown as a fall of wandering flatlanders or a dopping of off-course sheldrakes. Why, if we *were* related, did I feel this innate, full-grown, whole *otherness*? And even worse, why did abandonment by a family that surely wasn't mine, seem utterly devastating?

Fam-i-ly (fam'e le, fam' le), n., 1. parents and their children considered as a group, whether dwelling together or not. 2. any group of persons closely related by blood, as parents, children, uncles, aunts, and cousins. 3. all those persons considered as descendants of a common progenitor.

The longing was intensifying and the worst part was that it didn't have a face. I knew that I wanted *something*. I tried to cross the bridge, not for something to be touched or something tangible waiting on the other side, but for something unseen, illusive. I thought maybe everyone had this feeling inside them—of being pulled along in the rapid currents of a river; trying to lift your head above the surface, not because you're drowning, but, to see the banks for the very first time; to identify not only the trees and rocks and grasses as you floated by, but to see the place, to locate it in your life, in time, to give it a name. It was not likely something lost, but just something nameless, or at least something to be identified to make some kind of sense out of it, to give it meaning, to harness it into a frame of reference.

I tossed in bed trying to divert my thoughts from the immediate problem. "People did it every day," I thought, punching my pillow and cussing into it, "people leave their families, even stable, sane families. They get married, go away to school, escape from the hole. They simply walk away."

Stop thinking! Get some sleep, I commanded the achy place in my head. Now all the lesser, unjust things my oh-by-the-way-we're-moving parents dropped on me, usually at one o'clock in the morning, seemed relatively minor: moving in the middle of the night, leaving everything, never living in one place (other than Maynard Bald) long enough to make a single friend; making me go to nine different schools by the time I was fifteen; bringing two more babies home, when they didn't take care of the two they already had. All of these were only minor offenses when standing next to the two mammoth ones—pretending they were my parents and walking away from us, abandoning us at every selfish whim.

Regardless of the different towns, the nights on the road to strange places, the cheap apartments rented, the nights of waiting for them to come home, we always returned to Maynard Bald. Mother didn't like being away from her mama and daddy *or* her brothers. They were anchors, her grounding. The moves were tolerable as long as she could have contact between moves. Morley was close enough to Maynard Bald for her to know that her brothers could come if needed. It was akin to a newly-walking baby veering away from her mother to a strange place, even to a different room, but needing to come back to Mother's security, touching her, then off to explore again.

All the places we had lived away from Maynard Bald seemed like long vacations. Once we spent two months in Fort Walton Beach, Florida, where we lived in an isolated little stucco house on the beach. My father had retrieved me from Morley Mountain where I'd stayed most of the summer with Grandmother Evers. He drove all day and into the night. I was seven, and had never seen the ocean. We arrived after dark, and I couldn't see the ocean, but I could hear it. I sat up whimpering all night the first night. Mother pleaded with him, "Joe, just let her sleep on the floor at the foot of the bed in our room.

Just until she gets used to the house. She won't wake the baby. Please, she's scared." He refused, and I sat up in bed for three nights in a row listening to the unfamiliar sounds of the waves trying to crawl ashore and watching silhouettes of tiny lizards scurry across the adobe wall.

After Fort Walton Beach, we returned to Maynard Bald for a short time before moving to Anniston, Alabama for three months. I didn't go to kindergarten and by the time I was in the second grade, I'd attended three elementary schools. The next few years brought a series of moves: back to Fort Walton Beach twice; to Muscle Shoals, Alabama; to Harlan, Kentucky; Huntsville, Alabama; Franklin, Tennessee; and Hazard, Kentucky. We stayed in each of these cities and towns for only a few weeks, sometimes a couple of months, and between each one, we returned to Maynard Bald.

Looking back, I tried to remember when I realized that *other* families, normal ones, did not traipse all over the country moving like a band of nomads, lying to neighbors and school personnel. Other parents didn't disappear for months. Other parents didn't disappear at all. Ever. My parents' disappearances were the second-most grievous and unforgivable of all. "What kind of parents abandon, simply walk away from their children? What kind of parents lie to their children or pretend to be the parents of their children, when they aren't, or drag their children from state to state, or school to school?" I wondered. I started to sense my growing anger about the whole situation and wondered if it might not be forgivable at all.

Mother had been gone for nine months, and my father for almost as long, except the time a month ago when he stopped by briefly to see if Mother had come home and to cut her dresses to pieces. Anger had replaced fear. "Look at it this way," I thought, "at least I'm staying put." It was too stressful to feel angry all the time. I felt guilty and figured I should start working on at least a partial forgiveness of my parents. I knew it would be impossible to summon up a cross-your-heart and swear-to-sweet-Jesus kind of forgiveness, but it seemed I should try to work something out or at least make an attempt; not a full-fledged forgiveness, understandably, but an *almost forgiveness*, just enough to take the curse off my soul, enough to let me sleep at night. One day in May while Grandmother and I sat on the back steps, I told her of my plan to *try* to forgive my parents.

Grandmother Lillie said, "You're giving yourself over to lies. An *almost forgiveness* is half-hearted and sinful and will not work. You should not waste even one thought on it. It's just like *almost alive* or *almost sorry*. You cannot almost forgive someone."

Most times, I didn't know the meaning of having an unspoken thought, but just the very idea of coming face-to-face with Mother and Daddy about such a subject made me want to go to bed and pull the quilt up so tightly around my face that I would smother to death and be done with it.

I rehearsed my speech standing in front of the bathroom mirror a hundred times, forming my words just right. The perfect words in an order that made sense. And I could not shake or cry or get the jerk in my throat that makes it impossible for any words to come out. But I knew when the time came, and even without a dally in my thought, my voice would stay pushed down inside me somewhere, cowering so deeply in me that it could never squeeze itself hard enough to be heard.

At the exact moment I released my secret of working to partially forgive them, I knew I'd given my grandmother the perfect opportunity to launch into one of her you'll-never-get-into-Heaven sermons designed specifically to induce a minimum of three days of guilt.

Her face changed. And I saw that a fit of Psalms was coming on as I watched her shake her head and slide back across the counterpane and prop herself up just right for a powerful delivery. She wiped snuff juice that gathered at the little wrinkles at the corners of her mouth.

Her sermons were usually found hunkered down behind a soft and pretty voice spouting wisdom of the mountains, or growing flowers, or the ways of the Cherokees. They were carefully disguised. But without warning and stashed right smack between her stories of the folds of McCloud Mountain and the cut of the French Broad River, a Psalm or a Proverb would jump up and take hold of me. Lillie Dabney Halverston could cloak her sermons brilliantly, especially when I was young. She could conceal a moral in such an unlikely subject that I was already taken in before I knew it. I was sure my grandmother was put on this earth for the sole purpose of concocting plots with Solomon and David to bring on just as much guilt as possible for one little woman to spread around.

Sometimes, instead of hiding behind a Psalm, her words were packed cleverly into a riddle or a song or a dithyramb. She could call up words from the scriptures or any other book she'd read in her lifetime to suit every whim. These were proof of her points, evidence of her knowledge, and support of her correctness. I lay in bed at night before sleep thinking for sure that my grandmother was an imposter, and that she was really some other being reincarnated from another time, hiding in the body of a scrawny, little lady living in east Tennessee.

She had magic in her and ditties that could lull me out of my senses and at the very same time make me feel guilty about every little sin I had ever committed. Her words closed in on me and for a little while relieved the fear struck in me sometimes when we didn't know where Daddy was. Those same pretty words could spread through me at night before sleep dusting me with the same feeling I had the first time my mother plaited a grosgrain ribbon into my hair.

Grandmother ranted, wailed, and quoted scriptures about sinning and getting right with the Lord—unbelievable of someone who'd never stepped one foot inside a church. She declared, "When my heart is unsettled or my head is troubled, I sit in the woods and give myself up to the quiet of the shadblow and the hickories, or I get someone to drive me up to Eagle Bluff where I can sit high for a while. Get my thoughts untangled."

When she began her sermon with Psalms or Proverbs, I knew she intended to have my full attention. "Lunda Rose," she sighed, "Remember the six things hated by the Lord and the seventh being an abomination to him?"

As hard as I tried, I couldn't remember what she'd preached to me since I was six years old. I couldn't call them up no matter how I rummaged through my head. "*Seven? Seven?*" I whispered to myself in a futile effort to recall. These had not held up well in my memory.

"The seven things, Lunda Rose?" she questioned, trying to give me clues and scare me at the same time. She waited, squinting at me and twisting her lips into a bitter pucker indicating not only her dissatisfaction, but also that she could wait all night for me to retrieve the seven vile deeds that offended the Lord.

"You're headed down the wrong, spiraling road," she'd say. "I've tried to teach you how to take mind of yourself, and, now, right in front of me, God help me, blasphemous words and poison are pouring out of you about a half-hearted forgiveness and making special deals with the Lord."

She put her fingers under my chin and turned my face toward hers so that I looked right into her pale, gray pupils as wide open as a night highway. She whispered in a soft voice as if someone in the next room was not supposed to hear.

"The seven vile deeds that offend the Lord? What are they?" When she realized the clues weren't helping and that her attempts to scare the deeds into my memory weren't working either, she began chanting them so precisely that you would have thought she'd written them.

" *A proud look, a lying tongue, and hands that shed innocent blood, a heart that deviseth wicked imaginations, feet that be swift in running to mischief, a false witness that speaketh lies, and he that soweth discord among brethren.*"

"Well, great," she said, "this whole family is spinning off straight down to Hades. Now, you listen to me. Promises made to the Lord when you get yourself into a sorry mess amount to just plain lying and under-handed bargaining. You let that notion leave your head this very minute." She rubbed the corner of her mouth with her handkerchief.

Even though I knew Grandmother was right about everything, I wanted to hold on to some of my forgiveness, little pieces of sweet pardon, stashing them and hoarding them to dole out later when they were needed like aces in a poker game. "*Where* in the documented list of sins was the sin of making orphans of your children?" I wondered.

"Anger will turn on you, and the wreckage is ugly," she said, standing up and putting on her apron, an indication that she was finished with the discussion. The weight of the truth, the *correctness* of what she said, spread through me like an unfurling fit of temper.

"Total forgiveness may be just too much to ask," I thought, but didn't say. I preferred to think of my present work on forgiving my mother and my father as more like one of those promises you make to the Lord when you're in a pitiful mess and you say, "Lord, if You will just let me live through this, I swear I will never sin again, or cuss, or hate anybody, or pretend to be sick to get out of washing up the supper dishes, or hold a grudge against my worst enemy or any relative. I swear I will stop lying to Robert Joseph and Elda Kate about being adopted. I promise to stop smoking, stop chewing tobacco, stop dipping snuff, and stop tinting my hair with Maudie's henna rinse."

Such a promise had to be worth something to the Lord. It was not one of those false promises that even the preacher at Habersham wouldn't be able to keep. In the years it would take for such forgiveness, I could take comfort in knowing I was working on it, and I wouldn't stay up nights worrying about it. This was not one of those lying promises that made me feel guilty about making such a promise to the Lord in the first place.

It was a down payment of sorts until I could muster up a full forgiveness. It had to be worth something. This deal required a lot of work, and I intended to give myself a few years. I'd been collecting my anger for years, saving it up like four-leaf clovers to stick between the pages of the Bible, hoarding it in the event that I would need it someday. I figured God wouldn't bind me to such a promise when he realized the full significance of what Mother and Daddy had done.

Once more I thought through the predicament and decided to test the most serious first: they'd lied to me, and lying was the most deceitful of all their shameful offenses. I repeated to myself and tried to remember, "I must. The seven most vile deeds? Think. What are they? Lying?" I knew if I was going to have any peace at all, I had to pardon them, at the very minimum, for not confessing that I did not belong to this family. Later, I could work on the lesser infractions, their minor, but still unkind deeds: my mother taking my best Lakenvelder rooster by the feet and slinging him all over the yard and clear into the woods and wringing the necks off of my dye-colored baby White Wyandotte Easter chicks just because they grew up. Who would do such a thing? And the time we moved away forcing me to give up my honey-colored dog, Beasley, a female mistakenly named, who had at least two litters of pups a year. Mother said she gave Beasley to Uncle Hoboch Lewis a few days before one of our middle-of-the-night moves. That was a bold-faced lie. When we returned to Maynard Bald a few months later and visited Morley for Mother to see her mama and kin, I asked Grandmother Evers how Beasley was doing at Hoboch Lewis' place. She had no idea what I was talking about.

And there was the time when we got up in the middle of the night and moved to Alabama, leaving behind my blue Schwinn bicycle and every other puny thing we had. Some of these pardons were going to take some time, but if I succeeded at forgiving the big one, the lesser ones would be easy. I repeated inside my head, "I must. Seven most vile?" I thought if I could convince myself of the wretchedness of their lies about such matters, that it might help the Lord see the gravity of it. Yes. Now I remembered the second of the vile sins that offended the Lord: a lying tongue.

But, the more I thought about it, I came to think that Grandmother was right, and I was only lying to myself. Besides, if I could manage a full, proper pardon, I wouldn't have this urgent need to leave this family.

At every opportunity, Grandmother chanted dithyrambs about forgiveness, or grace, and sometimes, in hope of sending me running to the library or to her own books, she would quote Shakespeare's or Milton's lines about rue, "the herb of grace," she said, looking sideways at me to detect any signs of guilt. She saw that her constant chiding was beginning to pay off.

The shape of my memories surprised me as I got older. There was always that faint line between what I really remembered and what I just thought I remembered. Grandmother said, "Your memories are the most valuable things you own. If you don't think you have enough of the good stuff, just make them up. Imagine them. Give yourself over to them and imagine them just the way you want them to be and your mind can deliver anything you want. The funniest thing about memories though, is that we usually throw out the soft and the easy and the sweet ones—throw them out like supper scraps, but we hang on to the bad memories for dear life, hoarding them up like apples and walnuts in the cellar when we're readying for a hard winter."

Grandmother said, "Sometimes though, remembering is just one deceitful, fickle shape of imagining. Be careful. Memories will sometimes cheat you. They can take different shapes just like that neon glass your daddy melts and stretches to make his signs. They're just that watery and unfaithful if you don't keep them reined in. The good ones can escape your hold and be gone in a second. You have to snatch them back when they start to leave you. And, if you set your mind to it, they can be shaped and molded just the way you want them."

My anger had passed the seething mark. Nine months had gone by since the fight when Mother had left. Early one chilly morning in May, I turned off the tiny heater in my bedroom and tore through the house, hoping to make it to the road before the school bus driver blew the horn. My chronic tardiness annoyed Grandmother and embarrassed Robert Joseph.

The front door was open, and Mother stood just inside. Her black hair fell across her cheek as she leaned over to set down a small vinyl valise. As she turned toward me, she swept her hair back, tucking it behind her ear with one figure, and when she faced me, I saw the evidence of that awful night in August—a scar across her right cheek to the corner of her mouth. She looked frail, gaunt, her deep-set eyes lost between her cheekbones and brows. When she saw me, her face relaxed giving way to a slight smile. In that single moment, all sins were forgiven, all anger surrendered.

I didn't go to school that day, nor did Robert Joseph or Elda Kate. Grandmother left our house as soon as Mother arrived. Maudie was asleep in the sound-proof bedroom at the far end of the house. She had left Toad Dobson in Baltimore and returned to Maynard Bald and was living with us again. Mother told me not to wake her. Ruby Grace had stayed at her own house most of past nine months because she wanted to avoid Daddy in the event he returned, and she knew that Grandmother was with us. It was obvious Ruby Grace had missed Mother. During those nine months, she had written countless letters that were never mailed, since we didn't know Mother's whereabouts. I thought that must have been Ruby Grace's way of coping.

For most of the morning, Mother sat with Robert Joseph, Elda Kate, and me in the front room. She didn't talk much, but listened to Robert Joseph's and Elda Kate's endless questions without answering, but instead, changing the subject or redirecting the conversation. They didn't give her much of a chance to answer, telling her in rapid succession of all that had happened since she'd been gone. She wasn't ready for questions or answers about herself, and she listened to them attentively. Occasionally, I saw her looking at the three of us, studying us as if we were strangers. She said nothing of the broken furniture, and later as we followed her into her bedroom, she said nothing about the cut dresses spread across her bed.

For a solid week, the three of us followed her from room to room like starved children. Even Maudie and Ruby Grace couldn't get enough of her. Maudie talked about herself, and Ruby Grace talked about her inability to cook a decent meal. After Ruby Grace left one evening, I saw the stack of never-mailed letters tied with a ribbon and left on the dresser.

No one asked Mother where she'd been for nine months or asked any questions at all about those nine months. Not one of us cared. Our father's name was not mentioned. Mother's presence preempted everything else in my mind; this was a time to savor. She had come home. We were not orphans.

.

Only Two Reasons to Stay Married to a Man

I loved the sound of my grandmother's name: *Lillie Dabney Halverston.* But most people in town nodded their heads, touched their hat brims and said with the greatest reverence, "Good day to you, Miss Lillie Dabney." She insisted that Dabney be included when anyone addressed her, since she was never proud of taking the Halverston name. She nodded back ever so slightly and lowered her eyes just a bit as if she was the Queen of Maynard Bald.

It was June, 1963. School was out for the summer. Since Mother's return, I'd stayed at Grandmother's most of the time. I preferred it. I loved our conversations, and every night we read to one another. She'd stayed at our house for nine straight months, and although she proclaimed it was to "make sure everything ran smoothly and to see that we made it to the road in time for the school bus," I knew the real reason was to contend with Daddy if he came home.

Not one thing about Lillie Dabney could have

been called *ordinary*. She had enough spine for the whole Cherokee Nation. Everybody knew she was a force not to reckon with twice if she was riled. She said, "I have to be true and keen-minded and knowing because I'm a Cherokee. Sometimes I have to be as mean as a penned-up foxhound. Sometimes I have to be stiff in the lip and steadfast because I'm a Halverston. Other times, it's because I'm a Halverston, that I just have to be still."

Grandmother was a small, thin woman with a bigger-than-life presence. She didn't think of herself as small, and took offense when it was implied. She was certainly exercising the power of her imagination if she ever pictured herself any way but skinny. I doubted that she ever had a bit of extra flesh that could be gathered into a pinch.

Older folks said she'd always been peculiar and a little wild, like a hungry, feral cat that wanted your offered, table scraps, but wouldn't come close enough to snatch them up. An old neighbor, Jerome Higgenbotham, had known her since they were children, and he told wonderful stories about her. Listening to him one day as I sat on the back step watching him deadhead flowers, I was sure Higg had always been in love with Lillie Dabney. He revered her. I could hear it in his voice.

Higg said, "I recollect that even when she was young, nobody could believe that she'd ever come close enough to a man to hear his heart, much less be tamed into marrying him. She rode through town bareback with her hair flying and folks here just didn't know what to think of her. She broke every rule and sometimes even tested the law. We could never quite figure why a woman like Lillie Dabney would marry a man like W.O. Halverston.

"Lillie Dabney was just sixteen years old when she married your grandfather. W.O. never treated her well from the start. None of the Halverstons treated her with respect. Every single one of them brought her enough misery to be found in a lifetime. They never accepted her as a part of their uppity bunch. They thought W.O. had married beneath him and called her *an ill-bred Indian* and declared that she would never give anybody the satisfaction of changing.

"The Halverstons were a snobbish clan," Higg said to me once when he was painting the porch. I was surprised and wondered if he had considered that *I* was a Halverston. He told stories of how they were a high-strung, lord-it-over pack with heaps of money back when Ira Odell Halverston, as a young man, first made his way from Virginia to east Tennessee. Higg said the Halverstons came by their money around the 1890's by raising tobacco, breeding Tennessee walking horses, and of course, the Halverston recipe for heavy absinthe.

"Those Tennessee walking horses are fine, valuable horses, and the Halverston's had the best Tennessee Walkers around," Higg bellowed, throwing his head back. "Yep, they're fine working horses all right, but temperamental. They're bred to have five different gaits that are born right into them so the tobacco growers can maneuver them up and down and through the crops and between the tobacco rows with a strut so smooth you'd never know you were in a saddle. Your great granddaddy could turn a Tennessee Walker on a spot of spit, and so could W.O. and Lillie Dabney. That's how W.O. met up with Lillie. She convinced him that he could have a full conversation and come to a good understanding with a Tennessee Walker just by knowing how to squeeze every muscle in his legs. 'Talk with your thighs,' she'd tell him."

Grandmother told stories when we were alone about her Cherokee mother whom she called *Angawela*—the Cherokee word for *woman of the sun*. To the Cherokee people, Angawela was a term of affection, and often used in place of *mother*. It was the only Cherokee word I'd ever heard my father use and possibly the only term of adoration that ever came out of his mouth. The Halverstons didn't use such words. I'd heard my father call his mother Angawela only two times: once when it slipped out on Christmas Day when she presented him with the white birthday cake with cement icing, and, once when he was trying to sooth her after accidentally swearing at her. Both times when Daddy had let the word of endearment slip, he'd glowed with embarrassment. We pretended we hadn't heard.

Although my grandmother never talked about being a Cherokee in the presence of any Halverston, except me, she talked of her own Angawela teaching her to ride without a saddle and showing her how to find and identify plants used to make medicines. Her face changed as she talked of her mother the same way it changed when she talked about my father.

Grandmother's small frame gave the impression that she was frail, but that was a misconception. She lived on a diet of nuts, berries, fruits, and vegetables. She maintained that she could survive on only a diet of apples. She didn't eat meat. Maybe it was because she didn't have teeth. There wasn't a single time in her life when she was sick.

Only Two Reasons to Stay Married to a Man

Grandmother wore her course, straight hair in braids, carefully wrapped and pinned with bobby pins so her braids hugged the back of her head. Her skin sagged and hung there on her bones like limp, bleached muslin. I imagined that her hands had not always been calloused and boney and shrunken. Even if she occasionally had to take on the messes handed her and making her look older than she really was, she was beautiful.

She must have been born with white hair. When she smiled at me, I didn't know she was supposed to have teeth. She ate less than a mouse, so I figured she didn't need them for eating. Her dresses were starched and white. Sometimes around her waist she tied a white apron with tiny pockets. When a dress or apron didn't have a pocket to hold her handkerchief, she'd use a safety pin to pin it to the inside of her dress at her bosom where she kept valuables that were too precious for her black vinyl pocketbook. Her bosom and black pocketbook hoarded more secrets than most folks' cellars.

Every piece of cloth in her possession was white and most everything was starched so stiff that there wasn't a chance of a wrinkle finding its way to any bed or bureau drawer in the whole house. Everything: her dresses, aprons, tablecloths, counterpanes, sheets, and curtains were as pure and smooth as any wedding dress.

We called her *the Queen of Clorox*, and we complained constantly about the smell. Her house smelled of it because she mopped the floors with it. She used jugs of bleach like they were filled with water from the creek. Until I was ten years old, I thought the scent on her was bottled perfume and probably came in a fancy blue bottle like *Evening in Paris*.

My grandmother didn't move a fraction of an inch in any direction when she slept. You would have sworn she didn't breathe. And because she slept fully clothed and wearing her shoes, you would have sworn she was about to get up and go somewhere. She pulled her arms across her chest and lay there looking as if she was in a coffin, snoring louder than any man, and when she got up, she'd smooth the counterpane a bit with her palm making it look like no one had ever been on the tall, black, carved bed.

I learned early on that Lillie Dabney Halverston didn't trust in much of anything outside herself. I supposed that she could not trust in anybody after marrying into the Halverston family. Oh, she favored the Lord and trusted him in her own way, but she never asked anyone, not even the Lord, for anything if she could help it. She only asked Him for things when it was absolutely necessary, when she needed help pulling in the reins on her life if she felt it was spinning out to Mercury.

Her fussiness over cleaning and bleaching things until they fell apart was her own special way of feeling she had control of something in her life—scrubbing something to the point of disintegration was simply a means of control. "Just a shred of control," she'd admit. "When I see I'm losing sound footing or that I might need a little help, I just sneak in a few *pleases* and *wants* and *thank yous* to the Lord. I try not to be asking Him for something all the time. I don't want the Lord thinking here comes sniveling Lillie Dabney again whining about one thing or another, wanting Me to fix a problem, cure what ails her, or get her out of some kind of trouble. No, Ma'am! You cannot go pestering the Lord all the time. I only ask Him for just the few favors I need. Just enough to get by. Nothing more. Can't be bothering the Lord all the time about things that are trifling."

She was honest and high-minded to the point of being pure uppity about it. And she did not lie. At least, not to me. I thought she occasionally got the truth of things jumbled up with some tiny little lies, but the confusion was unintentional, and everyone pretended not to notice.

"That sometimes happens to people as they get older or meaner or more forgetful," she'd say, "now you just remember, Darlin', that memory and imagination sometimes wear the same dress. That's all right, though. It doesn't matter which one is taking hold of you, as long as you never carouse with the devil. That's when your memories and things you've only imagined can turn to *lies*.

"And never, never feel sorry for the devil. Not one bit of pity. He'll pull you in and fool you every time. He'll cheat you. Memories can cheat you sometimes when you get them wrong, but imagination is usually a kinder sort. It can prod you to create art. Memories can do that too, but you have to make sure they are *true*.

"Try not to hold on to or even imagine the bad things. Don't let them ball up in you and fester. Just let them go. You have the command over both of them. Make up your own truth when you need to," she'd say, "that's imagination, when you have it on your mind that you want to just sit down and bawl your eyes out, make up some ditties, or stories, or songs. One hundred percent guaranteed to make you feel better and help lift you over the slough. Make your memories and your mind's eye treat you right, the way you want them to. Hang stuff on them and pluck glitter out of your dreams each night to wrap around your favorites."

Grandmother wasn't like the others in the family. I figured she wasn't really a Halverston anyway, since her only transgression was marrying one, from whom she'd made a partial recovery after the divorce. The family didn't take to her from the very beginning. She knew there wasn't one of them who would take an extra breath to help her. I wondered why she birthed five babies before she figured out she didn't like W.O. very much. I asked her why she stayed married to him for all those years when she didn't even like him and especially after she found him out.

She said, "There are only two reasons to marry and stay married to a mean man: fear and love. When I finally came to know that I no longer felt either one for W.O., I had to let him go on back to his mama at Jacksboro. One morning I woke up and the dreadful, deadening truth of it all came to me. I knew I had lost my fear of him and any love I'd ever had for him. You can tell right off when fear leaves you, but when love for another person passes out of you, especially if it's gradual, you may not recognize it. When you truly love someone, something happens to your sorrow and to your fear. They take on a different face when they're felt for someone you love instead of for yourself. They're wider and deeper and self doesn't seem to hurt so much. When my own sorrow started to weigh on me more than his, I knew love had left me. I was worried about how I would care for five children, that's the only thing in the world that I've ever feared. But, I thought about it for a while and decided being rid of him and being shed of the Halverstons would be worth any worry or sacrifices they cost me."

As I listened to her, it occurred to me that my grandmother and my mother were alike in at least one respect—both had married Halverston men and both were miserable because of it.

She only talked about one of her five children— my father. You'd think he'd ridden into the world one Christmas Day on a gilded chariot. She'd say Joe this and Joe that, bragging really, when she went into town to Shelby's to buy snuff, always insisting that Mr. Shelby wrap the Bruton box in brown paper. She'd whisper to me, "I don't want every shirt ruff and nodding lady in town knowing my business." I knew the shirt ruffs and nodding ladies were not concerned with her business, especially her brand of snuff. Most of the sentences spoken at Shelby's Grocery and Mercantile or in the parking lot started with "I" or "My" and ended with "me" or "myself." Most people listened to Grandmother going on and on about her Joe to be polite, and then they would go on with their gossiping and bragging about their own children and their grandchildren or sometimes, about how their tobacco crops were doing this year and how much the harvest in the curing barns would bring at auction.

It seemed to me Grandmother had only one minor flaw: she wasn't very objective about her youngest son. When other relatives called him selfish, uncaring, aloof, and even mean; she defended him saying, "Joe's none of those things; he's highly-strung, I'll give them that, but that's often misread. He's intense, and what he does is solitary work."

Once when we were walking to Powell's Five and Dime to buy her garters for rolling up her stockings, I told her I'd heard a relative (whom remained nameless) say, "Joe uses people, and once he's used up a person, once they're spent, used like an extension of his own being, he throws them away."

"Do you think that's true?" I asked.

"Any relationship uses people, Darlin'," she said as casually as if she was commenting on the state of Pearlie Butters' dahlias, "not necessarily in a harmful or negative way, mind you, but we all seek out another person because they bring something to us, to our lives. Except family, of course; we don't have much say over zygotes and gametes. Everyone *wants* something. And that's all right."

"Think about what attracts you, draws you to another person—to the people you like to be around. Take your friend, Ova Gay, for instance. Why do you like to be with her?"

"Well, because I like her."

"But, why do you like her? What does Ova Gay bring to you that makes you want to be with her?"

"She's fun and easy to be with, easy to talk to; she cares about me. She listens to what I have to say. But, that doesn't mean I use her."

"Yes, it does. You use her as your confidant, your listener; you know she cares about you. It's not a bad thing. You just have to think of it differently. Now take someone with whom you have nothing in common—no similar interests at all. Think about what could compel you to want to spend your time with that person."

I kept thinking of my father even though

Grandmother said her concept of *using* people didn't apply to relatives. She impressed upon me constantly that thoughts didn't usually come to our brains fully-formed like Aphrodite springing from the sea foam. They have to incubate; to put down roots and feelers that creep along the surface looking for just the right place and time to plug in, to anchor, to take hold.

Shelby's seemed to get farther from Lillie Dabney's house with each trip we made. She was small and feisty, and seemed to be moving in fast motion most every step she took. Trying to keep up with her wore me out. When I was little, I had to run beside her to keep up, but when she saw I was falling behind, she'd stop, put her hands on her hips, and say, "Now, hurry it up, Lunda Rose. They could roll up the streets before we get home."

She considered walking across town and back before daybreak and enduring misery of any kind to be acts of virtue. I didn't see how suffering and sore feet were going to change my standing with the Lord in any way. She declared that cars were unreliable and expensive, and that she would never want nor have one of the contraptions if it was given to her free. I suffered through the same declaration when electric fans appeared in the window of Robard's Hardware.

She railed against the mess of the world caused by highfalutin machinery made for lazy people. Even in July and August when it was boiling hot in her house and no one could sleep because there wasn't a current of air moving in the whole state of Tennessee, she preached about electric fans that would suck lazy people right out through their windows.

Grandmother walked in high gear everywhere she went. Her white dress and white shoes made her appear larger than she was, but they helped me see her coming long before she arrived at the door. I saw her riding in a car only a few times, and those times were usually when she rode in the sheriff's car. I suspected she enjoyed riding in the backseat of the patrol car because it aggravated the sheriff.

When I fell behind, especially when I was little, on what seemed like one of our hundred-mile marches across the county, she'd say, "Don't dawdle. Pick up your step. We'll be home before you know it. I've got things to do."

After each long walk, and when I just wanted to collapse into a heap and never take another step as long as I lived, Grandmother would slip into the front room and take a crisply-starched, crochet-edged handkerchief from a drawer in the sideboard. When she thought I wasn't looking, she'd ease the snuff box from the brown paper, pour the brown powder into a cotton, draw-string pouch, wrap the pouch in the lacey handkerchief and pin it to the inside bosom of her dress.

Later, the Queen of Maynard Bald sat at the kitchen table under the dangling, naked light bulb, where I sat across from her. One of us would read. The room was filled with the smell of boiling evening primrose roots. I was never quite sure of exactly what she did with the tea of the boiled primrose roots. She said, "It's nothing short of a liquid miracle to pour on the hollyhocks, makes the blooms brighter; the leaves greener. It's a sweet elixir, without the alcohol of course, for sipping in the evening when I sit on the porch and watch the mountains swallow up the sun."

I examined the hollyhocks she claimed to water with the evening primrose tea to see if they were brighter. As I glanced at her, I saw her gently, carefully pack her left cheek with Bruton snuff and slip the draw-string pouch back into the bosom of her dress. I pretended not to notice. Why did it matter any more than the truths that slipped away from us or the forgiveness that was not given? We gave and kept just enough as was necessary, choking out the rest like weeds.

*   *   *

I discovered that my father could pull bent truths and sometimes flat-out lies from mid air. Some were the best lies you could have ever heard; they resembled fantastic stories—so incredible, as if you were being plopped down in the middle of them to become a character; they made you *want* to believe them.

Mother was truthful about most everything, except me. It was just that sometimes, like Grandmother, she didn't really realize what was true and what wasn't. After living with Daddy and listening to his tales, she couldn't be faulted.

I didn't know why they couldn't just admit the truth about me, and I could put this whole relations thing to rest. At least I wouldn't stay up at night worrying about being related to Aunt Winnifred Wilfreed Halverston or Cousin Maudie Halverston.

I liked the notion of being related to my grandmother, my mother, my two sisters, and my brother. It was the whole idea of being related to other Halverstons, those I called *the unhappy ones*, that kept me up nights. These were uninvited people, who seemed to be in constant combat with the world.

They wandered through our lives. Not one of them had a destination or any purpose that they could identify. Their unhappiness was chronic.

The gene question was one I continued to bring up before the Lord, but He did not do one thing about correcting His mistake. He didn't bother to send me even a hint to imply that He was working on it or, at the very least, thinking about it. He just let me stew down here without giving me one sliver of a sign.

About two months after Mother returned, I was at Grandmother's helping her corral what she called, her *English garden*, that she'd substituted for grass. It was July and unusually hot, but already, barbed burdocks and spotted joe-pye weeds were suffocating the foxgloves and hollyhocks. Aunt Winnifred and Maudie were there and had been embroiled all morning in a quarrel over whose responsibility it was to help Grandmother with such a task, since neither of them liked nor knew the first thing about plants.

"I'll do it myself," she snapped, "Lunda Rose and I will do it."

As I tackled the joe-pye, she pulled at burdock weeds, being careful to save the roots, claiming the Cherokees harvested and boiled them into a tea for purifying the blood, healing skin problems, soothing the stomach, and relieving gout. Occasionally, she'd stop and stare off, and I knew she was thinking about Winnifred or Maudie.

She slowly shook her head from side to side and closed her eyes, indications of her bafflement and annoyance. She said, "Lunda Rose, I know you don't understand Winnifred or Maudie. Sometimes I don't either. Both have troubles. Winnifred is the most disagreeable of all the Halverstons. Even though she's my own daughter, I see that she can be hateful. I don't understand it. Elease wasn't that way—two daughters with the same parents, but completely different temperaments. Winnifred is vain, self-centered, and in constant disagreement with everyone. She can't get along with a husband. She's been married four times. Men can't tolerate her for long periods, so when a husband protests or refuses her, she divorces him, and is off without as much as a second thought, looking for the next victim to marry her and cater to her wiles. Oh, she's charming in the beginning, before the wedding, but before the cake is eaten, she finds her newest husband's Achilles heel and starts to exert pressure, to manipulate. She puffs up, pouts, and is given to theatrics when she doesn't get her way, and if those don't work, she starts to belittle him. The worst of her traits, though, and the two she has in common with Maudie, are her wicked tongue and her belief that she knows everything. Winnifred can be malicious too, but Maudie is never malicious, just hurting.

"The difference in how I react to Winnifred's and Maudie's hatefulness is that I can make justifiable allowances for Maudie's, but, at times I think Winnifred enjoys being miserable and contemptible. There are people who thrive on their stores of misery. Maudie has reasons for being unhappy: she's never been on firm ground since the day she was born, no real sense of where she belonged, or even of who she was. Elease was sick and couldn't care for her. She's never known her father. Of course she had the father she'd made up. I pleaded with Elease to tell the real father that she was pregnant, but she refused.

Consequently, he never knew she'd been born; so Maudie made up the daddy that she wanted: a daddy who never missed sending her a package for her birthday; a daddy from a prominent family of attorneys in Nashville; a daddy who, after his law practice was firmly established, would summon Elease and Maudie to Nashville.

"And of course, that poor man, whoever and wherever he is, can't be blamed for failing to come forward, since he didn't know he was a father. I don't think it would be a good thing if he met Maudie as an adult. She's become bitter with a collection of Halverston traits that cause her discontentment. If she was able to meet her father, she might spit cuss words at him the way she does at us sometimes. On the other hand, though, we might just be surprised.

"When she was a little girl, so beautiful, so brilliant, I was ecstatic thinking this is the way it should be for a little girl without her parents. But, when Maudie was a teenager and these traits and behaviors started to show themselves, I saw the makings of what I call *the toadying shift of a female*— smiling and rolling her eyes and puckering her lips up just right to make any man near her lose his wits to the point of not being able to recover them."

"Why did you let her do it?" I asked.

"Oh, Darlin', I tried to convince her, and Winnifred too when she was that age, that there were other ways to get what she wanted, rather than manipulating or spouting sweet, outrageous, sometimes untrue words from lips smeared with *ruby-slipper red* lipstick bought at Powell's Five and Dime or using a tone of voice a little sweeter than was necessary for the truth."

"Maudie has seldom mentioned her mother in all the years she's been at our house," I said, as I tried to pull a burr out of my hair. "I barely knew Elease because you didn't allow me into her room, but I knew I felt a fondness and a deep sadness for Aunt Elease. I only remember seeing her in bed and you telling me that when she took her ailment, six men were required to carry her on a make-shift gurney to the big carved bed in the first room at the top of the stairs."

Grandmother stared off as if she was visualizing that day years ago. She said, "Even with all six of those strong men struggling and sweating, the trip up the long, narrow stairway carrying Elease and a stretcher almost killed off every one of them. The only thing that kept them all from tumbling backwards down the stairs with Elease perched on the stretcher like Venus of Willendorf was that Elease wasn't very tall. They heaved and swayed from side to side, cussing and thudding against the sides of the stairwell like a bunch of soused 'possums. When they sighted the big, carved bed in the room at the top of the stairs, they practically sprinted to it to set the stretcher down. The six of them, all red-faced and wet with sweat, ran down the stairs before I could ask them to help me shift Elease into place.

"Elease was always eccentric, but, unlike Winnifred, she was kind. After Maudie was born, the *slough of despond* grabbed her and never let her go."

Grandmother was the only one of us who knew the secrets surrounding Elease. Even when I was a little girl, I knew not to ask questions. Most times, when I did muster up enough courage to ask, I was either ignored or immediately told to hush up. Once I went to the top-of-the-stairs bedroom and found the door had been left open to Elease's room, a place where I wasn't allowed. Grandmother said, "She's sick, and you'll disturb her if she's sleeping."

On the floor next to the bed were a wash pan of soapy water, hand towels, and a new bar of rosemary milk soap. I only saw her from a distance, lying there, eyes closed, in the huge, black, carved bed, a lifeless, mammoth form under the counterpane. She was on her side. I could see her long black hair, a feature of most of the Halverstons. She didn't move or say anything, but I could see she was awake. She had the distinct, beautiful features, especially the cheekbones, of a Cherokee.

Grandmother said that after she gave birth, she left her bed only for short periods to sit at a small table in the bedroom to eat her meals and wait for Maudie to be brought in. Finally, when Maudie was still very young, Elease didn't stir from her bed at all. Grandmother cared for Maudie full time, and seldom took her into Elease's room to see her, saying the child was confused and didn't recognize Elease as her mother. When Aunt Winnifred was between husbands, which was most of the time, she lived with Grandmother and helped with raising Maudie.

After Elease died, six stout men were summoned again to Grandmother's house to move her body to Belcher's Funeral Home. I wasn't allowed to watch and was banished to the kitchen, but I could hear the men and Grandmother trying to figure out a way to get her body down the stairwell without having to remove the handrail or a wall.

The stairwell was narrow with a curved landing where the stairs changed directions. One of men said a stretcher was out of the question. "Moving a body is different from moving a live person," he said, "the handrail will have to be removed." Another said that even if the stairwell was straight, there was still only enough room for two men on each end of the stretcher, and that four men were not strong enough. Cratis Roache opened his carpenter's measure with the ease of one fold of a bellows to determine the stairwell was 38 inches wide. Cratis shook his head. Finally, they rigged four thick quilting poles, that were cut making them short enough to make the turn at the landing, and wrapped her in a large quilt, making a knapsack of sorts, where her huge body was swaddled, molded and rolled into a shape that would fit between the walls of the stairwell.

I watched and listened through the cracked kitchen door, and regretted it from that day. The low murmurs of the men discussing how they would move her and the sounds of her body thudding against the stairwell wall would stay with me the rest of my life. It took over two hours of six men struggling, directing, and contending with Grandmother's instructions interspersed with sobbing and wailing.

Cratis made the mistake of asking Grandmother if she had been able to reach Maudie's father to tell him of Elease's death.

"Maudie does not have a daddy," she snapped.

Embarrassed, he backed away and wiped his forehead with a handkerchief pulled from his bib pocket, while at the same time giving him the chance to look away from Grandmother. I wondered how closely related Elease was to the Virgin Mary, whom I'd heard about in Sunday school. Elease having a baby all by herself seemed like the same Sunday-school story to me.

Grandmother and Maudie were smart, and both had huge vocabularies. I knew who to ask when I wanted a definition of any word in the English language. I would ask Grandmother first, as Maudie always seemed to be annoyed by questions. Once I overheard a woman in Shelby's Grocery talking to another woman standing in front of the milk cooler. She used a word I didn't know. That same day, when Grandmother and Maudie were together in the kitchen, I asked, "What does *illegitimate* mean?" Grandmother stared at me in silence, twisting her mouth the way she did when she didn't know the answer to a question. I looked at Maudie, who glowed like she was lit on fire. Her neck was splotched red.

"Where did you hear that word? Where did you hear it?" she yelled.

"At Shelby's. A woman in Shelby's."

"Don't you ever use that word again. Do you understand me?" Maudie screamed grabbing my arm.

It was hard to imagine that my grandmother was also Maudie's grandmother. I knew it must be true because Elease was her daughter. Grandmother said Elease had died of consumption, what everybody else called *tuberculosis*. Many of the coal miners in Maynard Bald died of consumption: Grandmother said it was really *black lung* or what people in the mining camps called *coal dust poisoning*, when they withered away to mere skeletons and labored for every breath before dying. Elease didn't *wither away*. I thought Grandmother must have made a mistake about her diagnosis.

The only problem now was Maudie. I thanked the

Lord that she hadn't heard Grandmother's response to Cratis' question about her daddy. I found myself feeling sorry for her in those months after Elease's death. Just as I began thinking that she was becoming nicer, that we might even start to like each other, she'd curse at everybody who spoke to her, slam doors, and spend days in her room without coming out.

In the days before Maudie came to live with us, I'd only been around her when I went to our grandmother's. I thought she was one of the strangest persons I had ever known, more strange than any of my other kin. It worried me that we were related. Maybe she was dropped into the wrong family, too.

Grandmother said, "She's your daddy's niece, and he'll take her as a member of the family, if she will just keep a rein on her anger and try not to be so hateful." Grandmother said once, when I asked her why Maudie was so mean, "There are things that are much worse than death. One of them is being left behind."

Only Two Reasons to Stay Married to a Man

The Red Pontiac

"Grandmother had made her way just fine," I thought as I sat on the rock step and drew in a deep breath, savoring the faint scent of the fading phlox. I was contented and reveled in the stillness, the calmness.

It was late summer, 1963. Daddy had returned a week ago without incidence. He appeared unperturbed, collected, mute. Mother seemed unafraid, almost relaxed.

They'd been apart for nearly a year, and now they behaved as if nothing had happened. No one offered explanations or excuses for why my father had behaved the way he had. Now it was harder for even Grandmother to defend him since Mother's nine-month absence and the visible scar across her right cheek—a permanent reminder of that horrible night and the damage done a year ago.

We didn't ask questions. "Maybe it will last," I thought. I leaned back against the cool stone, closed my eyes and listened to the droning of cicadas. I would never forget the sound. The whirring brought back a vivid memory of something that happened at this exact time of year ten years earlier.

I was very young, but it became one of my clearest and most indelible memories. It was the hottest summer in the Smoky Mountains that anyone remembered, 1953, thick and wet, clothes stuck to skin, and the only sound cutting the air during the day was the drumming of cicadas.

Even in those early days, when we lived in the Petticourt house on Old Depot Road, we knew it was just a matter of time before someone in our family ended up dead or, at the very least, in prison. I started to put this together, reaching a full conclusion about it all by myself without any help from my grandmother. It just stood to reason, since every male who came through the door toted a pistol stuffed in his pants. All of them: my father, the uncles, the cousins, all male blood relations on both sides of the family, and almost every man or boy who came to the house to see my father about his work carried a loaded gun. Mother insisted that business-related matters be handled outside or in the workshop.

Eventually, it would happen though, and I learned early on that if any one of them was asked why he carried a gun, he would not be able to tell you.

It was just after her mother died in April of 1953 that Maudie had come to live with us. For a few weeks after Aunt Elease died, Maudie lived with Grandmother and Winnifred (whom Maudie called the *aunt at large*). But three Halverston women living in proximity of one another proved to be impossible. Maudie needed to finish high school, and my father thought living with us was a good idea to give Grandmother some relief. Mother was almost six months pregnant with her fourth baby and asked

Maudie to help her with cooking and housework.

No one in the family had displayed a glimmer of happiness since we'd moved into the Petticourt house. My father had been gone for weeks. Mother cried most of the time, and Maudie grieved for her own mother. No one slept.

What we heard during the night was the roar of pickup trucks going back and forth from the sheriff's office to the depot, which was only a short distance from our house. We learned from *the Maynard Bald Press* that Mr. Ralph Winslow at Flat Hollow had broadcasted on his ham radio that he was the disabled father of nine children living in the mountains near Maynard Bald, Tennessee. A young nun in Indiana got word of Mr. Winslow's plea and alerted the news media and service organizations. Since Mr. Winslow's broadcast, boxes of goods had arrived by the trainload—food goods, clothes, toys, school supplies, dishes, pots, pans, bed linens. Hundreds of boxes were arriving from all over the country, giving Sheriff Rosemund's temper enough torque to move a train.

"Who does he think he is? He has no idea what he's stirred up," Sherriff Rosemund ranted to a newspaper reporter. "This town would never let a family go hungry."

All night long the steady stream of pickup trucks continued back and forth from the train station to haul all the goods to the sheriff's office. The same air hung over us without moving, smothering us with heat, moisture, and unfamiliar sounds. Everyone in the house was sleep-deprived, which added to the already seething agitation and growing hunger for what we didn't have, the craving that rose up in each of us. My own hunger was for something I couldn't name, my wanting for something unknown to me.

The summer afternoon that presented itself to my father on that August day, a mere matter of hours after arriving home in a red convertible that we'd never seen before, was irresistible for rolling down the top and trying to persuade my mother to ride in it. *Shameful*, Mother called it, from the minute she laid eyes on it. Yes, this was the same father who disappeared as quickly and unnoticed as the evening's last slant of daylight across the kitchen wall. Vanished one day and home again weeks later with no mention to my mother of where he'd been.

I don't know when I stopped believing that each time my father walked out the door, he would eventually come back. I don't know when I understood the concept of headlong carelessness or stopped believing that somewhere, deep down inside him, there was a decent man. I did not arrive at this important fact overnight by just waking up one morning believing something that wasn't in my head when I went to sleep the night before. No. This notion was a long time coming, and it came to me gradually, filling me up a little bit at a time. Growing. One of those things that pushes on your heart day after day until it seeps into your soul like an underground leak.

And sometimes in dreams I would think I had found the opening of a well that I could look into like a window to find the leak. I wanted to find it. To see it. But I was afraid to lean in close enough to peek over into the hole. And when I did call up enough courage to lean forward, squinting, shaking, the water was too deep and too dark.

Back then and for years after, I believed there

must have been a little bit of good in him because my grandmother birthed him; it seemed reasonable that since he was her baby, he must bear some resemblance to a decent person. I did not trust, however, that when he left for a neon job in Kentucky or any of the places where he told us he'd worked, that he would ever come back to us.

Each homecoming was filled with elaborate stories that made it impossible to remember why we were mad at him. Even my mother was drawn in by his tales of the Green River in Kentucky, and how, on a neon job at a motel along the river, he'd fished a water moccasin out of his toolbox. How at a downtown hotel in Pikeville, a man in the room right next to my father's, was found shot with a hotel pillow used as a silencer. His stories were fraught with mystery and parts left out, but Daddy jumped from one outrageous happening to another, each one more exciting and unbelievable than the last.

"Well, who shot the man in the next room? And why for God's sake?" Mother asked trying to slow him down.

"Helen, how should I know?" Daddy glared at her, irritated by the interruption. "The hotel maid found him after someone called the front desk saying there weren't any glasses in the room. Her screaming woke me and there was all the ruckus afterwards: the ambulance blaring coming after a dead man, when all they needed was a coroner; then the police sirens; and all those people in the halls. They knocked on every friggin' door in the hotel. Everybody was asking questions."

Grandmother's excuses for him played in my head like a memorized script, "Joe's always been reckless, defiant. Since he was just a scrap, he's never been afraid of anything. Sometimes he gets wild and a little mean, but he doesn't mean anything by it. Not really."

I imagined how her face changed, as it always did when she talked about him. She didn't talk about her other children the way she talked about my daddy. In fact, if a stranger was listening to her, he'd assume Joe was her only child. Her only near-perfect, shameless, rogue child.

Back then, when we were all younger and unknowing, it was easy, as it is for most young children, to see our father as loving, protective, flawless, without faults. Over time, though, all of us, and even our mother, became less tolerant, and our indifference toward him and his recklessness grew. The only times our indifference couldn't rescue us was when fear rose above it, pressing on us like we were being held under water.

My father was lost somewhere in a place where he didn't belong; not a fault of his own. If Grandmother was right in her defense of her youngest son, it wasn't that he was mean-spirited or even uncaring—she insisted that he was merely thoughtless and, at times, selfish. Later I would hear my mother say to him over and over that he was like his own father—never thinking of anyone but himself, and after he'd used up a person, once they were spent, he threw them away.

Thinking back on it now, the occasions I remember most vividly showed off behaviors that resembled the spasms of flight of a lost butterfly. Unpredictable. Random. Searching. Chaotically moving in one direction and then jerking to another. Never decisive or satisfied with his path. It was that recklessness; that winged carelessness that kept my mother, and all of us for that matter, in a constant state of torment.

I was near the edge of the woods where I'd spotted a hognose snake. To get a better look at it, I tried to coax it out of the weeds with a stick, but when I lifted it, it fell to the ground and plopped over on its back, lifelessly showing its white belly to imitate death. It was during this delicate operation of capturing the snake that I saw the red car in front of our house. I ran to the front porch and looked through the screen door. I tried to pull it open, but it was swollen in the wet heat and wedged fast in the jam.

Mother stood in the far corner of the room, crying, her face wet and red, and her eyes puffed up. I pressed my face against the screen. There was always that desperate look on her face. The ache in her voice. The familiar plea. Head down. Whimpering like a hurt animal. The next minute swearing at him and more crying. Always, the crying.

"Joe, how could you? How could you do it? How could you do something like this? Where have you been for these days and weeks? I've been out-of-my-mind with worry about you and about these babies and about the one inside me. Now you're here, Lord, help me, talking like nothing's wrong. Weeks without a word, but now, you show up with a brand-spanking-new red car! I can't believe it. Did you get a blow to your head that you haven't told me about? That's it, isn't it? You've had a strike to your brain in one of those places you go and never tell me about. You've been in a brawl, and somebody has knocked you senseless. You've had a brain accident. What else could make you buy a new car when we have the children?"

My father looked at her, and just for a second, a peculiar look came over his whole face. I thought she might have gotten through to him—that he might have thought about how she cried when he wasn't here. And just for a moment, he studied her.

"Awh...Helen...you're fussin' over nothing," he said trying to change the subject. "I don't want to hear you anymore," he snapped, sounding as if the words were coming from someone else. "Stop asking questions. You ask too many questions. Just shut up."

She looked at the floor and closed her eyes. She stroked her belly and held her hands under her belly as if scooping the baby into her arms and rocking her back to calm.

"You know I have to go away to work, to make a living. I'm doing what I can for you and the babies, and all I hear is your constant yammering. What you need is to get away from here. Wha' da you say we take a trip to Texas after the baby comes? This year, 1953, will be our best year. When the baby comes, you'll be okay. Maybe we can see one of those little armadillos, and we'll get Lunda Rose and Robert Joseph each a pair of real cowboy boots—gen-u-ine cowhide with pointy toes. Maudie can look after the children while we're gone. She needs to work for her fare around here anyway. We'll have a great time. You've always talked about goin' to Texas. And wouldn't ya love to see one of those little animals covered with armor, see it up close? Now stop crying!"

Mother kept her ironing board set up in the kitchen all the time now. She used to prop it up in the pantry, out of the way, unless it was Tuesday, her usual ironing day. For months, she'd kept her mama's cameo brooch pinned to the front of her blouse— sometimes she pinned it close to her throat, or on her sleeve, sometimes to her apron. I'd watch her touch the carving gently with her middle finger as if reading Braille. Lately, she needed to iron something almost every day, and it didn't matter if it was an unkind, wet, 100-degree day.

Her belly rubbed against the ironing board. With every word, her iron slammed into the maternity smock that she worked on. Most of the time, the iron didn't even hit the blouse. She cried without making a sound as she hit the board with the iron. Daddy hated it when she cried, and she knew this. She'd mastered crying silently.

She stepped from behind the ironing board so her whole broad figure showed. She pulled at her pleated, orchid smock, holding both sides away from her and looked like she was taking a bow in a ball gown. She said, as she curtsied, "Look at me, Joe. Look at me. The baby will come before you know it. Already, I look like two swollen moon pies melted together, a Guernsey ready to deliver. And you want me to go for a ride in that hideous car. Lord, I would deliver right on the curve coming out of the dip. How could you buy a car?" she whined, shaking her head. "A red car? A car without a top? What's happened to you? Where did you get money for it?"

The vein in his neck bulged. The one at his right temple throbbed as if it would burst. "I told you I didn't buy that car. A man owed it to me for a favor I did for him. Not a penny for that car, I swear. And look." He pulled from his pocket a roll of bills and spread them on the table: $20's, $50's, $100's. Mother started to cry.

"Joe, what have you done for this? God, help us! What have you done?"

"Nothing. Just a favor. A big favor I owed a friend. Not only did he owe me for the favor, but I got paid for making a big sign—red neon for a job in Roanoke. It was a huge job. You know how they bring the big money. My friend was real grateful. Said he didn't know how to repay me. Now let's go for a ride around the depot. Let's have some fun. Get the babies."

"Joe, you're lying to me. I can't ride in that car," she said shaking her head, never looking up. "That car makes me sick. It's red. It doesn't have a top. It has the head of a Cherokee Indian on the hood. What will the neighbors think? They'll think we're just common Heathens. We're behaving like crazy people! I cannot ride in a red car with a Cherokee Indian on it."

"Stop it, Helen. Why do you go on and on about that blessed hood ornament. It's just a piece of chrome. There's an Indian's head on all Pontiac cars. Pon-ti-ac. You got it? Just because you have all that Cherokee blood running through you doesn't mean every Indian is a Cherokee. Pontiac was some famous Indian chief from up north. It's a Pontiac car. Will you shut up about the car. It's a Pontiac. How many times do I have to tell you? What difference does it make? See, it says it right on the car. PON-TI-AC. Come on, Helen, forget that. Let's have some fun. Get the babies. You'll be fine. You've got a long way to go yet. Expecting doesn't mean you're an invalid. Clean up your face. Let's go."

"No, you go on," she said without looking up.

"Just take the babies around the loop. I can't ride in a red car without a top on it. It has an Indian on the hood. Joe, where did you really get the money? Lord, that car is so red with an Indian's head on the hood. I will never ride in it." I wanted her to stop talking about the Indian's head, but she brought it up again and again. I held my breath and prayed she'd think of just one positive thing to say to him.

Daddy's face grew redder. Sweat ran down from his wet hair. He closed his eyes and took a deep breath. In a low voice and hardly moving his lips, he said, "Like I've told you a hundred times, a man gave me the car and the money for a favor. And I got paid for the Roanoke sign. Some work I did for him. Stop questioning me. What difference does it make?"

On that August day, she couldn't keep her crying from him. She slammed the iron across the board, fidgeting with the cameo near her throat, and making the little snubbing sounds that babies make after a long cry.

"Helen," he whispered, squeezing her name through his teeth. "Stop your never-ending whining and that bloody ironing," he yelled as he grabbed her right hand to stop the iron. He stood directly in front of her on the opposite side of the ironing board, looking her straight in the eyes and pressing hard on her hand keeping the iron on the blouse.

"Just tell me what you have to be whining about all the time?"

"You're hurting me, Joe. Stop it."

"I want you to look at me and tell me exactly what it is that you're whimpering about all the time," he said calmly, pressing his hand harder over hers holding the iron on the blouse. The blouse started to smoke. Tears washed down her face. She grabbed at his arm trying to free her hand. Flames burst from the blouse sending Mother screaming to the sink where she grabbed a kettle of soaking beans flinging them over the ironing board and the kitchen.

She cried and held her hand. I started to cry.

"I'm okay," she said, bending toward me. "You see, I'm fine," she said holding up her hand. "Take Robert Joseph now and go on with your daddy."

Daddy eased toward the screen door, pushing it. It was stuck. He stepped back slowly raising his leg and with one blow kicked it off its hinges. The screen door fell across the porch. He stepped across it and walked to the red car, picked up a loose rock from the steps and slammed it into the Indian head on the hood breaking it clean in one easy swipe. "Is that better?" he yelled.

Mother stepped onto the porch and across the screen door to watch us get into the car. She'd wrapped the extra cloth of the bottom of the maternity blouse around her hand and wrist.

"Be careful with them," she said, her voice choking. "Make them sit down when you pass the tracks and the depot. Don't get too close to the trains. Make Robert Joseph sit down. He won't do it unless you make him. Lunda Rose, watch out for him. Make him sit. He'll want to stand up to see the train."

Daddy said, "Lunda Rose, Robert Joseph, get into the car. We're going for the loop." I looked back at her and steered Robert Joseph to the red Pontiac and into the front seat. I didn't want to go. I wanted to run back to her and tell her not to be afraid; that he wouldn't hurt her. He saw my hesitation. "Lunda Rose," he ordered, "Get into the car." I climbed into the back seat, sliding across the seat to get a better view of my mother. Robert's hard-soled shoes danced across the front seat, and he clapped his hands wildly. "Daddy, let Robert Joseph come back here with me," I pleaded trying not to cry.

"He'll be fine where he is," Daddy let out a whoop and yelled as if nothing had happened, "Let's go for a ride around the loop. Let's have some fun." *The loop* was the name we'd given the one-lane dirt road that circled through the hills around the depot and the tenant houses. Some railroad workers lived in the little houses, but mostly they were just rundown places with beds for miners who'd been sent by the mining companies to take care of the coal cars.

There was an excitement about the business of the depot—the hurried movements of the workers and passengers, the smells of burning fuel and the heat of summer, the sounds of machines and bits of over-heard conversations. All of it fused like the droning whir of a million cicadas.

If we got there at the right time, we could see the engineer and watch the motion of the iron wheels and hear the burst of the whistle so painful that I'd cover Robert Joseph's ears. Maybe we'd get there in time for *the Southland*, the passenger train from Corbin, Kentucky. Some of the south-bound passengers would have boarded in Cincinnati, Covington, Louisville, and Berea before reaching Corbin. We'd see people waving from the windows, the pretty people.

According to my grandmother, the train depot in Maynard Bald, Tennessee, had more activity than a fat city. Most of the trains hauled coal from the mines, but, once a day, *the Southland* came through, and once at night, *the Flamingo*, the North-bound train starting from Atlanta. The train that moved people was a beautiful sight with carriages the color of midnight blue trimmed with lettering, serifs, and thin scrolled lines painted the color of gold. The livery colors for the massive engines were red, yellow, and gray.

I loved seeing *the Southland* with its elegant people with perfectly-dressed children; those children who never got dirty or spilled things; little girls wearing frilly dresses and boys wearing little suits making them look like miniature men. The heads of the beautiful people flashed by. I liked to imagine where they were going in the midnight blue carriages. I could see the ladies through the train's windows. A few wore lovely hats with shading brims and magnificent feathers. Sometimes they would wave with hands in gloves. I imagined they were headed to Atlanta to buy new hats.

The dirt road was the ride of a roller coaster—one of those rides when your belly feels all tingly inside and you think you won't make it over the next ridge. I loved to ride the loop road. A car without a top was better than the *Flying Dutchman*, the roller coaster at the Knoxville Fair that made you want to feel the feeling over and over again—the feeling that your stomach was jumping up into your chest.

The dirt on the road was bone-dry. The stretch nearest the depot was black from coal that sifted off the coal cars. Daddy said poor people stole coal from the train cars left parked on the tracks at night. When the Pontiac passed, the dust flew up leaving a black cloud that sifted down like black rain behind us.

Daddy drove fast. He yelled, "Feels like a roller coaster!" as he threw both arms straight up releasing the steering wheel. I was scared. Grandmother said he'd always been daring. "Since the time he could walk," she said, "wanted to do everything fast, never afraid of anything."

Just as the depot came into sight, two linked engines approached pulling a string of coal cars that stretched so far the caboose was not visible. Painted on the engine and each car was L & N RAILROAD. Daddy said it meant *Louisville and Nashville*. The engineers waved and the whistle was so loud you thought it would split your eardrums. Another train with CLINCHFIELD RAILROAD painted on each of the cars, each loaded with coal, idled on another track. The engineer pulled the chain holding the whistle open. Robert Joseph covered his ears and started to cry. From behind him, I cupped my hands over his ears. All I could think of was the look on my mother's face as we were leaving.

There was excitement at the depot. Railroad men climbed on the engines and hung from the trains railings. All the hurrying and business of it. Escaping pressure hissed from the engine; heat and the smell of something scorched rose up from the tracks and through the platform. A noise rippled through every car, one and then the next, as if it was a single heartbeat. People on the platform stood back.

I stood up in the back seat and waved to the engineers. One of them touched the bill of his striped cap in a make-believe salute. We were next to the station; the engine idled. Passengers were getting off and boarding. He left the car engine running as he lit a cigarette and studied the train. Robert Joseph stood up in the front seat. The train started to move, slowly at first, then building speed. Daddy studied it. We could see the great wheel braces. The sounds grew louder. Robert Joseph squealed with excitement.

"Lunda Rose, you sittin' down?" Daddy yelled as he threw the Pontiac into gear, never taking his eyes off the wheels of the train.

The Pontiac started to move slowly, slowly right up alongside the engine. The engineer saluted and waved and pulled the chain to sound the whistle. He waved again and smiled. Then his face changed. He stared with a strange look on his face, a fixed, scared look, as if he was examining us.

"Faster, Daddy," Robert Joseph squealed. "It's getting ahead of us." Daddy leaned into the steering wheel and bent forward, looking back and forth at the train and the road ahead. The Pontiac went faster. "Sit down, Robert." He couldn't hear me. I leaned over and swiped the backs of his legs, motioning for him to sit down. He whimpered because he couldn't see out. He wailed.

The train sped faster; the smell of burning fuel rose from its underside. Daddy's knee stiffened as he pressed his shoulders forward. The Pontiac went faster and faster. Daddy leaned into the steering wheel. The vein at his temple moved up and down, his face red and wet with sweat. "What a stupid, stupid man to think he can go faster than a 1953 Pontiac," he yelled. The Lucky Strike hung limp from his lip and moved up and down as he swore and jerked his head back and forth.

We flew beside the train at the same even speed. FAST! FAST! FASTER! Robert's mouth was open. His screams were hushed by the sounds of the train. The engineer started to wave his arms and motion to us with terror on his face. I could tell he was swearing. Shouting. Red-faced. He wielded his fists motioning for us to go away. He thrusts his fist in desperate bursts into the air. Daddy pressed harder on the gas pedal. We flew faster and faster. The train picked up speed. The Pontiac picked up speed. The Pontiac was on the loop right next to the iron wheels of the great engine running alongside it, keeping the same speed. Faster. Faster. Daddy leaned in, his chest pressing on the steering wheel.

When I looked, Robert Joseph was sitting, eyes and mouth wide open, hands over his ears. I looked at the engineer. He was waving. Shouting. Swearing. I looked at Daddy, laughing with his head thrown back, both hands clutching the steering wheel. The Lucky Strike laid limp across his lip as he bent farther into the steering wheel. He was wild with the thrill of it.

He yelled, "Look at that poor, stupid man. Thinks he can go faster than a 1953 Pontiac. Dumb as sheep." Daddy shouted, "Go for it, *you* imbecile."

The engineer waved his arms, motioned violently, and pulled on the whistle chain. His mouth was frozen in horror, as he pulled down on the chain. Daddy ignored him. His foot pressed heavier on the pedal. We raced alongside the iron wheels. Robert was screaming. I knew now what he was doing— trying to beat the train to the crossing—determined to cross in front of the engine. The Pontiac crossed the tracks seconds before the great engine.

Daddy stopped and smiled and lit another Lucky Strike and attached it to his lip. "That poor, stupid boy didn't split the atom, now, did he?" I looked at Robert Joseph sitting on the front seat, unaware of what had happened. Black dust sifted down on us and lay like tiny black crystals on Robert's blond hair. He was still and calm and trying to tie his shoelace.

It was then, looking at my father sitting there with that wild look on his face, not thinking for a second of all three of us dead, that I became my mother and my grandmother. In that moment of silence, in the shrill, steady silence, I began my years of covering, shading, apologizing, excusing, forgiving.

Looking back, it was at that moment that I started to think of my father differently: not as someone I was forever waiting for; not as someone who would take care of us; `not as someone who would always come back to us; but rather, as an unwelcome visitor who took up too much of the air around us, whose presence carved out a deep well and left a hole when he was gone.

Mother must never know. She must never know about the loop, that Daddy had outrun and crossed by mere seconds in front of the train with Robert Joseph and me in the red Pontiac.

The cicadas droned on—a steady, pulsating whining like wheels on a wide stretch of wilderness highway. Droning on and on after waiting all those years to resurface, to break the silence—whining as though nothing extraordinary had happened on that August day in 1953. Mother must never know.

The Glory of the Mean Year

I would keep the secret of outrunning the train. Other unimaginable things happened around that same time.

I knew one thing was true. No matter how long I lived, I would never forget the months surrounding Elda Kate's birth. Tensions mounted. Agitation seethed just below the surface. No one talked. Mother was especially silent. It seemed she was distressed over one thing or another that whole, seemingly never-ending year of 1953. Some things were meant to be remembered, perhaps to prepare us for things to come.

That time in my childhood, those months before the birth of my sister, seemed to have stretched over a lifetime, but time, like size, was distorted because I was a child. Everything seemed big because I was little. Houses. Stairways. Rooms. Furniture. Even people. Time was distorted: days, weeks, months; they all seemed the same. When my father disappeared for what seemed like years, those periods when Mother was the most distraught, I had no concept of whether a week or a month had passed. I was little, my only yardsticks of time were my birthdays and Christmases or the last house I lived in.

I would learn eventually that the mind remembers most vividly the things that summon our emotions. We, of course, remember the positive moments like birthdays and gifts and cakes. But moments, even brief ones, of fear or pain or loss will be remembered always. Eons after we've forgotten long-ago, intense joys, we will remember the most brief and fleeting sorrows.

We must have lived in the Petticourt house for at least a hundred years. In reality, we lived there about two and a half years; two and a half years we would all remember. By the time we moved from the Petticourt house, all of us were ready to leave it behind. Living there marked a time when our lives would change forever.

It wasn't a particular event that prodded us to call this year, 1953, *the mean year*. We referred to it that way long into our adulthoods—*mean* because there was never enough of anything and because everyone in the family seemed angry. There was a long string of happenings that made it unforgettable for all of us. What made the events from September through early December indelible for us was that it was late in Mother's pregnancy. Not only was she sick for most of the nine months, but she seemed unusually fragile, vulnerable. In September, Dr. O'Brien recommended that she stay off her feet and have as much bed rest as possible until the baby came.

Daddy was away most of the time and only passed in and out of our lives. It could have been entirely spoiled, but what happened in December seemed to smooth the glaze making the first eleven months of the year seem more distant. For Maudie, Ruby Grace, Robert Joseph, and me, the time will never be completely forgotten, but perhaps just memories faded. For our mother and father, it was a time of unimaginable turmoil.

Ruby Grace was sick most of that year. I tried to think of a time when she wasn't sick, although no one could say exactly what was wrong with her. Maybe it was our family that made her sick. Sadness clung to Ruby Grace, and when she left a room or a conversation, sadness lingered there like stale air.

Standing by the stove, mother waited for the perfect time to take the cornbread out of the oven. She was so swollen with pregnancy that her belly got in the way of everything she did. She could barely reach the stove. She didn't smile, and she never laughed out loud like she used to.

The smell of her cornbread filled the whole house, and even waffled outside. No one made cornbread like hers. She learned from her mother, and she bragged that her mother taught her when she was just a young girl. She said, "The secret of making cornbread is a perfectly-aged iron skillet, just the right size and seasoned black. Sometimes, old man Higgenbotham appeared on the back porch with a dozen brown eggs and said, "Thought you might need some eggs. Don't want to interfere with your supper." She usually slipped a big wedge of cornbread wrapped in a dishcloth into his hand to have with his brown beans and sliced onions that evening. He always accepted.

Reluctantly, Maudie had unpacked her bags over a period of five months and taken over the drawers of the bureau in the bedroom upstairs as if she intended to stay. `Some people in town, who didn't know our family history, mistook Maudie for our oldest sibling rather than our cousin.

After her mother died at the end of April, 1953, Maudie forbade anyone in the family, even Grandmother, to talk about her or even mention her name.

Now my cousin divided her time between our house and Grandmother's. She seemed more hateful at Grandmother's, probably because that's where she remembered her own mama.

Maudie made each of her appearances with the drama of a summer storm. Each time she left a room, I looked at my grandmother's face, and looked about to see what was broken or overturned or missing. Maudie did exactly as she pleased, leaving strewn messes to be cleaned up, repairs to be made, breakage to be pieced back together.

Grandmother told me about genes—how your genes were passed to you from your mother and father; and how you even received them from your grandparents and their parents. Surely, since Maudie and I had the same grandparents and great-grandparents, we must have some of the same genes. I stayed awake at night worrying about just how akin my genes were to hers.

Maudie was smart. I figured her intelligence, her beauty, and above all, her way of speaking, must have come from Elease, although I never heard Elease speak. Maudie used beautiful words. And although her voice was loud, and she talked incessantly, it was at the same time, lovely, almost musical, except when she spat cuss words at everyone around her.

She passed in and out of Grandmother's house

and our house at odd times—any time of the day or night that suited her. Always unexpected. I spent a lot of time trying to understand Maudie, what made her who she was, and where she belonged. After she'd lived with us for a considerable time, I suspected that she was really a Halverston. Proof of my theory that I was not, became more pressing.

Grandmother said, "Maudie has a foul tongue and temperament and, at times I have suspected that she harbors a troubled soul. It has worried me since she was a little girl, and it worries me that she is forever restless and unhappy—never pleased about anything on this earth. I'm afraid she will never be happy, because, she has never, nor will she ever, allow it."

Maudie sat in the kitchen one day about three months after she'd moved in and pushed her hair away from her cheeks and declared, "I swear, I'm going to leave this one-horse town." I said, feeling very confident with my facts, "I know there are at least five horses in this town. The First Methodist preacher has at least three that he bought for his daughters." Maudie looked at me, rolling her eyes and with a sigh blew a stray wisp of hair away from her face, "Hush up, you little nymph! I'm not talking to you; I'm talking to myself. Get away from me and stay away from me."

When Maudie was ranting so that no one understood her, I escaped by asking to stay at Grandmother's, where I slipped away to the parlor, took off my shoes and socks, and pushed the revolving library easily with one big toe. I wondered why I had to be around a madwoman who got left with the Halverstons by mistake. I knew we would never be rid of Maudie. And I didn't trust that some of those crazed genes had not found their way into me. But what if Maudie really belonged to this family, and *I* was the mistaken one? Here only temporarily? Perhaps we had both been left here with these strangers? I hoped that I would come upon some sure, reliable evidence of which one of us really belonged here.

I wondered how Daddy could stay away most of this whole year with the baby coming. He always talked about the baby and referred to *it* as if she was something not real. He hated Mother this year and told her that he hated her at every chance.

Around the end of October he marched into the house after being away for weeks and ordered Mother into the car, the despised red Pontiac. They were gone for hours, and Maudie, Ruby Grace, and I took turns through the night looking out the front window, waiting. It was long after daybreak, and I could hardly stay awake for my turn as sentinel, except that Ruby Grace and Maudie had dutifully stood watch and threatened that my life would be pure agony if I so much as closed one eye.

I yelled to Ruby Grace and Maudie, "They're back!" The three of us watched as Mother rolled herself across the seat closer to the car door, and Daddy, red-faced with anger, pulling at her from outside the car. When she drew back from him, he pulled back his fist, his anger lifting him from the ground in a dance-like spin. He drove his fist into his other hand, and dropped his head, closing his eyes to gather himself, to control himself. His lips were moving. Mother was saying something to him. In a single movement, he spun toward her grabbing her hair and jerking her head back. He pulled her by the hair out of the car. She hit the ground head-first, the side of her face hitting the black gravel. Again, he pulled her head back revealing her wet, bloody face covered with black grime. She pleaded and held up her arm to protect her head from his blows. Finally, he released her hair and her limp body fell face-down on the ground, her arms wrapped around her head, her knees drawn up to protect her pregnant belly. Silently he stood over her.

I squealed in horror, but Daddy did not look at me as I beat the window with both my fists. Already, Maudie was running toward them taking the rock steps in what seemed no more than three long bounds.

By the time Maudie reached them, Daddy was lifting Mother, pushing her back into the car. I could see Maudie's arm gestures, and she was yelling at him, pleading with him, but he pushed her away. He slid behind the steering wheel and drove away, Mother slumped beside him.

Maudie paced. Ruby Grace and I watched her. We knew something awful was about to happen. I started to cry. Ruby Grace started to cry. Maudie was quiet; instead of screeching at us to shut up, she said in a calm voice, "Be quiet. I'm trying to think."

She dialed the operator. "Operator, get me the sheriff's office," she said with no excitement in her voice. "Hello. Sheriff Motts, this is Maudie Halverston. I'm at the Petticourt house, at Joe Halverston's place. Joe has gone crazy. He's taken Helen in the car. I'm afraid he'll kill her. Get over here. Look for them in the red Pontiac. Stop to get Lillie Dabney on your way over here. She can reason with him. Talk him down."

In minutes, the patrol car was in front of the house. Grandmother was in the backseat. Sheriff Rose was already out of the car and up the rock steps. Grandmother followed him in. She looked small standing next to him. The leather strap over his gun had been released.

"What's happened here, Maudie?

Still with no alarm in her voice, she said, "Joe's in a fit. He's taken Helen in the car. I'm afraid he'll kill her this time. Helen thinks there's another woman, so she got Sudie to drive her to Jellico where she could see for herself. Not only did Joe find her spying on him, but worst of all, Joe thinks the baby is not his. You know Joe Halverston. He will kill her. He's already pushed her out of the car and knocked her around. Her head's bleeding. If he does come back and finds you here, he'll shoot all of us."

"Now, just slow down, Maudie. Where do you think they went?"

At that moment, the Pontiac appeared in front of the house. The sheriff put his fingers on the snap of his holster as he walked toward the door. Mother and Daddy had reached the top rock step.

"Come on inside, Helen," the sheriff said, holding the door open with his left arm, his right hand on his holstered gun.

Before the sheriff could stop her, Grandmother was behind him.

"Let me talk to him," she said, pushing past the sheriff and looking up at Daddy. Square on. Looking right into his face.

"Lillie, get back into the house. I will do this. It'll be alright," he said, as he put his hand on Daddy's shoulder, saying, "Come on with me, Joe. Let's talk about this."

Maudie, Ruby Grace, and I watched them through the window. They stood by the patrol car talking. After about fifteen minutes, Daddy got into his car and drove off. Sheriff Rose came back, stepping just a few feet inside the open front door. The screen door had not been put back since Daddy kicked it off its hinges a few months ago.

"You'll be all right, Helen. He won't be back. I told him I was issuing a restraining order against him, that he was not to come near you or this house. Told him the only reason I wasn't arresting him today was because I didn't want his mother and his children to see it. I just told him that about the restraining order to keep him away from you for a while." He glanced at Grandmother, who was unusually quiet.

Mother sat on the couch while Maudie tapped her face with a wet washcloth and then with a cotton ball soaked in alcohol. Grandmother, Ruby Grace, and I surrounded her watching Maudie's every move. "Five Halverston women in one room," Maudie said, "well, this might not happen again for another century."

As young as I was then, I will never forget the look on my father's face that day. He was a madman—not because Mother hated the red Pontiac, nor because he thought she was influenced by her sister, Sudie. It wasn't that he imagined every man was looking at her. It was something else; something I wasn't old enough to understand. Years later I would understand why he flew into a rage every time one of us mentioned the birthing being close.

In the early morning of December 4th, I heard Maudie talking to Dr. O'Brien on the telephone and later, our neighbor, Higg, showed up in his truck.

Mother turned to wave to me through the truck's back window as they drove away. That night Maudie shoved Hershey's Kisses at me as fast as I could swallow them. She folded newspaper and cut endless strings of hand-holding paper dolls. As soon as she saw I'd had time to start thinking of my mother, she'd pull out more Hershey's Kisses.

That year, 1953, was a mean year—a sad, awful year, except for one day in early December. Maynard Bald had a foot of fresh snow, and, out of this year shaken to pieces, came one glorious thing: something even better than perfection—a baby girl.

When Mother arrived home with the baby, it was as if the world had tilted off its axis. Everything had changed. Halverston women could be in the same room without pouting, quarreling, threatening—even Maudie was different.

The baby had two cribs: a full-size crib in mother's room for nighttime and a cradle-size crib near the big window in the front room. Mother said she had to have plenty of light. We were drawn to the front-room crib as if it bore ripe, sugar-laden, golden persimmons. At least one of us was with the baby every hour of the day, even as she slept.

When Elda Kate was nine days old, I was alone with her in the front room. Mother had just fed her; Maudie brought her in and placed her in the crib on her back, saying she'd be back in a few minutes to turn her over to her stomach. I watched her thinking she was the smallest, pinkest creature I'd ever seen.

Suddenly, I sensed someone else was there.

"What color are her eyes?" Daddy asked from the doorway. Before I could answer, his long stride made him seem to glide across the room toward the crib. I tried to call out, but I could not.

He stared at the baby for a long time, the way you study a person you think you know. She looked at him. His face softened. There was no throbbing vein across his temple. He turned to me and put his index finger to his lips. "Shusssssssssh," he motioned.

He was gone. I was the only person who knew he'd been there. That evening while they peeled potatoes in the kitchen, I heard Maudie say to Ruby Grace, "I think the baby might be the miracle we've been waiting for. This just might be the beginning of the golden year."

Tethered to Wanting

Girl On Fire

It became easier to forget the houses and towns we'd lived in. Most of them became just faded memories. From September, 1954, to March, 1956, we had lived in Fort Walton Beach, Florida, twice (in different houses) and in Anniston, Alabama returning between each move to Maynard Bald.

Another memory that would never fade was of what happened in December, 1956. We'd lived in five houses since moving from the Petticourt house. In April of 1956, we'd settled into a house on East Central, one of the nicest streets in Maynard Bald.

Daddy had become more unpredictable. More fitful. Mother had become more forgiving, and even though he was away from home most of the time, she showed little interest in his whereabouts or what he was doing.

About once a month I'd look around me to take inventory of my belongings. I'd ask myself, "What would I take with me in the event a middle-of-the-night move happened, and I could take only five things?" They would have to be small, of course. The decision was easy: a torn photograph of my mother as a little girl with Sudie standing behind her and Purcell and Weir beside her; a letter Daddy sent from England before I was born; a tiny neon mistake that Daddy shaped into a plump bird; a beautiful stone worn smooth by water and found in the creek; and an arrowhead found in Luther Bain's plowed field after a rain. Of course, I didn't count my quilt from Grandmother as one of my five things. I would find a way to take it regardless of what was left behind. Usually, I folded it flat and sat on it. Daddy never noticed as he yelled at us to "leave everything."

It seemed we'd lived in almost every house in Maynard Bald. Some people keep track of their lives using a calendar or a diary or special dates like birthdays or weddings, but I learned to retrieve my memories by recalling which house we lived in.

We lived in the house on East Central for only a short time. It was a tiny, white house on the east fringe of town. At least what paint was left on it was white. We called it the *Methodist house* because the property was owned by the trustees of the First Methodist Church. Eventually, a paved parking lot and a building so large it would raise the Presbyterians' eyebrows were built where our house once stood. Years later, it would be difficult to sit in the grand oak pews of the magnificent church, especially if for a night funeral, something common in east Tennessee—having something as sad as a funeral after dark. When in the church, all I could think of was that my bedroom, by my approximation, in those years long ago, was exactly where the choir members stood in their long robes trying to sing some obscure song put down by Charles Wesley—sounding like each member was singing a different song.

During our time in the Methodist house, Mother seemed indifferent, almost contented. Daddy passed through and out again like the winter storms that came over Caryville Mountain. He was usually around just long enough to get everybody all stirred up, and then he was gone again, leaving our house turned up-side-down like a fallen nest of nettled wasps.

I was getting pretty good at imagining things the way Grandmother taught me, and I could conjure up all kinds of happenings in my mind's eye of happy things and exciting things and interesting and different sorts of folks that I knew must live beyond the mountains, maybe as close as Jellico.

When I could find enough pop bottles to sell to Mrs. Agee at the store on the corner, I'd buy a pack of paper to make a drawing book; drawing helped my imagination and also helped in keeping *the Great Nothing* from lingering too long especially during the bitter cold and darkness of December. The Great Nothing was Grandmother's term for the winter despair that, by her account, afflicted most Halverston women.

Some nights, I would lie awake for hours convincing myself. Imagining. When Grandmother said that I could make my imagination work for me, I had to look long at every memory as it passed through my mind. I examined each one until one I wanted to hang onto came by. Most of the time, memories get crowded out by new notions our brains have to deal with. That's the way of a memory— sometimes an idea comes like skipping a stone across water with only tiny parts of its surface touching, brushing the water's face. One that I always snatched up the second it came to my mind's eye was the image of my blue Schwinn bicycle. It was a girl's bicycle, one without the bar at the straddle. SCHWINN was painted in cursive gold letters that ran down the center bar. It was bright blue and shiny because I wiped it every evening with a dishcloth. The paint was without a single knick or scratch. It was the only thing I had ever owned that wasn't something someone else had thrown out. It was the one thing I was ever perfectly sure had been bought brand new and especially for me. I got up at daybreak every morning just to ride my bicycle before getting ready for school. I wondered why I had to go to school in the first place, especially since Grandmother knew everything and could tell me all I needed to know.

When the warm days were gone and the coal dust from the cook stoves started to settle down on everything like a soft gray blanket, I parked my bike by the house and went to ask Mrs. Agee if she had any spare cardboard boxes I could have to cover my bicycle. I didn't want any rain, snow, or dirt on it. And I didn't want the neighbors' dogs rubbing up against it or peeing on the tires. I intended for it to stay new-looking forever. When the snow bent the cardboard boxes, I shoved it off to make sure my make-shift, cardboard garage stayed put.

One morning in early December, I went outside and kicked the cardboard and watched the snow cave in over the shiny spokes. "What was the use in trying to keep the snow off of it?" I wondered. Realizing the futility of a collapsing, cardboard garage, I had to ask myself why it was so important to me in the first place. I had more pressing things to worry about.

The pipes were freezing under the house because the electricity had been cut off. It didn't matter anyway. There wasn't one thing in the Frigidaire except a half bottle of ketchup, an almost empty jar of mustard, and some cucumber concoction for Maudie's face. I just wanted to crawl under my quilt and holler my head off.

My blue Schwinn bicycle was prettier than any other bicycle in the world, and I flew like the wind on the paths in the woods and up and down the dirt roads. Sometimes I would ride into a part of the woods where it was dark and there weren't any paths and I'd have to slow down. I could pedal fast, the same way I could run fast. I'd show off for Grandmother when she sat swinging on the porch. Disappearing into the woods, I'd holler, "Look at me. Look at me, Grandmother." She'd jump up out of the swing and wave her white, lace handkerchief and smile showing her snuff-stained gums until the woods gobbled me up.

It seemed my blue bicycle and fast legs, and my mother were the only things I ever thought I could show off. I liked to show off my mother. She walked to my school one time to get me, and the whole class whispered, "Who's that?" Without offering an acceptable explanation, Mother had come to retrieve me just before math class. All she said to Mrs. Troutman was that I had to leave school early that day. I remember just feeling happy that I would miss math class.

I knew something was different. There wasn't much talking on the way home, but that wasn't unusual. There was something peculiar in her movements, and when she did offer empty talk, there were pauses in her sentences, as if she guarded how many sentences she was willing to give up. This was a trait she shared with her brothers—one that showed itself only when she was nervous.

After we got home, she moved faster than usual, with a certain urgency, like a hen gathering her chicks, tucking them under her wing before a brewing storm.

For supper that night we had fried chicken and mashed potatoes. I wondered how she came up with chicken, but then decided not to ask. She baked cornbread in the black skillet, and there was a bowl of green peas that no one ate. I hoped Daddy would eat the green peas. He was the only one who liked the foul little things.

Elda Kate dawdled at the table. Mother didn't eat. I figured she was waiting for Daddy to come home. She cut up Elda Kate's piece of chicken in little, bite-size chunks hoping she would stop lolling and finish her supper. She could dawdle through an entire meal, especially when it came to eating something like peas or any other food that was green.

It was getting dark, and Daddy wasn't home yet. Robert Joseph was pushing peas around with his finger, and Mother was determined to make him sit there until they were eaten, even if it took all night.

She set up her ironing board next to the table—a sure sign that something was wrong. The outlet for the iron was on the side of the socket holding a naked bulb over the table. Mother was upset about something because the unfolding of the ironing board was usually the first indication that something was about to happen, like a meteor hurling itself into the earth or Daddy bringing some stranger home.

I couldn't understand why anyone would spend all that time ironing a pillow slip, when somebody's head was going to bury into it and wrinkle it up that very night. I imagined that Grandfather and his number-three wife, Louise Maple, slept sitting up, probably sitting as straight as fence posts in their beautiful bed to keep from messing up their starched pillow slips. That was the only way those white pillow slips could hold the starch and not have a single crease or wrinkle in them.

I learned early that ironing was good for staving off aggravation and the Great Nothing, or just about anything else that ailed you. It worked every time for my mother. Pillow slips and aprons were good, but if she was agitated in a whole, tearful, deep, awful way, she needed something more important to iron like a counterpane or kitchen curtains. The only place to plug in the iron was at the kitchen light bulb that dangled over the table, and with every thud of the iron against the ironing board, the naked bulb flickered and swung back and forth.

More curtains were ironed at the kitchen table than it seemed we had windows to cover. Mother could see everything from that single spot under the dangling light. Sometimes, it seemed like she was held fast in that place for most of the day. She didn't miss anything. She could see how Robert Joseph was doing with his peas. She could watch the pots on the stove. She could see when Robert Joseph and I were teasing Elda Kate. She could look out the window to see if Daddy was coming up the road. Mother stood watch over just about everything while ironing a pillow slip.

We knew the look on her face. The one she wore when she'd been fettered to the ironing board for days. Robert Joseph helped Elda Kate off of the seat of folded quilts. What a mess! She had dropped peas and little bits of chicken all over the quilts.

Grandmother would be very upset if she saw them after the time she spent stitching them up. She was convinced that if she didn't finish a new quilt by the fall of every year that we would all freeze to death. She knew our electricity was cut off half the time and she was mostly right, we would freeze if we didn't have the quilts. Even Mother was very protective of them. She didn't notice that I'd grabbed them to put under Elda Kate at supper. I figured it was a good thing Grandmother set up her quilting horses in the spring and stitched through the summer and into autumn, saying she must finish before the first frost. Always, the quilts were left behind when we'd cram ourselves into the car leaving everything to take off in the middle of the night. I managed to rescue *my* quilt each time without Mother or Daddy noticing.

It was long after dark when Daddy came home. He came in, walked straight to look out the kitchen window that faced the road. He said, "Get the kids into the car." Without so much as looking up or changing the rhythm of her ironing, Mother said, "I am not going anywhere with you, Joe, and the children aren't either. We're fine right here."

He looked at her in disbelief, and the vein in his right temple started to bulge and move up and down like it had its own set of throbbing lungs. He stood fixed, looking at her for what seemed to be a whole, long night, and his eyes turned on me sitting at the table and trying to let on as if neither of them was in the room.

"Maybe I have to repeat myself," he said in a low voice as he moved toward the table and slowly eased his pistol out of the back of his waistband. He slid the gun toward her across the table. The cadence of the thudding iron did not change. Her jaw started to shake, to quiver like she was trying to hold her mouth closed, but something was trying to pry it open from the inside. The cord attached to the dangling light bulb moved with the iron. Her eyes never left the pillow slip.

Daddy's temple vein looked like it was about to pop out of his head, and I prayed she'd look up and say something. "Let's just go, Mother, don't say anything, let's just go now," I begged. I was deafened by the jingling sound made by his fingers turning over and over in his pocket and the sound of the iron cord banging against the light bulb. Then the only sound was deafening silence. Daddy brought his closed fist down opening it in time to release a pocketful of bullets onto the table. The iron rested on the pillow slip and there was a smell of scorched starch.

Mother stood motionless, crying with her eyes fast on the gun and the table covered with bullets. "Joe, don't do this. I can't go. You have to let me stay here. Go on without us. We're not going," she whimpered. "I'm leaving you. You are sentencing these children and me to lives of constant wandering. I'm leaving you to have this life all to yourself."

He stood behind her and put both his arms around her. His tall body and long arms swaddled her like he was holding on to life itself. "Now Sweets, you know that can't be true. You'll never leave me. You can't leave me. Where did you ever get the notion that I would let you go anywhere without me?" He picked up the iron, still holding her close to him. Her body went limp, and she tried to silence her sobs.

"I'll go, Joe. I'll go," she sobbed.

"You'll never leave me, Helen. Never. And if those

mountain-boy brothers of yours are putting that foolish notion in your head, you just tell them this for me, "There isn't a place on this earth where I can't find you. Not a place where you can hide from me. Not Morley. Not Egan. Not Anthras. Don't ever, even for one minute, think that I won't find you, Sweets. Tell your brothers that for me."

I hated the smell of scorched starch as much as I hated the smell of the newly-painted green car that reeked of stale cigarettes and something else I couldn't identify. It was the same smell always there in the dead cars where Robert Joseph and I played in the field next to the house. Mother warned us not to go near the dead cars. She said, "There are snakes living in those cars and in the kudzu growing up through the floorboards. Those heaps of metal are full of snakes. Besides, it makes you smell like oil and brake fluid. Stay out of those cars," she warned.

When I found a little snake in an old Buick that I was especially fond of in the car cemetery, I brought it home and hid it in a shoe box I'd punched holes in and kept hidden under the bed. After all, who was afraid of a little grass snake? I did think a short while about Mother's warning; I surely didn't want to smell like brake fluid or an old dead car.

I knew we weren't going to get ice cream. We left everything, even the quilts. I figured this must be an important trip for Mother to leave the dishes on the table and the ironing board standing. The smell of burnt starch lingered in the kitchen. There was barely enough time to think about the five things on my latest heart-broken-without list.

Daddy first drove to Grandmother's to drop off Ruby Grace and to talk to Grandmother about Ruby

Grace staying with her. Maudie was already there. It was clear that Ruby Grace wasn't happy about the arrangement. Given Daddy's mood, I thought I shouldn't balk too much about not being allowed to stay behind with them.

We rearranged ourselves in the car. After we got comfortable in the back seat, as comfortable as a body could get next to Elda Kate with mashed peas all over her, we stopped just outside of Maynard Bald. Of all the people to see parked along the side of the road in the middle of the night, there was Daddy's brother, Uncle Ogan, with his wife, Edith, and their three children.

Carl pulled in behind Uncle Ogan. Carl had worked for Daddy and Uncle Ogan at the neon shop since he was thirteen. Now he was eighteen, and no matter where or how many times we moved, Carl moved with us. I couldn't remember a time when he wasn't around. Carl was as permanent as Maudie.

Daddy, Uncle Ogan and Carl stood behind the car talking. Finally, Daddy slid across the front seat to the steering wheel and Robert Joseph moved to the front seat. The back seat was crammed full with Elda Kate, Mother, and me practically on top of each other. Mother refused to sit next to Daddy in the front.

Daddy always owned a Cadillac, and the cars' colors changed as easily as chameleons' colors. Since he had a place to paint large signs, it was easy to drive his car into the shop and change the color. Today it was green. Tomorrow it could be pin-striped. This one was a 1955 sedan that had changed overnight from black to a horrid hue of green. He drove it like a kamikaze, wide open down the dark country roads. Uncle Ogan and Carl barreled behind him. All three of them lived under the notion that they were above the law; that laws like speed limits and the prohibition of toting loaded pistols didn't apply to them. Maybe they *were* above the law, at least in Maynard Bald.

I was scared. Not because of the speed or the darkness, but because I wondered if there would be a time when we wouldn't return to Maynard Bald. How could my mother leave the dishes on the table and the ironing board standing? How could she leave my blue bicycle? What about my red skirt with the hem cut on the bias? I'd put that on my extended, prioritized, heart-broken-without list with my red banlon sweater set.

Aunt Sudie gasped for breath the first time she saw my red skirt cut on the bias and my red banlon sweater set. I also had matching red leggings. I thought she was gasping because she was overwhelmed by the beauty of seeing them all together. She said it was the ugliest getup she'd ever seen. I wondered what Aunt Sudie must have been thinking to say such a hurtful thing. I just chalked it up to the fact that Aunt Sudie did not have an appreciation for beautiful things.

The car sped down the country road with Uncle Ogan and Carl staying right with us. We turned onto a bigger road that had more road signs and occasionally, we'd pass closed cafés and motels where everything was dark except neon signs for beer or vacancies. The headlights fell on a big sign that said, "WELCOME TO ALABAMA." I didn't know where Alabama was or where we were going. I didn't know why we left our house without as much as a brown paper bag from Cas Walker's Supermarket. We didn't have a grip, what Grandmother called a *valise*. I thought that was such a strange word. She used a lot of strange words. All I could think about was leaving Tennessee and leaving my blue Schwinn bicycle.

Occasionally, Daddy would signal for Uncle Ogan and Carl to pull over, and I could hear their muffled talking behind the car, but I couldn't make out what they were saying.

I started to fidget and squirm and worry. It seemed like hours since the last stop to fill the coffee thermos and go to the restroom at a combination diner/gas station. The road was straight. The sky was wide open with a million blazing stars.

I was given the seat next to the door. The glass felt cold against my cheek. I prayed for sleep. I ran my fingers across the door and felt the door handle and an armrest with an ashtray in case someone in the back seat wanted to smoke. I pushed in the cigarette lighter, thinking it would be fun when it flew out like a piece of toast. It did not pop out. It started to glow. I waited. I saw the whole ashtray start to glow with a halo of orange. Smoke began boiling out filling the back of the car. It was burning with an awful smell. Flames flew up setting Mother and Elda Kate into a panic. I started to feel sick. What would he do? I started to pray, "Lord, please let me die in this fire and please save everyone else."

Daddy started cussing and raving. A little bit of light from the dashboard lit the side of his face and the vein in his right temple had already started to bulge. He pulled off to the side and turned the engine off. Ogan and Carl pulled in behind us, but stayed in their cars. Daddy sat there looking straight ahead with smoke pouring out of the ashtray while Mother and Elda Kate were screaming like banshees. They jumped out of the car. Mother was holding onto Elda Kate who was squalling to high Heaven. I didn't take my eyes off Daddy.

Without so much as a hint of change in his face, he jerked the door open and poured cold coffee from the thermos into the ashtray. He squatted down on his haunches so he was at eye level with me.

"You listen to me, Lunda Rose," he said in a low voice, as if the words could hardly find enough room to pass between his teeth. "I have a whole hoard of important things on my mind right now, and I don't want you breakin' up my bloody-blessed concentration. Do you hear me? I don't want to be looking back here or through the rear-view mirror and seeing that you've set the blessed car on fire! Do you understand me?"

Every joint in my body locked, but I knew because he was squeezin' the life right out of his words, and he was showing restraint, that he would not hurt me. Not with everybody watching. Maybe Mother would insist that he not kill me. Elda Kate cried. Mother stood there locked in place. Watching. Finally, they slid into their places in the back seat. He looked at me and said, "Go to sleep and don't let me hear another peep out of you."

The window felt cool as I pressed my face hard against it, and every time I saw even the dimmest light fly by, I wondered if this was it. Was this where we'd end up?

As we sped down the back roads and past sparsely-scattered farmhouses with dimly-lit porches, trying to stay awake was painful. If I fell asleep, there's no telling where we would end up. We were just little specks flying through space like lost gnats looking for a place to land. The way he drove, we could be in Mississippi by morning, flying right by Alabama without a notice.

As I tried to fight off sleep, a dark heaviness weighed on me. I felt sad and at the same time a bolt of excitement ran through me and welled up inside me so that every time I dozed off, a muscle would jerk me back. If the Lord was truly listening to me, I wouldn't be crammed into this stinking car speeding through the night with a bunch of crazy people. I had been patient hoping God would realize his mistake and send my real daddy to find me. It looked like I was going to have to contact the Big Creek Gap Home and School for Orphans in Frakes, Kentucky, again to see if I could get a room there for a while. Daddy wouldn't let me stay with Grandmother, and anyway, he'd know where to find me. I imagined just what it would be like with my real family. They probably lived in a perfect little town in North Carolina or Virginia or maybe even Atlanta. A place where there wasn't any spit on the sidewalk or a stove that needed a few chunks of coal. Bet there was a bed piled high with quilts, where you could go to bed without wearing the clothes you wore to school that day. And it would be the same perfect bed every night.

I was scared that night; licked my lips until they were raw and wondered how our lives would be different if we could choose, while still in the womb, where we would be born, picking a place and maybe picking our parents or our family or siblings or hair color. I would have chosen Maynard Bald. Grandmother said, "It's not a place that defines you, it's the *days* that happen to you while you're there."

I thought of all the houses we'd lived in and the endless procession of gun-packing relatives, from both sides of the family, through those houses and through our lives. Many times Grandmother said, "When you want to understand your dreams, study them, and be aware of the *feeling* you have when you wake from the dream. It's the *feeling*; it doesn't matter whether it's joy or fear or anger; whatever your feeling, your emotion, that's what your dream is really about. Then you think of what's going on in your waking life that parallels that same emotion." I wondered if she meant daydreams, too. Or just night dreams?

She was good at deciphering dreams. I thought it must be the same to interpret people and houses and rooms—and for some reason, I thought of my grandfather—I tried to think of the way I felt on encountering him and the room with the big, perfectly-made bed. Always empty. A drowning emptiness. It was that same emptiness of the Methodist house.

Our ride into the night was a trip that I would have rather saved for another day, when I wouldn't have been so tired. If I hadn't been tired, I could have talked to Daddy over his right shoulder to make sure he didn't go to sleep at the wheel. He rolled the window down as far as it would go and his hair blew across his forehead. A limp cigarette hung on his lower lip. On the seat, there was a thermos of cold coffee and four packages of short Lucky Strikes that he'd share with Uncle Ogan and Carl.

I knew as fast as he was driving, we could end up wherever we were headed before he had a chance to fall asleep. "Try to think of something else," I told myself. I could hear Grandmother's voice somewhere inside me. "Imagine the dark away," she'd say. "Make something up that your mind can hang onto, something good." I thought of playing the piano with Mrs. Ayers. But that thought was pushed out in a second and in rushed the dithyrambs. They'd run loose through my head like I invited them in. Ditties. Always going on about one thing or another, but she could take a tale and tell it in a way that swallowed you up whole, and you'd forget about everything else.

I wondered if every family crammed themselves and everything they could carry into their cars and moved in the middle of the night. Surely, other families didn't move leaving everything—their dishes on the table, their ironing boards, their clothes, and even their blue bicycles and red skirts cut on the bias.

Girl on Fire

The Chattanooga Ironing Board

I buried myself so far down under the covers that I could hardly breathe. Not wanting to get out of bed, I stayed there trying to press myself so deeply into the mattress that I would burst through and roll across the floor. I remained there for a good hour listening to my own uneven heartbeat and wondering how we were going to get out of this miserable mess.

At that moment, I hated Mother for giving in to him. Or was it my father I hated? I thought of the possible truth of what Lillie Dabney said, "Only two reasons to stay married to a man: love and fear." Which one was it for Mother? Maybe both? Definitely fear and maybe love, too. Were they nouns or verbs for her? I tried to convince myself that it wasn't important, but questions about Mother started to torment me: "Was she weak or just scared? Did she love him? That was the answer—of course she loved him," I thought. Why had I not thought of it before? Fear wasn't powerful enough for her sacrifices, but love was a different story altogether. I tried to imagine my mother without him. It was impossible to even imagine. I'd heard her tell Aunt Sudie, when she thought I couldn't hear, that she'd die without him. Even when she'd declared to Sudie that Joe Halverston was going to kill her, she'd weep that she loved him using the same breath of air. I'd read stories of old people who'd been together for a long time; one would die, and, in just a short time, the other would die, as if death came from living without the other.

Before I opened my eyes or rolled over to see where we were, I was thinking about him. He had a way of ruling not only a person's life, but also her thoughts. My father had a kind of meanness living in him somewhere in a secret place where its only company was carelessness. He was a man who did not care the least bit about a single thing in the world. It was there in the emptiness of his eyes, or maybe hiding in that little pulsing vein on his right temple. He did not care about anything, not even himself. And he was never scared. Of anything.

There was a haze of gray in the room, like the mountains in August just before dark, when there's barely enough light left to make out silhouettes or possibly shadows, but only the things holding up well in your memory, not those you can really see.

I eased out of bed and parted the curtains to look out the window. My heart dropped inside me. I couldn't breathe. "This was surely what Hades looked like. We have arrived at the Death Valley of the South, or maybe purgatory," I thought. How could red dirt look so *unred*? I plopped back into the warm spot and pressed my back against the wall at the top of the bed, trying to get a hold on where I was. Last night seemed like it happened a long time ago. Maybe the vision of a bunch of crazy people crammed together like turkeys in a thunderstorm was just a dream.

Mother sat in a winged-back chair that spread from behind her shoulders and made her look small. She opened her eyes, and I could see she'd been crying.

"Mother," I whispered. "Where are we? What is this place? Where are we?"

"Stop it, Lunda Rose. Go back to sleep. It's all right. Everything will be just fine. Go back to sleep."

"I guess I'm supposed to take some kind of comfort in you telling me everything is all right? Where are we? It's gray. There aren't any mountains out there. There aren't any trees as far as I can tell. No mountains. No trees. No nothin'. Nothin'. It's ugly. Why are we here? Why did you come with him? Again? You promised you wouldn't. Why can't you stand up to him? Why do you let him drag us all over the place and back to Tennessee to stay a month, or a week or two, and wham, just like that, we're lifting off to some nether world? Again."

"Lunda Rose, that's enough. Hush. I don't want to hear it."

"You just go on then and stand for it. For him. Never mind that we don't have a blessed thing to our name! You're always taking up for him. Making excuses for him. Defending him. Why does he have to go wandering all over the United States to make neon signs? Why do you have to trail behind him dragging us with you? Why do we have to go with him? You are as selfish as he is. He doesn't want us, and I wonder now, if he is more important to you than we are."

"I'm not sure why we're here," she said with as much indifference as if she was talking to a perfect stranger. As if she hadn't heard what I'd just said.

"Why can't he get a job selling life insurance or working in the mines? Something normal." The back of the big chair rose six inches above her head and the sides of it spread out wrapping around her making her look frail and vulnerable. I felt sorry for her in a way that hurt down in my gut. I swallowed hard and tried to push down the smother-hold mounting in my throat. Not two minutes ago, I hated her, and now I just wanted her to show some indication that she was alive.

"Go back to bed," she said. "It'll be all right. Your daddy needs to work here for a while. There are trees out there." She repeated it, as if repeating it would make it true, the same way she told us over and over when we crossed the Alabama border that we'd see how beautiful it was, when in reality, there was only red dirt as far as you could see.

"They just don't have any leaves on them yet. Stop whining. We'll go back to Tennessee in a few weeks. Stop fussin'. You'll wake Elda Kate and Robert Joseph, and we're all dead-tired." Her voice trailed off with a faint hiccup, that telltale evidence that comes out of your throat after a good cry.

"There are trees!" Mother said. "Why, this is the middle of town, and it's smack in the hold of winter. There just aren't any leaves on them. Stop whining and fussing. We'll be going back to Tennessee before you know it. Besides, look at it this way: No Halverstons here! What do you think of that? No Halverstons!"

"Mother, we're all Halverstons."

"Don't be smart with me. You know what I'm saying. No Maudie. No W.O. No meddling mother-in-law. Seems like paradise to me."

"I don't know why I had to come to this forsaken place, when Maudie and Ruby Grace were allowed to stay with Grandmother," I snapped.

Lillie Dabney can't take all of you. Besides, Maudie and Ruby Grace have to stay in school."

"School," I shouted, "what about my school; doesn't my school matter? I'll never catch up."

"Yes, you will. We'll enroll you next Monday. That'll give you a week to settle in."

On the second day in the big house with the strange smell, Mother woke in a fit, as if her brain was undergoing some kind of spasm. "Help me put clothes on Elda Kate. Find her shoes." I wondered what clothes she meant, since we'd left what few things we had that resembled clothes. As we were leaving, she'd grabbed the only cup Elda Kate would drink from and a ragdoll that Elda Kate never let out of her sight. She jammed everything she could into her big, straw pocketbook, and, what she couldn't cram into her pocketbook, she stuffed into her brassiere: her two prized cameo brooches; $23.84 from an oatmeal tin stashed behind the coffee cups. She threw her iron and a little skillet into the straw bag. I was more thankful for the skillet than an iron or faces carved in shell. Cameos and an iron; just what we'd need on the road.

I covered Elda Kate's dirty dress by buttoning her coat. Robert Joseph's clothes were too small. He tugged at his pants and the collar of his pullover. I had a coat that had belonged to Ruby Grace. It was long and covered all my clothes, so I wasn't too concerned about the way I looked. Elda Kate's coat was warm enough for this part of Alabama. Robert Joseph had a mackinaw that was too big for him and a little toboggan hat that covered his ears. As long as he was warm, I didn't care how he looked either. Mother didn't seem to notice.

I saw her face, and knew she had a mission coming on. The three of us marched in tandem down the street. We marched right into the gray of Alabama as if we were part of a grand parade. It was a strange gray. Everything blended together becoming the same ghostly shade of gray. There wasn't any color. When I squinted the way that helps when you want to see how much contrast exists in your view, all I could see was a blank slate.

The sky, the trees, the ground, the pavement, and the sidewalk all ran together like the shapes you try to make out when night settles. There were no mockingbirds. No birds at all. There wasn't a blade of grass, but only packed, red dirt. A few spindly pine trees surrounded the house. Spent pine needles covered most of the ground, making the absence of grass less noticeable. I couldn't help feeling just a bit excited to see the expanse of bare, red dirt. I figured when spring came, I could plant watermelon and cantaloupe seeds without having to do a lot of work.

I could hear Grandmother's voice as clearly as if she was standing next to me, "When your fingers are in the dirt, you can't think an evil thought." She was right. When I sneaked the spoon from the kitchen drawer and dug and turned dirt all day, I could think of nothing else, except what I was planting. In Tennessee, I used to dig grasses, weeds, sod, moss, and sometimes a wild flower from Mrs. Pruitt's garden, something I'd learned from Aunt Florence Nell at Morley. I planted them in my own secret place. I had to remember to put the spoon back into the kitchen drawer, so Mother wouldn't know I'd been digging with it. It was her gravy spoon. She'd stashed it in the straw bag, too.

There was one tree that stood naked and alone in the Alabama yard. Mother said she'd never seen such a tree. There were broken shells under it—a whole sea of cracked, gray shells. It wasn't a tree that I knew from Tennessee. When one of the girls who lived down the hall overheard us, she said that it was a pecan tree, which explained why there weren't any in the Tennessee mountains.

Along the edge of the red-dirt clearing, that was supposed to be a yard, was a wall of tall pines. A straight row of sprawling shrubs grew in front of them. The girl from the apartment down the hall, said they were called *fetterbushes*, and that when spring came, their clusters of pink flowers would draw in hummingbirds.

I wondered just exactly where we were going. Mother had that driven look all right. She didn't know this street or this town. Wherever we were headed, we would have to walk there.

"There's a hardware store down the street," she nodded. "Saw it when we came into town. I have to get an ironing board. We can't go about looking like we weren't raised well."

It was important to Mother that we appeared to be well-raised and perfectly-ironed regardless of moving in the middle of the night wearing the only clothes we'd brought with us. She took every opportunity to bring to our attention the importance of our appearances.

"Button Elda Kate's coat. Make sure she stays warm."

She found the hardware store at the corner of Parker and Lee. She marched in like a queen wearing her cameo brooch and with the three of us trailing behind her. She cleared her throat and straightened the cameo brooch at the front of her dress. She easily reached through her open coat keeping her fingers on the cameo. She coughed slightly to get the attention of a small man wearing a long-sleeved, white shirt and a yellow and white polka-dotted bow tie. "Sir, I need a new ironing board," she said.

The man stretched his body forward to look over the cash register counter at her, and his eyes scanned the line we formed behind her. He cleared his throat and straightened his body; he paused for a long while studying the situation. Again, she straightened her body and stretched her long, thin neck to make herself appear taller. She was five feet and nine inches tall and appeared somewhat imposing when she stretched to reach her best posture.

He said, "Yes, Ma'am, we have a new line of fine ironing boards. Just got 'em in last week from Chattanooga. Highly adjustable. And seeing that you're a tall woman, Ma'am, you can raise it to suit you and your back won't start ailin' you after a stint of ironing. They're on sale for a mere $2.95." Mother wiped a wisp of hair away from her face. She made herself even taller, almost formidable, as she straightened her body again and stretched her neck and fingered her cameo giving her an air of nobility. She opened her purse, took out a coin pouch, and started to count quarters laying each one on the counter. Robert Joseph pulled at his pants and grabbed his crotch; he started to dance and moan. I whispered to him, "You have to wait just a while. Just a while longer. You have to wait. Listen to me. We'll be home in just a few minutes."

"Two dollars...two twenty-five...two fifty," she counted as the quarters slipped under her thumb and onto the counter. She stopped counting and looked at the clerk and at Robert Joseph, who squeezed his eyes shut in an effort to diminish his increasing pain. The salesman paused for a while and said in a low voice, "Excuse me, Ma'am. I think I told you the wrong sale price a minute ago." He straightened his bow tie, fumbled with a few small papers next to the register, and said, "Why, yes, our finest ironing board—came all the way from Chattanooga, only $2.50 for Monday only."

Mother looked at him and put her fingers delicately on the cameo and said, "Why, isn't it delightful that this happens to be Monday?"

She strutted out of the store with her neck stretched high, with the grace of a whooping crane, and with a brand new ironing board under her arm. An ironing board brought all that distance from Chattanooga. I held onto Elda Kate's hand and Robert Joseph was under my feet. He yelled and moaned, "I have to pee."

"Good grief, you'll just have to wait. It's only a little farther to the house." I wondered why boys let the urge to pee just slip up on them and ambush them with a surprise attack. No warning at all. And then he moaned like he'd been struck with pain and agony, and danced and hollered like he was on fire. He whined and held his crotch all the way home.

Mother set up her new Chattanooga ironing board even before she took off her coat. She covered it with towels she'd found in the house. I couldn't imagine what she planned on ironing. We didn't have any curtains, or underwear, or bed sheets: the things she usually gathered when she needed to iron. She'd iron anything made of cloth if her misery had settled on her hard. I figured she'd find something to iron, and I was right. I went with her as she marched down to the end of the hall where three single girls lived. They invited us into the living room of their apartment: simply furnished with only a couch and two chairs. Against each of three of the walls was a table that held tiny collections: a collection of salt and pepper shakers, one of tiny porcelain dogs, and a collection of rocks and crystals.

"Thought you might like to have your blouses ironed. Save you some time for other things. Fifteen cents a blouse, ironed perfectly without one wrinkle, the way your mothers would like them."

As Mother detailed pressing pleats and ruffles, I could hardly notice anything except the collections. Obviously, these were girls who did not move in the middle of the night. Charlsie was the one who insisted that we come inside, the one who told us about pecan trees and fetterbushes. "Do you like rocks?" she asked. "This is calcareous limestone," she explained picking up a large rock carved in the shape of a ram's head. "It's called an *effigy*. Very old. From New Mexico. You can hold it," she said handing it to me.

*   *   *

Carl did not follow us directly into Muscle Shoals the night we arrived. He showed up three days later driving his Studebaker that looked as if it'd been pieced together from scrap tin. The driver's door was dark blue and the other door was washed-out blue. "No, no, Lunda Rose," he corrected me, grinning, showing his bad teeth. "Not washed-out, but more *cerulean*," he said proudly. "Saw that written on the paper label of a paint can. Same color of blue."

The fenders were dark green and gray. The top and hood were the burnt red of parched dirt. As I walked around it, Carl grinned and said, "Ain't it something to look at? Think of it as *a jubilee of color*. Beautiful."

It didn't seem to matter that we moved like a band of strays in the night, Carl always found us. It was unclear how he, Uncle Ogan, and my father communicated. We seldom stayed in one place long enough to have a telephone.

"Drove all night and stopped for coffee only when I'd see an all-night diner. Almost fell asleep a couple o' times," Carl said, as he stood holding the refrigerator door open. I wondered how he knew where the kitchen was in a house he'd never been to before. He spread mayonnaise on his sandwich. It appeared to me that every time we moved, Daddy and Carl seemed already familiar with the towns and houses that were new to us.

I knew we wouldn't stay long in Muscle Shoals, because Mother was unhappy. "*Secrets* again," I thought. Something was terribly wrong—something hidden from Mother and from us. I hated it. Nobody liked this red-dirt fire pit except Daddy and Carl. The two of them worked all night and slept most of the day. It was cooler at night, more tolerable for working with the heat of the cross burners. Carl usually woke up before Daddy, and I'd hear the sound of the jubilee of color; grinding, as Carl struggled to get it into reverse.

One morning Mother, thinking Carl had left, sent me to the attic room to get the pillowcases for washing. The bed was made. I thought that strange for Carl, since nothing about him was neat. I hadn't heard him crank the Studebaker that morning. For some reason, I felt as if someone else was in the room. With the stealth of a cat, I sank to my hands and knees to look under the bed. Shrieks of laughter and other sounds I couldn't control rang through the apartment.

"What is it?" Mother yelled as she ran up the stairs. The shrieks of shrill hybrid sounds coming from me were jumbled turning to laughter as Mother reached the doorway. I moved toward the bed and threw up the counterpane. I was on my knees looking under the bed while pointing with one finger and trying to cover my mouth to hush what was about to come out. Unable to hold my tongue, I yelled in a half-giggling and half-squealing voice, "What in the pit of Hades are you doing under the bed, Carl?"

"Hush, Lunda Rose," threatened Mother. I bawled and pointed and covered my mouth. Still squealing and laughing, I looked square at Carl's face. There he was, sprawled under the bed on the bare, wood floor wearing all of his clothes, his boots, and his coat. His eyes, streaked red, were open now. He looked like a knot of wires strung together like a pitiful bug with too many joints. His katydid legs started to stretch, and his head moved a little as his eyes fluttered. He rolled his head across the chicken-feather pillow. His mouth started to move, but no words came out.

"You're sleeping with a chicken-plucked feather pillow," I yelled, "and a blessed, week-old, yellow T-shirt, a filthy mackinaw, and holy blue jeans. You imbecile! Who, but a boy from Morley Mountain, would sleep on a bare floor with no quilt or mattress, when there's a perfectly good bed right here? You are unbelievable." I shouted as I stood up and looked at his pointy-toed, yellow cowboy boots sticking out from under the bed.

The counterpane was smooth with one pillow missing from the bed. Carl tucked his legs a bit and rolled himself from under the bed like a lazy dog that had been disturbed. He looked at my mother and me without any sign of embarrassment. He said, "I never sleep in a bed. Never have, not even at home. It's too dangerous. If somebody walks into the room, you're right out in the open to look at. Why, anything could happen. Just too dangerous. Never sleep in 'em."

The edge of his lip curved upward like it wanted to form a grin that started at the side of his mouth. He fumbled with the buttons on his mackinaw. Finally, he poked at the sleeve of his undershirt where a pack of short Camels appeared like magic from the folds of the rolled sleeve. "Got any matches, Sissy?" he asked me. Mother said, "Carl, don't be teasing her. She's already in everybody's business. You just make her more sassy-mouthed."

"Why would I have matches?" I looked at the floor and hoped he wouldn't tell Mother I smoked.

Mother frowned. "Lunda Rose, stop quarreling with Carl, and watch what comes out of your mouth. He's only teasing you."

Carl sucked on his cigarette as he rolled the pack back into his sleeve. I thought it was funny how he rolled his sleeve with one hand to show off the red tattoo spelling "ROXANNA."

"Ah, Helen, don't fuss at her. If she just wasn't so meddling and busy all the time. If she'd stay out of my business, she wouldn't be in trouble with you and aggravating everybody to death. A person can't even pee without her knowing it. She asked questions about bloody, ripping everything. She's in everybody's business, and she shouldn't be. Someday, her questioning and prying are going to land her in more trouble than she can wiggle out of. Send her to school. That's where she should be. Those Alabama girls will take some of the sass out of her. All she has to do is open her mouth. They'll know she's from Tennessee. They can smell out a new girl. Smell Tennessee on her as sure as if she'd had it written on her."

"No. I'm not going," I shouted.

Mother shot Carl a look. "Carl, why do you taunt her?"

She cupped her hand around the back of my neck and pointed me toward the stairs. We marched at attention down the stairs and into the kitchen. The only sound was our hard shoes on the bare floor. When I was straight in the chair, and, when I stopped struggling with the strands that had fallen loose from my tight braids, she leaned over to put her face in front of mine. She said in a low, but frustrated voice, "Lunda Rose, you have to leave Carl be. Give that boy some peace."

I whined, "Mother, what fool sleeps under the bed wearing his mackinaw and his pointy, yellow cowboy boots?"

"Stop it, stop it right now! It doesn't matter if Carl wants to sleep naked in his boots in the backseat of his Studebaker! It is not your business. Let him be."

I was dismissed from sitting at attention and flew out of the kitchen slamming the wood screen door already broken from all the slams that had come before. It bounced several times beating against the frame. Pouting outside was better than pouting in the kitchen. In a while, I'd forget Carl. I'd be distracted by other thoughts.

The next morning Mother went to a phone booth to call the principal to tell him she was sending me to school by myself on Monday, and that she'd be over in a few days to fill out the forms and sign papers. She didn't have any intention of doing either.

I wore to school the same skirt and sweater I was wearing when my father yanked us from our house in Maynard Bald. I saw there was no way out of it despite my protests, and once I entered the huge steel doors of the Wilson Elementary and Intermediate School, I was sent directly to the principal's office, where I sat in an over-heated condition for two hours because I refused to take off my long coat. I wanted to crawl into a little hole and pull the ground in over me.

Mr. Blain was busy threatening two boys who had been truant for two days. He asked my name and sent me to Mrs. Armstrong's class, where I sat in a back corner and refused to talk or do any schoolwork. Everybody turned and stared. I closed my eyes and hoped that I would become invisible or disappear. At lunchtime, I hid in the girls' bathroom and cried.

At 3:15 p.m. when the bell rang, I was still

crouched in the bathroom. After the sound of voices disappeared, I ran home, bawling my head off. I flung the door open and stood there wailing like a banshee. Mother couldn't believe what she saw.

"What's happened?" she cried. "Your braids are gone. Cut! What's happened to you?" I cried that night until I was sick. Mother never sent me back to Wilson School.

*   *   *

Carl said he found the Studebaker at a car graveyard in Tazewell, Tennessee. Said he worked out a good deal. Showing a half grin and his bad teeth, he leaned toward me like he was going to tell me a secret. "Don't you think the jubilee of color is much akin to a beautiful woman?"

"You must be just plain crazy," I snapped. "I hope you've never told Roxanna that she looked like the Studebaker."

"ROXANNA" was tattooed inside a big heart on his left arm. He bragged that Roxanna would be right there on Morley Mountain waitin' for him when he got back to Tennessee. Carl didn't know much about females. I doubted Roxanna Murdoch would be waiting for him or pining away for him when he returned to Morley.

Carl was smart. It was as if he could read my father's mind, as if my father communicated with him without words. Maybe it was because he'd worked for him for so many years. I wondered if Carl knew the secrets Daddy held so close. "He had to know," I thought, "he's never beyond earshot of Daddy, especially when they're at the neon shop.

Carl knew the strange tree in the front yard was a pecan tree. He said pecans wouldn't grow in the mountains because of the altitude and the cold. He knew things about engines and wrenches and about curing tobacco. He knew things you'd never suspect would be of interest to him like how to grow a Christmas cactus on a window sill. But he didn't know the important things Grandmother knew, like what the Cherokees used to commit suicide or that only love or fear would keep a woman with a man. It was obvious that he didn't know one thing about women, or color, or fashion, although he boldly announced to everyone that the color of his Studebaker was, more accurately, *cerulean*; the proof was on a paint label.

While I watched him working under the hood of the Studebaker, I looked at the old building behind the house. It looked as if it had been, at some time, a three-car garage. The heavy double doors had padlocks on them, and we'd never seen anyone go in or come out of the old building. Carl said it belonged to the landlord who owned the apartment house. I wondered what was in the garages. Daddy asked the landlord if he could park his truck there, but he said Elias McNeely on the third floor paid him to let him use the building for storage. I had seen my father talking to the landlord and Elias McNeely a couple of times, but each time, they'd stop talking when they saw me.

As I handed Carl a wrench, I noticed one of the three padlocks was open. Carl was lying on his back on one of those gurneys mechanics use to roll themselves under cars. He couldn't see me. When I walked into the unlocked bay, I saw that the walls between the bays were open at the tops. I could easily climb the wall to see what was on the other side.

Robert Joseph was whimpering, and Carl was impolitely hollering, "Hand me the flashlight. Hand me a wrench." I grew even more scared and nervous, but I had to see what was in those garages. Maybe it was something Daddy was hiding. More secrets. Mother had repeatedly asked him to take us to the neon shop in town. He continued to say, "It's not a place where you'd see anything of interest to you. Besides, it's dangerous. When I'm not there, Ogan is working; cross-burners are lit."

"Be quiet for a minute," I said to Robert Joseph as I scaled the wall on the left of the first bay. I could scale a wall like any boy, but regretted that I was wearing a dress resulting in splinters piercing my calves, hands, and bare feet. The problem was that I was straddling two bays about 12 feet off the ground, and I didn't know how to get down. What if, when I made it into the locked bays, I couldn't get out? I fully expected that Robert Joseph would start screaming like he was on fire if he realized I was gone.

The second bay was filled with hundreds of boxes. I had to know what those boxes were hiding, and I scaled down the wall sliding the tips of my fingers between the boards to hold on. My hands were stinging and bleeding and full of splinters.

I had a horrible thought that I might not get back to Robert Joseph before he discovered he was alone. I could hear him whimpering already and calling my name. I imagined the wrath of my mother flying upon me if she knew I had left Robert Joseph by himself. Worse yet, what if Daddy came home while I was stranded twelve feet in the air? I looked up. How would I scale over the wall to get out? I had to get back to Robert Joseph.

The hundreds of boxes were filled with cartons of cigarettes. Every brand imaginable. "I risked my life and the wrath of my daddy for friggin' cigarettes," I thought, as I checked for cartons of short Lucky Strikes and short Camels, the ones without filters that left yellow stains on your fingers. I contemplated who the principle mourners would be at my funeral. Stacking the boxes along the wall, I built make-shift stairs. When I got to the top, I said, "Lord, just help me drop down these 12 feet to the ground without breaking my leg or my neck, or without killing myself, and I swear I will walk with Mrs. Pruitt to the Beech Street First Baptist Church every Sunday and Wednesday night for the rest of my life without complaining or sassing my mother. Amen."

I left a carton of short Lucky Strikes on the dash of Daddy's car. I left the carton of short Camels on the dash of Carl's jubilee of color. The carton of filtered Salems were for me. Carl and Daddy asked if I knew anything about the cigarettes they found in their cars.

"Nope," I said, "wonder how they got there?" Carl's grin started to form at the corner of his mouth.

One day in April, a letter came addressed to my father and postmarked Maynard Bald, Tennessee. The return address read "W.O. Halverston." Daddy tore the envelope open and read it silently.

"We have to go back to Tennessee," he said without looking at any of us. "My work is almost finished here anyway."

I couldn't believe it. Home. School.

"What does the letter say, Joe?" Mother asked,

without looking up from her ironing.

"Never mind the letter. We're going back. That's enough."

I tried to imagine what my grandfather had written in the letter. I figured that particular letter was important to get Daddy's attention the way it did. But, I didn't care what was in the letter. I just wanted to go home.

Later that day, I overheard Daddy telling Carl to "pack up. There's a problem with one of our clients in Cincinnati. We'll leave the families in Maynard Bald and go on north to take care of the matter. Tell Ogan I've had a letter from Dad, and we have to leave tonight."

I longed for home, and Grandmother, and her dithyrambs with their hidden meanings. If I listened closely and concentrated, I could pluck their meanings right out of my head.

I don't know exactly how long we were in Alabama, but there are some things in this life a person just never gets over. It seemed we were there for months, and it was a narrow world there—the gray, red-dirt world of Muscle Shoals, Alabama. I had attended only one miserable day of school, but we were there long enough for Mother to set her ironing business into motion. I worried about missing school. I thought of calcareous limestone and dreamed of living in a place long enough to collect something. What would that feel like? I knew that missing school didn't matter.

We left Alabama in the middle of the night, just like we'd left Tennessee and every other place we'd ever lived. "Leave everything," Daddy said. I wondered what he was talking about. There wasn't anything to leave.

It was around 1:00 a.m. when we turned onto Main Street as we were leaving. Daddy said, "I have to stop by the shop to check something. It won't take long. You and the kids wait in the car. I'll just be a few minutes." He left the engine running and went in through a side door. Carl's Studebaker was parked in an alley at the side of the green building that resembled a warehouse. Uncle Ogan's Cadillac was parked in front next to us. I examined the outside of the building. It didn't look the way I expected the sign shop to look; it was large, but the doors were small, too small for large signs to fit through. I was in the backseat with Mother and Elda Kate. Robert Joseph had fallen asleep on the front seat.

After about 20 twenty minutes, Mother said, "Lunda Rose, go to the side door and see what's keeping him. The door was cracked about two inches. I heard Daddy and Carl talking. As I opened the door, Daddy turned quickly toward me. "I said to wait in the car," he yelled. I ran back to the car.

"Well, what's he doing?"

"I don't know," I told her.

"Did you see him?"

"I saw him talking to Carl. Mother, that huge building is empty, except two telephones on the floor."

"Empty? What about boxes of glass tubes, cross-burners, tools?"

"It's empty. There's nothing in there."

We saw Daddy walking toward the car. When he slid under the steering wheel, I looked to check the vein in his right temple. He said nothing. Mother was silent.

I still had a worn-out $20 bill stashed in my shoe for emergencies, something Lillie Dabney taught me. But I was leaving Muscle Shoals with more than I brought with me. I had changed. I'd learned that people are not always who they appear to be or who you want them to be or expect them to be. My mother understood this too.

Mother had plunged her iron, her gravy spoon, and the iron skillet to the bottom of her huge pocketbook as we were leaving the apartment. She stuffed her two beautiful cameos into her brassiere. And before closing the door, she turned and looked back at the Chattanooga ironing board standing like a metal sculpture under the dangling light bulb in the kitchen. On a line strung across the kitchen, hung the pretty lacey blouses that belonged to the girls at the end of the hall. Starched. Perfect. Not a single wrinkle.

The Sloth of the Willow

As soon as I opened my eyes and sucked in a deep breath, I knew where I was. The smell of turned, fresh dirt woven with the smell of compost and turkey litter and laced with the distinct scent of *Clorox* was a fragrance I knew. It was a scent lodged forever into every crevice of my memory.

From the bed, I could see the wallpaper painted in creamy white roses with specks of yellow at their centers. Grandmother said the smoke-stained wallpaper in the bedroom was as close to growing a Cherokee Rose as she would ever get, and she reminded me that there were at least 39 shades of white.

"Too cold to grow 'em by the porch, so I just grow 'em on the wall. Seems like they favor places south of here. A long time ago someone gave my mama a Cherokee Rose brought from Georgia. She tried everything she knew to get that little sprig to grow in this part of east Tennessee. She said it was the altitude and late spring frosts that the plant couldn't tolerate. My mother told stories of the Cherokee Rose being *a rose of life* because it changed from one color to another before it wasted. Yesterday, it had been one shade, today another, tomorrow another shade. Just like people. Just like lives. And it has to like where it's planted."

Even without my eyes fully focused, I saw the bureau lined with the blue perfume bottles with *Evening in Paris* on their paper labels. I wanted to linger there in the bed and savor the scent of the air and the pillow slip. Grandmother loved the scent of *Evening in Paris*, just like my mother, although lately, Mother had taken a liking to a fragrance called *Tabu*. Traces of *Evening in Paris* lingered in Grandmother's dresser drawers and on her handkerchieves. Sometimes it was hard to detect perfume on her because the mixed scents of *Clorox* and soap were too strong.

I jumped up and ran straight to the front porch and there they were—the mountains.

"There you are, my sleepy Sweets," she said as she cupped her hands around my cheeks, pulled me to her, even though I was almost her height, and planted a big kiss right on top of my head. I thought for a minute she'd picked me right up off the porch boards. I felt as though I was suspended in space with my feet dangling. Floating. Her lips made a loud smacking sound, and her arms held me fast for a long time. I did not resist.

"Come sit with me in the swing and let's watch the mountains get morning sun on them." I snuggled close to her and could smell the earth and *Clorox* and just a slight lingering of snuff mixed with *Evening in Paris*. It was too early in the spring for the trees on the mountains to be greening up, but they were as pretty as they were when I left them. I had memorized every single ridge and fold and curve of the place where the mountains reached up and rolled right through the sky. I knew the exact dip where I could find the dog star in August, and I knew how every rolling line and gap looked in the gray of December.

There were a few places on the mountains where some leaves were just trying to get out. She told the same stories every year at this time of how the trees struggled, trying to leaf out. "Trying and looking everywhere for spring," she said, "at this time every year, I watch the mountains and the orchard and try to look ahead with a good feeling in me, that certain feeling inside me that spring is coming. You know we're getting close when the equinox comes, and then you have Easter and Decoration Day to look forward to. And daffodils. Of course, daffodils. Won't be long 'til I'll have to go to the mountains, back deep into them, to get my hickory chicken mushrooms. Yes, ma'am, you can only cut hickory chicken mushrooms on one day of the year: April 15th. That's the only day they're at their peak. I'll fry 'em up in a little bacon fat for you. Now up in Kentucky, they call them *dryland fishes*, but here we call 'em *hickory chickens*."

She rambled on and on, and I realized I loved and missed the sound of her voice almost as much as the sweet scent of her. "Did you remember the equinox this year?" she asked. She planned her whole life around the vernal equinox. Every year, as far back as I could remember, she had explained it to me in the same words she used the year before and every year before that. I was home. A bad dream was coming to a close.

I sat next to her in the swing and listened to her stories as if I'd never heard them before. She planned her garden and what she would plant this year. Her face lit up as she presented a complete history of almost every tree and flower she'd ever planted.

She told stories of hoop-skirted daffodils and the Cherokee rose, of how she learned from her mama that cutting blackberry brambles back to the ground the first week of July would prevent the dastard things from ever growing where they weren't welcome.

She told her favorite story of when she was a girl and learning to run a bull-nose plow as easily as any man in the county. She talked about taking apple scions in the dark moon of February from her prized Tennessee Black Twig apple trees to bury in a tub of loamy dirt in the cellar for tongue grafting onto new rootstock in April. "Keep them in the root cellar 'til grafting time. Of course I put them in a cellar where there aren't any apples stored from last fall. Shouldn't store the fall apples with anything I'm planning to plant in the spring. Gases from the apples will kill 'em for sure."

It didn't matter a whit what she talked about as I closed my eyes and listened to the cadence of her voice. I wondered where she went in her brain to pull up so much knowledge. She rambled about the calm brought on by the little yellow orchids of the lady slipper. "It has an effect that lulls your mind to good thoughts like the valerian flower. Good for calming," she declared. And she talked about the bliss of choosing the perfect morning when she'd feel the warmth of the sun on her face for gathering yellow trillium to sooth her eyes—something the Cherokees did.

Her voice spread through me as if it was my own, but far away, as if it was only a dream. She talked about the sweet scent of wisteria and the taste of May Apple jelly and in the same breath she'd talk about the Cherokees knowing what plant to use for every purpose. "A Cherokee knows the roots of the May Apple can put you down. The only thing to use for suicide. I know of more than a few who stashed it back for that very purpose."

She knew everything there was to know about the spring equinox, and on which Sunday Easter would fall. I didn't mind hearing the same story year after year. She'd say, "Now I've already told you that spring comes with the vernal equinox in March of the year. That means it's the time in the heavens when the sun is just right over the equator to make the time that it's daylight the exact same as the night is long. Usually happens about March 21st. It's only because of the equinox and the full moon that we know which Sunday is going to be Easter every year. If Preacher Conroy didn't have a calendar, he couldn't figure it out. Well, I guess he could look it up in the Bible, if he knew where to look. It says right there in the Bible that Jesus rose up again and somehow we were all to know that Easter would come on the first Sunday after the first full moon after the vernal equinox." Sure enough, Easter has been at the right time every year since Grandmother taught me about the fat moon that comes after the equinox. She taught me about dryland fish mushrooms, medicinal plants, grafting apple trees, and how to behave around wild animals. These were things Cherokees were privileged to know.

She talked on and on with the same excitement that she had every spring when she spoke of such things. I never wanted to be away from her again.

Who would teach me important things? The things that really mattered? Her talking was continuous. I said nothing. She asked me questions and answered them for me, but I didn't mind that either.

Occasionally, I'd jerk myself back. "What about getting away from this insane family that was not mine?" I thought, "what about seeing for myself what's beyond the Mississippi?"

The branches on the willow tree that stood close to the house were turning the first clear, light yellow-green color that came every spring, the transparent color that seemed to vanish if you looked away and back again. Grandmother called it *chartreuse*. She used beautiful words like *chartreuse* and *fuchsia* and *saffron* and *vermillion*, but she was careful always making sure she explained every new word as if I were still a little girl. I didn't interrupt. As far back as I could remember, she'd simply made up her own words when she couldn't find the words she wanted to get her point across, the same way she made up her own songs, her own dithyrambs, her own memories, and often, the particularities of her very own soul—her essence—as if she'd picked them from a store shelf or an abundant garden.

I heard a cat-like mew coming from last year's tangle of vines at the south end of the porch. A catbird, the shy cousin of the mockingbird, appeared only for a moment. As we moved back and forth in the swing that hung from a rusty hook; she wrapped her shawl around me and occasionally her talking would slow down. Each time she looked at me, really looked at me; it seemed she was seeing me for the first time. She studied me. "Did she see the changes?" I wondered, "could she see that I was different?

Sometimes, without warning, she again took my head in her hands, drew me close to her bosom, and smacked another big, loud kiss right on the top of my head.

Since I was a little girl, Grandmother had told me stories of Proteus, the Greek god, who in *the Odyssey* changed his shape time and time again simply to be who he needed to be.

"People can change," she'd say, "transform themselves to become who they need to be or want to be—to come to their way of being in the world." She readily referred to herself, trying not to be suspect of attempting to change another person—a goal, she assured me, that was unachievable.

She told the things about herself she'd like to change: "Oh, I have reason to refrain from criticism," she said, "to withhold my sarcasm, to avoid gossip with Mrs. Pearlie Hille Butters. Just work on them a little, you understand?"

I knew it was someone else she hoped to change. She closed her eyes as if digging deep for her memories. "As hard as I have tried, I will go to my grave abhorring loud noises, crying babies, barking dogs, and unlit kitchens. And when people turn away from me when they're speaking or don't keep control of their children." More than once, I'd seen her tap a young mother on the shoulder at Shelby's Grocery and demand that she reign in her children.

"And I have to work on offenses—not letting myself react with undue sensitivity to every little thing," she nodded, "most things that offend me are trite and shouldn't matter: the preacher coming 'round, for instance, doling out guilt the way Southerners dole out courtesy; neighbors as nosey as spinster sisters," she'd whisper, "and things that I know are unimportant, unexpected visitors, and people who strive to keep themselves in endless states of dissatisfaction. All are minor offenses."

"If I were Proteus, how do you think I would transform myself?" I asked her. "Guess. What do you think I'd become? I know exactly the shape I'd take. It's like making a wish. Go on, guess."

"You would be smart to recognize that some things just need to be left alone," she said, "what it comes down to is that everything in life is constantly changing. I learned when I lost my Little William that even death and loss are as much a part of life as growth and love. No matter what confronts you in your life, you push through it with hope; you listen to your own heartbeat like you've never listened before. Remember, too, when you're thinking about all the things you'd like to change about yourself and in your life, that yes, maybe Lucille Frawley needs changing and maybe there should be a road blasted through a mountain, but sometimes there's a sweet appeal in leaving things alone in their imperfection, ignoring the small fractures in the glaze. And sometimes, something damaged might just reappear in a new form."

"I would be myself," I blurted out. She stared at me pushing her tongue against her left cheek to rearrange a trace of snuff. "But not myself now, the way I am now, but after I change over time—myself with a larger notion of who I am and where I belong.

"Maybe I do belong in Maynard Bald. As many times as I've thought of my escape from Maynard Bald, from these mountains, I think now that what I really want is to escape *to* the mountains. And *to* myself. As long as I'm enough. I just want to be enough. I want to be able to face my father, or anyone for that matter, without staring at my shoes. I want to come to the coliseum whole and in a little pain. A little pain is a good thing; it motivates you to seek relief. To keep moving forward. A little pain will give you courage. I don't want to be without it completely. I want to speak my piece without wearing shoes that hurt, without that little bit of induced pain. I don't want to wear them for even half a day without allowing myself to take them off or permitting myself to sit down to relieve the pain."

"You have changed," she said, "but memory and familiarity, and sometimes, habits tie us up with a string—tie our lives together, our worlds, whether it's what we want or not."

I felt torn—one minute I thought I'd figured things out, but the next minute, I was faced with self-doubt and obstacles. And at the moment I started to think every solution was within reach, a barrier would grow up in front of me.

Just as I started to think everything was right with the whole world, here came Maudie, prancing up the walk in her usual interrupting way. Maudie preferred living with Grandmother. She said, "I can't pull out my suitcases every few months when your daddy has a mind to take off in the middle of the night."

"I'm going to leave this blessed family," I told her.

"Dearie, you don't have a bloody chance of getting out of here," she said with certainty, "you're just dreaming. Our grandmother's been putting crazy ideas in your head, again. Don't believe it," she taunted, "not one of us will ever leave here."

I couldn't bring myself to care much for Maudie.

As far as I could tell, the only thing Maudie and I had in common besides our name was our grandmother, and I secretly resented that we shared her. I never came right out and said it, but I knew Grandmother wasn't real crazy about being her grandmother either. Oh, she was smart alright, but not in the way Grandmother was smart. Maudie was what our kin called "a Halverston, through and through, with a sharp tongue and an inflated sense of prerogative." Grandmother said, "Maudie's tongue is run solely by anger, but we can't fault her for that."

Grandmother was smart in different ways, probably because she'd lived so much longer than any of us, and because of her mama. She said, "People like us make do and get by no matter what we're dealt in this life. No matter what comes our way, we face it off square in the eye. We're born that way. It's natural. It's the way things are."

Then Grandmother started talking about Decoration Day and getting some of Ova Gay's mama's pretty, red, crepe paper flowers dipped in paraffin. "I try to get some every year to take to Little William's grave," she said, "and to Elease's."

Maudie sat on the porch with us and started filing her fingernails with an emery board. "*Unbearable Luscious Raspberry*," she said. "My new fingernail polish," she announced, pulling a little bottle out of a sack of big pink hair rollers. "Ruby Grace is giving me a body wave tonight."

"Maudie, the way you interrupt absolutely everything with your nonsense drivel about Toni body waves and your latest toenail color is disrespectful, and no one cares anyway," I snapped.

She rolled her eyes and plopped herself down in

the straight-back chair on the other side of the porch. There she landed looking like a pile of red and pink, except for her pedal pushers that were lavender. It was clear that Maudie never intended to do one bit of work in her lifetime that required the use of those newly-painted, luscious raspberry fingernails.

She carried on a full talk with us without once looking up. Maudie held her left hand out to admire her manicure, and said, "Grandmother, why don't you call it by its true name? The day is Memorial Day. And I swear, it does not make one bit of sense to go through all the trouble of taking flowers to someone who is dead, when a dead person can't even enjoy or appreciate a bouquet of flowers. It is crazy and just plain wasteful."

Grandmother looked at her without saying a word. Maudie could spoil anything, and I knew, if I could see into Grandmother's head that she'd be thinking about slapping Maudie clear down to the Jacksboro cemetery for speaking of the dead in such a disrespectful way.

I felt surprised that I was happy to be back in Tennessee. But after all, it wasn't Tennessee at the heart of my contempt; it was the constant moving. Mother had rescued her iron and her cameos from Muscle Shoals, and I hadn't had a great fondness for anything we'd left behind this time. Even if I had to put up with Carl and Maudie always bickering with each other and everyone else, I was at least with Grandmother.

I listened to her ditties and wondered how anyone could be so smart. I smiled as I thought of her dithyrambs. She helped me think things through. It used to rankle me when she chanted those meaningless rhymes and told stories of kin that I'd never heard of and didn't want to know. She chanted the same stories and ditties over and over. Being away from her made me think of how much I missed her and how much I missed her ditties that sounded like songs, and I paid attention now.

I heard her in the next room. She hummed and whispered her sweet songs until I fell asleep each night. She hummed as we made spoonbread in the evenings. She said, "Ah, Sweets, remember, the world gets narrow when you're journeying toward something; it gets wide when you're journeying away from something. Take back roads and side roads, but never lose where you're going or where you've been." Yes, I was certain that she knew everything.

I stayed with her while Mother looked for a new place for us to live. It was hard to find a house in Maynard Bald that we hadn't lived in before. Funny thing, though, we never lived in the same house twice.

I wished we could have lived with Grandmother, but my mother wouldn't hear of it, saying she would sleep on the side of road on a bed of rocks before she would live with my grandmother again. "I lived with Lillie Dabney while Joe was in the Army Air Corps during the war," Mother said, "Joe thought it was a good idea for Ruby Grace and me to live with his mother while he was away. 'It'll be good for all three of you,' he said. I won't make that mistake again.

"It was long before you were born. Ruby Grace was two years old. Joe left New York Harbor on April 10, 1944," she said, "he was stationed in England and crossed the Atlantic with almost 12,000 troops aboard the *Queen Mary* from New York to Gourock, Scotland.

"I never felt like Lillie Dabney wanted me there, nor Ruby Grace for that matter. I hid Ruby Grace's dresses, all of her things, really, to keep her from washing them in Clorox.

"She steamed open my letters from Joe, and tried to lick and reseal them leaving snuff traces on the envelopes. At first I felt sorry for her. I knew she missed him. It took weeks for letters to reach us, and that deepened her worry, but I started to think that, rather than missing him or worrying about him, she resented that he didn't write to her as often as to me."

*   *   *

When the warmth of spring came late to the mountains, when the willows turned chartreuse, Grandmother called it *the sloth of the willow*—cold springs when the leaves and blooms struggled to make it to a true green. She would put her hands on her hips as she looked from the porch. She talked on about the days when the cold of winter would pass and the trees and plants would turn certain colors. She explained, "Sometimes, spring just gets arrested, just stops, growth and time can't move on. Winter lays a hold on April, and it seems to be paralyzed. Everything is caught and held fast in place. If you pay attention to the willow buds, you'll see a change that's hardly noticeable. There's no sudden jolt, but a gradual, emerging surprise like the coming of evening or the summoning of a faint memory, often, not realized until the arrival of solid darkness or the full bloom of recollection."

I thought the same thing could happen to people. It had happened to Carl. It seemed as if he never changed or got older. He was held suspended in time just like the willow. It didn't appear to me that he was working to change anything about his situation. Nothing about Carl or his life has changed since he came to live with us. He came home with my father one day and stayed. He didn't live in our house, other than sleeping on the floor beside the couch sometimes when Daddy needed help with a blueprint for the neon. He said he never wanted to go back to live at Morley Mountain. That was obvious, since he came all those years ago; he didn't mind that he was overstaying his welcome.

Daddy said he needed Carl to help him make neon. I wondered what needing Carl to make neon signs had to do with him living with us, and moving with us everywhere we went. Sometimes, when we packed ourselves into the car and took off to another state, Carl would be waiting for us at the other end.

I watched him when he was working with Daddy. He wasn't as tall as my father, who was six feet, four inches; Carl was wiry, whereas my father was slender, willowy in a graceful, but strong way. Both were considered handsome. People said my father was a handsome man, that he looked like the Dabneys, rather than the Halverstons. He had the dark features and angular facial structure of the Dabneys. He looked nothing like his father or his brother, Ogan. Neither of them were tall, and they were stocky in their builds. I asked Grandmother if he looked like the Dabneys when he was a little boy. She said, "He did."

There were some things about Carl that were just like my father: the way he held his cigarette between his thumb and index finger; the way his mouth curled at the edge when he grinned; an angular face with high cheekbones—all just like my father, with a few exceptions—my father was always dressed nicely even when he was working, and he had straight, beautiful teeth, amazing really, since he refused to see the only dentist (whom he called a *horse dentist*) in Maynard Bald. Carl smiled only when he wasn't conscious of it. His bad teeth showed when he laughed, and when he realized that he was laughing, he closed his mouth. His clothes were shabby and usually dirty from spitting tobacco juice. When he wasn't working, he could be found in front of Colley's Pool Hall, where he and the other boys there, spit all over the sidewalk without showing any signs of shame whatsoever. They had a certain way of moving, as if in slow motion, occasionally turning around to look at a girl walking by or to look at cars with out-of-state license plates, those traveling north on Highway 25, probably going farther than Jellico.

In a strange way, I felt sorry for Carl. I wondered if he really had a family or a home except with us. He said he came from Morley, and sometimes he talked about his mother, but I think he made up those things about coming from Morley and about his mother sweeping around him when he was sleeping under the bed.

I suspected that Carl was dropped in with the Halverstons by mistake just like I was; that he was cursed somehow. Sometimes, when Carl laughed a certain way or had a particular look on his face, I saw it plainly, and I thought he *did* look like my father. Yes, it was another mistake.

I imagined Maudie was dropped into the family intentionally. Robert Joseph and Elda Kate didn't belong to this family either. I felt sad that they were too young to know that they were in the wrong family, and I felt certain that Ruby Grace's inclusion was deliberate. That part was not a mistake. It was true. Ruby Grace looked like our father and moved through space like our mother. She had a way about her that made her connected to these people. It was something I knew for sure. When sad or scary things happened, or when Daddy came home and started breaking up the furniture, Ruby Grace seemed to let these things go unnoticed. Most of the time, she just disappeared into her own little world. That world that Grandmother called narrow. She had a way of disappearing like magic when any ruckus started. Mother said she was just like our father. I wondered where that magic world of hers was.

I knew for certain that I was not meant for the misery and misfortune of this cursed bunch of crazy people. It *was* a big mistake. At every chance, I searched the faces of my mother and father looking for some resemblance. I listened closely to their voices, especially to my mother's laugh, thinking I might hear my own. I searched my grandmother's face and voice, and even the way she moved her fingers and wrists. I looked at my own hands thinking they might look long and limp and able like hers.

Sometimes, in the mornings, Grandmother sang her silly, senseless little songs to make me laugh. We giggled as she'd tell stories she'd made up which usually came on when she was put out or nettled with something or somebody. That was just about all the time. At times her ditties were hard to follow, but most of the time I'd figure out at least pieces of them. She'd rattle dishes in the dishpan and the songs would give up her secrets. She'd spit them out as quickly as they popped into her brain. A wild fire that couldn't be stopped. She made up hundreds of them. They grew more complex as I got older. She chanted:

Always listen to the dithyrambs, Darlin'.
Listen to my ditties. Listen closely.
Hold them to your bosom and think.
Mother's not what you think.
Pious, pretty, little thing with a veil.

Sometimes at night, I wondered where my real family was and what my true mother and father were like. They were probably living up in Kentucky somewhere enjoying perfect mornings and near-perfect evenings. Probably had a big verandah with a swing and chickens in the yard. Bet they had a big bathtub with purple, stick-on, rubber daisies on the bottom. It was a tragedy how big this mistake was. I imagined that my real family was one like Ova Gay's; that my mother could make red, crepe-paper flowers and my father came home every night with a magnificent mistake that had morphed into a glass rose or a swan.

The Sloth of the Willow

The Double-Wide Tombstone

In four years, from March, 1957, through July, 1961, we lived in Muscle Shoals, Alabama; Huntsville, Alabama; Harlan, Kentucky; Franklin, Tennessee; Hazard, Kentucky, and a third and fourth time in Fort Walton Beach, Florida, each time, returning to Maynard Bald between moves.

In some of these places, I didn't enroll in school. At several schools, my attendance lasted only a short time. As soon as they started to ask for school transcripts or shot records, Mother would pull me out, as those records were always left behind. By the end of the school year in 1961, I had attended seven elementary schools and a junior high school. After being in eight different schools, no one had any idea to what grade I belonged.

When we returned in June, 1957, from our third stay in Fort Walton Beach, there wasn't time for Mother to find a house in Maynard Bald. It was good thing; in less than a month after returning, Daddy woke us in the middle of the night and told us to get into the car. Since our return, Robert Joseph and I had stayed at his mama's, along with Ruby Grace and Maudie. Mother and Elda Kate had spent the month at Morley with Grandmother Evers. Daddy had already picked them up.

"Where are we going this time?" I asked Mother as I got in next to her.

"Florida, again," she said with no hint of excitement in her voice.

I was used to it now: being hauled out of bed at ungodly hours; having my father bark staccato, one-sentence commands which included "Don't ask questions." Usually, it would happen about 1:00 a.m. I learned eventually that this particular departure time gave my father two advantages: it insured that the neighbors would have gone to bed and wouldn't see us leaving, and it would give us a considerable number of hours to travel in darkness.

Leaving everything didn't bother me anymore; and the one true thing I was certain of each time we moved like a summer storm in the night, was that if we weren't leaving Tennessee, we would be headed for Tennessee. We never moved from one place to another without first returning to Tennessee, never knowing if we would stay a few days, a week, or years. I liked going toward home better than going the other way.

We didn't stay long in Florida that time. As usual, we got up in the middle of the night and crammed our bodies into the Cadillac, leaving everything in the house. We left dishes with food still in them on the table and pots on the stove. I glanced back through the house as we fled our brief stay in Fort Walton Beach and thought that it looked like a family had just gotten up from supper and left to go to the store on the corner. "At least," I thought, "we could have cleaned up the mashed-potato pot and the iron frying skillet before we took off to another state."

We drove straight through the night and into the next day. I didn't mind leaving this time. I didn't like Florida any more this time than the three times before, or any more than I'd liked Alabama. There weren't any mountains; the earth was as flat as a cornpone. It was the hottest, wettest place on earth; everyone perspired like open spigots. Florida's only redeeming feature was that it had an ocean, but apart from the Atlantic Ocean and the Gulf of Mexico, I could get along without it. The ocean made a relentless racket. I figured I had gotten by all these years in the mountains without a big Atlantic Ocean, so I would do just fine without it.

In July of 1961, we moved to a house on Prospect Street. All of us were tired of moving. Mother was never content away from her family. Now she visited Morley when Sudie called to say she was coming to get her. Oddly, Daddy didn't appear to mind.

I arrived at Grandmother's one day in July to find that Daddy's sister, Winnifred, had left her husband and taken over her old room at Grandmother's. This was disastrous. Maudie didn't have exclusive claims to the Halverston eccentricities. No sir. She shared these rights equally with Winnifred. Grandmother had explained that Maudie's anger was never malicious and could be excused because she didn't really *want* to be hateful, she just couldn't help it. But Winnifred's anger showed itself in a vindictive way—and she enjoyed it. She had, at some time over the years, threatened or blackmailed everyone in the family—

everyone except her mother and her brother. She did not scare Lillie Dabney nor my father one whit.

That night I slept in the room where Elease had died. Grandmother seldom opened the room even when Maudie was away. I thought of the day in 1953 when Elease's body was swaddled in quilts, the sound of her body thudding against the wall as Belcher's men carried her down the stairs.

When I awoke the next morning, I hoped not to see Winnifred nor hear her voice. I felt strange, as if my brain had separated from my body. I'd spent only a few minutes with Winnifred the night before, and consequently, had gone to bed with a splitting headache. Holding my tongue around her was nearly impossible; it required work, as did merely contending with her.

"Silence is a numbing poultice," I repeated over and over inside my head what Grandmother had told me to recite when frustration took hold of me, when I couldn't help just blurting out whatever first came to my mind. The inability to hold our tongues was another inherent trait, a curse common to every woman with Halverston genes.

Interrupting my thoughts of how to silence myself, Grandmother tore into the room first thing that morning, saying she needed to go to the Jacksboro Cemetery. I didn't understand why all old people liked visiting cemeteries. For Grandmother, it was a celebration: something you looked forward to and got excited about. When I questioned her, she presented her standard speech of how most mature persons shared a history with a cemetery. It seemed to me to be just another way to celebrate death.

Jacksboro was about five miles west of Maynard

Bald. It was too far to walk, although Grandmother had been known to walk there if she wanted to go badly enough, and, if there was no one around to drive her. She hated riding in cars, called them *motor vehicles*, still despised them to this day, and said they weren't to be trusted. She hadn't trusted them since her very first ride in one. She had her own ideas about *devices*, as she called them. Devices included just about anything in this world that could make your life easier, or more pleasant, or more comfortable. She referred to window fans, motor vehicles, and electric mixers as devices and declared that an electric window fan would suck her right out the upstairs window. She had peculiar notions about anything that had a motor, engine, or used electricity. And God forbid that any person would claim ease, or pleasure, or comfort, or fun as her own by using such devices. It didn't matter that it was smoldering in the upstairs rooms. In summer, I thought I would surely suffocate. I was glad it was too far for us to walk to Jacksboro. I liked riding in motor vehicles. She was determined to go to Jacksboro on that day even if she had to walk. I prayed she would find someone to take us.

She marched directly into Colley's Pool Room. Her black vinyl pocketbook hung on her right arm. I stood behind her. I was old enough to be embarrassed. We entered the pool room cautiously; it was like finding our way into a dark cave; like being plunged into dark waters. The cigarette and cigar smoke made it hard to breathe the thick air, air that seemed depleted of oxygen. No other place in the world smelled like the pool room. Grandmother said it was the hot dogs and onions, but I didn't think she was right about that.

There was silence as every shadow of a man turned to look at us through the smoke. We were not on friendly ground. I couldn't tell who they were in the dark. Her figure was clear to them because she had on her white dress and her heavy white shoes polished to stand out as clearly through the smoke as shining fetters.

Women were not permitted in the pool hall, but she was an exception. Every man in the place stopped talking and turned to look at us. The silence lasted forever until Otis Longmire behind the counter asked, "What can I do for you Miss Lillie Dabney?"

"I need someone to drive me down to Jacksboro. Thought maybe one of these hard-working boys could drive me, since they're all on their breaks from their chores."

"Who'll take Miss Lillie Dabney and Lunda Rose to Jacksboro?" he asked.

There wasn't much of a clamor of volunteers. Otis Longmire banged his hand, clenched into a fist, like a gavel on the counter, changing his question to a command, "Elmer, you're going down to the Jacksboro Courthouse today."

"I'm going to the courthouse directly," Elmer Heatherly spoke up. "I'll take her and her granddaughter down that way if they don't mind riding in my pickup truck."

As we slid out of the truck at the cemetery, Elmer said that he'd go on to town and take care of his business and come back to the cemetery when he was done. I watched as Grandmother tried to pay him for driving us, and I saw him shaking his head and waving his hand in a refusal.

We took the same path we'd used for years, since I

was old enough to walk. Along the west border and under the ancient oak branches we made our way to the Halverston plots. She stopped and became still.

"Do you hear that?" she asked. "The song of a thrush, or maybe a mockingbird imitating him—five notes that mimic five black keys on the piano, and if you listen, you'll hear a trill that mimics mountain music."

She explained, as she did on each of our trips up the hill, that the white oaks and Eastern red cedars were only along the borders of the cemetery because of their roots. "There aren't any maples; their roots invade; and no walnut trees; their roots poison." Occasionally, she stopped at the oldest Halverston stones and read them aloud: "Jacob Halverston died in April, 1862, at the Battle of Shiloh (the name of the meetinghouse just north of Savannah, Tennessee, on the bank of the Tennessee River), and Howard Halverston died on January 8, 1815, at the Battle of New Orleans, when Andrew Jackson butted his Tennessee Militia against the British. It was this battle," she explained, "that gave Tennessee its reputation as the Volunteer State when 2000 soldiers from Tennessee marched with Jackson."

"These are all Halverstons. Where are your people?" I asked.

"My people are Cherokees; they're buried up in the mountains. A few are buried in the little cemetery at Crouches' Creek."

She was careful not to step on graves. She made sure we passed by the gravestones that she wanted to touch and talk to. I was patient and watched as she ran her hand over Little William's headstone. "WILLIAM IRISH HALVERSTON" was written on the stone, a small, white, marble tombstone between Horace Halverston and Edna Elease Halverston. She stayed in that particular spot for a long while and talked to the little boy she'd lost years ago and to her daughter, Elease, who died when she was only 32. She studied me for a moment and inhaled holding it inside her as if trying to capture a tiny wisp of air holding the scent of red cedar. She bowed her head and talked to Little William, and then her allergies started to bother her.

We climbed farther up the ridge and arrived at another row of Halverstons' graves. W.O. had died a little over two years ago in 1959. We lived in Huntsville, Alabama, at the time, and only Daddy came back to Maynard Bald for the funeral. Grandmother attended his funeral and sat next to Louise Maple.

W.O.'s grave was at the end of the row, and I knew Grandmother would deliver a speech at his grave just as she had the other Halverstons. "He was the father of my five children," she'd say, "I owe him that."

As we approached the end of the row, I couldn't believe what I saw. There on Grandfather's double-wide tombstone, his number-three wife's name, that he'd had etched next to his years ago when they'd selected the stone together, was gone. Where "LOUISE MAPLE HALVERSTON" was once etched was now a blank spot, as smooth as the polished granite. Grandmother stared at it in silence. She was expressionless and looked down at the ground like she was thinking. She shook her head.

"What happened to it? Where did the words go? Where is "LOUISE MAPLE HALVERSTON?"

How can a name just disappear off of a tombstone?" I asked.

Grandmother, still blank-faced, seemed unable to speak. She shook her head, set her mouth at an angle the way she did when she was frustrated or needed time to think. She said, "Your Aunt Winnifred has gone too far this time. She's crossed the line. I'm certain that Louise Maple will have her put in jail." Grandmother had a way of placing emphasis on *your* Aunt Winnifred, as if I was related to her and that she was not.

The most vengeful of all the Halverstons had set to work in her meanness. Aunt Winnifred Wilfreed Halverston, Grandmother's own daughter, had hired someone to sandblast the name of Grandfather's living, number-three wife cleanly off of Grandfather's beautiful double-wide tombstone.

I thought Winnifred had reached her low point when she falsely accused her preacher husband of stealing from church funds. Once she even threatened to kill herself if her husband left her alone again during a thunder storm. Even when someone sat with her during a storm, she wept, cowered in a corner, feigned fainting, and paced in the cellar.

I used to think Aunt Winnifred and Cousin Maudie were mean-spirited until Grandmother explained to me that Maudie couldn't be faulted; she was just trying to find someone to belong to. But Winnifred was a whole different matter; not only was she mean-spirited, but as I got older, I saw that she was outright bitter. She was a female version of William Oscar Halverston and his daddy, Ira Odell— mean to the marrow, to the core. A wickedness that went clear down to their very insides.

"Lord, help us all; help me, Jesus," Grandmother said. "It's true that W.O. was sometimes a loathsome soul, especially in his younger years, but he's dead now and has no reins over Winnifred or her rip-stomping ways or her hate-filled deeds. She is a woman bent on getting revenge any way she can get it."

Aunt Winnifred was all ticked off because Grandfather's number-three wife, Louise Maple, had found a boyfriend. And now, with W.O. dead for over two years, Winnifred, his only surviving daughter, believed that Louise Maple didn't deserve to be buried next to Grandfather.

Winnifred hired Orville Dabney, her second cousin on Lillie Dabney's side of the family, to sneak down to the Jacksboro Cemetery and sandblast Louise Maple's name cleanly off the big, double-wide tombstone. We figured it had to have been Orville because he earned liquor money when he needed it by digging graves for Belcher's Funeral Home and by sandblasting marker stones for Claiborne Monument Company. Besides, Orville was afraid of Winnifred and would commit to anything she wanted.

It was a pitiful shame, too. Grandfather was married three times that we knew about. Lillie Dabney was the first. His second wife, who we didn't know, lived in Kentucky. Louise Maple was his third wife. She still lived in Maynard Bald and maintained a long-term friendship with Lillie Dabney even after W.O. died. For a short time, when Lillie Dabney fell ill and needed looking after, W.O. and Louise Maple took her into their house and cared for her.

Two years after his death, all three of his wives were still alive. But, to insure his beloved Louise

Maple was next to him in death, they had gone together a decade ago to Claiborne Monument Company to pick a special stone. And now, he was in his grave for all of eternity with not one of his wives beside him.

I felt a little sorry for him, seeing as he had no say over the matter. The double-wide tombstone didn't look right with a big, blank space to the left of W.O.'s name.

"Why would Winnifred do such a thing?" I asked, "is it legal for a daughter to deface her father's tombstone after he's dead just because she doesn't approve of her stepmother?"

"Honey, none of this is legal or moral. But illegal or immoral—neither has bothered Winnifred in the past. She must have caught Orville Dabney in a drunken stupor and in desperate need of whiskey money to get him to do such a thing," Grandmother said still shaking her head. I thought even a man like my grandfather should have the say over who would lie next to him in the cemetery.

I wondered if sandblasting a name off of a tombstone was against the law. I supposed it didn't matter, anyway, since the deed was done. And, as Grandmother said, "Winnifred doesn't care a donkey's nickel about the law, but I know Louise Maple won't have any trouble at all taking out warrants for the arrests of Winnifred and Orville." I thought Grandmother was embarrassed to have a daughter the likes of Winnifred. I wondered how W.O. felt about his daughter when he was alive.

Later I learned that Grandfather paid Claiborne Monument Company $365.00 for the largest rose-colored granite slab that could be hauled by a freight train all the way from South Dakota. He paid Wesley Claiborne an extra $36.00 to etch his name and birth date and Louise Maple's name and birth date on the huge stone. He paid an extra fifty cents per inch to have dogwood twigs and blossoms etched around each of their names.

"They'll both be arrested by morning," Grandmother said, "and Winnifred deservedly so, but Orville just does what Winnifred orders him to do. That's a shame, too, at least for Orville," she said, "it's unfortunate that he has to go to jail because he's too scared to say 'no' to Winnifred."

I saw that Grandmother felt sorry for him. She said Orville claimed to be disabled with black lung from working all those years in the coal mine at Morley and would not survive with his kind of disability if he was put in a damp cell in the bowels of the jailhouse at Jacksboro.

"Of course, if he's paid in cash, he isn't disabled," Grandmother declared. I didn't know what she meant by that, but it wasn't like her to speak ill of someone on her side of the family. She usually clammed up when I asked questions about the Dabneys, especially her father, and she only talked about her mother when I pressed her and when we were alone. When I asked questions about her Cherokee relatives, and when I asked if Dabney was a Cherokee name, she stopped talking. She talked more openly about the Halverstons and lately when I asked questions about Winnifred's and Maudie's doings, she answered.

"Do you think they'll arrest Aunt Winnifred?" I asked.

"Honey, if they had put her in jail for every illegal thing she had ever done, she would be rotting there right now. I wouldn't put anything past Winnifred. She isn't turned like your daddy or any of my other children. It's hard to say what she'll do, and it's hard to know what Sheriff Rose will have the nerve to do. He's just like Orville: scared senseless of her. He'll probably let her be. She's threatened him too many times and shown him her fits of temper too many times for him to stand up to her."

In the early evening, my father sat across the table from Sheriff Rosemund Motts waiting for Winnifred to return from Knoxville. Winnifred knew things about Rose Motts that he wanted to keep private. It seemed Winnifred Halverston had collected secrets not only about every relative, but about almost everyone in Maynard Bald.

Sheriff Rose's presence was only a show of force to try to scare Winnifred. The truth was that he was just as afraid of her as everyone else.

Grandmother and my father were the only ones unafraid of confronting her. At least that's what we thought. Daddy had never let her bully him even when they were children.

When Winnifred arrived home, she showed no hint of surprise seeing her brother there in the kitchen with Sheriff Rose and Grandmother. To Winnifred, her brother and the sheriff were just two more men with weaknesses: secrets that made them vulnerable and that gave her power and protection.

"Mama, I believe you're right about what drives Winnifred's meanness," my father said calmly as he tipped his chair on its two back legs, "yep, what drives her is jealousy and resentment—not just of me, but anyone who has something that she doesn't.

"Joe, my dear little brother, what do you have that

I possibly could be jealous or resentful of?"

"Our mother," he said.

Winnifred's face stiffened emphasizing its angles and her deeply-set eyes. "Don't bother me with the whining and wailing of Louise Maple over that farce of a tombstone," she said in a low voice, "Louise Maple is not going to lie down there for all of eternity in the Jacksboro Cemetery next to our sweet daddy. I will see to it. Don't threaten me, Joe. I know your secret—what your real work is. You don't scare me. And, Mama, you don't scare me either. And, Rose, you just go on home and get some sleep."

That night, I lay in my bed feeling sorry for my dead grandfather and wondering what power, what secret Winnifred held over my father, a man who wasn't afraid of anything.

I thought about the rose-colored, double-wide tombstone, now blank to Grandfather's left, and how it was a pity that he had to lie there on the ridge top at Jacksboro all by himself for all of eternity.

The Glass Roses

There were a few brief periods as I was growing up when our lives were somewhat calm. One of those times was just before my fourteenth birthday in August, 1961. We lived in the house on Prospect Street in Maynard Bald. For a while our parents seemed more settled, almost as if they were happy. They appeared to have lives *with* one another and *with* us. It seemed as if we were meant to share the same house. We'd lived in the house longer than usual and were growing accustomed to sleeping through the night without fear of being dragged out of bed to take off to another state.

My father seemed more tolerant. He spent more time at home. Most nights he spent drawing blueprints for signs. Sometimes I'd watch him bent over a drawing that he'd spread over the living room floor and wonder if my grandmother had really given birth to him. How could it be that a skinny, frail, little woman could give birth to such a baby? Their insides weren't turned much the same either; Lillie Dabney was a gentle, southern lady, but no one would call my father a *gentle man*; people called him other names that weren't meant for me to hear, but never to his face.

They were both smart, but different kinds of smart. Grandmother was smart from constant reading. Her mother taught her what she couldn't learn from books. She was mindful of the ways of the Cherokee people. This wasn't something the Halverstons talked about, since her five children had the Halverston name firmly attached to them.

My father saw the world differently from other people, and most of the time, it seemed he carved his place in it with a serrated blade or a gun. But when I watched him working with neon, or working on a painting or drawing, I saw just beneath the surface, another man—a more human man, one who could whip out a sheet of paper and a paint brush to perform magic.

Once I found an injured American kestrel, a beautiful bird of prey with vibrant colors and exotic markings. His injuries appeared only minor leaving him slightly stunned and temporarily immobile. I was sure he had encountered, in mid air, a golden eagle or another male kestrel.

I begged my father to sketch him; to capture the image of the magnificent bird before he came to his senses and took flight. My father gathered chalk pastels he used for preliminary color sketches for the neon signs, collecting only the colors needed to rub with his thumb to blend cinnamon-red, umber, and gray. Then, as if he had *imagined* it onto the paper, it instantly appeared as life-like as if you could touch its cinnamon feathers and rufous back and tail. He drew blue-gray wings and its mustached black-and-white face without so much as glancing at the bird.

Struck silent, I watched, not wanting to take my

eyes off the kestrel, or the drawing, or my father. The kestrel began to move his head rotating it slowly from side to side as if it rested on a pivot. He seemed to be surveying all that surrounded him.

After no more than ten minutes, he lifted himself into the air with ease and disappeared into a stand of white oak trees. I couldn't take my eyes from the spot where I last saw him, hoping he would reappear.

He did reappear only a few minutes later in an opening next to the white oaks. He hovered briefly on fast-beating wings before disappearing again. I wanted to run after him, but I did not, perhaps because I knew this time he was really gone. He would not return.

Daddy said I should have the drawing, since I was the one who found the bird. Grandmother usually laid claim to his drawings, laying them flat in a pile on the floor under her bed, handling them as if Leonardo had drawn them. "They won't survive otherwise," she said, "not the way Joe treats them."

I tacked it to the wall in my room with thumbtacks and moved it from house to house each time we moved. In all our middle-of-the-night moves, I managed to jerk it off the wall and roll it up so that over the years, it became creased, torn, and full of holes on all four corners.

Eventually, Grandmother insisted the kestrel drawing be added to the stack under the bed despite the constant chiding from Winnifred and Maudie declaring the pile of drawings "as worthless as the glass sculptures on the revolving library."

"You and Lunda Rose make a fuss over unimportant things, Mama," Winnifred snapped. "All of you dote on him, and he hates all of us." Both of us ignored her. We considered the notion that she knew nothing about fine art.

* * *

All the nodding ladies of Maynard Bald dolled up on Saturday mornings to strut down Main Street and peer through the windows of Balloff's Clothing Store knowing full well they weren't going to buy anything. They usually had their shirt-ruff husbands sit in their cars parked in front of Colley's Pool Room. Sometimes the husbands with their hair all slicked down with Vitalis would see one of their neighbors, whose wife was also looking in Balloff's window. They'd get out of their cars and stand around after promising their wives they wouldn't spit on the sidewalk. Eventually they'd make their way into the pool room reserved only for men. Once the husbands disappeared into the dark abyss of the pool hall, the only way the wives could let them know when they were ready to leave town was to send word through a small window resembling a speak-easy window in the side alley, where women were allowed to place orders for chili dogs without going inside.

Belcher Tidwell carried a tin can in the breast pocket of his jacket, and occasionally pulled the left front of his coat away from his chest leaning into it to spit. It was clear from the smell of Old Spice mingled with the aroma of pool-room hot dogs smothered with onions that the wives had made them clean up a little for Saturday morning strutting. On a hot day, the smell could travel the whole block.

Sometimes, I heard the nodding ladies whisper about my grandmother: How she was just a Cherokee acting real uppity since she married a Halverston. If I hung around Shelby's Store and let Grandmother go on about her business, I could hear some of the old folks, those who had known her since she was a girl, whisper as she walked slowly down the row with the shelves of flour and cornmeal. She looked at Mr. Shelby, "You out of Martha White Self-Rising?" Without looking up, Mr. Shelby pointed to the bottom shelf. She seemed disappointed that he actually had what she wanted, knowing that he would never run low on Martha White Self-Rising.

Mr. Marlow leaned over and whispered to Haskell McCulley, "Must be that Lillie Dabney is going to bake a blackberry cobbler. Remember her back in the days before she was married. Folks here just didn't know what to make of her, but she turned every head in town. "

Haskell said, "Yeah, W.O. didn't know what to make of her either. She's set him on his heels a few times. I remember one time when she almost killed W.O. Found him with another woman and almost beat the old geezer to a pulp with his lover's high-heel shoe. No one could even imagine how Lillie Dabney came to get that high-heel shoe off of that woman. After that, stories were told for years that W.O. had puncture wounds all about his forehead and ears and even down his back. He was learning just what he'd gotten himself into marrying a woman like Lillie Dabney. Wasn't two months before that marriage started to fester."

I watched her face to see if she had overheard them, certain that she had, but she just ignored their gossip and stares and tilted her head back a little with a flair of southern uppityness and paid Mr. Shelby for her snuff and flour. We walked on down Main Street and stopped at Balloff's window to admire the new ladies' handkerchiefs that had just come in, probably a new shipment just in from Cincinnati.

Lillie Dabney always carried on her person a delicately crocheted handkerchief usually of white linen, and sometimes, there would be a crocheted border in the palest pink or the softest lavender. Her handkerchiefs were a mystery. I saw them appear from mid air and each one was carefully unwrapped from a loose knot at the top. Like magic, rose hips fell away revealing the small box labeled, "BRUTON SNUFF." At Shelby's Grocery, they always wrapped her box of snuff in a brown paper bag. I sometimes saw her sneak it into her crocheted handkerchief, and I marveled at the way she managed the delicate operation without anyone seeing her. "Why was that little box such a big secret?" I wondered. No one cared that she dipped snuff, but I supposed she did have an image to uphold.

Her pocketbook, like her handkerchiefs, held valuables and secrets, and when I was little, both entertained my imagination thinking they must hold secret letters or maps, or maybe jewels belonging to wealthy, long-dead family members, maybe she'd copied down a Cherokee legend from her mother or scribbled a universal truth disguised as a dithyramb.

Once, when a piece of folded paper fell out landing under the porch swing without her seeing, I waited one hour and forty-five minutes, hardly taking my eyes away until she went inside to start supper. I ran with the paper to the woods and unfolded it to find a verse from Isaiah:

The Glass Roses

When you pass through the waters, I will be with you; and through the rivers, they shall not overwhelm you; when you walk through fire, you shall not be burned, and the flame shall not consume you. For I am the Lord your God.

This seemed peculiar for a Cherokee and for someone who'd never been in a church. I didn't think of her as being religious, but instead, I thought of her as *spiritual*. Like everything else in her life, she dealt with things in her own ways and on her terms. She defied anything that didn't make sense to her. I thought the verse from Isaiah must have been her way of coping with the death of a child, possibly a verse someone had given her at Little William's funeral. That was something precious enough, valuable enough, to be guarded even as she slept.

She allowed herself only a few hours of sleep a night as if going without sleep and working, or at least, moving fast for 18 hours a day, were virtues, and I pondered how depriving yourself of sleep and working until your body pleaded for rest would get you into Heaven or at least get your name on the list like Grandmother said.

Lillie Dabney lived in an old, two-story, white house just at the edge of town. Unlike my maternal grandmother, who lived at Morley Mountain, she didn't live on a farm, although it was far enough away from the heart of Maynard Bald to give the feeling of living in the country. She had her independence although she didn't drive. Our house and Shelby's Grocery were within walking distance. She had a garden. But most importantly, she had privacy, which she valued more than hollyhocks or Cherokee roses.

Except when Elease was alive, or when Winnifred

was between husbands, or when Maudie was passing through, Lillie Dabney lived alone and preferred it that way. All five of her babies were delivered in her upstairs bedroom by the Cherokee midwife, Emma Still Meadow. W.O. was not present for any of the births except one, my father, Joseph, who was the youngest. After my father was born, W.O. dropped by only occasionally, leaving her to raise five children all by herself in the big, white house that he paid for.

I had always felt that her house was more mine than any of the houses I had lived in with my parents. It was surrounded by a fence with peeling, white paint. It encircled the entire house and the front and back yards, although she refused to call them *yards*, and insisted that she did not have and would never have a yard. She utterly detested and never used the words, *yard* or *lawn*. "They should be called *gardens*," she'd say, adding "the concept of a *yard* is ridiculous."

In summer there were hollyhocks of all colors and almost twice the size of Mrs. Hanover's hollyhocks next door. They grew along the fence and provided prized privacy.

The garden was filled mostly with wildflowers and plants with names that only she knew and could pronounce. There was no room nor desire for grass. Grandmother called it an *English garden*, saying she "hated grass, and we should never forgive Thomas Jefferson for going over to Europe and coming back to America with the absurd notion of a *lawn*. Manicuring and fussing, always cutting, trimming, or some other unnecessary form of alteration, all, in my opinion, just plain ridiculous, contrived and unnatural," she contended, "imagine concerning yourself with something as trite as the height of a blade of grass. It's just some peoples' way of feeling they have control over some tiny aspect of their lives," she explained, "when their sons have been sent off to war or the Russians have launched a *Sputnik*, they can keep the height of their grass in check."

Hollyhocks and echinacea took over everything. There were lots of bees, and every spring and summer when I was little, I ran around the gardens barefoot. I was stung 11 times in one summer, and Grandmother would dampen her snuff with her saliva and wrap it in a soft cloth. She called it a *snuff poultice*. As soon as it touched my swollen toes, I felt relieved. The heat and the swelling disappeared, and I could go to sleep.

The house, like the fence, was white and peeling, and one of the oldest houses on the north side of Maynard Bald. The location of the house provided everything desirable: it was close enough to Highway 25 to see every passing car; it was about 100 yards from the creek where the Martinelli boys gathered rocks for building their houses; and just above the creek were the train tracks that any time of day or night signaled activity.

My favorite place in the house, besides the room where I slept, was the parlor. No one was allowed in the parlor except Grandmother and me. She discouraged everyone else, including my father, from the room for fear someone might touch something. I couldn't recall her having a single visitor who wasn't a blood connection.

When my father was in the house, he stayed in the kitchen, and sometimes when Grandmother had other visitors, I'd slip away into the favored room to be alone. In the evening, light streamed in through windows that faced west and rose two inches from the floor to just a few inches from the ceiling.

When Grandmother and I were in the house alone, she would stand silently at the parlor windows for hours, the same way my mother worked at her ironing board, as if she was waiting for someone. I knew both waited for my father.

As the sun faded, she stood a few feet away from the window, as if she didn't want to be seen by anyone passing on the street. As darkness came, she moved closer to the window, and the lights were never turned on in the parlor, which made it possible for her to survey the goings on outside without being seen. Since she didn't have a radio, television, or telephone, her window watching served as entertainment of sorts. The only other activity that engaged her more fully was reading.

My favorite thing in the entire house (besides my bed that was handmade by Grandmother's uncle) was the revolving library: a massive, towering thing of black walnut that spun on a 300-pound steel beam that spiraled like Archimedes's screw toward the ceiling. It was not a secret that the revolving library came from the Maynard House. Melvin Maynard, whose family settled and named Maynard Bald, was said to have been in love with Lillie Dabney before and after she married W.O. Halverston.

When I was little, the revolving library seemed enormous, and it seemed to reach almost to the ceiling. It spun like the carousel of painted horses parked in the customer parking lot of Lyon's Supermarket the first week of every September—it spun round and round just like our lives, except the painted ponies wound their way back to the same place each time just to start out again to go nowhere.

I used to pretend that I could wind it up making it turn round and round on its pintle revealing 20 compartments, supposedly for housing books, although there wasn't a single book in the room. All of her precious books were protected on built-in shelves in the adjoining room. She rarely permitted anyone into that room either, except a few close friends and even fewer close relatives, for fear they would bother her books or ask to borrow one. Her most prized were on a middle shelf at eye level so they could be admired, but not touched: a copy of *Ulysses* that she read again and again writing notes in the margins about Proteus, a leather-bound copy of *A Doll's House*, and *27 Wagons Full of Cotton: One-Act Plays of Tennessee Williams* that she had sent to Nashville to have bound in ochre-colored leather. It was only in the last few months that she decided to send her copies of Joyce's and Ibsen's works to Nashville by way of Sheriff Rose, saying the pages were brittle and falling out making them difficult to handle. Only classic literature was proudly displayed next to the Southern literature. She also took pride in showing off the newly-bound books, but still, the books by *modern writers,* as she called them, or by non-Southerners remained wrapped in brown paper and relegated to dusty resting places under her bed.

The bookless shelves of the revolving library displayed the most glorious things in the house. Any person allowed into the room was held spellbound—pulled in, mesmerized by the sight. The shelves were lined with glass sculptures and fragments of neon signs that reflected and refracted beams of light that streamed through the towering windows, casting shadows and twisting the light like prisms casting hundreds of tiny rainbows twirling in pirouettes. You could read them as clearly as images in puddle eddies or shadows through dappled light.

Grandmother told stories about each piece, every piece made by my father. I wanted her to go on forever; she would grin and show her gums when she talked about them and her voice softened. Sometimes she stopped in the middle of a story and looked out the window.

When she was busy and others weren't around, I would lie on the floor in the parlor just a bit under the revolving library. I took off my shoes and socks and crossed my leg at the knee and pushed it with just my big toe. Round and round it would go; the speed of its turn depended on the weather and humidity. In late afternoon, the glass forms threw light and colors against the walls and the sound of the ball bearings as it turned on its axis would remain in my memory as clearly as the whirring of cicadas.

As I got older I recognized, not only that my father was different, but that he was an artist. In all my growing-up years, when I sat on the floor next to him night after night and watched him sketch designs for neon signs, it never occurred to me that melting glass was as much an art as painting a canvas.

It was hard to think of him, not as a stranger shrouded in secrecy and mystery, who passed, uninvited, in and out of our lives, but rather as a real person with his own view of the world, his own goals, his own fears. I watched him bent over torch burners with the rubber tube between his lips to manipulate the flow of air to shape the neon letters. When I needed something positive about my father to hang onto, I imagined him as Vulcan, master of the arts of fire. Grandmother had read stories to me of Vulcan and other Roman gods for as long as I could remember. Vulcan was her favorite because he was a lesser god and despite all his shortcomings, he made beautiful things.

It became more and more difficult to see the man who transformed sticks of glass into beautifully-lit signs and tiny glass sculptures as the same man who could push my pregnant mother to the ground or kick the screen door off its hinges. This was where all the boundaries began to melt as though creating something beautiful lightened the shade of darkness.

We never knew where or how my father learned to turn sticks of glass into works of art. In fact, at the time, we didn't think of what he did as extraordinary. Looking back, I realized that I never knew anyone, except my father, who made neon signs. He made every sign in Maynard Bald, Tennessee, and probably most in the small towns north to Hazard, Kentucky, and south to Chattanooga.

Neon glass would stay forever in my mind, as would the birth of each neon sign that I'd seen him create. I had watched him as long as I could remember. When I was young, he permitted it as long as I didn't ask too many questions or get too close to the flames or the hot glass—what he called *liquid fire*.

Boxes of hollow glass tubes in eight-foot lengths lined the walls of the shop where he worked. I watched as he scored the tubes cold with a file and snapped them apart hot, forming angles and curves— the most wondrous cursive letters were born like flaming red vines bursting from the heat. The birth of a child could not have been more magnificent: like a sorcerer, he pumped the sealed tube to create a vacuum; filled it with neon gas for red or argon gas for green or added a tiny droplet of mercury for blue. He could make any color by using phosphor-coated tubes. Then, like a magic show, he short-circuited the tube with a high-voltage current and the result was a spectacular light show.

It was listening to him when he was *bending* glass, as he called it, that I learned how to think things out: planning each step, the sequence, the concentration, and above all else, taking time. It was from watching him that I learned how to apply planning to other important aspects of my life. "You can't just hang around waiting for life to happen to you. You have to take up a pencil and write it out," he'd say. Make yourself a plan, a sketch, or a blueprint—a map to get where you're going. Think of bending glass for a sign and of living a life as puzzles for your mind—much akin to your grandmother's dithyrambs, but not as tedious."

I watched as he placed the hot glass on a blackened wood block to cool. Occasionally, there were accidents or the *magnificent mistakes* as Grandmother called them: when a tube was faulty or from impurities or from oxygen left behind. The finest mistakes would become exploding roses (my favorites) or mermaids if the glasses were red; swans or plump birds or bud vases shaped like honeysuckle vines if the glasses were white or florescent-lined. I learned that argon inside a white or florescent-lined glass would be purple with a droplet of mercury and light added. When the mistake was made from green, florescent-lined glass using argon, it became a vine of ivy. I listened as he explained every experiment or mistake. "Mercury energizes the molecules of the florescent coating making the color deeper, richer," he explained. Once when a glass tube filled with argon and mercury broke on its way to becoming a sign for a motel in Florida, he melted the pieces into a colony of drifting frogs with dangling glass tentacles for legs streaming from them like strings of purple fire.

Grandmother's explanations of the *magnificent mistakes* were not exactly the same as my father's. Neither were they exactly from a scientific perspective. She declared the glass roses the most miraculous. "They're like the mistakes you make in your life that turn you in an unexpected, sound direction; not at all what you first intended," she said, "then by some minim of fate tending toward a miracle, you arrive at a place as if you've been plucked out of an ocean and hurled there by Poseidon himself."

The transformer caused the lights to flicker and interfered with the telephone and all things run by electricity. My father leaned over his cross-burners and yelled over the characteristic buzzing sound of the current and the hum of the transformer. I never tired of hearing him say, "The light in neon signs is made to glow by simply lighting a gas with a discharge," or of hearing him tell me hundreds of times that the first neon sign in America was made for a Packard car dealership in 1923, the year after he was born.

Growing up, I was allowed in the neon shop only when there were no other men there; usually that occurred only late at night. I could show no signs of potentially falling asleep because it was too dangerous, and he couldn't stop what he was doing to take care of me. Long rubber tubes hung from his mouth, and, sometimes in just minutes, the sound of the flame lulled me to a state of serenity where there was no outside world, but only this place where art was being born. The times when I could stay awake, I watched him wait until the flame was right, when he would gather a long piece of glass from an eight-foot box, and as he sucked in as much air as his lungs would hold, and his lips tightened around the rubber tube, I knew it was definitely magic. The glass curled and waved like water and, almost instantly, he would have formed "MOUNTAIN INN" or "BIG CREEK GAP MOTEL." But the real magic came when he corked both ends and fused a current to it. It hummed and glowed and, sometimes, flashed on and off: things like "BUD'S PLACE" and "LUCILLE'S STOP" in red and "COVE LAKE MOTEL" flashed green. "LYON'S SUPERMARKET" glowed white and yellow with thousands of light bulbs flashing on and off creating the illusion of a moving arrow. When I walked by Lyon's Supermarket on any of the 15 days when the giant sign was being installed, he would call to me from atop the building and throw down coins for a Coca Cola or a milk shake.

My father needed drafts—sometimes a second, third, or fourth draft of the images that would become neon signs. He had large bolts of butchers' paper that he unfurled across the floor late at night getting ready to draw the letters. He worked on blueprints only at night. Sometimes it was hard to stay awake so late, but I sat by him as he hunched over the rolled-out paper. Usually around 1:00 a.m. he tucked his legs under him and started to draw—a sketch of the letters "MOTEL MAYNARD" would appear, so perfectly drawn that it looked impossible that a human hand had produced them. The times when I saw him frustrated and angry, when he broke up furniture, paced, and swore to himself, were times when he made mistakes. Usually, it was a misspelled word that would take hours to correct, depending on the size and where the error occurred. I tried to help him with his spelling, but it was hard to let my father know when he'd made a mistake. His errors were not because he didn't know how to spell, but because his concentration was intense, and he would fail to step back to view the whole word, rather than just one letter. Looking at the whole word was difficult because of the large scale of the signs.

I tried laying the dictionary close by, but that didn't seem to work. He would go right on and leave the "e" out of "TAVERN." I knew he would start swearing, and I prayed he would open the dictionary and discover his mistake all by himself.

After the sketches were finished, he placed each section of the large script, usually one letter at a time, on the coffee table or the kitchen or dining-room tables, and sometimes when the signs were large, he drafted them by unfurling the bolt of butchers' paper across the hardwood floor sometimes from one room to another.

With a wheel that made a perforated line and using blue chalk, he transferred the sketches of each individual letter onto a long scroll where they were connected to form words or the complete sign. Around daybreak or a little before, he would finish, untangle his legs from underneath him, and stand smoking his one-hundredth limp cigarette. He would grin at me as he rolled up the endless scroll, and if he had not made mistakes, he'd wink and remind me not to mention to my mother or my grandmother, or my teachers that I'd stayed up all night.

When he left the room, I looked at the coffee table with each letter etched into it by the perforating wheel. Mother would be very upset that "MOTEL MAYNARD" was etched into the coffee table. With letters etched into the wooden tables and misspelled words that made him break the legs off of the furniture, we had a new coffee table or dining table almost every week. Sometimes, he would dispose of them without replacing them, and other times, he would simply forget or lose interest, which happened often. And no one ever reminded him.

On my fourteenth birthday, August 6, 1961, my father came to pick me up at Grandmother's. He said we were going to the neon shop, that he had a surprise for my birthday. I had to cover my eyes before going inside. He led me to a high stool, told me to be patient, and to keep my eyes covered. I could hear the click as he turned off the lights. He kept saying, "Keep your eyes closed. It's a special surprise for your birthday." I clenched my eyes with the strangest feeling of excitement. He had never been around for one of my birthdays, and he had never presented a gift to anyone except my grandmother.

I tried to peek through my fingers, but it was dark in the room. I heard the sound of the transformer and the hum of the electric current. It was the lulling sound that I recognized. I opened my eyes to see "LUNDA ROSE" in large, red, cursive letters glowing beyond belief.

I could hardly wait to show Grandmother. She

would place it on a shelf on the revolving library. Maybe it would fit on a shelf above the glass roses where the light would treat it as a prism. Or maybe she would find just the right place on a shelf next to the plump blue bird or the purple bud vase. Or perhaps it would find its place next to the glass swan. "The light must hit it just right," I thought.

I called to her from the bottom of the stairs. The stairs were steep as in most old houses. I held fast to the handrail with my other hand clutching the glorious red glass. Grandmother called from the top landing. I looked up at her, and the toe of my clunky loafer caught on the lip of the step. Just as she called, "Stay there. I'll be down. I'm coming down," I stumbled and fell; the glass crashed against the wall. And there all over the stairs were a million little pieces of broken red glass. It was gone forever.

Grandmother said, "He'll make another one." We looked at each other, and we both knew it wasn't true. He would never make it again. There would never be another red name, a name the color of pigeons' blood, a name made just for me, one that hummed and glowed in the dark.

Tethered to Wanting

Turn Your Ear Inward:
An Early Step to Solitude

It was in early fall of 1961 that Ruby Grace announced that she wanted to marry David Martinelli, whose family was the only Italian family in Maynard Bald. David delighted in telling us stories of how his small Italian family ended up in the mountains of Tennessee; how the Martinelli's came over from Sorrento and Amalfi around the turn of the century. Once in America, they made their way to Mobile, Alabama. Roberto Martinelli, David's father, was only 17 when they arrived in Maynard Bald. It was the Tennessee limestone that drew them out of Mobile. In Italy, their trade had been stone masonry, and Mario Martinelli had already taught his sons, Roberto and Luca, the art of building houses from beautiful stones.

With their father, the brothers combed the river banks and creek beds first in Mobile, and eventually following the river to Huntsville, then traveling east and north to Chattanooga and on to Knoxville in search of stones most like the colors and matrices of those they practiced cutting in Italy. Once Mario laid eyes on the limestone that lined Jellico Creek that ran through the dead center of Maynard Bald, he announced, "This is it, boys. We've found our house rocks. This is where we stop."

David leaned in and his voice grew louder. We sat in the living room on that fall day listening, mesmerized as he told how his uncle and father carried the stones, the colors of yellow and sienna seen on the shell of a quail egg, moving them in wooden wheel barrows the distance from the creek to the site of their father's house, the first to be built. It took 14 years to complete houses built for Roberto and Luca. These were the first stone houses in Maynard Bald. Soon after finishing the first two rooms of the first house, Mario and his two boys began Maynard Bald's only stone masonry company, later growing to include a brick company and a cement block company.

Later in the fall, after Ruby Grace's announcement of her intention to marry David Martinelli, everything about her seemed to change: she was more withdrawn, distancing herself from the family, hardly speaking to any of us unless taken by surprise or waylaid as she passed through the house. She went to great lengths to keep David Martinelli's family from ours and ours from his. She was sick most days, but could never tell us what was wrong with her.

For several years, a certain melancholia had begun rising in her, usually showing its first signs soon after the autumnal equinox in late September as the spans of daylight grew shorter.

Ruby Grace paid little attention to our grandmother's warnings that it was in late September

when we could expect the onset of the Great
Nothing. Shaking a knotty finger close to our faces,
she'd say, "It shows its ugly head without warning and
fuels the making of poor choices, faulty judgments,
and bad decisions."

Ruby Grace rolled her eyes and winked at me as
Grandmother delivered her Great-Nothing speech.
She didn't approve of the upcoming marriage.
"You're just too young, and you'll feel differently in
the spring when the Great Nothing isn't attaching
itself to you."

By Thanksgiving, the darkness of the season and
the coming of winter loomed over us with the
heaviness of a new moon. Ruby Grace's decision to
marry David Martinelli came as no surprise, but it was
inconceivable that she would consider leaving
Maynard Bald or that she believed David's father
would permit him to leave.

It was clear Ruby Grace was marrying to escape,
but to leave Maynard Bald was the worst betrayal.
"How could she leave us?" I thought, "how could she
leave the rest of us behind? How could she just run
off leaving the rest of us here to worry about our
mother and to clean up the messes?" I found myself
arguing with her and saying hurtful things to her at
every opportunity and without provocation.

"You'll learn that men hate sick women," I blurted
out, pulled it from thin air for lack of anything else to
get her to talk to me. Arguments or stupid comments
were better than no talking at all.

"Well now, when did you get so smart about
men?" she asked in a calm voice.

"No, I'm not smart about men, but I'm smart
enough to know that men don't like broken things

they can't fix. Grandmother told me that."

The engagement was short. In the first week of December, Ruby Grace and David Martinelli married in front of the Justice of the Peace at the Jacksboro Courthouse. Grandmother, Mother, Maudie, Delilah Martinelli, and I attended. Ruby Grace wore a pale gray suit she'd sewn herself and a matching pillbox hat with a wisp of net that fell over her face. She was beautiful. Striking. Tall, six feet without shoes. David was six feet, three inches.

My crying was so loud, the Justice could barely be heard. David's mother cried, but in a polite way. Grandmother was still sulking because Ruby Grace had ignored her warning about marrying in December—"Close to the winter solstice, the shortest day of the year," she railed, "you couldn't have chosen a worse time, Ruby Grace."

"Why would you say such a thing?" Ruby Grace had snapped, "the decision has been made. I am happy. Even in December and away from Maynard Bald, I will be all right, and I will be happy."

They left the following day for a December honeymoon at Niagara Falls, where it was so cold that for a solid week, they hardly ventured outside. Immediately after returning, Ruby Grace and David moved to Chattanooga.

After Ruby Grace moved, I spent more and more time with our neighbor, Mrs. Pruitt, and her daughter, Miranda. It was safe there, and I loved hearing her talk about Tchaikovsky and Dvorak and prothonotary warblers.

"Tchaikovsky is hard, but it's a good thing we have Tchaikovsky in winter," Mrs. Pruitt said, as she tilted her head back and closed her eyes as if she was falling off to sleep. I thought her Tchaikovsky music sounded grand, almost noble—all that sound compressed into one piece. The Russians must have liked that. Mrs. Pruitt said Tchaikovsky lived a long time ago. The music reminded me of a dream; the same dream that runs through your head all night and seems to never end or have any resolve. No beginning, or middle, or end.

Maudie complained that listening to Mrs. Pruitt's records was just plain painful, and there was no way to escape it since it was too cold to stay outside. "A painful noise coming from the Victrola," Maudie called it. She pleaded with Mother to make me turn it off.

At every opportunity, I played records borrowed from Mrs. Pruitt. I delighted in listening to them when I was alone in the house. Times alone were rare. Noise was eternal at our house because of the number of people. When I listened to the records with the volume loud enough to drown out whoever was in the house, it made me feel like I was alone, which I preferred. But, when not listening to records, I loved the silence of my bedroom. I could think.

The room was a pretty room. And, it was comfortable, except in winter—when no heat reached the room, and it was freezing. I had a small electric heater that I was allowed to turn on only when I was in the room, but not in bed. This, understandably, made getting out of bed difficult. I usually spent at least ten minutes seized with dread.

I studied the wallpaper that Mrs. Longmire must have put up while she was in some sort of loss of herself. The designs ran together when I squinted. I admired the collection of colored bottles on the dresser by the window. Most of them I had found. Mrs. Pruitt had given me three of them. I liked the way everything behind them, especially the wallpaper, was distorted when I looked through them.

It was a nice house except the wallpaper and lack of heat. Our earlier houses were smaller, with the exception of the Petticourt house. The Longmire house was large with spacious rooms and halls like mazes. I built a rat maze once—complete with partitions and a glass ceiling, but when I told Mother I could study how different rewards and factors influenced learning and memory, she squealed, "No rats. Absolutely not."

I tried to explain that they were really mice, not rats. She said, "We are not having rats nor mice living in this house. Don't bring the subject up again."

Being alone didn't occur often, and when it did, especially in summer, I wallowed in the precious time and didn't squander one second.

Mother said the Victrola was going to ruin me. "I swear, Lunda Rose, your time would be better spent if you turned off that noise box and read a book. Stop listening to that noise, all that squealing! Please read a book. Mother slammed the iron back and forth over the pillowcase. She said, "I think better when I'm ironing. And I can block out the music."

From my room, I could see the shadow of the cord dangling from the ceiling and moving with her rhythm of complaints. Still, without looking up, she directed her scolding and discontent at me and at Maudie sitting at the kitchen table filing her nails while conjuring up images from la-la land of summer days and picnics at Looneys Island Bluff with Toad Dobson. "I swear I am cursed with a house full of sassy girls. All this work to be done. And not one of you is doing anything to help me with housework. Maudie, don't you have your own room to look after? Do you ever think of anything besides boys? What will become of you girls?" she scolded, referring to Maudie and me, and exempting my sister, Elda Kate, simply because she thought her too young to do housework.

"Just look at you!" she said looking at Maudie, "filing your nails at the kitchen table with the ill manners of a heathen and twaddling on and on with daub about traipsing to the mountains with that smooth-running Toad Dobson. And you," she said, turning toward my open door, "listening to a woman screeching in a foreign language. I should be rid of the whole lot of you. You're a piffling bunch. I should have birthed boys. They aren't near the worry and grief that you girls give me," she yelled, slamming the iron against a crocheted doily that she had already ironed at least five times. Mother did not understand that opera can be translated without knowing Italian, and that violins have words and a language of their own.

"Lunda Rose, turn off that noise. Joe will be home any minute, and he'll smash that record into a million pieces. Why do you bring those screeching recordings home from Mrs. Pruitt when you know something could happen to them. You wouldn't be able to replace them. What would you tell Mrs. Pruitt? How many books and records do you have under your bed? How many? If your daddy hears even a peep of that sound coming from your bedroom, he'll yank those records and the Victrola out of there and destroy them. Lord, maybe that would be a blessing and give us some peace."

"Opera, Mother. Those recordings are called *opera*."

"Don't sass me. Turn it off!"

Maudie ignored Mother and continued her yammering although no one was listening. "Maybe Toad and I will drive up to the Pinnacle or Coalter Shoals and have a picnic of tomato sandwiches. Of course it would be closer to go to the Cumberland Palisades, but I hate that winding road to Jellico. I don't imagine there's a stretch more than the length of a town block on Highway 25 that doesn't have a vomiting curve. I suppose I could ask Toad to drive slower around the curves. But then he'd say I'm bossy, and we'd argue, and the picnic would be ruined. Folks from Jellico call the Palisades *High Cliffs*. Did you know that? We could have our picnics on the bank where there's a great view of the cliffs. He's promised to take me to see the Obed Wild one day."

"Maudie, could you think of something other than Toad Dobson long enough to peel potatoes for supper?" Mother snapped.

"I'll take care of the potatoes as soon as my nails dry," she said, fanning and blowing her red fingernails, then holding them out limp like a begging dog.

Mother's voice grew shrill. The thuds of the iron were closer together. Her fussing had a certain cadence with the same rhythm as the thuds of the iron. The slamming of the iron became louder as her irritation with Maudie grew. Maudie's drivel about the picnic continued as she named the other possibilities for potential picnic sites. "Maybe we can go to Paint Rock Bluffs on the north bank of the French Broad.

That isn't too far from Knoxville. Or maybe Chilhowee."

"What a circus!" I thought. It reminded me of Mr. Neville teaching Chaos Theory. It wasn't his own theory, of course, but when he explained it, he said, "To understand Chaos Theory, just think of watching a butterfly in flight. It isn't the flight of a bird, deliberate with a destination. The butterfly's flight is jerky and random and unpredictable. It's chaotic."

I thought, "If Mr. Neville came to this house, he wouldn't have to use the butterfly again, ever, to explain chaos."

I longed for one minute of peace, of silence. I was impressed by silences. Grandmother loved to talk, but she knew *when* to be silent. She learned it from her mother. She called it *being still*. She said, "Silence is necessary to know yourself. It is required to know someone else. If you sit silently in a room with another person, you'll know about that person. You'll learn all that's important. Lack of silence can kill you. It can kill a relationship. It can kill thought. It can kill creativity. Silence is required. Solitude is the partner of silence. Solitude is necessary too. When you're alone and surrounded by silence, turn your ear inward. Listen to yourself. Listen to your own voice deep inside you. Listen to your thoughts. Listen to the voice that never sleeps."

That was it! With Maudie living in the house, who could be expected to have any peace, a thought, or a relationship with oneself, whatever that means. Or any creativity or a single moment of silence? I tried to remember if there were any of those things before she came to live with us. She wailed about something constantly, carried on like a yeaning sheep.

Maudie continued her endless, piffling nonsense about her picnic journey with Toad. "Constant, blithering nonsense," I thought. She knew my father would put a stop to her plan. And all that planning and thinking she was doing would be for nothing. Daddy often reminded her that even though she was his niece, she would abide by his rules just like the rest of us.

"Maybe we'll get an early start and drive up to Virginia. Maybe Meadows of Dan, you know, there on the Dan River," Maudie said.

I heard voices from the porch. "It's Joe," Mother whispered without raising her eyes and still ironing the same doily. "Be still," she whispered to Maudie. Maudie blithered on. "Shut up, Maudie!" Mother said in an excited whisper. "Be still. Listen."

I walked to the kitchen just in time to see why Maudie had fallen silent. Carl was there. And Daddy stood behind him filling the whole door frame.

He was six feet, four inches tall, and it looked effortless when he grabbed the top of the door frame with both hands and looked up at the ceiling while holding a cigarette between his teeth. This gesture seemed to anchor him to the floor. Mother never looked up. "Helen, stop ironing!" he commanded. "I don't want to come home to the endless slamming of that iron. "

He turned his eyes toward me. "What is that bloody racket?" he shouted. I backed into the bedroom as he walked toward me. "It's nothing, Daddy. Just a record from Mrs. Pruitt. I'll turn it off."

"Well, now, Mrs. Pruitt is going to be very unhappy, isn't she?" he mumbled as he pushed past me, still holding the cigarette between his teeth

"No, Daddy, don't break it. I won't play it again. I'll take it back tomorrow. Please, Daddy. I can't replace it. It's not mine."

He walked past me and pressed the needle into the record. The needle scraped across the record and ground into it stopping the turntable. He lifted the record and read the label. "What is this supposed to be?"

"No, Daddy," I cried as the record hit the floor and his heel crashed down on it. He looked at the Victrola and took a draw off his cigarette. He turned and walked out through the kitchen. Carl stood there silently. Mother ironed. Maudie, Elda Kate, and I fell silent. No one moved for a long time after we heard the car door slam and the engine start. I sat on my bed and tried to think of what I would tell Mrs. Pruitt.

Maudie went to her old bedroom that she once shared with Ruby Grace. Even at the far east side of the house, in the cold room with the piano left by Mrs. Longmire, I could hear her crying.

Turn Your Ear Inward

A Walk in the Snow

All the things about my father I had tried to deny could no longer be ignored. Deep down, I had known this for years, but through those years, I was either too young to understand it, or I didn't *want* to believe it—that my father, the artist who created beauty, was also a man who was capable of turning a monstrous side to us.

The thought had been forming, getting stronger for years. Now it was indisputable. The full, undeniable proof of the man my father was, came to me later in December of 1961. The evidence flew in my face, and there was no doubt this time. The knowledge came whole and certain and looked me square in the eye, pushing everything else from my mind. It was true that he occasionally turned other facets of himself toward us—a lighter, more human side, creative, but the one we saw most often took up the most room and was the darkest. Grandmother said, "Every human has a dark side." But I didn't want to believe that.

Mother's relatives kept their distance, staying put on Morley Mountain—festering, their hatred for my

father swelling like an open sore. Mother didn't go to
Morley as often. Her sister, Sudie, came to our house
at least once a week, sometimes twice or three times a
week. I was sure it was to bring news of
Grandmother Evers, and also to see for herself that
Mother was all right. Weir kept the truck battery
charged, but Mother discouraged the uncles' trips to
Maynard Bald for fear they would encounter my
father and someone would be shot.

Daddy despised Sudie. I knew it by the way he
changed every time he saw Mother and Sudie
together. He watched them. He resented the
pleasure Mother took in Sudie's presence, but most of
all, he hated her influence. She encouraged Mother to
learn to drive, to get a job, to voice her opinions.

Sudie was a coal miner's widow at twenty-six. She
and my mother had the same striking features: black
hair, porcelain skin, angular cheeks, thin and tall with
long legs that reached to their elbows. When people
mistook one for the other, they easily assumed the
other's identity. Mother was different after she'd been
with Sudie, as if she'd taken on a strength that didn't
belong to her.

Sudie talked openly to Mother about Elton and the
mine explosion that killed her young husband and
five other miners. One day at our house, she leaned
closer to Mother and said, "I never really loved
Elton." She quickly changed the subject when she
realized Mother didn't know what to say. "What are
you afraid of?" she leaned in and asked her in a
whisper.

"Well, it's not Joe, if that's what you're thinking,"
Mother snapped. "What scares the wits out of me is
looking into the hollow of this existence and realizing

that all the air has been sucked right out of me, smothered, as if my life has been wasted in the darkness of the mines without going near them."

"Good Lord, Helen, I was prepared for your answer to be Joe, or the Halverstons, or copperheads, or Black Widow spiders, or just plain old dying. I'm glad we got that straightened out," she said trying to pare down the seriousness of the answer. "Anything else that scares you?"

"Well, yes, if you must know. I'm afraid of senility; next to that, of being without a home; of not being loved by anyone, of being left, and of dying alone. But those fears are common to all of us. Aren't they? And I know it sounds strange, but I'm afraid that I haven't reached far enough."

She looked at Sudie trying to read her face. "Like every mother, I'm afraid for my children, afraid of the lives they might have. I don't want them to end up like me—with a life without meaning."

"What are you saying? Your life has meaning. You have four children for pity's sake."

"I know. I didn't mean that."

Sudie leaned closer. "Do you know the difference between having *meaning* in your life and *purpose* in your life? They're different you know. I've given this considerable thought since Elton died, well, really, since Elton and I married."

I could see over my book that Sudie's announcement surprised Mother. She stared at her without comment.

"Meaning, you see, is what a person finds in the present, at this very moment. It's passive and stays within you; like loving and longing. Purpose, on the other hand, belongs to the future; it's set aside to be acted upon later. It's active and springs from you like drive and determination. Meaning involves other people and purpose is a solitary thing—something that isn't shared. Purpose is having inner work to do, something deep inside you that steers you with conviction through the days and keeps you up at night thinking about doing it. But meaning, that's a different thing entirely. It's a feeling of having a hole inside you filled up, and it requires the help of other people to bring it to you, to fill you up.

"What?" she whispered, "I think that Elton's death affected me differently than I suspect the death of a husband would affect most women. I didn't love Elton when we married, but now I've come to think that sometimes, and only for those of us who are very fortunate, someone comes into our lives *without love* and changes us forever."

* * *

It seemed like Ruby Grace had been gone for years, when it had been only a few weeks. Maudie had left for Baltimore with Toad Dobson.

I watched and listened; I tried to figure things out on my own. Mother and Daddy had bickered almost every day during the weeks since Thanksgiving, even in the days before and after Ruby Grace's wedding. Mother cried most of the time. When I asked her what she was crying about, she wouldn't answer, but would shake her head from side to side and cry harder. When I asked, "What can I do to help you, to make you stop crying?" she'd shake her head and sob into her cupped hands. When she tired of being asked, she looked at me and said, "No one can help me." When I glimpsed her sitting alone, she seemed unreachable.

Mother and Daddy could not stand to be around each other, always fussing and carrying on, and at the same time, they couldn't bear being away from each other. This kind of *love* was impossible to understand. Mother cried even in the night. She cried when he was at home with her, and she cried when she was without him.

I had been looking at the situation all wrong. It seemed to have nothing to do with how much they did or did not love each other, but rather, the source of their problems came down to what one did not know about the other—*secrets*, always holding onto them, hoarding them, and whether real or imagined, secrets were like pain, as real to the bearer as breathing. Secrets were deadly. They imploded my family, backfiring—causing each deception, each wrong, each little lie, and sometimes even the good intentions to fold in on themselves. And even imagined secrets and deceptions ultimately nurtured distrust as surely as if it had been grown in a petri dish.

I realized as I got older, that, ironically, much of Mother's suspicious nature regarding men was cultivated by her father and brothers. The Evers men were handsome and spirited. Women found them charming and were drawn to them. I had heard that even my mother's father, John Evers, was known to let his eye stray in the direction of a pretty woman.

I was young when my grandfather died, and I can remember only three things about him: he was handsome with a beautiful, deep voice; and he was scared witless of storms, keeping a rocking chair and mining hat in the cellar where he gathered practically every person in Morley, at least as many as could squeeze into the cellar. Once the cellar door was closed, he rocked steadily in his rocking chair, singing as loudly as he could sing, until the storm passed.

The Evers' suspicions of everyone outside of Morley were bound to them as tightly as their own flesh. This seemed perfectly senseless to me. Secrets, suspicions, and distrust were hard work. In my mother's case, I wondered why she would want to stay with someone she didn't trust? Mother had her own secrets, too, which nurtured her distrust of my father. Years later, I would learn one of her most fiercely-protected secrets—that she was expecting Ruby Grace before she and my father married. Had her brothers known about the pregnancy, they surely would have killed my father right then and been done with it. They probably would have killed Mother, too.

Lately, my father's absences lasted for weeks and at times stretched into months. When Sudie or anyone asked about him, Mother would reluctantly speak of him; and if she said anything at all, it was to make excuses or offer explanations. She would say she didn't know where he was, but believed he was in Harlan, Kentucky, working on a sign for a café.

It was when he started talking about having a spell of work in Pineville, Molus, or Elcomb, that Mother knew he wasn't telling her the truth. "I know the areas around Molus and Elcomb, Kentucky. There's nothing but mountains and hollows," she said, "the folks up there surely would not have a bit of use for a neon sign. I am not stupid, Joe."

Also, he told her he was taking a bakery sign to Savannah, Tennessee, just north of the state line juncture of Mississippi, Alabama, and Tennessee, and that when he delivered the sign to Savannah, he was driving on to Muscle Shoals to take care of a matter there.

"Lies, just lies," she whispered, barely moving her lips.

When she did go with Sudie to Morley to see her mother and brothers, she stayed only a few hours before asking Sudie to drive her home. She would begin to fidget when the uncles started asking questions. Her brothers, one by one, probed for information as to Daddy's whereabouts; each brother thinking he was the only one questioning her, and she lied easily, telling each one that she was fine. Each of the five interrogations concluded with the whispered question, "Do you need money?" And she would lie with a confident "no", too proud to tell them the truth.

I looked at Mother and my father when they were together and felt sorry for both of them, and I wondered which one would kill the other. It took me a good while to figure out that when Lillie Dabney came to get me in the middle of the week to spend the night with her, that something was going on that was supposed to be a secret—a secret I, especially, was not supposed to know. For years, I thought everyone spoke in a whisper when they were inside their houses.

Although my brother, sisters, and I were now old enough to take care of ourselves, I knew that Grandmother was still scared for us. And although we knew all the signs, I took a certain solace in knowing she would come. She said, "When your mother and daddy start quarreling, just get out of the house. Make

Robert Joseph and Elda Kate get out. Get out and stay out. All of you. Go next door to Mrs. Pruitt's until they settle down or leave."

One evening in December just before Christmas, my grandmother appeared at the door, and Mother seemed unusually pleased about her arrival. I was happy to see her, although, unlike when I was little, I knew now that when she came to collect me and insisted I spend the night at her house, something was wrong. Finally, I realized that my father stopped at his mama's each time there was a blowup at our house— not that he divulged any information, but he knew his mama wouldn't question him; he could calm down and think more clearly. Gather himself. She'd give him coffee and blackberry cobbler and sit across the table in silence without interfering.

She said, "Get your nightgown and come home with me tonight. There's snow in the clouds, and you can get to school easier from my house. Come on, all three of you, get your pajamas."

I knew the situation was dire when Grandmother showed concern for Elda Kate.

"No, Lillie," Mother said. "I'm thinking of calling one of my brothers to come down and take Robert Joseph and Elda Kate to stay with my mother for a few days. It'll be alright if Lunda Rose stays with you."

I hoped the snow would be light. It was Monday, and every Tuesday, the girls played basketball in the gymnasium. It was the only day of the week that the boys' coach would give up the gym to the girls. I had been deemed the center forward for one of the two girls' teams, and I was sure that I was the answer to the entire future of girls' basketball.

A Walk in the Snow

Folk-and-square dancing was held after school every Tuesday. Mrs. Hannah Clotfelter would put a scratched, 45-record on a portable record player to play *Green Sleeves* over and over. Then she would put on a German polka until we complained. Against her own preference, she resorted finally to a piece with a Scottish fiddle, and we were praised for our amazing footwork. It did not matter if you could hold a beat or if you stumbled all over everybody, or if your left foot was out when everybody else's right one was out. Sometimes, Mrs. Clotfelter would play a 45 of a square call that was even more fun because the caller always told you what to do—

Now, pass on under and swing your girl. Now to the right. Now parade and twirl her left.

I liked knowing where to move and what to do. I liked hearing the calls. There was something happy about the caller's sound. I wondered what the man on the record looked like, and I imagined him holding his fiddle and tapping his foot. Mrs. Pruitt always corrected me when I called it a *fiddle,* saying it was really a violin, and that the only thing that made it a fiddle was the kind of music played on it.

That night I stood at the window in Grandmother's parlor and felt relief in being there. It was late, and there was barely enough light to see the snow coming down. The snow was building fast, mounding against the west side of each porch spindle. Basketball practice and folk-and-square dancing would surely be cancelled. I wouldn't mind missing basic algebra class and the dreaded few minutes of Mrs. Alley making us stand at attention like little children to quote the B-Attitudes. Those two things alone were reasons enough to long for snow.

Basketball practice and folk-and-square dancing negated the agony of the B-Attitudes. I wished for a foot or two of snow on Wednesday.

There was just enough light from the porch light to see that the snow was already over six inches deep. I sat at the parlor window with my elbows propped on the windowsill. The snow came fast, a wet and heavy one that stuck to branches and power lines. Grandmother stood back in the darkness so as not to be seen from the street. She was especially unsettled, adamant that the room should stay dark, saying we would sit in the kitchen to read. I used to think it was to save on the electric bill, but I learned that the habit was to keep check on the outside world without being seen. Standing back a few feet, she gazed out the window half the night, always looking and waiting for something or someone.

My eyes tried to close as I watched the snow falling in the beam of the porch light. Finally, she said, "Better get under the quilt now. Got to rise up early." She stretched out beside me still wearing her clothes and shoes. She didn't turn down the covers, but perched atop the quilt and counterpane penning me beneath the sheets making it difficult to move. Just as I started to doze, she jumped up and snatched her pocketbook from the bureau, lacing her arms through the purse's straps and placing it atop her breasts.

It was late. I hoped Grandmother soon would settle down and sleep. I heard her breathing heavily. Her body went limp. "Finally," I thought. I tried to be still and not to think of the B-Attitudes or how Mrs. Alley fussed when I left out one.

There were noises I couldn't make out on the

front porch. I jerked, briefly seized by fear that it might be Daddy. Someone was crying. It sounded like a whimpering puppy. Yes, that was the sound—one I remembered from years ago, blind puppies under the house, crying for their mother's milk. I looked at Grandmother to see if she roused. She didn't. I was held there, frozen. It was the sound of a woman crying—faint sobs, sad and desperate. They grew louder and louder, then softened to only a whisper, and then to a low, rapid plea. Snow smothered the sounds as it had hushed the sound of the creek and the train.

Grandmother sat straight up in bed as if rigor mortis had just grabbed her whole body and flung it like she was sprung from a slingshot. She sat looking at the door as if preparing herself. She did not call, "Who's there?" She sprang to her feet, her white shoes hitting the floor as if she'd jumped from the ceiling. When she eased the door open, there in the blowing snow stood my mother and Daddy. Mother was wearing a paper-thin coat. Daddy had on his warmest, biggest mackinaw.

Mother was silent as he pushed her from behind. She sat at the kitchen table and buried her head in her hands. Her face was red and wet. She begged, "Please, Joe, let me borrow a coat from your mother. I'll freeze to death. I'm already half-frozen. Please, Joe, leave the gun with your mother. I'll do anything you tell me to do. I won't do it again. Don't make me walk any farther in the snow."

Daddy went to the dark parlor to look out the window. Mother pleaded with my grandmother to try to talk to him, to try to get the gun. "He'll listen to you, Lillie," she whispered. "He's forced me to walk in the snow without a decent coat. My feet are numb."

Our house was on the west end of town just where the outskirt meets the farm country. She leaned toward Grandmother and whispered, "The sheriff and his deputy were making their late rounds looking for cars stranded in the snow. I knew the sheriff would stop, thinking how strange to see two people walking in deep snow in a place like the west end— out in the country. It was especially odd to see someone walking late at night in this weather without a real coat, or gloves, or boots. They knew something was wrong.

" 'Are you two all right?' the sheriff yelled from the window of the pickup.

"Joe held his pistol in the pocket of his mackinaw. He whispered, 'Say you're all right, Helen, or I'll shoot all three of you.'

"I tried not to cry out, not to needlessly endanger the sheriff and the deputy. I wanted to shout, 'stay there. Don't come any closer.' I was afraid they would see I was crying. I called back to them, 'We're all right. We're on our way to Lillie Dabney's. Our truck hung up in the snow a piece back.' The sheriff got out of the truck and yelled through the blowing snow, 'We'll give you a lift home.'

" 'Stay there,' I prayed.

"Joe yelled back, 'It's okay; we're not far from my mother's house.' He said, 'Helen, tell them everything is okay and let out a little nervous giggle the way you do when you can't think of anything to say. Make them think you're all right, or the last thing you'll see is blood all over the snow.' "

Daddy went back and forth from the kitchen to

the parlor to look out the window. He came back into the kitchen and without looking at us or saying anything went out slamming the back door.

I heard Mother whisper, "Lillie, plead with him not to make me go on. I have to have a coat. I can't walk anymore in the snow. He will kill me if I stop or fuss. Ask him to leave the gun with you. Try to reason with him. He'll listen to you. Please, Lillie."

Grandmother started to cry.

Hours passed. He didn't come back. Mother had shed her clothes and shoes. All night she sat by the stove wrapped in an old robe and a quilt.

"Lillie, listen to me. Joe will kill me if he thinks I know anything about his business. I don't know anything. I don't want to know."

"Know what? What are you talking about? What are you saying?"

"Listen to me, Lillie! Joe is hiding something. I don't know what his secrets are, and I don't care, as long as he doesn't have another woman."

"Why do you think he has never allowed me to drive or even learn to drive for that matter—just one of his ways of controlling me, of keeping me from knowing anything about him. Why do you think he doesn't permit me to go anywhere without him, or to be with other people? Why do you think he can't bear it when I'm with my family? Or anyone? He views other people as threats and competitors. The times when he's come home and didn't find me there, he's flown into fits of raving madness, breaking the legs off the furniture and breaking up anything in his way. His rage is out of control. I'm afraid of what he'll do next."

Mother eased toward the back door to look out

the window. "When one of my brothers or cousins comes to drive me to Benge's Grocery or to see Dr. O'Brien or when I leave the house to do perfectly innocent things, I have to be back in the house before he comes home."

"What's happened that's thrown him into such a rage?" Grandmother asked. "Why is he making you walk? And with almost nothing to keep you warm?"

"I wanted to know what he was doing night after night. He never says anything, and I know something is terribly wrong. I knew he was leaving. He was in a hurry. Irritated. Paced without a word. Finally, he said he had to deliver a neon sign to a cafe in Harlan, Kentucky.

" 'In this weather?' I asked, 'and this late?' He acted so strangely. After he left the house, I called the Bottoms Store. Got Merlin Messer out of bed to fetch Caudill to come on down here to drive me to Harlan. Since Joe's truck had a lift crane and possibly a neon sign on it, how hard could it be to find him in a place the size of Harlan?"

Mother talked in only a whisper, "Joe left the house about 11:00 p.m., and it was about 1:00 a.m. when Caudill got to the house. We headed out to Highway 25 on that frozen, winding road over the mountains to Harlan. We could hardly see the road. Neither Caudill nor Joe Halverston are one bit afraid of an icy road. We didn't come upon a single car and crossed into Kentucky about 2:00 a.m.. The southern edge of that little town has always been known for crimes in the train yards and around the mines. Further into town the streets were lined with decaying buildings with broken neon signs, flashing lights, cheap motels and juke joints. About two blocks down the main street, there was a motel of small cabins with a still-lit neon sign that said, MOUNTAIN LODGE. There in the shadows was Joe's truck parked far in the back. I knew he had a woman in there. I asked Caudill to park about 50 yards down, and turn off the lights.

"We waited in Caudill's truck. The light was on in the cabin where the truck was parked, but we couldn't see anyone. It was still snowing. Caudill was worried he'd get his truck hung up in the snow. He kept the engine running so we could stay warm. He started to worry about running out of gas. We heard voices farther back in the parking lot, loud voices of men arguing and getting louder. There were gunshots muffled by the snow. Four pops of smothered gunshots. I knew the sound. Caudill and I jumped out of the truck and ran in the direction of the sounds. There beneath a red neon sign were two men lying motionless on the pavement. A spreading puddle of blood forming a wide circle grew from beneath one of them. Blood oozed from the other man's ear and from the left side of his mouth. People came out in their nightgowns; some were no more than half-dressed. It was quiet with only the deafening silence of snowflakes falling to the ground. They all stared. No one moved close enough to the men to see if they were alive. The motel manager came out and ran back in to call the police. As the circle of on-lookers formed, and the pools of blood grew around the two men, it became clear that an ambulance wasn't needed. Everyone just stood there looking at the lifeless bodies. As I looked up at the gathering of people, there, across the circle of spectators, stood Joe, looking from the back of the crowd and holding a bottle of Coca-Cola in each hand.

"I thought, 'Oh, Lord, please don't let him see me or Caudill,' but he looked across the dead men and across the viewers and saw me. His face stiffened, becoming more angular. Looking at the ground, he walked slowly toward us and asked calmly, 'What are you doing here, Helen? How did you get here?'

"Then he saw Caudill. I told him Caudill had brought me. 'I was worried about you, Joe.'

" 'Tell your brother he can go on home,' he said, still looking at the ground, vein bulging, blinking fast the way he does when he's trying to control himself. 'You'll ride home with me.'

"All I could think of as I slid across the seat was 'tonight he will kill me.'

"Joe drove around the mountains like a madman. When we got home, he pushed me out of the car. He said, 'Helen, you're so bloody curious about Harlan and its goings-on, let's just go to Harlan! Let's *walk* back! We'll have ourselves a little walk in the snow.'

" 'No, Joe, we can't, not in the snow,' I begged him, 'it's too far. We'll die.'

"All he said was 'You're so interested in my doings, why don't we just walk it? Maybe you'll learn something.' "

Daddy didn't come back to Grandmother's that night, nor that week. Mother stayed until daylight. She found an old pair of boots and struck out from Grandmother's to walk home, telling me that she'd be fine, that I was to stay with Grandmother until she came for me. This was a time when I most felt my anger toward Ruby Grace for running off to Chattanooga and Maudie for leaving for Baltimore. Oh, I knew Ruby Grace couldn't stay with us now that she was married, but "why did she have to move to Chattanooga?" I asked myself.

"I have to go home to see about Robert Joseph and Elda Kate," Mother said. But when I asked Mrs. Hanover to use her phone to call our house, there was no answer. Not even an answer from Robert Joseph or Elda Kate. School was cancelled that day and the three days after, which brought a warm Saturday when the snow started to melt. Still, no one answered the phone at our house.

After supper the next Monday evening, Grandmother's neighbor, Mrs. Bertha Hanover, knocked on the door to tell us Mother had called from the telephone at the back of the Bottoms Store at Morley. Mrs. Hanover was to tell us that she was sending Caudill to get me. Robert Joseph and Elda Kate were with her at Morley staying with Grandmother Evers.

At first light the next morning, Caudill sat with the truck idling in front of Lillie Dabney's house. He was bundled in a heavy wool work jacket that struck him at mid thigh. I had a thick coat and my quilt that I spread across both our laps. A slow grin started to form at the right corner of his mouth. The truck's heater didn't work. He said nothing. I knew the trip would be another 32-mile struggle against silence.

When we arrived at Morley, Caudill drove directly to Hoboch Lewis' house and dropped me off. Aunt Lettie explained that the reason was in case my father was watching their houses, he wouldn't know in which house my mother was hiding.

The uncles had agreed that Mother should not stay with Grandmother Evers. "That's the first place Joe Halverston will look," Purcell insisted, "Helen will move from house to house, rotating among the five of us, not staying more than one night in the same place."

Sometimes she would break the rule and stay two consecutive nights with Weir and Florence Nell. I spent the night wherever mother slept. Both Mother and I preferred being at Weir's. It felt safe there. All the uncles were protective, but Weir was the most ill-tempered and protective of them all. He also harbored the greatest loathing for my father.

After dark on the day I arrived at Morley, Hoboch Lewis walked with me to Weir's house to see my mother. We stayed that night at Weir's, where we sat until 2:00 a.m. in front of a coal-burning stove listening to Mother's and Florence Nell's stories of when they were girls.

On my second day there, Mother said we would stay at Weir's for another night.

It was Weir who first saw the figure of a man standing on the road at the curve just past the Bottoms. Weir was walking home from the mine with three other miners, each coal-blackened and carrying a metal lunch bucket. The other men reached their houses and signaled goodbye with the slight movement of one finger. Weir walked on past his house to the place on the road where he had seen the man, but when he reached the curve, there was no one there, and he didn't see anyone walking in any direction.

He came into the house and went to a wash pan where he soaped up his hands and face before sitting down for supper. "Thought I saw someone out on the road a while ago, but couldn't make out who it was. You and Lunda Rose stay put inside for the next few days. Don't go wandering over to the store or to Mama's or the brothers'," he said as he filled his plate.

After supper, Weir sat down on the only padded chair in the whole house. He always sat there after eating. It was close to the stove. He rolled himself a cigarette, and Florence Nell poured for him a small shot of whiskey in a glass that came to her new and full of snuff. Mother, Florence Nell, and I sat at the table discussing Florence Nell's special recipe for the jar of applesauce she had opened that evening saying that she had been saving it for winter. "Made from yellow transparent apples," she smiled, "and that single apple seed there on top is my trick. Apple seeds hold just a trace of arsenic, but using just one to bleed in a pink color is the secret for flavor."

Weir came to his feet as if something had startled him. He held out his hand motioning for us to stop as we moved toward him. He signaled us to stay back as he slowly walked to the other side of the kitchen and reached behind the Hoosier cabinet retrieving a Colt 44 Russian. I followed him to the front window where he eased back the curtain with one finger.

Even without a car or person visible, Weir knew who was there.

"Stay back, Helen," he commanded. "Joe Halverston will not speak to you or lay eyes on you," he said, stuffing the gun into the front of his pants then tugging at the sides of his belt, pulling it up in an effort to secure the pistol.

My father stood on the other side of the door, but did not knock. Mother and I followed Weir despite his warning. He eased back the curtain.

"Get on back to the kitchen, Helen, so I can open the door. The sight of you will just kindle him. He doesn't know which house you're at. Go on back there with Florence Nell and stay away from the window. You too, Lunda Rose," he whispered.

I didn't move for fear that Daddy was about to be shot. Or maybe it would be Weir.

My father stood silently on the other side of the door, but still did not knock. Weir could see the shadow of his shoes beneath the door. Leaning closer to the door, Weir said, "I have no business with you, Joe. And you have no business at Morley. What you're wanting cannot be found here." He said this calmly, with confidence, and with the tone of steadfastness possessed by all the brothers.

"Just want to talk to Helen. I've no quarrel with you, Weir." He said this without any malice in his voice.

Weir opened the door to see him standing as close to it as possible, as if he'd been pressed against the wood listening for any sound or sign of Mother. Daddy took a step backwards, slowly pushing the right side of his coat back just far enough to reveal the handle of his gun, a Smith and Wesson Model 19, given to him by his father.

"I just want to talk to her, Weir. That's all I want."

"Makes no difference to me what you want. Stay where you are, Joe. I have six children and my wife in here, but I'll shoot you where you stand. Get off my porch and stay away from my house. Stay away from Morley."

Weir took a step forward onto the porch; Purcell and Pinder came around the left corner of the house; a few seconds later Caudill and Hoboch Lewis appeared from the right. The only one of the brothers who spoke was Weir, who had always served as a collective voice for all five when Grandmother wasn't around.

"You got no business here that I can tell. Helen's business is her own," Weir said, closing the door. I watched through the window. After seeing Daddy's tall figure fade from sight at the end of the camp road, the other uncles walked on to their houses.

My father appeared there again the next evening, his tall, slender form just barely visible at the end of the one-lane road. He did not approach the house. He was there the day after that, and the next one, and the one after. For five days and nights, we were unable to leave the house. Weir made Mother swear she wouldn't go out during the day when he was at the mine.

I lay in bed those nights and relived the mess of the day when Daddy came to Weir's porch. It occurred to me that just because we hadn't seen him, other than on the porch and on the road those four days after, didn't mean he wasn't there. "What about the nights?" I thought. The only lights were around the mine and the tiny porch lights on a few houses.

I thought about Robert Joseph and Elda Kate; how they were just a short distance up the mountain with our grandmother, and they were unknowing about the whole sorry state of our family mess. I thought about school and wondered if I would ever go back; about Lillie Dabney and how worried she would be. But most of all, I thought about my father. I could not push the image of him from my mind. I had caught only a glimpse of him, only part of his tall figure, really, and a whole long shadow that stretched across Weir's porch. That same sad feeling welled up in me, and my thoughts drifted to a vague place and time that I linked to that same mournful feeling that came with a single story Grandmother had told when I was little—a Cherokee story about the wandering, lonely *Long Man*, Cherokee for *river*; a story about the Tennessee River that started its long journey in Paducah, Kentucky, and ran aimlessly until it reached Muscle Shoals, Alabama.

I needed to get back to Lillie Dabney. She was the one who made sense of things, the one who stood back to see things from a distance. She was the driver, the interpreter. It was she who made everything visible, clear. It was she who flayed open the mysteries.

It was Sunday and started to snow again.

The Long Way Back Home

Winter was hateful. I resumed reciting the B-Attitudes each morning which I thought should have been grounds for bringing a lawsuit against the school.

Our house was a hotel lobby where strangers passed through and occasionally nodded. As the naked trees began to show the first veils of chartreuse, temperaments began to improve. Sometimes there were small indications that Mother and Daddy still lived in the house. The walk-in-the-snow incident was hidden away with other harrowing memories.

In May, Ruby Grace and David moved from Chattanooga to Elcomb, Kentucky. I looked at a road map at the Fleet station and saw that Elcomb was much closer than Chattanooga to Maynard Bald. However, after six weeks in Kentucky, around the third week in July, 1962, they moved back to Maynard Bald, and David started work at the Martinellis' stone masonry company. It took only six months in Chattanooga and six weeks in Elcomb, Kentucky, to convince them to return to Tennessee and the support of Mario and the paydays of the masonry company.

It was not in Ruby Grace's nature to share information with others. Secrecy was another flaw in the Halverston genes. Ruby Grace didn't talk about her time away from us, nor did she talk about her first months of marriage. Grandmother said most of the Halverston women thought that knowing and keeping secrets gave them power and that divulging information, even meaningless information, was an indication of surrendering power or, at the very least, giving up something that belonged to them. Winnifred was a master. Grandmother remarked that Ruby Grace was under the same false assumption as every Halverston woman before her—that keeping secrets would endow her with some sort of potent leverage.

I wasn't interested in Ruby Grace's secrets. She was back. Maudie had left Toad Dobson in Baltimore, and divided her time between our house and Grandmother's.

It was around this time, later in the summer, 1962, that the face-cutting incident happened when Mother was gone for nine months.

We never knew where she went during that time. It was never mentioned again, but I was sure my father was reminded of that haunting night every time he looked at her. She made no attempt to conceal the scar with makeup.

After that horrifying night and after Mother's return, Ruby Grace continued to spend more time at our house than at her own. She avoided coming when she knew Daddy was at home. I knew her reasons for coming were the same as

Grandmother's—to make sure we were safe. She'd spoken with mother everyday by phone or in person since Mother's return. After a while, I began to understand how that incident had deeply affected Ruby Grace, although she never talked about it.

For almost a year, things seemed relatively calm. Maybe it had something to do with living in the same house, the Longmire house on Prospect Street, for a period long enough to feel like it was a home rather than merely a place for people to sleep as they were passing through. Or maybe, it was simply that we weren't moving every few months.

* * *

One night in October, 1963, Mother, Daddy and I had just watched the Huntley-Brinkley Report that had recently expanded from 15 minutes to 30 minutes of national and world news. Daddy never missed it when he was at home. Still, there was always the risk of losing the television to his attack if the rabbit ears wrapped in aluminum foil failed during the 30-minute program.

Once, when Elda Kate appeared with her class on a live broadcast of a children's program from Knoxville, just as a microphone was shoved in front of her and Mr. Bob asked, "What's your name?", the screen went snowy and diagonal bars appeared along with static. There was no time to fuss with rearranging the aluminum foil, Daddy's huge foot plowed through the screen, the picture tube, and the cabinet housing delivering one fatal blow.

On this particular October night, he was unusually restless. He asked if there was still coffee in the pot. When I returned with a cup of scorched coffee, he lit a cigarette, leaned back in his chair and casually announced that we were moving to New Jersey. "New Jersey?" I yelled. "I can't go to New Jersey. I hate New Jersey." He ignored me. Mother said nothing.

"Carl and his family are already there, and I've been working on a project there. Have your bags packed by Thursday," he said, barely looking at us. "You'll like it there. It's so close to New York City, you can see the New York skyline across the river."

For hours the next day I sat staring at my empty suitcase. Thinking. I was in high school. "Maybe sometime in this century I will graduate," I thought, "look at it this way, maybe they're starting to like each other. This could be the real *golden year*—a new start."

That night I sat in the dark. More thinking. I had never fully forgiven my mother and father for all the misery they had brought upon this family and upon each other. After all these years, I wondered if my mother's entire life would be spent living in fear of my father and moving every time an impulse nudged him.

Despite Grandmother's warnings, I still thought there was merit in an *almost* forgiveness. I thought it was a downright pity that we moved like a pack of convicts every time Daddy had a little change of thought. I was still fretting over things that happened years ago. His whims cost me my blue Schwinn bicycle. Back then, the blue bicycle and my red skirt cut on the bias were my most precious worldly possessions. I decided to just forget about all that past stuff. Grandmother told me years ago that I had too much to look forward to; that I shouldn't keep harping on things I couldn't do anything about.

I was still trying to understand the logic of moving at night and leaving everything. We had stuff strewn across every state in the East. It seemed more sensible that people who didn't own many things in the first place should hold on to the few things they did have. I supposed Mother and Daddy thought they'd have less to worry about. I wondered if they'd be better off if they didn't have *us* to worry about. Nevertheless, now, it was the possibility of not graduating from high school that was constantly on my mind.

Mother packed and showed little emotion, except she had her ironing board out almost all the time. Left it up right smack in the middle of the kitchen so everybody had to walk around it. Then, there was the blessed, constant thudding of the iron hitting the board. It was enough to drive a person crazy. I lay on my bed and covered my ears. I figured every emotion she had was thrown into that iron. She deserved to be left alone. We just stayed clear of her.

Daddy made all the arrangements for Mother, Robert Joseph, Elda Kate, and me to leave Maynard Bald on a Greyhound Bus to Newark, New Jersey, saying he was already working, that he'd drive there ahead of us and pick us up at the station. The trip was long with many stops, most of which were at night. I tried to sleep, but couldn't keep from worrying.

Carl picked us up at the station and said that Daddy was working. Now Carl was married and had a little girl one year old. His wife was expecting their second child. Before our arrival, my father had sent Carl to find a house for us. He explained that houses were impossible to find in the area. What he found was an apartment for us on River Road which bordered the Passaic River in Lyndhurst. The apartment house was owned by the Petrellis who lived across the hall. They were Italian, as were most of the people in Lyndhurst, except for a small Polish community. The Petrellis introduced us to authentic Italian dishes, and I learned to love the smell coming from their apartment; so began my love affair with Italians and Italian cooking. I had known the Martinellis back in Tennessee, but they weren't like the New Jersey Italians, probably because they had lived in Tennessee for so many years. The older Italians in New Jersey still spoke Italian. They listened to Enrico Caruso and Mario Lanza, and spoke using their hands and sounding like they were in constant arguments, although they called them *discussions*; sometimes they called them *conversations*.

New Jersey was a culture shock. I wasn't prepared for my enrollment in school. It was a bombardment of options. I registered for Latin I and German I that would prove to be difficult because I had to catch up. I'd never attended a school this large. I had difficulty adjusting. When I spoke, everyone turned to stare. I assumed it was because they'd never heard anyone from the mountains of Tennessee before. On Fridays, I went to the auditorium with Ellen Segal, Benjamin Weiss, and a few other students I didn't know, while, what seemed like the entire student body, went to Sacred Heart Church on Ridge Road and St. Michael the Archangel Church for catechism instruction. We were the students who were not Catholics.

After a few weeks, I loved New Jersey. Daddy came home in the evenings. There wasn't any quarreling. I was befriended by Georgette Gagliardi and Maria Shapinsky. The nicest boy in my Latin class, Mario Damato, had noticed me, even talked to me. John F. Kennedy was President. The universe was perfect.

Mario invited me to his house to introduce me to his family and have pizza made by his grandmother. She didn't speak English, and pinched my cheeks as she smiled and said, "*Crescere bella*," which means *grow beautiful.* Mario's parents treated me as if I were a beloved relative. Sometimes he came to my house, but not often, and not when my father was at home.

I missed Lillie Dabney and Grandmother Evers and Ruby Grace. At times, I thought I felt a little tinge of missing Maudie. "No, that can't be true," I thought.

One Saturday in early November, when Mother and I were alone in the kitchen, she said, "Lunda Rose, I'm pregnant."

"What?" I backed away, staring at her. "You can't be," I said, unable to close my mouth or say anything more.

"Are you happy? I thought you'd be happy. Your daddy is thrilled," she said. "it's just what we need—a baby." Her voice had a different quality, one of excitement. I wanted to ask, "Do you know how many women have thought they could save their marriage by having a baby?" I didn't ask the question. It would have been hurtful and served no purpose.

She looked pretty. Almost beautiful. Young. I reminded myself that she was only 38. Still, at sixteen, it was hard to imagine my mother pregnant.

At first I was angry. Shocked. But after I thought about it for a while, I thought, "Great, Elda Kate's birth brought us peace for a while; my father is happy about the pregnancy; this could be the real *golden year.*

But, it also could be a *mean year.*"

Two weeks later, Mother was taken by ambulance to the hospital. It was during the day, and Mrs. Petrelli called the school secretary to ask that I be sent home. I knew before Mrs. Petrelli said it that she'd lost the baby. We didn't know where Daddy was. I called Carl, but he pretended not to know Daddy's whereabouts. Carl took me to the hospital. Mother was devastated. "Look after Robert Joseph and Elda Kate," she said, "until your daddy gets home."

Five days later on November 23rd, President Kennedy was assassinated. The entire nation was stunned and mourning. I watched the funeral on television—the riderless horse, the boots turned backwards in the stirrups, images never to be forgotten.

Daddy came home on November 25th. It was impossible to read his feelings. Mother was ordered to stay in bed for three days after Carl brought her home from the hospital. Daddy seemed attentive. When he wasn't looking, I examined the vein at his right temple. It wasn't bulging.

As the months passed, tension and apathy grew side by side in our house. The winter months brought the Great Nothing for me and what the doctor called *reactive depression* for my mother. She went about her days as if nothing was wrong. Sometimes, signs that she was alive surfaced and there was arguing about Daddy's absences. Mother started to worry about affairs. I started to worry about more serious things.

I could do all the worrying I wanted about staying in school long enough to graduate or about Lyndon Baines Johnson's safety. I worried about that dot on the map, a little place I'd never heard of called Laos;

Walter Cronkite kept getting everybody all stirred up over Laos. Every evening he talked about Laos, Vietnam, and Cambodia. I looked all of them up on the map in the library at school, and when I saw how tiny they were, I figured there wasn't much worrying to be done over them.

I thought my worrying time would be better spent on more worthy things: strip mining in the Tennessee mountains; having clothes to wear to school without having to hand wash my blouses at night; trying to understand why kids at school were mean to Ellen Segal. I worried about my dog that we left in Tennessee when making our move to New Jersey.

"Cripes," I thought, "I have to give up worrying. It doesn't take me anywhere. It's fruitless. It feels like I'm running in circles on a single path along a single edge to end up where I started."

It seemed that the sensible thing to do was to focus all of my skills and energy in the art of worrying on more important things like what my father was doing or living in one place long enough to get an education. It was bad enough I had not forgiven them for leaving my dog behind, but the real problem, apart from my father, was that I didn't know when Mother would wake me during the night and tell me to get dressed.

The night I'd dreaded came the following summer in the first week of August, 1964, when Daddy announced we were moving again. The announcement came late on Friday a few hours after the 6:30 evening newscast. That night he seemed especially agitated and preoccupied. The Huntley-Brinkley Report had been usurped by Walter Cronkite. Instead of his usual shouting commentary on what Mr. Cronkite was reporting, Daddy was silent, pensive.

He was restless and occasionally opened the curtain with his index finger as if he was expecting someone. He straddled the recliner's footrest that he used as a tray of sorts between his knees where his cup of coffee and cigarettes were within his arm's reach. He indicated to Mother that he was proud of how much planning he'd done in the last three months to avoid moving during the night. She stared at him in disbelief.

"You'll like where we're going," he said, "a little place up north, Oneonta, New York—a place where you can lose yourself." Mother stopped ironing.

"You'll like it. Not too big. Not too fast. It'll be a new start."

I questioned just how many new starts we would need to find one we wanted to keep. It was unlike him to offer explanations for anything, but then came the most surprising thing of all—this was the first time I had ever heard even a hint of concern about how any one of us would like a new place or how we would *feel* about moving.

Mother paused and shot him a look of disgust. She said nothing. I wondered how she could keep silent, when the next day she would pack everything that would fit into her brassiere and her big straw bag, and, if there was enough room in the car, into a suitcase. There would be a clamor for brown paper grocery bags. I tried to keep a few bags stashed for this type of emergency. I had sorted through my things to determine what would fit into two brown paper bags: my big, pink, plastic hair rollers, two blouses, both frayed at the collars, my pink, fuzzy house shoes that Ellen Segal had already worn out before they ever came to me, and two plaid skirts with box pleats. Of course, I had my five things that I would never give up, except the kestrel drawing that I'd given to Grandmother for safe-keeping. I'd replaced it with a gold cross pendant that Mario had given me. My five never-leave-behind things were small. I would sit on my quilt.

Robert Joseph made a fuss about leaving his drums that he was rarely allowed to play because we lived in an apartment. It was absurd that he had them at all—an attempt on Mother's part to make us seem like a normal family. I secretly hoped they would be left, as it seemed to only frustrate Robert Joseph and Mother that he had them, but wasn't allowed to play them. He was constantly beating on a table or his thigh or the refrigerator, or anything near him.

A week later at close to 3:00 p.m. on Sunday, we packed everything that would fit into the newly-painted black Cadillac. This was a fairly new Cadillac, a 1964 model that was originally black, then painted two-toned blue, and now, it was black again. He got new license plates. The taillights were mounted on black and chrome fins two blocks long. I thought it would be nice if the taillights opened like two trunks for more valise space or brown-bag space.

As big as the ugly thing was, there was hardly enough room for five people. Daddy said he'd come back with a truck to get the furniture. I knew that was a lie. My father didn't care one iota about material things.

I worried about starting in a new school. This would be my third high school. I was hoping we could stay put for a while, since I had only nine months to go before my graduation. I was numb and sick to my stomach when I thought of school in another strange place. If we kept moving, I would never graduate.

Daddy had to pull off twice saying he needed to sleep for a while. He'd sleep for about an hour, then he'd rouse, light a cigarette, drink coffee and we'd be on the road again. He made several stops to use pay phones.

We arrived in Oneonta in the night. There weren't many street lights or porch lights. The place didn't look like much of anything, not many neon signs nor businesses. Daddy stopped the car in an alley behind a row of houses that were all alike. We entered through the back door of one of the houses and climbed an interior back stairway. A large mixed-breed dog barked from the top of the stairs. Daddy called the dog by name, "Rufus, shut up, stop barking," he commanded, as he leaned over slapping the leg of his trousers in an attempt to have the dog come to him. Clearly, Daddy was familiar with the dog, and it was obvious he'd been to this house before.

The tiny wreck of a house was owned by the company where he worked. It was furnished with sticks of make-shift furniture. The rooms were cramped, and there weren't enough beds for all of us. Mother said we could make do if we worked at it. Robert Joseph slept on the couch. Elda Kate and I slept in a double bed in the smaller of the two bedrooms. I was too tired to fuss much about the living arrangement. Besides, I wasn't as worried about where I would sleep, as where I would go to school.

Not one of us had the nerve to ask Daddy where

Rufus came from. He didn't like dogs. I thought back to years ago, when I set my nightgown on fire trying to take care of my dog that Daddy hated. I was around nine. It was one of those times when he hated everything and everybody. A time when each room in the house seemed to hold enough air for just one person.

The dog was suckling a late litter in mid October, when, in a sudden cold snap, the temperature dropped from 62 degrees before sunset to 21 degrees at 9:00 p.m. The dog had given birth in a small space under the house. There was only enough room for me to bend my body to get inside, and crawl on my belly for the last few feet to the puppies. I was small, and it was easy. I could hear her puppies crying. Daddy had heard them and warned me, "Do not go under the house during the night to see about those yelping puppies."

As soon as I was sure he was asleep, I snuck out barefooted and carrying a candle; headed directly to the hole in the foundation where I could squeeze in. I waited until just before crawling through the tunnel formed by the foundation rocks to light the candle. I could hear them crying. There were four of them, little blind things crawling over each other trying to suckle. As I used my elbows to back out, the candle flame touched the nap of my flannel gown sending the almost inaudible sound, the catch of ignition through my whole body—the sound of flashpoint vibrated through me. I slapped at the flames and tried to roll in the dirt, but there wasn't enough room. I contemplated burning to a crisp rather than waking Daddy. Finally, the flames and the light were gone, and I lay there in the dark in the dirt in a shroud of fear smelling of burnt hair and thinking the movement of my heart would lift me right off the ground.

Now, I watched him and resented that he actually seemed fond of Rufus. The dog liked him. And, my father was the only person who could approach Rufus without the dog barking.

On our third day there, in the evening as Daddy was leaving to go to the shop, I mustered enough courage to ask, "Where'd you find Rufus?"

Daddy looked stunned and paused for moment.

"The man in the downstairs apartment works at the neon shop. He owns Rufus. Got him because they needed a watchdog at night at the shop. Now we're using spray paint, so he brought Rufus to the house until that's finished." I wondered why a neon shop would need a watchdog.

My father didn't talk about his work in Oneonta. He didn't like questions about anything, especially his work. Mother said Carl worked there, too. Already, when we'd been in Oneonta for less than a week, men from the company came to our house, usually at odd times, always at night, and they talked to Daddy outside. I wondered if it was because we were not supposed to hear their discussions, or, if it was because Mother would not permit the meetings to take place inside.

Daddy and the *neon men*, as Mother called them, were always dressed in suits, white shirts, and ties. As many times as I had watched Daddy fire and bend neon glass back in Tennessee, I had never seen him working on a neon piece in a suit and tie.

Carl and his family lived in a small house a few blocks from our apartment. They had moved to

Oneonta two months before we arrived. Now he and his wife had two little girls. I agreed to babysit a few nights a week for Carl to take his wife out to eat. He said his wife was unhappy; she didn't like New York; she didn't like moving.

Carl stopped by often to talk to my father. They usually talked outside, but one night in late August, when we'd been there almost two weeks, Carl came inside, saying Daddy had driven to the neon shop to get something he'd forgotten. Unlike my father and the neon men, Carl wore jeans and T-shirts, never a suit and tie.

"Can we talk, Helen?" he asked, throwing his head back just slightly indicating he wanted to talk outside.

"What do you want, Carl? What is it? We can talk right here."

I went to the next room and sat on the bed. Mother and Carl were barely audible; it was impossible to make out what they were saying. I moved across the room and pressed my ear to the wall near the half-opened door. I moved closer to the door, but still could make out only a few words that didn't make sense. It was like the game I used to play with my friends as a little girl—where you sit in a circle and whisper in the ear of the person next to you, passing it on, and when the story reaches the last person, it doesn't resemble the beginning story. I struggled to fill in the parts I couldn't make out.

Mother spoke in a whisper, and Carl's voice was just a bit louder. What was he telling her? She shushed him as he tried to console her. I leaned in closer to the open door.

"Helen, why do you fret and worry so over Joe? I promise I'll get him calmed down. Just give him some distance and stop challenging him, stop accusing him. Joe has a lot on his mind right now. That's all it is. He worries a lot. That's all. It'll get better."

There was a long silence. In a choked, slow, deliberate whisper, she said, "My life is a scourge, a bitter cup that Joe Halverston has served me. I'm bound to him, Carl—bound to a man I can't stop loving. I know there's another woman. Now I'm losing myself; I'm on the wane. A downward spiral. And you're telling me *he* worries. Are you out of your mind? Have you taken leave of your senses? Joe Halverston has never worried a minute about anything or anyone in his whole life. Not even himself. He values nothing."

"You're wrong, Helen. Listen to me. He worries. He just doesn't let it show. In his line of work, a man can never show what's inside him. He'll never show you he's afraid or worried. He can't do that."

"Carl, now you're talking pure nonsense. What are you talking about? What are you saying? Joe doesn't know what it means to be afraid. He's never been afraid. Never. He isn't capable of it."

"Helen, start thinking. Get your head out of that dark hole! Wake up! Use your head! You don't know, do you?"

"I know that I'm married to a man I don't know, a man I can't trust."

Carl lowered his voice to a whisper. I struggled to be perfectly still and quiet, straining to hear him.

"He worries! You just don't get it, do you? You really don't know. He does it for you. He kills people, Helen. Joe kills people. Yes, he kills people! A killer for hire! That's where he goes when you think he's with another woman. You don't think he worries?

There are always those trying to get to him. Why do you think he moves you and the kids in the night? Joe is always on the move. Sometimes for a job. Sometimes he's on the run himself. To stay alive."

"It's not true! Not true!" she whimpered. There was a long silence. I could hear her chair moving as she stood up. Her words were louder, clearer. "Don't you ever say he does it for me; don't ever say those words to me again."

I couldn't keep my body still. I couldn't breathe. I stood at the other side of the wall frozen with Carl's words cutting through me. Everything was blurred.

*   *   *

Daddy didn't know that Mother knew. Mother didn't know that I knew. She didn't confront him after she learned his horrible secret. She went about her days as if nothing had changed. I did not. I cried and worried. I wondered if Mother would go secretly to the police. I wondered if I should tell the police. Even if they believed it, they'd patronize me and send me home after telling me, "Don't you worry. We'll take care of it."

Mother was scared and in denial. She pretended every time he left to supposedly finish a neon job, that she believed him. She became increasingly passive, not confronting him or questioning him. She didn't accuse him of affairs. "Maybe she has confronted him," I thought, "maybe she's persuaded him to stop. 'He will quit if he loves me,' Mother has told herself."

Like my mother, I wanted to believe he had stopped, but deep down, I doubted it. Things appeared calm on the surface for a few months, but then they started to argue and fight. Daddy became more explosive, violent even. Most of the time, I felt like our house was about to erupt.

He didn't come home most nights until about 4:00 in the morning. Sometimes he was gone for days. During those times, Mother cried a lot. We had a steady diet of Jell-O, chocolate cake, bread pudding, spoonbread, and brown beans.

I dreaded the very notion of starting my senior year of high school in Oneonta. I thought of getting on the school bus on the first day of school. I thought about the look on every school secretary's face over the years, when I showed up in the office to enroll. Each asked, "Where's your mother?" I explained that I could do it myself because my mother had no car. I would tell them my name, birth date, and where I came from. They would ask for my birth certificate, shot records, and school records. I would explain, for the one-hundredth time, that all of those things had been lost in our move. In truth, they were just left behind.

I started, once again, writing letters to the Big Creek Gap Home and School for Orphans in Frakes, Kentucky. Even though it was in Kentucky, it was the closest home for orphans I knew in proximity to Maynard Bald. I had been writing the Head Mistress of the school since I was in the fifth grade. For years, she had replied to my letters in a business-like fashion always starting with:

Dear Miss Halverston,

I am very sorry, but you do not qualify for admission to Big Creek Gap Home and School for Orphans. Students can only be placed in our school by order of the Commonwealth of Kentucky.

Now, at seventeen years old, it was especially hard to convince the Head Mistress and the school administration that I was an orphan. It was getting harder to explain all the different postmarks. The explanations I'd offered over the years: that I lived with my grandmother just across the Kentucky-Tennessee state line; or that I lived with my great aunt in Kentucky, just didn't work any longer.

Oneonta was small, old, pristine. Here, fall came early, and the large oaks and maples that lined the streets were ablaze. The lingering scents of summer had faded to make room for the sweet, distinct smells of fall. Only occasionally, was the smell of the railroad yard at the edge of town noticeable. There was something deeply sad about Oneonta. It was a town where hundreds of railroad tracks converged. It was a hamlet between two hills. On one hill was New York State Teachers' College and on the other was Hardwick College. Almost every house in town housed college students. I envied them.

The high school was a large, new, sprawling building at the edge of town. It had the look of an industrial building, modern, but not memorable, similar to the shirt factory back in Maynard Bald.

I looked at the new faces in the hallways. I was numb in my aloneness, and that sick feeling started to well up in my stomach. Even though my Latin teacher at the last high school in New Jersey pleaded with me not to engage in another year of Latin, I was informed at enrollment that no credit would be given for a single year of Latin unless Latin II was completed.

One Thursday in late September, at the end of Latin class, a girl with big hair and huge, horn-rimmed glasses walked with me to my locker. Another girl approached with a smile, while mumbling that her father was forcing her to take Latin. "Hi, I'm Maisie Weitz. Would you like a pack of Trident? My daddy's a dentist and gets this stuff by the truckload. Oh, I'm Maisie, and this is Aggie, Agatha Boyers really. We call her Aggie. Heard you're from Tennessee? How did you ever get to Oneonta?"

Maisie's mouth never stopped moving even though it was packed full of braces and Trident. Aggie's mouth never stopped either. Aggie was one of the few seniors who had a car—a brand new, white, 1965 Mustang. After her mother's death five years ago, her father had hired a dorm mistress and turned their large house into an off-campus residence for college girls.

Aggie and Maisie became my friends. After school each day, we each boarded separate buses. Aggie was not permitted to drive her car to school, but around 6:00 p.m., she would arrive at my house after picking up Maisie.

She never came into my house. Neither did Maisie. I liked it that way. I waited for the sound of the horn. We would giggle and rush off to cruise Main Street even though all three of us were failing Latin II. The next weeks were filled with hayrides only for the seniors and football games, where we pretended we were having a good time even if we were so frozen we could hardly move.

On the Wednesday before Thanksgiving, the three of us arrived at my house after a bonfire pep rally in a field west of town. I could see my mother's silhouette as she stood in the front yard. It was cold, and for her to be outside was an indication that something was wrong. Aggie rolled down the window and I leaned across her. "What's wrong?" I asked, my voice breaking as I prepared myself for what I was about to hear.

Mother asked, "Can you drive me over to the tracks to look for Joe?" I was horrified that my mother was about to divulge what I'd worked so hard to hide.

"Is Daddy all right?"

"Oh, I'm sure he's just fine. I just want to see something for myself."

"Oh, no," I thought, "this is going to be awful."

"Sure, no problem," Aggie said, before I could think of a way to keep this from happening. I slid into the backseat with Maisie. Mother sat in front. Aggie and Maisie talked nervously to her trying to ease the tension. I hoped they wouldn't ask questions, and I hoped Mother wouldn't divulge too much information

We were at the edge of the track yards which were like a big city within a little town. Mother knew exactly where she wanted to go. I glimpsed at her face as we passed under the streetlights. She looked old. Her face seemed drawn. Her voice was different. "Turn here on Iron Street. Slow down a little. Stop here. Turn your lights off." Silence fell over us. Mother was fixed on the huge tail fins of the black Cadillac parked on the street lined with small older houses.

"Lunda Rose, get into the Cadillac and drive to Manford's Station. He keeps a spare key under the mat. Park behind the buildings at Manford's so the car is out of sight. Take the key and hide it. Your daddy will come home mad. Don't give him the keys and don't tell him anything about me. He cannot find me. I'll be okay. Aggie will call you."

"Mother, don't make me do this. I can hardly drive. I can't even steer the beast. I don't have a driver's license. What if I get stopped? What if I hit something ? I don't even know how to get back home. What if Daddy catches me? He'll kill me. Please don't make me do this."

"Go on," she said. "You can do it. You have to do it. Hurry. You'll be fine. I'll be fine. Everything will be fine. Take care of Elda Kate and Robert Joseph. Aggie will call you and tell you what to do."

"We'll wait for you to pull out," Aggie said, "I'll go ahead of you. I have to make my curfew."

I fumbled in the dark until my fingers touched the key under the floor mat. I slid behind the steering wheel, clutching it tightly to steady my shaking. I pressed my forehead onto the steering wheel and talked to myself and shook.

The car was massive, a barge on wheels. "How could Mother ask me to do such a thing?" I asked myself, "knowing I can't drive a car, especially not this beast." I prayed, "Just let the old thing keep running after I crash into something. I don't care how bad it is, as long as it runs."

I managed to stop shaking by holding tighter to the steering wheel. I thought my arms would shake loose from their sockets. It was starting to snow. "Try to find the knobs for the lights and the windshield wipers," I whispered. "Stay calm. You can do this. You can do this. You have to do this."

I cranked the engine, closed my eyes, and backed out slowly without turning on the headlights. Somehow, the monster missed the other vehicles. I drove a short distance and turned on the lights. The tail lights of Aggie's Mustang disappeared as she turned the corner. I was alone.

Driving slowly through the maze, I tried to find a way out of the labyrinth of tracks and dirt roads. After three dead-end streets and three times of breathing deeply and talking up my courage before backing, I left the field of railroad cars and made it back to residential streets and eventually back to Main Street. As soon as I turned onto Main, the lights of Oneonta were visible. I prayed for the first stoplight to turn green. It stayed red. I stopped at the intersection. There were no other cars on the road. The snow was coming heavier than before. The street lights revealed Daddy's German Luger on the seat beside me. "Oh, no," I cried, as I shoved it under the seat.

I turned the corner and saw Manford's Station. The surrounding lot was empty except for a tow truck. I slowly drove to the back of the station and parked the car between the building and the tow truck. I took the keys and the gun and walked to the street to look back to make sure the car wasn't visible. The walk home was only about two blocks. The snow was coming heavily, a wet, dense snow.

I stood in front of the house. The lights were on upstairs, and I tried to look through the windows for signs of Elda Kate or Robert Joseph. I hated Ruby Grace for leaving us. I needed her. She'd know what to do.

"What if Daddy made it home before me?" I thought. I went to the back stairs and listened for any sounds. It was dark and quiet in the stairwell. I put the gun under the first step and made my way up to the landing. I leaned against the back door for a long time just listening.

I did not feel any contempt for my father. What I felt were the same fear and deep sadness I felt those years ago under the mahogany desk. Only this time was worse—I felt I had betrayed him. "Oh, I'd kept the secret; I'd not gone to the police; I'd played a passive role in assisting Mother in her surveillance, but now I was entrapped in a problem with no solution and no winner.

Elda Kate and Robert Joseph were asleep in the front room. I quietly woke Robert Joseph and motioned for him to go to the back room. "Daddy is going to come through the door anytime now. You have to help me. We have to hide the gun before he comes. We cannot let him find that gun. You know he will find Mother. We have to hide the gun and the clip in different places."

Robert Joseph whispered, "On the ledge behind the chest of drawers." "No, not in the house. I have it. Get your shoes and coat on and find something to dig with. Daddy will be walking, so you'll have to watch for him while I take care of the gun. I'll bury the gun and the cartridge in separate holes."

Robert Joseph found a big stew spoon for digging. He stood watch, and I dug shallow holes through the snow and barely into the ground. The dirt wasn't frozen yet because of the leaves. "Quick, get a broom," I yelled when I saw my footprints all over the yard. I swept and the prints disappeared beneath the new snow.

We could barely see. We hurried up the stairs. "Keep your clothes on and get into bed," I ordered. I remembered the nights I had gone to bed wearing my clothes.

My heart wanted to jump out of my body as I drew my knees up under my chin and sat on the bed trying to think of what to do.

"Are you sure it's covered?" Robert Joseph whispered from the next room.

"Yes. When Daddy comes home, don't say anything. Even when he talks to you, let me answer him. No matter how scared you are; let me talk for you. Daddy will never realize you're not talking. It'll be all right. Pretend you were sleeping. He won't even notice that you're wearing clothes. Don't be whining or carrying on so the neighbors might come."

"Sh.h...h...h. Hush. He'll hear us. We have to listen for footsteps." My body was frozen. We were quiet. It was a long time before we heard the sound of his footsteps and the back door opening.

For a long time he stood in the doorway. He just stood there. He walked in the dark to the back room where he and mother slept. Rufus didn't bark. I saw the light come on and there was a long stillness. I tried to stop my own shaking. My body wouldn't be still and my sounds wanted to burst out of my throat.

He walked to my bed and touched my shoulder.

"Where's your mother?"

"I don't know."

"Lunda Rose, I know you drove the car. Where is it?"

"I didn't. I don't know, Daddy; I swear."

He walked into the back room and there was silence. There were sounds of rummaging and the sounds of wire clothes hangers scratching the metal bar. The sounds stopped.

Robert Joseph and I made it to the bedroom door

at the same time. Daddy didn't look at us or say anything. Without speaking, he pulled the chest of drawers from the wall, looked behind it, and slowly slid it back. He took a pair of scissors from the top drawer. "Crap!" I thought, "he's going to cut up her clothes again." There was only one dress and a blouse in the closet. The dress was a light shade of blue and just below the collar was her precious cameo. He unpinned the cameo and placed it on the bed, carefully, as not to damage it. After he cut the dress and blouse exactly the way he'd cut her dresses before, he picked up the cameo letting it fall to the floor, as if not to notice. We heard the cracking, like the crunching of egg shells under the heel of his huge shoe.

"The car is behind Manford's Station," I blurted, "the keys are under the third step out back."

Daddy walked to the kitchen, and, as we watched, he removed the receiver of the telephone and turned it to remove the tiny receiving transmitter. He walked to the hall phone, unscrewed the mouthpiece, took out the transmitter and slipped the two tiny pieces into his coat pocket just like before, the same thing he did every time Mother left. We heard his long steps down the stairs.

"Get into bed," I told Robert Joseph. "He'll be back soon."

As we whispered from our beds, we listened for his footsteps. We listened. My body jerked when the telephone rang.

"Hello," I whimpered into the phone. There was no sound for a few seconds. I heard Aggie's voice. "Hello. Hello," she yelled into the phone. "Is anyone there? Lunda Rose, is that you? Hello. Hello."

"Aggie, Aggie, don't hang up! It's me. I'm here. I'm here."

I heard the dial tone.

The phone rang again. Aggie said, "Lunda Rose, I know you're there. I'm coming to get you. Meet me outside as soon as it's daylight."

It was just after daybreak when I saw the Mustang. I could hear the snowplow on the next street. Aggie barely stopped as I ran out and jumped into the car. Her voice was high-pitched and broken. "Your mother is at the old Oneonta Hotel, that old brick building downtown. She's using the name, Evelyn Andrews. Room 35. She's instructed the desk clerk to let you go up to her room. No one else. Where's your daddy?"

"I don't know. Don't worry. He's probably at the neon shop. How are the roads?"

"Do you think he may try to follow us?"

"No, we'd see his car. How could we miss it?"

Aggie drove into town slowing to get a look down a narrow alley behind the old hotel. The snow was too deep. She let me out on the side street and I walked around the corner to the front entrance. The smell of the lobby matched the long, purple drapes. The wooden desk was high almost hiding the man sitting on a stool in front of the key box.

"Evelyn Andrews? I'm looking for Evelyn Andrews."

"Go on up. Room 35. Third door on the left."

Mother met me in the hall and hurried me into the room.

"Where's your daddy?"

"I don't know. He has the car but not the gun. Robert Joseph and Elda Kate are scared. I'm scared.

We buried the gun. When he finds you, he'll kill you."

"Yes, *if* he finds me, he will kill me: he's that mad. I followed him. I know what he does. I know what he did at that house. And he knows that I know."

Mother looked at me as if waiting for me to ask what she was talking about.

I hesitated. "What do you know?"

"Never mind. It's not important. He will not find me. I'm leaving Oneonta in a few hours. You stay with your daddy. Do what he says. You know he'll never hurt you or Robert Joseph or Elda Kate. He'll take you back to Tennessee. Don't be afraid to go with him. I'll be there soon. I'll be fine. Go on. Don't be afraid."

I walked to the side street where I'd left Aggie. The Mustang idled in the same spot. Mounds of dirty snow flanked both sides.

Aggie was silent as we drove back to the apartment. She didn't ask questions, and I was relieved. I asked her to drive by Carl's house to see if Carl's car was there. It was parked in front of his house, where it was blocked in by snow.

"Lunda Rose," Aggie said, "there's something I think you should know. I wasn't going to say anything, but I think I have to tell you."

She pulled over and stopped on a side street far enough from my house that Daddy wouldn't see her car. The parked cars were packed in by snow, and she stopped in the main lane and left the car running. Turning in her seat to face me, she said, "It was on the news this morning that a man was found shot at the address where we drove your mother, where we saw your dad's car. I haven't said anything, and I won't. The police are asking that anyone who saw or knows anything to come forward. Didn't you say his gun was in the car, and you and your brother buried it? Well, your dad didn't have his gun, but don't say anything about the gun if anyone questions you."

"No," I said, trying not to show my shock, "I won't." All I could think of was the certainty that Daddy owned a second gun, maybe a third. My father was never without a gun.

"Aggie, you worry too much," I told her. "Go home to Thanksgiving turkey."

"Come home with me," she pleaded. "Come and eat with us. You know how my mother cooks. She'd love to feed you that awful veggie stuff she makes. You're the only person who'll eat it. It thrills her."

"You know I can't leave. Remember, when you call that you won't be able to hear me, but I'll hear you. Daddy took the transmitters out, but he'll be listening, hoping it's Mother calling. I'll see you on Monday."

I got out of the car, and watched Aggie drive away. When she was out of sight, I started to walk toward the house. Daddy's car was parked in front. I hated that ugly car. I thought about how much it looked like a hearse.

At the top of the stairs were Elda Kate's and Robert Joseph's brown paper bags. Rufus barked as if he'd never seen me before. Daddy ordered us into the car. It started to snow again. I sat in front.

"We're going back to Tennessee," he said. "I need to take care of things."

He drove to the neon shop on the way out of town. Leaving the car running for heat, he slid out of the black beast. I watched as his long legs moved through the snow toward the door. That deep sadness swept over me as I watched him walking, looking down. I was confused. I thought, "How can I feel sorry for him as the anger wells up inside me?"

When he got back into the car, he turned and looked at me and said, "Your mother is making a terrible mistake. She doesn't need to hide from me."

I talked continuously as we drove through the night. I knew he wanted me to tell him where she was hiding. I talked in rapid fire about everything that popped into my head. I thought if I stopped talking that he would nod off, since he had been up at least thirty-six hours, possibly longer. Or he would have an opening, an invitation, an opportunity to ask about Mother, a chance to probe for information about her.

Even the fear of Daddy falling asleep couldn't keep me awake. Nothing I thought of to talk about kept my eyes from closing. Robert Joseph and Elda Kate slept on the back seat. I talked on and on not making any sense at all. We could hardly see the tail lights of the car in front of us. The last thing I heard him say before I fell asleep was "We're not staying on the Pennsylvania Turnpike. They'll close it in a while to plow. It's just as well. This car is pretty easy to see. We'll take the old highway to find a motel. They've probably plowed it by now. We'll stay on the old road. We'll take the long way back home."

The Shape of Something Removed

When we arrived in Maynard Bald, I felt sick in my stomach. Our trip back to Tennessee brought a deep surge of dread that cut to the quick. But, along with the dread, came a delightful excitement. I was tethered to the mountains and this life and this mistaken family like the willow was tethered to winter, held fast by them. There would never be a possibility of leaving this family. I was as mercilessly bound to it as a half-open, shriveling bud.

When I was ten years old, I decided I couldn't do anything about being dropped into the wrong family, and even at that young age, I was sure these mistaken parents would thwart any notion I had of leaving Tennessee. At fifteen, under the mahogany desk, I knew for sure that I had to leave.

I would have to change my life plan. My plans devised years ago under the persimmon tree and later under the desk just weren't working out the way I thought they would. I figured the persimmon-tree plan must have been unrealistic anyway. I needed to rethink my escape. An awful sense of guilt poured over me. "Why should I feel guilty?" I thought, "why should I feel guilty for wanting freedom? For wanting what was outside the mountains and for wanting a life outside this family?"

I remembered something Grandmother had said several years ago when we were having a discussion at her kitchen table; actually, it was more a lecture than a discussion. She said that guilt was a picture of the past, and that I should give it up and think about *now*. "Think of this very moment and of what's to come," she said, "the present and the future are where your mind should be. Humans are the only species who can plan for the future. You should take advantage of having such a brain." After she'd let me think it over in silence for a good five minutes, she reappeared in the same spot, crossed her arms and said, "Lunda Rose, I've always believed that guilt is a nasty leftover of our past, and worry is just an imagined, useless hanger-on that torments us over something in the future that hasn't even happened and may never happen. Neither of them does us one bit of good. You should know that by now."

Immediately, I returned to my interrupted guilt. "How could I even think of such things?" I whispered to myself, "escaping this place? Leaving this family? What about Robert Joseph and Elda Kate? What about my mother?" Ruby Grace made it out of this family. And although I was happy that she'd made her escape, I had not forgiven her for leaving us. Robert Joseph and Elda Kate would not forgive *me*.

I relieved some of my feelings by telling myself that most of my plans were just dreams. Maybe this family wasn't a mistake after all. I knew that my dream of coming home from school to people who smiled and asked about your day was just that: a dream. The part of my plan to find out what was on the other side of the mountains had become real, and it wasn't all I expected. Even outside the mountains, I belonged to the same family.

I couldn't worry about the past anyway. My job now was to plan tomorrow. If I could make it 'til May and graduation, I would find a way out of this family.

Daddy dropped Robert Joseph and me at Lillie Dabney's house. Knowing he couldn't leave Elda Kate with his own mother, he took her to Grandmother Evers' house. Elda Kate was the image of our mother, and Daddy's mother did not care much for either of them.

Daddy's face looked tired and old, but he did not look disheveled. He did not look like a man who had not had any real sleep for two days and nights or like a man whose stomach had not had anything but coffee. I wondered how a man who never carried a valise managed to keep his suit and white shirt in order. I imagined he carried a fully-packed valise in the trunk of the car.

When we arrived at Lillie Dabney's, he didn't offer her an explanation of what had happened in Oneonta. She didn't question him. He picked a roll of bills from his pocket and said, "Take care of them for a while, Mama. I have business in Atlanta. I'll be back soon, maybe in a few days, probably before Christmas. Don't fret. I have to meet a man there. It's important. Shouldn't take long." He talked to Grandmother as if Robert Joseph and I were not in the room, and he deposited us there with Lillie Dabney like we were boxes of summer clothes to be stashed away in her storage room until warm weather when he would come for them.

It was the end of November. Maynard Bald looked the same as it looked when we'd left for New Jersey. Returning after all this time was like watching a color movie fade to black and white. The people and surroundings appeared in different shades of lifeless, muted gray. I was angry. I was scared. The Great Nothing teetered across my body as if my body was a fulcrum and depression was a see-saw. One thing for sure, my father and the neon signs were in living color. The buildings looked pale and lifeless posed against the great mountains. The town was gray-stricken like the leavings of a dream, the kind when you wake up and just can't remember. All the memories and the same feelings of when I was a little girl welled up inside me.

Maynard Bald had a certain beauty about it and alongside the beauty was an ugliness and a darkness. A numbness came with the feeling. It was a weight pressing against me like the dark presence of something great, and when I looked, there was nothing. Grandmother called it *the slough of despond*. She described it as *the malaise of the spirit* that is, for some, their worst enemy. "It can paralyze you," she warned.

It was as if we had left only yesterday. Daddy's neon signs glowed and flashed at every café, hotel, and store in town. Some of the neon tubes on the signs at Colley's Pool Room and Shelby's Grocery were broken. The letters that Daddy had painted so perfectly across Hack's Auction House were peeling. Most of the hundreds of bulbs that made the arrows atop Lyon's Supermarket appear to be moving were broken.

"The arrow is crippled," I told Walter Lyons as he pushed the cash drawer.

"You're Joe Halverston's girl, aren't you?" he asked.

"You should ask my father to screw in a few hundred white bulbs to make your arrow do its pointing like it used to. It looks awful." I knew that Walter Lyons was one person who bore a grudge against my father. Only a few years ago, Daddy had pointed a gun at him and threatened him. The colors of the neon were more beautiful than I remembered.

I knew we would never return to Oneonta. I wondered where Mother was, and if she was safe. She was too afraid to come to Tennessee. Since neither Lillie Dabney nor Grandmother Evers had a telephone, she would not be able to contact me. Grandmother Lillie had never allowed a telephone in her house, but maybe Mother would call the Bottoms Store at Morley and have Merlin Messer send word to Grandmother Evers or to one of the uncles.

I told myself over and over that Mother was safe as long as Daddy couldn't find her. Where would she go? Maybe she'd go to one of her brothers. Purcell and Caudill had left the Morley coal mines for Ohio, and Weir had given up coal dust for a job in a steel mill in upstate New York. Pinder and Hoboch Lewis still breathed the dust with the help of whiskey. I hoped, even now, that the brothers would never come face to face with my father. All of my uncles were just as fearless and unforgiving as my daddy. Their guns were just as big. And they had not forgotten. Although they'd left Tennessee, Weir,

Caudill, and Purcell still carried their guns. Only, now, their guns were concealed. Each of the uncles still bore serious grudges against my father, and their contempt for him would be reignited once they knew what had happened in Oneonta.

Returning to Maynard Bald High School would be the easy part. At least I didn't have to write more letters to the Big Creek Gap Home and School for Orphans in Frakes. I wasn't fond of the notion of living in Kentucky, anyway. I didn't have to make up stories about my birth certificate and school records. Mrs. Davis, who ran the office at Maynard Bald High School, knew me. Mrs. Davis ran everything from the office to the coffeepot to the standardized testing.

All I thought of was graduation. Part of me wanted to graduate and never look back. And part of me doubted that I'd ever leave.

I wrote across the front cover of my notebook, "LOOKING TO MAY." I knew I had to focus on graduating and making sure nothing went wrong. I tried to think only of positive things: my old dreams and plans passed through my mind; I thought of graduation; I dared to imagine going to college. Grandmother's dithyrambs played in my head. I imagined Mother was safe. I pictured the day when I would leave Tennessee; to my surprise, my dream of someday leaving competed with wanting to stay.

Mr. Morton, the Principal at the high school, remembered me from when I was in this school before moving to New Jersey. He asked Mrs. Bivens, the guidance counselor, to take care of my classes, credits, and schedule. I was faced with the problems of transferring credits from Oneonta and receiving credits for the German and Latin classes I had taken in New Jersey and New York. The only foreign language taught at Maynard Bald High School was French. Mrs. Bivens rolled her eyes and asked, "Lunda Rose, why in the world did you enroll in German and Latin?" I said, "Because Latin is a dead language and the German language sounds the most like the way I speak naturally."

"What are you talking about?" she asked.

"Mrs. Bivens, I know that the way I talk is the way I will *always* talk. My words are not sing-songy. German is not sing-songy. It's flat and straight just like a Tennessee tongue. Latin isn't spoken anymore except in the Catholic Church. I could learn these two languages without trying to force my mouth to do the impossible. What happened for Eliza Doolittle will never happen for me. My way of speaking is the way I will always speak; I will die with the same speech pattern you hear right now."

"I will never understand you, Lunda Rose." she shook her head.

Mr. Morton called for me to come to his office one Monday morning. He smiled as he stood behind a massive desk cluttered with stacks of papers and cups of cold coffee. He leaned back with both arms clasped behind his head and said, "I've made arrangements at Lincoln Memorial University for you to interview on Saturday morning. I think you can get in. There are five seniors from Maynard Bald who have a chance. Can you go on Saturday?"

"Mr. Morton, I can't go! My mom and dad are out of town."

"I'll take you," he said.

"I can't go to that school. Even if they accepted my application, I couldn't come up with money to go to college. Lincoln Memorial University is too expensive anyway. I can't afford to go to a school like that. My parents can't send me to any school that costs a lot of money. I've thought about applying to East Tennessee State, but I can't come up with the money to go even to a state school."

"I'm coming over to your house to talk to your parents."

"I told you they are out of town! Besides, there is no house. I'm living with my grandmother for a while."

"Lunda Rose, where's your mother?"

"She stayed behind in New York. She's coming to Tennessee soon."

"Where's your dad?"

"I don't know. The last time I talked to him, he said he was going to Atlanta. No one knows where he is. Please don't try to talk to my mom or my dad. Forget about me going to college. Right now, I have more important things to worry about. I don't even know if I'll make it 'til May. I don't have fifty cents for lunch or clothes for school, and you're talking to me about visiting some high-follutin' school. The way things are going with the transfer, I don't know if I'll have enough credits to graduate. Instead of earning credits for German and Latin, I'm in a speech class and a typing class. Why in the world would Mrs. Bivens put me in a speech class at Maynard Bald High School? How can learning to stand up before people and spit out a bunch of rhetorical rubbish help me?"

"Now, Lunda Rose, don't get too big for your raisin'. We're doing the best we can."

"This is about more than hoping to speak in front of people or passing a typing class that will strap me to a chair and sentence me. This is about more than a life stint of nothingness and dying without doing anything. It is not about being accepted into a college that I can't afford. It isn't about money. It is about silencing something in me that I can't even name.

"Watch your mouth and your sarcasm. And you might want to think about changing your attitude. I am not your enemy. Your sassy mouth and your attitude won't get you anywhere."

"My sassy mouth and my attitude will do more for me than a typing class or a speech class."

"You're not showing much appreciation. We only want to help you."

"Help me? Help me? You can't help me."

"What is it that you want, Lunda Rose? What is it? Tell me. Think about what you want."

"You aren't serious, are you? Are you asking me what I want to be when I grow up? I am grown up, and I don't want to *be* anything. I want to *become*. I want to become a thinking woman who isn't scared all the time. I want to go to bed at night without wearing clothes. I want to become a person who uses correct grammar and doesn't have to fight and kick and bite and scratch for every single morsel of every single thing. I want a chance outside these mountains."

December was almost over and there was still no word of Mother. Daddy had been gone for more than three weeks. I wasn't surprised. I knew he would be gone longer than he said when he offered his lame explanation about going to Atlanta for a few days. I figured he was in New Jersey, New York, or who-knows-where trying to find Mother.

I started to sit by the window for hours. I thought

about what Ova Gay and I had talked about: that each of us leaves a space behind when we leave; an empty place carved in the shape of everything we were to everyone who loved and completed us. Our lives and selves grow out of the shapes of all the things removed from us: the longings; the selves we once were; all things unfulfilled, all that escaped us; all we didn't become; all things we had and lost; all things taken from us or left behind; the people who have left us—all the things that leave an empty space in the shape of something removed, leaving in its place a void—a well that never again will be filled. Even those who leave a space that is dark, deep, or jagged, they, too, leave a hole.

*   *   *

Mr. Morton threatened to expel me if I didn't attend school with some sort of regularity. "Lunda Rose, I have broken every rule for you," he said. "I can't push the limits much further. You've got to make some effort and stop fighting everything. You have to attend your classes. I will not make excuses for you any longer."

Ova Gay picked me up, and we passed the evenings playing *Rook* at Mrs. Pritchard's house. There I didn't spend too much time thinking about wanting a hot dog, or failing Typing, or if my mother was alive. Usually, there were games of *Rook* in the dining room and the kitchen. The house was always filled with squealing and laughing, as we played game after game into the night on weekends and until 10 o'clock on school nights. Mrs. Pritchard's house was too far away to walk, and I went only on nights when someone stopped in front of Grandmother's house and honked. I ran out to meet each honking driver as Lillie Dabney yelled from the top of the stairs, "Lunda Rose, you should be studying instead of playing the devil's *Rook* and carousing with delinquents." I waved to her as we sped away.

Christmas passed without fuss or celebration. Keeping me company for the dreaded holiday were Robert Joseph, Lillie Dabney, and the Great Nothing. I was happy to have it over. Grandmother made two of her infamous Tennessee apple layer cakes. The very thought of them terrified Robert Joseph and me. We couldn't save any for Elda Kate, because we never saw her; she stayed with Grandmother Evers. Robert Joseph called them mortar cakes. I feigned a lack of appetite, and Robert Joseph moaned and said his stomach hurt. We assured her that Daddy would be back soon, as he would never forget his birthday cake. His birthday was on December 25th, and since Christmas Day, she had stood at the parlor window looking, waiting.

The dreaded cake. We worried about what to do with the huge, ugly thing that she arranged perfectly on the hall table. With each passing day, the white icing became harder. How could he subject us to the dreaded white mortar cakes? There wasn't a dog to feed, and there were *two* cakes. But one was for his birthday. It remained untouched on the table. We smuggled the other one out of the house piece by piece. We admitted to each other that we ritually rejoiced as each piece met any trash can we could find within walking distance.

On New Year's Eve, I heard Daddy's voice and Grandmother's laugh in the kitchen. He promised to have cake later. He laughed and said, "Maybe I'll have a piece now with a cup of your coffee." I heard her crack the eggshells that she boiled with the coffee grounds.

Daddy sat on the white counterpane of the tall, carved bed. It was strange that he didn't look so big sitting on the bed. I turned away and started to feel the anger wrenching at my jaw and throat. I chewed the inside of my mouth. I couldn't determine if I was angry with him or angry with myself. My throat tightened, and I tried to swallow. Why couldn't I look at him and ask directly, "Do you call three weeks a few days? Did it occur to you that we have been waiting for you? Did it occur to you that Grandmother made a Christmas cake for your birthday? Did it occur to you that we have had to smuggle an entire cake, slice by slice, to the trash just to keep from hurting her feelings? Did you ever think of the second cake that's been hardening on the hall table for over a week while we waited? Did you know that your mother has waited at the window for three weeks—looking and waiting for you? Watching every car. Listening for your footsteps."

No words came out when I faced my daddy. As I remained almost choking on my muteness, Daddy looked at me and said, "It hasn't been much of a Christmas for you, has it?"

My muteness scared me almost as much as facing him with my questions. He walked to the kitchen, and I heard the sound of Grandmother pouring coffee through the sieve to filter the grounds and eggshells. Grandmother's words came fast with excitement, and I heard his fork bang against the plate as he tried to carve each bite of the white icing.

He explained to Grandmother that he had to go back to Atlanta, but that he would be back in a few days. Again, he pulled a roll of bills from his pocket and handed it to her. "Take care of what they need. I won't be gone long. This business in Atlanta is taking longer than I thought."

At that moment, I knew the real reason he came back. It certainly wasn't to see us or his mother or to eat the cakes made especially for him. He came back thinking Mother would be here. Not here in Maynard Bald, but at Morley with her mama or one of her brothers. I was sure he had driven to Morley to look for her before he came here.

And, I knew *why* he was going back to Atlanta. He said it was for his work.

"Well, right," I thought, "he doesn't know that I know about his *real* work." He didn't say anything as he closed the door behind him. He didn't want Grandmother to make a big fuss.

I watched her as she stood at the window. My anger deepened. It seemed that people were always waiting for him. Not that they especially wanted him to come. But they waited.

New Year's Day was sunny, but the cold was brutal. Grandmother celebrated the beginning of the new year in the first new moon of October, and she told stories about the Cherokee belief that the world was created in autumn. "1965 will be a good year," I thought, "Mother will come; it'll be a new beginning."

I heard the sound of the horn, and we were off to Mrs. Pritchard's house where four tables supported four games of *Rook*. The games lasted all day and late into the evening.

Mrs. Pritchard announced that the next day,

Saturday, January 2nd, the games would start around 7:00 p.m. I waited to hear Ova Gay's horn. Grandmother watched from the window. "Now, don't be too late, Lunda Rose," she said. "You should be sitting at the kitchen table with your school books."

There was a faint knock at the door. I leaped to the door expecting to see Ova Gay, but instead, my sister's mother-in-law, Delilah Martinelli, stood outside the door with the young, Evangelist preacher, the traveling gospel singer, Marshall Maggard. They just stood there without speaking. Grandmother moved toward the door, and her gaze met Delilah's. She looked at them and walked to the kitchen table and sat down. Delilah turned her head toward me and said, "Your daddy is dead. Shot. Shot in the head. Murdered." I watched her lips continue to move in what seemed like slow motion, but I couldn't hear her words. I looked at Grandmother as she let go of unrecognizable sounds, primordial sounds more ancient and elemental than language. She drew her crossed wrists to her breast and looked up. She wailed, "Not my boy. Not my baby boy."

The Eighth Cranial Nerve

Three days after Delilah Martinelli and Marshall Maggard came to Grandmother's with news of my father's death, Ruby Grace and her husband had taken charge of everything. News was sent to Sheriff Rosemund from the Knox County Coroner that the body was being retained pending an autopsy. An investigation was already underway.

Grandmother was inconsolable and did not nor could not leave her bed. Ruby Grace insisted that Robert Joseph and I come to the Martinelli house where David had grown up. Ruby Grace and David had been married for a little over three years, and had lived in Chattanooga for a while and in Elcomb, Kentucky for a short time. Since moving back to Maynard Bald from Kentucky, they had lived with David's parents, Delilah and Roberto Martinelli, in the large house while every Martinelli relative worked to complete a house for them on the four adjoining acres to the north.

"At least stay here until the funeral is over," she said, "until Mother gets here and things get sorted out." What she really meant was "until we figure out what to do with you." When I did not respond to her, she cleared her throat and straightened her body exactly the way our mother did when she wanted our full attention. "What I mean is that it will be better if you're with us until we find Mother. Look, Lunda Rose, I know this is hard for you. It's hard for all of us."

That night I could not close my eyes. I stayed at Delilah's house and Robert Joseph stayed next door in the unfinished house with Ruby Grace and David. I lay in bed and thought about my father being dead. I felt paralyzed, stunned, as if my body had been flung out to Uranus and ricocheted back. I felt as though each of my senses had been touched to an electric current and fried. I wondered when Mother would come, and I thought about just what it might feel like to be unafraid. I dreamed of what it would feel like to wake up in the morning without dreading the day. What would it feel like to think this is not the night my mother will die? What would it feel like to sleep in a nightgown rather than the clothes I would wear to school the next day?

Even with three days passing since my father's death, the fears still lived in me, gnawing silently inside me without giving me one minute of peace. In some ways, it was even worse than when he was alive, when he held us in clenches as tight as talons.

The funeral was to be at Belcher's Funeral Home at 7:00 p.m. I wondered if anyone outside our family would come. I had plenty of reasons to worry. I imagined Mr. Winfield Belcher and his three sons in their black suits scurrying all over the place. They smiled falsely even if there wasn't one good reason to be smiling at a funeral, especially a night funeral.

At 6:30 p.m. I climbed the steps of Belcher's Funeral Home with Ruby Grace and Robert Joseph while David parked the car. No one would travel the treacherous highway to Morley in snow to collect Elda Kate.

I stopped to gather myself before opening the door. "You can do this," I thought, "try to get hold of your anger, don't lash out, don't make a scene."

Mr. Winfield Belcher met us just inside the door and led us to family seats behind louvered panels. I was last to be seated, and Mr. Belcher leaned toward me and whispered, "Your daddy was a fine man. He will rest in peace in Heaven."

"What kind of sentence was that?" I thought, "what was he talking about? Heaven and peace? That was not true. My father would not rest in Heaven, and he surely wouldn't be seeing any peace where he would be resting for eternity."

The Belchers looked, moved, and sounded alike, and since they were all dressed in identical black suits with white shirts and black ties, it was hard to tell them apart unless you looked closely and tried to memorize some distinguishing feature like Ellis Belcher's chipped tooth or the way Herbert Belcher pronounced the "ou" when he said the word *about*. Not that it mattered. However, I wished that I had known which one I had accused of showing up on Grandmother's porch with a hammer and driving a nail through the front door to hold a wreath of plastic flowers. They aimed to please grieving families, at least until they were paid-in-full for a cheap casket, a register, and a few artificial floral sprays that they used over and over for funerals of those who were not sent flowers. Beside the guests' register was a standing

Styrofoam cross covered with fake flowers. The Belchers must not have known that Joseph Walter Halverston in his entire 42 years of life had never been inside a church. "If you need anything, anything at all, just call us," Ellis Belcher nodded to Ruby Grace.

I thought of the funerals I'd been to at Morley: Moss Rigney and Jerimiah Leadbetter who died in a mine cave-in; Grandmother Evers' brother, Melanchthon, "Lank" everybody called him, who died from black lung. Sudie told of how, when Melanchthon died at Morley, his naked body was placed on a long table. His wife washed him all over from a wash pan and dressed him in a black shirt and bib overalls. This was called *the laying out and dressing of the body*. His pocket watch with the long chain was placed in the watch pocket of his overalls. Copper pennies were placed over his eyes. His hair was oiled and combed straight back.

Mountain people celebrated death. They never would have admitted it, but it was true. They would say that the funerals and gatherings of kin following funerals were to celebrate the deceased's life. I never saw anyone cry at a Morley funeral. It was a time when your stomach was filled and you would see all the cousins you hadn't seen in a long while. And there was always family talk of topics such as getting new red chickens, of daughters who needed husbands with jobs, of the debt owed the company store, and how to make it through 'til the next payday.

There wasn't a funeral home or an undertaker at Morley. Folks there didn't think much of undertakers and embalming and such. They never would have paid money nor trusted anyone outside their family to take care of their deceased kin. This was not a funeral like those at Morley.

Grandmother was too sick to attend the funeral. Delilah sent her niece to look after Grandmother while everyone else attended. She had taken to her bed delirious and mumbling nonsense that no one could make out. The loss of her youngest son was more than she could bear, and Dr. O'Brien had to give her pills to calm her. I had watched her moaning and writhing in her sleep, and I worried that she would never wake up. Dr. O'Brien said she was steeped in grief and bedfast with a broken heart; that going to the funeral was out of the question.

At first, I'd said that I wouldn't attend the funeral. It would be too hard without Grandmother. It called for more than I could give. No. I had to go. I had to see for myself that it was true. "How would Mother handle it?" I wondered, Would she even come to Maynard Bald for the funeral? What if she couldn't be found and would not know about Daddy?" She didn't have to fear him anymore.

"Do I really have to look at him?" I asked Ruby Grace.

"Of course you have to look at him," she snapped, "if you don't look at him, you'll never believe it's really true."

"How would the undertakers fix his face to convince the viewers that a bullet had not gone in under his cheekbone and come out below the eighth cranial nerve?" I wondered. Questions bombarded my brain.

"What if the uncles killed him? Would the uncles come to the funeral? Grandmother Evers? Well, of course not. They couldn't be dragged here," I thought.

What if Aunt Winnifred demanded *a sitting up of the body* like the funerals at Morley? Without Grandmother or my mother present to make decisions, without thinking of Ruby Grace, Mr. Belcher might turn Winnifred loose. Winnifred could bulldoze her way right over Ruby Grace and Mr. Belcher. She would order an open casket and a viewing of the body? She would insist that the family receive friends. What friends? The only thing that would bring people in Maynard Bald or Morley to my father's funeral was curiosity. Oh, God. Every one of the kin will line up to see the hole in his cheek. I will have to hear Aunt Surrie announce in her reckless way, "Well pity sakes, he looks better than he did the last time I saw him, much better than I thought he'd look."

"Oh, help me! This could be worse than I'd even imagined. The uncles, the Belchers, and having to look at him," I thought, "there was Mother's arrival to worry about. What would that be like? Would she even come? Would she? At least she didn't have to worry anymore about him killing her."

My biggest worry was that the Belchers would not have done their jobs. I heard Aunt Winnifred whispering to Mrs. Pearlie Butters and describing every detail of what the coroner had told David, that the bullet had entered under his right cheekbone and come out the back of his head, that Daddy must have been lighting a cigarette at the time of the shooting, as a briefly-lit cigarette and a used match and matchbook were found on the floor next to him.

The picture running through my head made me want to run to Grandmother and to feel her stroke my hair and say, "Sweet Cakes, it will be all right." I jerked myself back to reality. I wasn't that little girl anymore. Winnifred's words ran through my head, scattering like shrapnel looking for a place to land. I could see Daddy's face in my mind, and I thought of a bullet running loose in his head.

I wanted to shut the picture out, but I couldn't. For some strange reason, I started to think about Mr. Neville teaching me about the eighth cranial nerve. It's the nerve in the cranium that enables the brain to experience sound. "Imagine," Mr. Neville said, "that our little brains are so magnificent that we can not only hear sounds, but we can actually feel them." He said, "Isn't it amazing that we can hear and feel sound at the same time. That's what you must long for and what most people miss. It's a part of the brain that makes something you hear from the inside of emotions, something you'll never forget, and something that no one else hears. It's solely yours— something inside you that lets you feel what Mozart and Beethoven intended. It's an emotional thinking where you feel and hear Mozart and Beethoven with your brain and not just your ears."

Mr. Neville said that when your eighth cranial nerve is damaged, your brain and your life will have holes, and that most people go through their whole life without even using their eighth cranial nerve.

I was scared when Mr. Winfield Belcher announced that my daddy was a fine man and that his loved ones would forever feel his absence. I looked around to see who those loved ones were. Grandmother was not here, and I figured she was the only person on earth who loved him, the only one who would feel his absence, the only one who would miss him.

Winfield Belcher was insistent that I sit in the family room behind louvered shutters hidden from the view of those in the main chapel. Somehow, Ruby Grace and Robert Joseph had been usurped, and I was seated between Aunt Winnifred and Cousin Maudie. Through the louvers, I had an unobstructed view of the casket and Reverend Habersham. Mother was not there. All of those in the family room were Halverstons and Dabneys: Uncle Ogan Halverston, David Halverston, Orville Dabney, a few Halverston cousins, a few distant Dabney cousins. Only one Evers came, Weir's oldest daughter. Carl sat in the family room on the other side of Maudie.

I asked myself, "How could he get himself shot? How could he leave us like this?" I craned my neck and tilted my head discreetly to see the casket. He did not look so big in the casket. One deputy whispered something to another deputy. Relatives were whispering. I heard the coroner talking to David even though Ruby Grace could hear. What was the big secret?

Cousin Maudie had arrived late and appeared at the door of the family room alone. Maudie casts the darkest of shadows on everything, as if things weren't dark enough. She could shade already dark situations to become unimaginable things. Maudie's presence was something you wanted to wake up from and thank God you were only dreaming.

When she heard me tell one of the Belchers to "hush up about my father resting eternally in Heaven," she said, "Now, Lunda Rose, have some respect."

"Respect for what?" I yelled. "Respect for

someone who was supposed to take care of my mother? Of us? Respect for someone who was supposed to cherish our mother and us? Respect for someone who might have taken the most cowardly way out of life? Should I have respect for someone who either committed so many crimes that someone killed him; or someone who wedged the uncles so deeply into their hatred that one or all of them conspired to kill him; or someone who killed himself because he couldn't do anything right? It doesn't even matter who did it. Anyway you look at it, he failed us. He failed in every way at everything he did. It doesn't matter who did it."

The uncles had every reason to shoot him. He was trying to kill their sister. The neon men had every reason to kill him because he could not be trusted. My mother had every reason to kill him because he wanted to kill her. His enemies had every reason to kill him because they feared and hated him. There was only one person who knew him, who didn't have a reason for wanting him dead. That person was his mother. Grandmother loved him unconditionally, and he destroyed her.

The Eighth Cranial Nerve

Getting the Misery Right

When the funeral was over, and while everyone was filing out, I asked Carl if he would stay there with me for a while and later drive me to Delilah's. He knew why. I wanted to force myself to inch closer, to see him in bright light.

When I looked at him held fast in his coffin, he didn't look as tall, as big, or as mean as he did standing. I studied his face to make sure it was really his. I leaned forward over the casket searching for the bullet hole, almost invisible, but there, under his cheekbone, about two inches` from his right nostril and covered with chalky makeup that formed a thin mask, was the tiny depression. I bent to look closer. To see if Winnifred was right about the coroner's report. Carl pulled me back. "Come on, that's close enough," he said. "What are you looking at?"

"I think it's ironic that the damage from the bullet is in the exact place on his face as the scar on Mother's face from having a piece of broken neon dragged across it."

I stared at him and wondered how he still made everyone miserable. How could this man, who didn't look at all menacing just lying there, continue to hurt so many people even after he was dead? How could he take from so many people? How could he use every person in his path? How could he keep robbing us from the casket?

Grandmother said, "When you reach the end of your life, it won't matter who you've loved, but only who has loved you." Something she read somewhere. I worried when I thought about my father. Worried for his soul. Had anyone really loved him? His mother loved him. Every person ever born has been loved by his mother. She was the one who'd cried for him, and I thought of what she'd leaned in to whisper in my ear at every funeral we'd attended: "They aren't crying for the deceased, but for themselves." I hated hearing her say that.

Taker! Taker! Taker! I thought as I stared into the darkness every night. He took the truth and melted it down, turned it and pulled it into small strands, and then let it harden just like the neon glass. When it hardened, it kept the new shape. Forever. Forever it remained just the way he formed it. Nothing could change the shapes of the neon letters except breaking them. After the glass letters were cooled and tempered, they remained in bar windows and on hotel roofs like they were etched into the very air where they rested.

Did I want to know the truth? Maybe the truth would be too hard. Did Mother know the truth? Did she know what he had taken from her? Did anyone know all he had taken with him like a vortex of water spinning down a drain?

On January 16th, two weeks after his death, Mother knocked on Delilah Martinelli's door.

December and January had had unusually heavy snowfall, and she was wearing snow boots and a heavy, long coat. Elda Kate was with her, an indication that she'd stopped at Morley. Delilah didn't know what to say to her, and neither did I. Mother offered no explanations of where she'd been. When I asked her, she said, "We can talk about that later. I came by to let you and Ruby Grace know that I'm here. Joe's car has been impounded in Knoxville until after the investigation. The sheriff is helping me take care of all that. I'm looking for a house in Maynard Bald for us, so the four of us will have our own house soon."

Within a week after Mother's return, we moved into a little, brick house on Dogwood Hill. Delilah and Sudie scoured their attics, spare rooms, garages, and second-hand shops for furniture. Ruby Grace found bed frames at Hack's Bargain Barn. Mother bought an ironing board and kept it set up in the empty living room. No one minded. It started to feel like a real home. The three of us were in school every day. I didn't know what arrangements had been made to retrieve the Cadillac from Knoxville, since Mother couldn't drive. I came home from school one day, and it was parked in the driveway, where it stayed parked, without being moved, for the next three months.

Around mid February, Mother started to look lost, sealed in the slough of despond that Grandmother talked about. The Great Nothing moved in. Yes, she knew what he'd taken from her, but she would never say it. I realized I was not the one who was lost, had lost. Everyone in his wake lost. Mother was the glass letter left the most broken, the most damaged. He sculpted her life just as if he had chiseled her from stone.

At times, I recognized my mother as the mama from my childhood, one capable of playing Dead Donkey or Monopoly; there was another side to her though, complex and hidden.

A small moving shadow fell across her face. "As pale and cold as alabaster," I thought, "I've been wrong about her all along; we've all been wrong. No one really knows her. It isn't the loss of my father; it's the loss of a part of herself—the part of her that did not become the person she intended to become."

At certain times and often, it was clear she was having a personal dialogue inside her head—I suspected she was daydreaming. And sometimes, when she talked about when she was a girl, she'd say impulsively, "Perhaps if I'd just waited at the trestle for the train to slow, I could have jumped onto one of those troop trains that wound itself around the mountains."

She surrendered more years than the others, except Lillie Dabney. She surrendered more of everything than the rest of us. Every part of her was his. She gave up the easiest, from just being tired, I suspected. The spot she filled in his path was at the center of his swath. The others in his world just overlapped or passed through when they didn't bother him too much or get in his way. We just stood on the fragile, wiggling lines of the boundaries, watching and dodging debris. Occasionally, someone would stray off course, too close to the center, where they would be flung back into their place with dead aim.

For months after he died, I watched as Mother

slipped slowly into the nothingness of that dark hole. He shaped her even from the grave. He stripped her of everything she had, and he only put back a legacy of need. He molded her dependency. "You don't need to know how to drive, when I can drive you," he told her. "There's no need for you to worry your pretty little head with working, when I will provide for this family," he said with all the charm it took to distract her. He cleverly contrived ways to convince her that molding her dependency was really his way of showing his true love for her.

She had no tools or scraps to try to rebuild her collapsed, broken life. She was damaged beyond repair. She did have vulnerability. She wore it like an award—one of those cheap ones, plastic painted gold, that are pinned on at the May Day relay races.

He taught her well. They learned their skills from each other and reinforced the other's weaknesses. She became more and more vulnerable. She wept and wailed daily. Some days, I wondered if she was rehearsing. Rehearsing misery. Practicing it. There were no words that could make her surrender her misery. She hoarded and guarded her suffering and pain like they were dark secrets, or sugar, or a grudge against a relative. She collected them like perfect maple leaves or pansies to press between the pages of The Bible. She was attached to her pain like old people get attached to habits and the familiar. I figure she gleaned a certain pleasure from her miseries. On days when she came close to the bottom of the pit, I wanted to write across her forehead, "DON'T KICK ME, I'M A VICTIM." That wasn't necessary. She broadcasted it like it was screamed through a bullhorn. Everyone around her fed her misery with their sympathy and attention—nourished it like it was a growing newborn. And as her miseries and vulnerabilities were practiced and strengthened, her spirit was melted down, molded, hardened.

His death stunned her into atrophy. Her wailing and plight worsened, and she became more intent on doing nothing and changing nothing. She cried constantly only giving up any misery when it was absolutely necessary to make room for more to seep in. Steeped in her agony, she seemed to be missing something though. It was anger that was missing. Always, anger had run rampantly through our house like a contagious disease. But Mother wasn't angry now that he was dead, nor was she angry when he was alive, but absent for weeks—the weeks when the house was cold, and Mrs. Pruitt gave us potatoes from her cellar, and Aunt Florence Nell would send Weir in the old truck to bring apples and green beans put up in mayonnaise jars. It amazed me thinking back on the times when there wasn't anything, she didn't seem angry in the least way. When he was alive, I ranted and shouted, "How could you stay so long with someone who would leave us this way?" Now that he was dead, I stood in the center of the room and shouted the same question.

"Don't be speaking of your daddy that way and in that hateful tone," she whispered. She defended him in the same delicate way and with the same soft southern accent she used for etiquette lessons. "Lunda Rose, a southern, mannered lady would not speak of the dead in that disrespectful tone. It's worse than an unpeeled tomato or raising your voice to your mother." She touched her throat reaching for something that wasn't there. "No, a mannered lady would not speak ill of the dead," she said as casually as if we were perfect strangers having a joyful, Sunday conversation on the verandah.

"Are you crazy?" I yelled. "We are having a conversation about my father, the man you married 23 years ago, the man you didn't know at all after 23 years, the man who has destroyed the lives of everyone in this pathetic family, and you're talking about bloody peeled tomatoes. What must be rolled up inside your head? Is there any reality at all, Mother? You have gone mad," I screamed. "You are driving me mad. Killing me!"

She turned her hollow gaze toward the road. She twirled her hair as she drifted away to that place. My anger started to slip away as she was slipping away. My sadness was for her sadness. I hated the things I'd said to her. I hated myself for saying them. Watching her scared me and tempered the anger that raged inside me. It was like yelling into the woods to hear your own voice fly off in every direction and be absorbed by the trees. Like releasing the birthday balloon's air and watching it fly away from you.

I looked at her face, into her deep-set eyes that seemed to be a paler gray. She fixed her gaze on the road like she was waiting for someone. It was then that I realized my mother was gone. Not to that place where she wanted to be, but to that place where she *had* to be. She needed the myth, the lie, the pain, the misery to survive in that place. She needed all of them to keep him with her.

Her despair worsened. Six weeks went by before she began to sit at the table and pick through her food. Sudie insisted that she get out, do things, talk to neighbors, learn to drive, get a job. She impressed upon her the importance of independence, saying, "The very first thing you have to do is learn to drive." She insisted that Mother should drive the dirt and gravel roads around the depot until she felt comfortable enough to drive on the main roads.

Mother shocked us by throwing herself headlong into learning to drive. She pestered Sudie to come every day to teach her. Mother loved to drive. She was unstoppable. Once she got her license, she shunned anyone who wanted to ride with her until she became more experienced.

She started driving almost weekly across the mountains through the hairpin curves of Highway 25 to Morley to see her mother and Aunt Sudie. Aunt Sarah, who lived across the line in Kentucky, would drive to Morley if she thought Mother would be coming up from Maynard Bald. Her brothers were there, too, but it was her mother, Aunt Sudie, and Aunt Sarah that she needed now. She needed women. Conversation. Consolation. Crying.

She enjoyed being at Morley on her terms, without worrying about getting home at a certain time. Only occasionally did she forget and look at her watch with a little gasp of panic.

Once she found the independence that came with learning to drive, and after she gained confidence that she could really drive herself to visit her mother and sister at Morley, she started her decline again.

Watching her transformation in the weeks after the death of my father, I came to understand that she had lost much more than her moorings. Her stability was questioned. Worst of all, he had taken to the grave with him all the misery she had come to rely on. Her misery had its own heartbeat. It had stopped.

Neither Aunt Sudie nor Aunt Sarah could engage her in their trials, crises, or sorrows. The ranters' corner at the Common Store at Morley couldn't draw her in. The obituaries in the *Maynard Bald Press* didn't interest her, whereas before, she immediately turned first to that particular page to see if she knew any of those who had died during the week. If she wasn't acquainted with any of the deceased, she would turn her focus to the surviving relatives listed for each of the departed, hoping she'd find at least one familiar name, hopefully a widow. Just *one* to console, to take part in her grief.

I surveyed the wreckage. The damage was all over her face—the unreachable look; the emptiness in her eyes, the hollowness in her voice. Now, she looked frail and just plain worn out. She seemed helpless, and I loathed that. Her figure and flesh weren't held up by bones. No bones. Only puffy white flesh like the woman in the blue dress in the painting that hung over Mrs. Pruitt's table.

Tethered to Wanting

Big My Want

On May 25, 1965, I walked across the stage at Maynard Bald High School to receive my diploma. I felt a certain incisiveness, a freedom of sorts, as Mr. Morton pressed it into my hand.

Mother did not attend. Lillie Dabney sat in back of the auditorium.

That morning an epiphany had seized me; it came to me directly and clearly that *I*, no one else, was standing in my own way. It was easy to become complacent, to let things bear down on me gradually, little by little, shaping and molding me, setting me in a permanent place; positioning and sculpting me like water running across a stone.

It seemed remarkably clear in which direction I was supposed to go: rather than focusing on trying to understand the adults around me, I needed to understand *me*.

I knew that when we were children, there was a specific time in our childhoods when we started to think about things outside our own minds—apart from ourselves. Later, we were supposed to reach a place of balance, weighing, shaping our internal worlds to mesh with our confines and other people.

313

An *identity*.

I had spent all this time trying to make sense of the adults around me, who seemed to me, even as a small child, to be insane, especially my father. It seemed the grownups closest to me had put an inordinate effort into keeping others from knowing them. I had tried to understand everyone else, constantly questioning why they did the things they did; who were they really; what was important to them; who and what did they love or feel passionate about; what were their fears; what did they *want*.

I observed the people around me and wondered, "How would they write their own eulogies or obituaries? What would they want to be said about them after they die? If they could pick the person who would deliver their eulogy, who would it be? To write or deliver a eulogy, you'd have to truly know the deceased. Perhaps a spouse or closest friend."

Then I thought of something peculiar that I'd never thought of before: my father did not have a single friend. Oh, he had his mother and his brother around him, and of course, Carl, was considered a relative just because he was always with Daddy. At his shop, my father was around the other men who worked for him, but I could not remember one unrelated person, except Carl, who had ever been in our house. As hard as I tried, I could not come up with the name of a friend, a neighbor, an acquaintance or even a salesman who had been inside our house.

I continued to think of the eulogy. I thought if you really wanted to understand a person, to know who they were; have them write their own obituary, and of course, let you read it. I tried it myself once, thinking much about how to capture the essence of a person in a single phrase of limited words. Perhaps eight. I walked through Jacksboro Cemetery and read the inscriptions on all the tombstones; all 597 of them. I had not paid close enough attention all those times at the cemetery waiting for Grandmother to deliver a speech at the headstone of every relative buried there. Sometimes she even presented monologues at the headstones of people she didn't know.

I had not been observant enough of what was written on the Halverstons' gravestones. When Grandmother lectured me about observation, awareness, and her favorite, *astuteness*, I had listened half-heartedly. She shook her finger at me. "Don't miss a single detail—not a crease in a linen or a mother-of-pearl button easing sideways through its buttonhole. Pay attention to everything."

On most of the tombstones were forgettable phrases: IN LOVING MEMORY OF; BELOVED FATHER, HUSBAND, BROTHER; IN HEAVEN ETERNALLY. Probably chosen in grief from the pages of a grave-marker book kept by the former undertakers, or Mr. Winfield Belcher, or the monument company. Some were probably suggested by preachers.

This notion of how much time I'd invested in trying to understand people bore down on me hard, but what struck me most about the realization was the gradualness of the bearing. Some things press upon you slowly, little by little, and some jar you into awareness.

We spend our childhoods trying to make sense of the world and how we fit into it and determining *if* we fit into it, and then, we spend our adulthoods trying to shape our imperfect worlds into those we *can* fit into, or at least tolerate. That was when my biggest awakening came: the understanding that it is our quest to shape our worlds to fit us, rather than shaping ourselves to fit the world, that begins all of our struggles *to control.*

I let my mother go. I wasn't sure where she went, but I imagined she had taken one of the side roads off of the road she gazed down from the parlor window. I called it the *longing gaze*—the look that came upon her when she stared beyond what was before her, beyond distance and through the tangible, as if she could see something the rest of us could not. She waited and expected. When the gaze came to her face, she was in that dark place where she lived most of the time now.

I let her go without a fight. I was tired of fighting, tired of struggling with lives that weren't mine, tired of wanting. I was sure now of what it was that I wanted. I was sure of what was holding me prisoner: my own expectations. It wasn't my mother, or her demons, or her side roads. And it wasn't this place. Maybe those were just things I had made up to console myself into thinking it wasn't my fault.

I wondered how comfortable I could be in my own attachment to the role of prisoner. I had longed for freedom. I had wanted it. I had been tethered to wanting. At times I wondered if I had grown attached to it. Longing had been my framework and my yardstick. Until now it had been my embryo, my skeleton, my context. For *what* I longed and *how much* had been the only variables.

"I would not turn into my mother," I thought. I looked into the bathroom mirror at three in the morning and saw my mother looking back at me. The most difficult and longest nights were those where, there, standing behind my mother in the mirror under florescent lights, was Grandmother wearing her scars like badges shining under the blue-gray of the lights.

I had held onto my memories, as if I somehow needed them, even the bad ones. They were all there, intact, with all their vivid colors. At times, I craved release from them. Night after night, I buried my head in the pillow and tried to identify my captors. I used to believe the mountains held me hostage. I had a deep fear that I would suffocate in the mountains. I envisioned time and time again being sentenced to endless years of sitting in front of a sewing machine at the shirt factory listening to the women around me hacking away from the cotton dust lodged in their throats and lungs. The coughs were like a deafening, fleeting dream when you wake up and never know what was there in the dark.

Grandmother had known the answers all along. She knew all the truths. I tried to remember her dithyrambs. "Remember the ditties," she said. "What did she hum? What were the riddles and songs that she made up when I was a little girl afraid of the dark?" I tried to remember. That night after graduation, as I half dozed, only temporarily falling into a real sleep with murky, shapeless fragments of dreams, I could hear the cadence that was hers alone; I could hear her chant:

> *Fear is the future.*
> *You are not there yet.*
> *Guilt is the past.*
> *You are never there again.*

Fear and guilt will hold
you captive.
Now will set you free.

What did it mean? Grandmother hated wasting lessons. "Wasting lessons is like spilling sugar," she'd say. "You can never salvage the sweet stuff. Once it's contaminated, wasted, just rake it into the garbage."

Since my father's death, she'd given up her lessons, her proverbs, her dithyrambs. Grandmother was an empty shell. A ruin. Her side road was not the one my mother took, but like my mother, she was gone. All she left behind were the lessons she taught me years ago.

I struggled to remember. I became obsessed with trying to remember the ditties, the words that, years ago, I dismissed as just silly songs and rhymes for my entertainment or to lull me to sleep after a bad dream. When I could recall the dithyrambs, most were shrouded in vagueness and doubt, and instead of recalling the riddles, all I could remember was the scent of lavender soap when she'd plant her face in my hair and make a repeated smacking sound as if she was leaving kiss prints all over my head.

Occasionally, she seemed her old self, when she'd rear up, surprising us with vitality and bursts of insightful advice.

"Listen to me," she said. "You are the only one responsible for your future, and fear is irresponsible. Set your mind and don't be afraid. Do not pull your head in."

With money from Grandmother and without telling anyone except Grandmother and Mother, I boarded the morning Greyhound bus for Knoxville.

The back of the bus was cold, and I sat next to a tiny, frail woman who coughed into her handkerchief and smelled of whiskey. I recognized the cotton cough, and she confided that she was traveling on to Nashville to stay with her grown son who would take her to Vanderbilt University Hospital for treatment of her respiratory ailment. After each coughing spasm, she sipped whiskey from a glass medicine bottle pulled from her pocketbook.

I found a two-room apartment just off Kingston Pike only a few miles from the Levi Strauss Company. The apartment was not exactly the find everyone was clamoring to get, but it would do until I could make some money. And I could tolerate any job to make enough money to repay the debt and stay away long enough to prove to myself that I wouldn't perish away from Maynard Bald.

On my first full day in Knoxville, I drew a deep breath and walked into the personnel office of the Levi Strauss Company and applied for a job.

"What kind of experience have you had?" asked a large, red-faced man looking over wire-rimmed glasses that appeared too small for his wide face. He looked at me, and when I didn't respond, he asked, "What kind of job are you looking for?"

"Any kind of job," I said. "I don't have experience, but I can learn whatever you give me."

"As young as you are, I'd be taking a real risk hiring you. Youngsters like you come in here every day. I spend time and money to train them, and then they find another job somewhere or a boyfriend. Usually a boyfriend. Either one, I lose!"

"You don't have to worry about the boyfriend part. Take a chance on me; you won't regret it, and you won't lose. I need a job."

"How do I know that you won't make a little money and take off up North? Or make a little money to pay tuition and go on up to the Hill?"

"What's the Hill?"

He studied me. "If you don't know the Hill, I won't be losing you to it. That's what we call the University of Tennessee! Guess since you don't know that, I won't have to worry about you working for tuition and taking off."

"Actually, I'm working to pay for a scroungy, two-room apartment," I said trying to keep eye contact.

"I'll try you tomorrow on the hook-and-eye machine. It's a monster. Dangerous. I don't usually put a new girl, especially a young one, on the hook-and-eye, but it's the only one I have open. It'll test your nerves. And mine. If you're afraid of it, it'll take your fingers off or you won't last on the job. One or the other. But you'll do fine if you stay focused and aren't given to distractions or daydreams. You get careless; you lose your fingers. I'll start you in training with Margaret Mave Mullins. She'll watch out for you until you're comfortable. She's a hard driver, but she'll teach you how to protect your hands. Better yet, she'll scare you crazy. If she thinks you can't stay focused or that fear of that machine can't make you pee your pants, you'll last less than a day. Just be fearful, careful and watch your fingers."

I worked at the hook-and-eye machine with the focus of a surgeon, never taking my eyes off of the monstrous plunger that drove the fasteners into the fabric with the force of a jackhammer. Bundles of denim crossed my lap and passed through my fingers until holes were worn in my blouses and my fingers started to bleed. When the supervisors were on breaks, Margaret Mave patched my fingers with bandaids and cautioned against having the inspectors see blood on the jeans. She had built up enough calluses on her own hands to protect them from the denim. Margaret Mave had worked at the same hook-and-eye machine since before I was born. The tip of her right middle finger, the one that pushed the right fly flap under the hook press, was missing. "Watch out for your fingers," she yelled every five minutes over the sound of the giant stapler.

I cried every morning in the shower. I wondered if it was the fearsome machine I was afraid of, or the notion that I might be there, in that same place for 20 years like Margaret Mave. That was my context. I needed a context. An environment. I thought of hunting for painted Easter eggs behind the West End Baptist Church when I was a little girl. As I ran through the woods looking for the colored treasures, I came upon a crumpled, wet, brown paper bag, litter thrown from a passing car. I picked up the bag and without looking inside, clapped it between my hands. Something was inside. I looked inside to find a gloriously painted Easter egg—smashed to smithereens. I sat on the ground with my head buried between my elbows and cried. I wanted to find another crumpled, brown paper bag. I wanted one more chance to recognize the painted egg. But when I came upon it, how would I know the difference between a crumpled, wet, brown bag and one with a painted egg inside?

I remembered what Grandmother had said, "You make your context. Everything around you, everything you do, and every person in your path will affect you somehow. Nothing is insignificant. Become a Proust. Observe every detail."

On the assembly line at Levi Strauss and in the shower at first light, I recreated myself. "People can transform themselves," I told myself. When I wasn't working on the beastly machine, I made up stories inside my head and took refuge in my daydreams. In the evenings and into the night, I sketched on scrap paper and constructed collages from old newspapers, magazines, foil from candy wrappers and cigarette packs, costume jewelry, and scraps of thrown-out fabric from Levi-Strauss. I crafted collages of broken glass from neon signs stolen from abandoned hotels, motels, and restaurants. I carefully glued every found treasure to scraps of wood or paper producing an endless series of images. I salvaged and gleaned from the wreckage of the past what could be recycled or incorporated into a new context, a new identity, a suite of collages of fresh colors and textures, the way I envisioned my new beginning, my new life, my new self. Grandmother said, "People shape you, but you determine your context and your outcome."

Memories, sketches, and collages became my maps. Not just maps of where I had been, but maps of where I was going. I'd written Grandmother's ditty in the homemade book given to me by my other grandmother as I left Morley three years ago. Her chant hummed in my head as I read:

"Take the back roads and the side roads,
But don't tarry long on the side roads
Don't forget where you're going,
And always remember where you're tethered."

The Good Enough Lie

By late July I'd painted the walls and cleaned everything in my apartment. After five weeks, all of my fingers were still attached to my hands, but fear of the colossal machine had not subsided. I felt like fear could be smelled on me the way an animal can detect when a person is afraid.

In the five weeks away from Maynard Bald, I hadn't driven back once or even called. I had written Mother and Grandmother to tell them about my apartment and my work at Levi Strauss, intentionally leaving out the parts about my fear of the machine and my unrelenting homesickness.

After I was confident that I wouldn't run home every time I felt a little displaced, I started to travel to and from Maynard Bald when I had more than one day off work: weekends and when I could swap shifts with Margaret Mave.

Maynard Bald was different. It looked smaller. The green hues of summer seemed dull, muted. No chartreuse like the early glimmer of the willow in spring; no pale, soft green like ripe cabbage heads; and no deep, rich green the color of shiny magnolia leaves. Grandmother said, "*You* have changed, not Maynard Bald." But, as the dog days came, she began to feel it too.

An insidious apathy had settled deep in the belly of Maynard Bald, arriving quietly and unnoticed, the way of most afflictions. No one even knew it was there: at least no one on the west end of town. Those of us on Dogwood Hill felt it welling up, getting fatter and fatter in the heat and laziness of August, gathering itself, collecting on the stubbled faces of boys hanging against the NO LOITERING sign in front of Colley's Pool Hall, hands in their pockets, wet, home-rolled cigarettes hanging limp on their mouths at seemingly impossible 90-degree angles, eyes to the sidewalk brown with the spit of tobacco juice. Those of us with mismatched clothes and bra straps holding on for their dear lives with the help of safety pins felt it. We felt the closeness, the threat, the ease of it.

Time and time again Grandmother poked with a knobby finger at the air between us and warned, "You just remember this, Miss Lunda Rose: apathy is as contagious as diphtheria, and it is a killer, lying hidden, skulking. It sneaks up on injured little nowhere towns like Maynard Bald and takes them out—not with any bawling announcement either, but coming slowly, without notice," she reminded me in a whisper, patting the corner of her lip with a lacey handkerchief. "Comes over you like dusk before the sky heaves out a solid cover of blackness; before you even suspect."

I wanted to believe everything Grandmother told me: that snakes didn't crawl at night; that you could slit and soak the tiny seeds of apples to leach out the pittance of arsenic to kill yourself if you should ever need to; that when the snout of Canis Major poked over the eastern mountain, it became harder to take a deep breath; that I was good enough all by myself.

Sometimes in August it became too hard to breathe. The heat was smothering. Then all I wanted was to coil back into myself like a baby armadillo. The nice thing for armadillos, though, is no matter how tightly they coil up, they have that little suit of armor—a hinged, segmented shell to keep them from breaking. And when they unfurl themselves after a near miss, it's like nothing ever happened; they just waddle away from the near-misses like they've lost their memories.

My apartment was unbearably hot making it impossible to sleep. I started driving from Knoxville to Maynard Bald every evening after work, and I slept most nights on Grandmother's porch where cool breezes found their way to us from the creek banks. She would fall asleep in a wicker chaise lounge on the porch as we talked into the night.

We talked about books, philosophy, the unrest in Southeast Asia, love, having babies. She even talked about my grandfather, and I realized, more than ever before, that Lillie Dabney Halverston possessed an innate shrewdness and a capacity for soundness that allowed her to keep her footing regardless of what was slipping or tumbling around her.

But, the most striking thing about her was the carefulness of her thinking, the exactness and precision of it. She thought things through and talked solutions over with herself—but only when she thought no one could hear her, only when she needed to hear the words or make a plan out loud, and when she was sure, or at least thought, I wasn't around to hear them. Actually, it was rare to hear her let go of a single reserved syllable to herself, since, if she could find someone to drive her, she usually perched on an overhanging rock on the side of Clinch Mountain to be alone saying, "legitimate thinking must always be done alone." She had other means of working out problems—I'd heard her lambaste Sheriff Rosemund Motts for pulling in one of the cousins, and she even spit analogies and long strings of acidic words at Mr. Benge at the store because he let the shelf run bare of Bruton Snuff.

*   *   *

Back in May, just a few days after my graduation, I was at the Tennessee Jubilee Drive-in with Ova Gay when J. Willard Willoughby yelled from his car to a boy I'd never seen there before.

"Want to go to a party on Saturday?" he shouted.

The boy eased out of his car and walked over to talk to J. Willard and two other boys with him.

"Who is he?" I asked Ova Gay.

"Hawkes Rivers from Jacksboro."

I couldn't take my eyes off of him. He was wearing perfectly creased khaki trousers with a pale blue shirt open at the collar. Handsome. Lean with a permanent grin and a confident gait.

He came over to speak to Ova Gay.

"This is Lunda Rose Halverston. She just graduated from Maynard Bald High. Came from upstate New York in our senior year. Hawkes is in his second year of pre-med at U.T."

The next day Hawkes called to ask if I wanted to ride over to the Jubilee for a hamburger. He called to ask the same question the next day. And the next.

Once I'd proven my independence, I started driving from Knoxville after work every evening, not just on weekends or when I had two consecutive days off. I'd watch for his car and dash out to meet him to avoid Grandmother's questions. She assumed it was someone in my class.

When she saw it was Hawkes, and from the first mention of my fondness for Hawkes Rivers, she'd paused making her voice more deliberate.

"Is he your reason for coming home every evening?"

"No, I've only known him for a short time, but I know you know his family. You remember his grandfather, Dr. Rivers, at Jacksboro?" She paused, trying not to show her disapproval.

"I know his father, Mosely, too. You don't want to keep company with the Rivers clan.

Never was she heard delivering a profane rail *outright* against anyone, not even against my grandfather after their divorce a hundred years ago, or Hawkes Rivers, or any of the Rivers. The way she did it indirectly was amazing—showing dissatisfaction, disapproval, and even anger with a smile, with the calmness and steadfast confidence of a seasoned prison warden, never raising her voice one decibel, so most of those she blasted weren't quite sure what had happened.

"I was reared by a mother whose temperament was so even, you wondered if her heart was beating," she'd laugh, "she never got herself worked up over things she couldn't do anything about. Maybe she did, but the important thing was that she didn't show it. I think her calmness and steadiness came from being comfortable within herself."

Grandmother gave the impression that she wanted me to leave Maynard Bald. She indicated, in a rather skillful way, that I should not form relationships with boys in Maynard Bald. Her methods were not subtle. I knew she still thought I would go to college.

"Sometimes there's a stymieing kind of thinking that can grow in these mountains," she'd warn, "It can rear up and grab you and the first thing you know, you'll be working at the shirt factory, daydreaming on 20-minute lunch breaks, viewing your existence as a loathsome burden, wanting always to be somewhere else, never happy with this moment or yourself."

"That is pure crap," I thought, but never said. I never disrespected her even when I disagreed or wasn't particularly interested in her cause. When she realized I wasn't as stirred or as evoked as she thought I should be over certain issues, or if a cleft developed between our views, she'd try to draw me out. That was part of the strategy, the training: drawing me out and into a confrontation, and if she was really successful, into a full-blown argument. She called it a *debate*.

"Find a more delicate voice for your anger, Lunda Rose. Make your voice the color of manna, the bread of Heaven," she said without looking up from her book, without changing her reading pace, without changing her tone or volume.

"Bread of Heaven? I don't think so. You're mistaking our Maynard Bald for some other place. You said yourself that you could feel the apathy, the complacency growing. This is Maynard Bald, and all the blessed manna in the cosmos, and all the bloody delicate language we could muster up, couldn't make it resemble Heaven."

Since I was a little girl, I'd never known her to fall silent. She alternated her conversation from the ills of apathy in two sentences and finished the paragraph with three unrelated sentences on the flavor and medicinal value of coriander. She added a pinch of coriander to everything: coffee, bathwater, molasses, even her Tennessee apple stack cake. In the middle of a discussion of all the reasons to avoid going to work at the shirt factory, I heard a recital of the exact ingredients of her Tennessee stack cake, the names of all the Tennessee apples; when they ripened; what they were good for—an entire horticulture lecture.

"Limbertwig. Dr. Matthews. Black Twig. Mountain Boomer. The Black Twigs ripen late," she'd say, "and hold up in the oven without becoming mush. Very good for apple dumplin's," she smiled, "douse with a sprinkle of coriander for the color. The perfect apple dumplin'!"

She knew it annoyed me when she talked about unrelated subjects in the same breath. When I was little, it was fun. It seemed like a game. But now it seemed like a provocation.

Her expectations were high, bordering on outrageous. Especially for me.

"You'll see," she said, "we'll find a way for you to go to college. You can go away to school and you won't have to work at Levi Strauss. We'll get the money somehow. Not this fall, but by next year. You'll go. I promise."

I started to think about being trapped here, refusing to believe there were ways out, out of the coal mines and away from the sewing factories.

"I'm not going," I yelled, "college is for creamy-skinned girls with skinny ankles and starched white blouses. I'm going to rot in this stinking town or in Knoxville or sitting in front of a sewing machine."

"Lunda Rose, choose more delicate language."

"Delicate language? What will delicate language do for me? Will it get me out of here? Or do you think it will make me more agreeable? More settled? More willing to settle for soft answers? Why, with this d-e-e-e-licate Tennessee drawl combined with the cotton cough, no one will understand a single word I say anyway. What difference will it make which words I choose? This is not the rain in Spain."

As soon as my words spurted out and echoed back to me, I knew I'd gone too far, sounding like a spoiled, thoughtless child in a fit of temper. I knew guilt would take hold of me, and I'd spend the night seized by remorse, wishing I could take it back.

"Go on to bed, Lunda Rose," she said, frustration levied on each word. "Tomorrow I'll talk to John McCarty at Peoples' Bank to ask if I can borrow the money."

"Don't do it!" I cried. "How would you pay it back? Let's stop talking about school! I don't want to go," I said trying to sound like I wasn't mad at the world. "Mother's going to be real disappointed, too. She thought I'd be out of here, gone for good. And farther than Knoxville, so I won't come home every evening."

"What are you talking about? Did your mother say that?"

"She made it very clear—said that once I left, I couldn't come back, that she didn't want me thinking I could run back and forth and, if I came back to

Maynard Bald, I'd better have a job lined up."

"That's ridiculous! You can come home any time you like. That's what you're doing now. Doesn't she know you're working at Levi Strauss? And you can come back to this house at any time, whether you're working or in school or not. What about Thanksgiving and Christmas and summer?" she asked, shocked, as if she didn't know full well that that was just the thing my mother would threaten.

"I don't know," I shrugged. "It doesn't matter. Tomorrow, I'll see Hawkes and ask him to marry me before he goes back to school next month. I already have my two-room, dream apartment. He could live with me off-campus. And puf-f-f-f-f. Magic! The problem will be solved! I won't have to worry about any of it."

"Stop your sarcasm," she said slamming her book closed, pursing her lips and tapping them with her fingers, biding enough time to push back the first words to her mind and to substitute acceptable ones. Southerners did that.

"That is exactly the kind of nonsense that will blaze its way to your mother, not to mention setting Mosely Rivers into a fevered spiral. You leave Hawkes Rivers alone. Your mother's enough of a problem without taking on the Rivers family. Mosely's already mapped out the next three decades of that boy's life. He's not going to have his plan raveled out by a girl from East End, or any girl for that matter."

I knew she was right. Hawkes took me to meet his father and his new stepmother, Dorothy Criel Driggers, once right after she and Mosely married. I had just met Hawkes. I didn't want to go, but he insisted. Said it was important that I meet them. I knew, when it was too late, that it was a big mistake.

They were sitting on the front porch there at the Rivers' house; Dorothy Criel barefoot, propped up in a double wicker rocker, fanning herself with a big, heart-shaped, cardboard fan with *Belcher's Funeral Home* printed on it and bawling that she was dying of a heat assault. Mosely's great white dog, Lancelot, a huge, nasty-tempered mongrel, snarled from beneath the chair as we walked up. Mosely made no attempt to quiet Lancelot as his lip curled up revealing his gray gums and as he let go of a barely audible growl.

"I swear, my body is like melting bubble gum— this kind of heat just softens you and will not allow any serious thought of any consequence," Dorothy Criel declared. "How are you, darlin' Hawkes?" she leaned to him absently shaping her lips against the air in an imaginary, fleeting gesture that would float past him unnoticed. "It's about time you brought her to us, to the far end of Jacksboro," she smiled.

Dorothy Criel was considerably younger than Mosely; not much older than Hawkes when Mosely picked her—plucked her right out of Flat Hollow away from her mama and daddy and her sisters— away from the whole family of close-knit Driggers' relatives who usually weren't eager or even willing to give up one of their females to an outsider. They didn't seem to mind that Mosely was much older and divorced from Hawkes' mother, since Dorothy Criel was marrying up. She seemed suited for her new place, her new status. He'd brought her from one kind of wildness to a different kind, this one more thrilling, but more dangerous. It was clear immediately that she doted with genuine affection on Mosely and Hawkes, without either of them outwardly returning the show of endearment.

Mosely hardly mumbled a word, and Dorothy Criel, in her attempt to fill the silence, never stopped talking. Not once. She talked about everything from the Rivers' thoroughbred Tennessee Walkers to how much she missed her younger, unmarried sisters still living at Flat Hollow. "Where are the sisters?" she moaned almost as a lament as her eyes sorted through the tops of the tulip poplars. "I wish they would come. Come to see about me, or if I might be needing something."

In some ways Mosely reminded me of my own father, both fear-striking men with heavy steps, lugging something hardened and deadened inside them. Both were silent, commanding men who'd never been separated from their guns.

Mosely was a man who wasn't born of a mother like the rest of us, a man you couldn't imagine ever being a little boy. He came out a full adult with a big gun and a whopping ego. When he did manage more than nods or shakes of the head, it was to order people around or cuss at them, even Dorothy Criel and Hawkes, who pretended not to notice. Mosely was high-handed, puffed-up. He demanded full-time submission from everyone around him, and it was known that he didn't give Hawkes one thing, not love, not attention, not approval, without conditions attached. And to make matters worse, Hawkes was his only child, and that alone was an impossible duty.

As difficult as Mosely was, as unknowable and disagreeable, there was a sadness about him, a vulnerability beneath all the noise he made, and sometimes when he spewed orders and commands and profanity, something in his voice fell away and revealed a different man, a frail man.

"Don't concern yourself with Hawkes Rivers or his daddy," Grandmother shook her boney finger, "They are not good people. Well, maybe Hawkes is a decent boy. But the others! They are people I don't want you around. Meanness collects around some people like mange attaching itself to a sick dog. Mosely has big plans for Hawkes. He has the boy's life all muddied up with his own. He thinks Hawkes will come out a doctor and step in when old Doc Rivers gets too old. Hawkes' granddaddy does a lot more in Maynard Bald than deliver babies and give out pills. Most can't be discussed. How a Rivers ever became a doctor is a puzzle. As for Mosely, the stench of his kind of meanness hangs in his spot long after he's gone.

This was the first time I'd heard her speak directly negatively about anyone, not bothering to couch her ill feelings toward the Rivers in a ditty. Clearly, she knew something about the Rivers family that I didn't.

Go to bed. We'll talk about this in the morning. And, Lunda Rose, we'll find a way. I'll talk to your mother. Now, go on to bed," she said kissing the top of my head the way she had every night I'd spent with her since I was four. When I leaned to her, I felt her stiffness, her frustration, the heaviness of the space between us, and knew, for her, the heaviness would linger there long after I went to sleep.

The next night Hawkes and I pulled into the last spot at the Tennessee Jubilee Drive-in where Wanda Rigney appeared at the car window with a wad of chewing gum clenched in her left jaw, a tiny order pad in hand, and a short pencil stuck through her ponytail. *What's New, Pussycat* rattled through the speakers above the restaurant window. J. Millard Hornsby and Clell Harvey came over and raised the hood to get a first-hand look at the engine of Hawkes' new car: a red, 1965, Chevy Impala Super Sport with more muscle than any car in a dry county of east Tennessee should be allowed. J. Millard yelled, "Hawkes, got yourself a monster car. You need 396 cubic inches and 425 horses to take these mountains?" He ignored the question. Mosely had bought it for him to take back to Knoxville in the fall to start his Sophomore year at the University. Hawkes seemed a little embarrassed by it, saying, "It's just another way my father keeps the leash in his own hands, even if it stretches clear to Knoxville."

J. Millard and Clell talked about horses and torque and how few medical books Hawkes would open next semester. Shaking his head in disbelief, Clell remarked, "This baby's built for Bonneville Flats—she's not gonna like the curves on the Jellico Highway. Maybe you can find a straight stretch of road long enough to open her up!"

"Hey, Hawkes. Take Lunda Rose to Knoxville with you, and she can coach you. Tutor you. Write your papers; even sit in on your exams if you can find some way to disguise her," J. Millard laughed.

"She'll probably be writing her own papers," Hawkes winked, knowing J. Millard's condescension bothered me. J. Millard, like Hawkes, was an only child. Neither had ever given a thought to their college money or from where it would come. I felt a little resentment toward Hawkes and J. Millard, not because they didn't have to work to go to college, but because both seemed to have a certain *expectation*. Hawkes said, "You take things much too seriously."

It couldn't be put off any longer. I had to tell him tonight that I was not—could not—go to school. I knew what he'd say: that he would give me the money for tuition. We'd had this same argument before. And he still didn't understand why I couldn't accept his offer.

"No one has to know but us," he'd laughed. "My father doesn't have to know, your mother doesn't have to know; your grandmother certainly doesn't have to know. It's just not a big deal to anyone except to you and your grandmother," he'd said over and over again in every argument since early summer.

I would wait until we were alone, if that was going to be possible in this century with every male within a 20-mile radius wanting to stick his head under the hood of Hawkes' car. The thought of telling him conjured up that familiar, awful feeling—that feeling of sadness, of longing for something that I didn't even know. The sick feeling in my gut was not a stranger, but like someone I knew well, the acquaintance you recognize from a distance and are not happy to see. It was unavoidable though—that dark longing with a hopelessness attached to it as tightly as a parasite clinging desperately to its pitiable host.

I glimpsed at Wanda with her hip thrown against the door of Mack Strothers' hotrod Chevy and at J. Millard and Clell leaning against the car. Mack looked up at me for just a second before snatching the pencil from Wanda's ponytail. She laughed and he bent over to whisper something in her ear.

I hoped he wouldn't come over. He was distant kin to Hawkes' stepmother. Dorothy Criel was from one of the Brass Ankle families that came up from

South Carolina and Mack was one of the Redbones from Louisiana. Most of the old families that had migrated from the Carolinas and Louisiana had settled in Flat Hollow way back on Cumberland Mountain near the Pellissippi River. A place isolated and unknown to those in Maynard Bald; a place where wrinkled-headed black vultures sat in bare-limbed white snags of river birches waiting for old dogs and chickens to die. This was a place where the cousins trained their pointers and occasionally trapped a coveted blue hawk or haggard, the mature, wild prize of their sport.

Mack and Dorothy Criel had all the striking features of their kin: flawless, pale, olive skin; tall, sleek, sturdy frames; and narrow, sculptured, perfectly-proportioned faces with high cheekbones and thin, angular lips. Those from Flat Hollow were so beautifully different in their look that they made outsiders jerk their heads short. But the feature common among them that brought silence and unbelieving, gawking stares was their eyes: large, deeply-set, round, penetrating and ranging from deep brown to hazel to a ghostly gray.

Seeing Mack Strothers made me think of my own dark-haired, gray-eyed cousin, Estel, who lived by himself back at Flat Hollow, refusing to step one foot into the deep mines. He kept a hunk of tobacco in his jaw even as he slept and told stories of the way his face felt when his beard froze, and what it felt like when he accidentally walked on the body of a dead bull struck by lightning and covered with leaves. He talked about the feeling of walking on flesh: soft, smoothed, melted into the contour of the ground; how even the red-headed, scavenging turkey vultures wouldn't touch anything struck by lightning. Estel kept to himself mostly, having little to do with outsiders and only came around his brothers and his daddy or other men in the hollow when they were training falcons or hunting dogs, both standing traditions taught to him by his daddy and our granddaddy.

A few times as I was growing up, I had been allowed to go with Estel and my other cousins to Shagham Bald and to Morley Cliff; to see them carrying their cadges, hauling up excited Sharp-shins and Red-tails and even one off-course Peregrine captured in North Carolina. Each hooded bird was kept in a separate cadge to keep him from killing any other bird that might come near him. As we approached the bald, the Peregrine displayed his distinct show of excitement: a frenzied bobbing of his head and pumping his tail up and down as if he were breaking free into a ritualistic war dance.

Once I watched Estel imping the broken feather of a Northern Harrier that had wintered in east Tennessee. Working the feather with his big, awkward hands, he attached a tiny hollow splint, a shunt of sorts that was hardly visible. "She won't even know it's there, he said. "Did you know she changes her shape in the air? Just like Houdini, she can alter it to the exact shape she needs to do her job."

He'd let me watch him care for the birds; even touch them, but the training and the hunt were only for those with birds. Only men. It wasn't until I was much older that I pleaded with him to convince the other cousins that I wouldn't crumble if I was permitted to watch the birds in pursuit. "This is the real spectacle, the true show," he warned. "If you hike to the top of the bald and start squealin' like a weaklin' sissy, you'll distract the birds and the dogs. My brothers will never let you near the falcons again. Understand?"

Estel and his three brothers positioned themselves on the open bald. He instructed me to stand about 25 feet away and motioned to me with his finger and a nod of our agreement. His Harrier was first to be taken from the cadge; the beautiful hooded bird perched on the leather gauntlet, heart pounding, covered head jerking from side to side in anticipation of the pulling of the hood. I could hardly breathe as I witnessed the release of the quarry. The slipping of the hood. Then the soar and the climatic stoop, wings tucked, neck straight. I stood there—as unaware, as mindless as the dove, stunned and seized by the vision of the resplendently beautiful horror of the strike, killing the prey with one mid-air blow.

Mack Strothers stood under the neon arrow with hundreds of timed lights that looked like the arrow was pointing to the Tennessee Jubilee. He was huddled with two boys I didn't recognize, but I knew they, too, were from Flat Hollow: the dead-tell signs were their tall, lean frames, their handsome, slim faces, their ease with Mack Strothers, their standoffishness, making sure they didn't cross the invisible line at the edge or come within ear shot of anyone who wasn't one of them. Flat Hollow people rarely came to Maynard Bald, so people in town didn't know them. The county truant officers knew to leave them alone. So did the sheriff.

"Hawkes, let's go somewhere to talk," I urged looking at the clock visible through the window of the restaurant."

"Let's drive toward Jellico. We'll find a place to talk. No one will be on the road this late," he said, backing out looking over his shoulder and calling to J. Millard that he'd see him tomorrow.

As we headed up Jellico Highway, I eased closer to him, as close as I could get leaning across the tunnel where the gear shift protruded from the floorboard. I played with the radio dial getting nothing but white noise with an occasional hissing spurt of WLS in Chicago or the broken voice of Cousin Brucie in New York City.

In a low voice he used when he wanted to avoid a subject, he said, "My dad thinks I should go to Knoxville a few weeks early. Settle into the dorm." Searching and fumbling for words, he said, "What do you think? Good idea? Buy books, get set up before classes start?" The lights of oncoming cars swept shadows across his face. He looked worried, or "maybe he's just tired," I thought, "or maybe Mosely's started grooming the eyas early, already shortening the jesses."

"There's someone behind us flashing his headlights. Must be J. Millard and Clell," he said, adjusting the rear-view mirror. "Clell must have persuaded Wanda to let him give her a ride home. I think he wanted to make sure Mack Strothers didn't take her home," Hawkes said tossing his head back with a laugh and leaning to check the side mirror.

"No, it's not a Chevy grill. I don't recognize the grill or the car. Probably just someone wanting to pass."

"Well, no one's going to pass on this stretch of road unless they aren't from around here," I said, "don't worry about him. Maybe he'll slow down and back off until we get to the foot of the mountain." The headlights of the car behind us dimmed, then flashed bright again. Dimmed and brightened. We felt the bumper tap the rear, then a hard ram.

"What's he doing!" Hawkes yelled.

The lights were blinding in the rear-view mirror. The car rammed the bumper catapulting us forward. Hawkes' chest slammed against the steering wheel. The car slowed a little falling behind us. We could see the headlights coming fast to our left trying to pass.

"Oh, no, not on this curve," I cried.

The car roared up to our left side in a blur. A blur, but in slow motion, every pounding second deliberate, every frame's motion stopped. A blue car I didn't know. The windows were up, the inside a dark abyss. The blue car moved from the darkness and was in full view slightly ahead of us in the on-coming lane. Hawkes fought the steering wheel to hold the wheels on the road. I saw the right back window roll down; and from the dark hole eased the barrel of a gun. The glass exploded through the darkness around my head, shattering, flying, driving itself into my skin. Numb and limp, my shoulders caved toward my chest. I sank back into the tunnel between the two front seats, my back against the floorboard. In the darkness, I felt the sting of the glass and the warmth of blood stream over my face. I smelled it and tasted it seeping into my nostrils and mouth.

I heard the roar of the car as it sped into the night. Hawkes rolled the car to a stop shutting off the engine and lights.

"Are you hit?" he asked slumping forward, laying his forehead against the steering wheel.

"No. Are you?" I sobbed.

"No, I'm okay. Just cut. We have to get off this road. They'll be back."

"What's happened?" I cried, running my hand across my forehead and temple trying to wipe the blood out of my eyes.

"You bleeding?"

"I'm okay. Just cut up!"

"We have to get away from here," he said, grabbing the long stick shift and throwing it into reverse. "They'll be back. Maybe a side road. We have to find a way off the main road. A place to hide where they can't see the car. In the hollow or ravine."

He spun the tires turning around, looking back for their headlights. He took the curves at breakneck speed as I buried my head in my hands, crying, screaming that someone was trying to kill us.

The hollow opened wide on the flat acres cradled at the bottom where there stood long, perfect rows of seven-foot tall white burley covered by great canopies of billowing white cheesecloth laid over the large, thin leaves that would become cigar wrappers. Randal Marlowe's place was cleaved between the ridges with the gossamer nets protecting the leaves from sun scald and looking like an unsettled cotton ocean where the precious leaves swallowed us up. The center rows were parted by a broad tractor path that led to the back of the barn. Hawkes drove between the shrouded rows and through the large barn opening, moving the car slowly under the ceiling of damp boughs, an umbrella sky of curing tobacco leaves, broad fans that brushed against the roof and hood swaddling us in darkness. Absorbing us. Submerged to hold our breaths. We could hear the rustle of the drying burley turn to stillness.

"Stop crying," he said, shutting off the lights and engine. "You have to be quiet! We have to listen. They'll be back!"

I tried to swallow back the spasms in my throat, gagging, suffocating as if I would explode with my silence. We heard the roaring motor of the car returning and the slowing of the engine. Then silence. The car had stopped. I stuffed my head into my knees to muffle the sounds trying to burst out of me. There were long spaces of drumming silence so profound that you may have the deafening of it once in a lifetime. Silence so absolute that even the vibration of the tree frogs and the beating of my own heart were mute.

We heard the engine start and the fading sound of the car speeding away. We sat in silence under the canopy of tobacco fans for hours. Neither of us spoke a word or raised our heads; and through those endless, pounding stretches of silence, all I could think of was how I would keep this forever from my grandmother.

*   *   *

The next morning was Saturday. Grandmother stood outside my bedroom door threatening that if I didn't unlock it, she would find her own skeleton key or her double-bladed wood axe. Horrified at the sight of my face in the mirror, I realized I couldn't hide from her.

"Hawkes and I had an argument," I told her through the door, cracking it just a bit. "I'm alright. I just want to be alone for a while to think through some things. I promise I'm fine."

Her sighs were precarious and heavy. "Something's wrong or you wouldn't be locked in there. What should I tell your mother?"

"Nothing! Grandmother, if she comes by, don't tell her about Hawkes. Just say I don't feel well. I'll be fine by tomorrow and I'll go by to see her on my way back to Knoxville."

Grandmother called from the bottom of the stairway, the inflection of disapproval apparent in her voice. "Hawkes is here to see you, Lunda Rose."

"Tell him to go away," I yelled lying wadded into a tight ball at the foot of my bed.

He opened the bedroom door slowly and quietly. I didn't raise my head or look at him.

"Get away from me, Hawkes. I can never see you again. Never. There is nothing for us. There never will be. Some things are so awful that they are unforgivable. Some things are so despicable, so wanton, so mean—and the ugliest thing about meanness is that it gets easier and easier until it becomes a part of you—so much a part of you that you can't do without it and you even forget it's there."

"What are you talking about? What have I done? I've done nothing!"

He looked down, closing his eyes and shaking his head from side to side. A young falcon, an eyas plucked from the aerie too early, too young to resist, but easier to train than the older blue haggard.

"You're just scared. Don't let this come between us. Please don't do this. It was just some boys from the hollow having a good time. We can forget it ever happened. We won't tell anyone. Ever. Don't let this separate us."

"I will never forget it. Hawkes, don't you see

what's happened? It was Mosely. Your father has hired someone to kill me."

"What? No! You're wrong," he said, backing away, his face contorted in disbelief. "You don't know what you're saying. My father would never."

"It's pure, raw evil to want another person dead. The meanness has attached itself to your father. It will never work for us. Don't you see that your father will never let anyone interfere with his plan? He will keep you in the cadge. In place. Safe. Safe from the pummel; from pugnacious sharp-shins that barrel roll out of the sky to wallop you straight on; safe from girls with pinned-together clothes and the wrong last names. A life with you would be one spent perched, teetering on a long-cuffed, calf-hide gauntlet, wearing a sewn Dutch mask. Don't you see? You'll never slip the tether. You'll never find the openness."

"You're wrong."

"It doesn't matter," I whispered, "you'll go on believing a lie that's just good enough to protect you from the truth. There's no other option for you and I understand that. But, there is another option for me."

"You're just scared."

"I am not scared. I am repulsed. Something has been chiseled out of me, Hawkes. You don't feel it. When the cage is big enough, you don't feel the walls against you. Feel the wires closing in, feel them getting closer and closer because there's no big clatter, Hawkes. It is a good-enough lie that you tell yourself about your father. What Mosely doesn't see is that he's lost you, not me. Like the blue haggard, the wild falcon with the Khan hood raised, the equator bells severed. The one flushed from the mew, harder to guide, with the loudest call, but then lost in the hunt.

Do you not feel the tension of the leash, the quiver of the acorn bells on the rufous-morph?"

Hours passed as I swayed, rocking on my bed, clutching my stomach in a sort of night-long grieving prayer that gave way to a purging, not of hate, but of sorrow. Mosely had taken the free-falling, torpedo stoop of the falcon: wings closed, diving, clutching, jesses trailing, altering his shape for the seize. As much as I wanted to hate him, instead, I was assailed head on with the same garbled dilemma as I had felt with my own father: one of feeling sorry for someone who has hurt me.

The first time I came out of my room, the next morning after Grandmother left a tray outside the door, I was unable to do the most basic things: eating, or talking or putting one foot in front of the other or thinking about anything beyond the walls of the house.

"I have to get into my car and drive back to Knoxville," I thought, "Monday morning I'll have to face the hook-and-eye machine. Focused. Without fear."

Grandmother wanted to talk. Any subject would have filled the silence. Without saying a word, it was as if she absorbed my thoughts and pain into her own body. She looked at me for a long time.

"Lunda Rose," she said, "you'll forget whatever it was that Hawkes did to you. Whatever happened to you! However he hurt you! He probably doesn't understand what he's done or hasn't done. Probably doesn't have the slightest idea what's wrong. Does he?"

"No."

"Know that men can't tolerate broken things or

damaged things—or things that can't be fixed or even the most minor problem that can't be solved immediately. They're designed that way. They scare easily. And the truth is that what lies deep within them is dreadfully frail and fragile."

The Good Enough Lie

Truths, Dreams, and Flat-Out Lies

The next morning, waking up in my own bed in my own apartment in Knoxville felt right for once. It was the first week of September, and there was the clamor of college students in my apartment house.

I didn't cry in the shower. It occurred to me while getting ready for work at Levi Strauss that my grandmother was a woman of truth and insight beyond what I even imagined. She knew things. She understood. She saw to the very core of things. She saw deeply into people. She liked things pure, simple, raw, uncomplicated. All the things she wasn't. She liked people who were straightforward, but she admitted once that she was not always as forthcoming as she preferred others to be. "People show you what they want you to see," she'd said.

Like every other member of the family, Grandmother was a master of denial and secrecy if they suited her, if she needed them. "Like solitude, denial is sometimes necessary—required," she said. "Pretense can color things a lighter shade. Sometimes you just have to let go of real truths and color things just a little lighter. Just a little lighter," she shook her head. Use imagination and you can have things the way you want them. Everything will be fine."

"Everything was not fine. Yesterday was not fine, nor the day before," I thought.

I could hear her words. "You have to be more positive, Lunda Rose. The winter won't be so brutal this year. You'll see. Things won't always be so difficult, Lunda Rose." It was always tomorrow, next week, next winter.

On this day, I felt different: contented, changed. I was gloriously happy as I unlocked the door of my fifty-dollar, lime-green, 1955 Ford. A three-speed on the column. It had the smell of brake fluid. Its gears stuck and scraped metal against metal sounding like grinding tectonic plates. But the real challenge to anyone who dared drive it was a clutch as sensitive and fragile as an aging woman. Once through the gears, though, you could sink into the smell of brake fluid and old upholstery and almost feel comfort in the familiarity of it.

Driving through South Knoxville, I didn't think of the hook-and-eye machine that severed fingers or the sound of women hacking endlessly from the cotton cough that crackled through their lungs and throats. I didn't think of Mr. Andrews, the floor supervisor who walked the aisles that separated the machines, stopping behind the newest girls, pushing them to work faster, pitting them against the clock to make quota, even though it was in this rush and in the haze of fatigue that accidents happened.

I smiled as I drove through the gate to the Levi Strauss parking lot. Now I knew the meaning of the look on Uncle Lank's wife's face when she dressed him in his black bib over-alls and placed coins over his eyelids preparing him for his wake. It wasn't the look of a woman who'd just become a widow, nor was it one of sorrow. It was the look of relief. There was a measure of contentment that came at the end of a struggle. I was content with my feeling. Certain. I could not settle for false answers or the shape and substance of this context. Even if the answers were exactly what I wanted to hear or believe, they were not good enough. Sometimes they were just flat-out lies. No, yesterday was not fine. Today would not be fine. Even if the winter was milder, it would not be enough.

I moved among the huge machines and bundles of denim. Forward without a backward glance. Somehow, I summoned enough courage, inhaled deeply, and walked past Margaret Mave to Mr. Andrews' office. The shrieking horn sounded for work to begin, and the factory hummed as the giant machines were started. I collected a check for three days' pay and waved to Margaret Mave from a long distance across the grinding of sewing machines. I saw her wide eyes and her sad smile and read them clearly. Clutching the steering wheel, I counted ten fingers.

Leaning forward, the steering wheel held my forehead. I thought of my father. "Joseph Halverston," I said out loud, enunciating, as if at that moment by saying his name, I had been freed from him. I thought of Hawkes' father, "Mosely Rivers," I said even louder and more deliberately than I'd spoken my own father's name, staring down at the floorboard, "A man who wanted me dead." Two men had almost rerouted my uncharted tether in that year,

1965, there in Maynard Bald, Tennessee, defining the length of the string and radius of my world, that small circle in the mountains of Tennessee. The seeds of wanting were sewn: wanting answers, wanting more than what was there, wanting to know *why* everything, wanting my real self.

The car started on the second try. Despite the expected wrestling with the column gearshift, I felt satisfaction and a little pride that I could drive a straight shift. I felt powerful. "How could I possibly feel powerful?" I questioned. "Lunda Rose, the champion of the confidence graveyard. Powerful? I've just quit my job; I have no money; and I'm headed to Cincinnati, alone, in a car that hardly starts or even runs," I said out loud, as if talking to someone in the car.

We tend to our own brains and the lengths of our tethers while sitting in the dark or standing in line at the grocery store. We cower behind our own shadows or in the kneeholes of mahogany desks, staying as mute as clumps of coal and as unseen as a pale shade of gray, and still we sigh and refuse to shed at least one shoe and finally admit that we are utterly alone with our busy, solitary brains and our unrelenting, unsettled longings.

At my apartment, I scraped the non-skid daisies off the old bathtub and packed everything into cardboard boxes I'd gathered from the Dempster Dumpster behind Cas Walker's Supermarket. I found an old canvas valise in the alley, and it held most of my things. The only things worth packing into the boxes were my collages and sketch diaries. The packing didn't take long.

The days and nights in Knoxville were not wasted.

In Knoxville, and years earlier, under the persimmon tree, I plotted my course, my life map. I continued my search for what was lost or what I didn't have in the first place. It wasn't until years later that I realized that there is only a very fine line separating truths, dreams, and flat-out lies. I could make things what I wanted them to be. Those were my grandmother's words. She said, "Sweetpea, everyone you cross paths with in your life will affect you somehow. People and experiences shape you and make you who you are. Somewhere along the way, you will figure out which ones to keep and which ones just suck the very life out of you."

I smiled all the way to Cincinnati, but about every fifty miles or so I'd burst into tears. I knew I could stay with my cousin, McCain, in Covington, Kentucky, just across the Ohio River until I found a job and a place of my own. It's easy to find sales jobs in big cities. I took the first job offered at Shillito's Department Store, the first and largest department store in downtown Cincinnati. It was a sales and cashier job in the men's department. It wasn't a thrilling experience, but I loved walking in the city at lunchtime and looking at the window displays—fantasies I'd never seen in Balloff's windows—snow-covered floors and backgrounds surrounding sleekly winter-dressed mannequins, and mechanical toys and animals that convinced children they were real, and painted horses that galloped on posts that seemed to shoot straight through the store ceilings to the sky.

In the basement of Shillito's was a pet department, where I spent my lunch break each day watching and listening to a gray parrot that the cage keeper had taught to talk and shriek wolf whistles. Every time a woman walked by, the giant bird shrieked a wolf whistle and declared, "I'm in love. I'm in love." One day I went during my lunch break to see him, and he was gone. The cage keeper said that someone had bought him. I knew the story wasn't true. I never went to the pet department again.

After Christmas, I decided Cincinnati was not where I should be. McCain urged me to stay for a few months longer, but I felt certain I would surely die from exposure if I stayed. I did not have the proper coat or clothes or temperament for such a place.

I was happy to say goodbye to McCain. I invited him to visit the family in Tennessee, even though I could see in his face that he would never go back. I assured him that Maudie had left for Baltimore with her fourth husband and that it was safe to go back.

In late January Maynard Bald was quiet, resting in shades of winter gray. Despite Grandmother's protest, I decided that since I had never been west of the Mississippi, I would take a Greyhound bus to San Antonio—far enough from Maynard Bald to keep me from running back when I got scared or needed something, and far enough that a long-distance call would be too expensive to ring anyone up crying about wanting to come home.

" 'I do not hate you;' that's what I would say to Mother first, before telling her of my plan to leave for San Antonio or asking the hard questions," I thought, as I sat parked behind the Cadillac in her driveway. "Why does she hang onto that blessed heap? Perhaps she needs it."

Mother seldom locked her doors. Certain she'd seen me, I entered without knocking, talking, as if she'd be sitting on the couch close enough to the door to hear me.

She was sitting in a chair in a far, dimly-lit corner of the living room. Her black hair was uncombed, pinned up away from her neck and from the collar of a pastel yellow robe with its ridges of chenille worn bare. She looked younger than forty years, her face flawless, pale against her dark hair.

I moved closer to her, and as she turned toward the window, I saw that she was wearing bright red lipstick and large, Bakelite earrings in the shape of quarter moons.

"Going somewhere, Mother?"

"No. Why do you ask?"

"You're wearing lipstick and earrings like you're dressing to go out."

"Oh, no," she shook her head, wetting her lips as if blotting her lipstick on a tissue, "I put lipstick and earrings on first thing out of bed. Makes me feel better."

I sat on the couch only a few feet from her. Every word, every sentence I'd rehearsed floated out my ears—not to be retrieved.

"I'm leaving Maynard Bald, leaving Tennessee. This time I'm going away for good, Mother. Well, not exactly for good—but far enough away and for long enough not to be tempted to come back when things don't go as planned. To San Antonio. I want to go somewhere I've never been before. Somewhere warm."

Her indifference infuriated me. She didn't say, "Don't go." Or "do you need money?" Or "do you have to go so far away?" No. She sat there with the same impenetrable look on her face, the same passive tone in her voice.

"You know how he died, don't you?" I blurted out, wanting to shake the words out of her, wanting to dangle her by the ankles upside down until everything inside her rattled and her hoard of secrets fell out onto the floor.

"What are you talking about? Are you talking about your daddy? We all know how he died," she said without looking up.

"It was you, wasn't it, Mother?"

She jerked her head back. Her eyes opened wider and she squeezed words in a voice that was little more than a whisper.

"Don't be ridiculous! You don't know what you're talking about. That's the craziest thing you've ever said and the meanest thing you've ever said to me. You don't know what you're talking about. You're crazy."

"You didn't pull the trigger, but you had someone pull it for you."

"Are you crazy?" she shouted.

"Maybe one of your brothers? Was it Weir or Purcell? Or Hoboch Lewis or Pinder? Caudill? Which one, Mother? Of course. It would have taken just a slight nod from you or your mama to have any of the five of them do it. Or was it someone in the coal mine who needed money? Or maybe you knew someone to call in New York when you were hiding from him? Of course! He died in Knoxville, and you were in New York. No one would ever suspect!"

"You, girl, have taken leave of your senses! You have read too many books! Why are you talking to me this way? Why are you being so hateful, making all this up? It's foolishness!" She started to cry. "You are mean. I loved your daddy. Do you really think I had

356

one of my brothers or a hired man shoot him? That's crazy! Absolute insanity!"

"It's not crazy if you're a woman afraid for her life. For once, tell the truth about him. Why are you still lying about it? Defending a lie? Tell me what is true. How can you protect all your secrets now? You couldn't survive with him alive and you can't survive with him dead. If you are holding that secret, it will drive you mad. That's it, isn't it, Mother? It isn't his death or living without him that's driving you insane; it's living with the lies. You've spent your whole life protecting your precious secrets, and in the end, the secrets, not my daddy, will kill you. You've been barely alive since he died; half here, just living along side your secrets—not burning them to the ground, but building a stone wall around them. You can't stand being here without him, can you? Bring him back even if it's just inside your head; put him between you and the real world, between you and life and you don't have to check out. At least by admitting it, you'd show some backbone—some signs of life left in you."

"Stop it! Stop it! I don't want to talk about this right now."

"You don't want to talk about this? When will it be convenient for you to talk about this? When will you land on this planet, Mother? Don't you see that if you don't talk about this, it will eat you up. Spread through you like a disease."

She cried louder. "How can you think these things? Even suggest them? He was not the monster you think he was," she said. "No one understood him. Not like I understood him. I knew things about him that no other person knew."

"Is there some kind of merit in knowing those things? I yelled. "Your secrets will always be there hovering over your bed at night, a shadow in your dreams or one staring back at you from the mirror, or words flying off the page of a resurfacing memory. Memories have a way of doing that—waiting there just below the surface to catch you off guard ten years down the road and in one of your happiest moments to step out into the open."

"Lunda Rose, do you hear what you're saying? Why do you have to analyze everything to death until you've bored it down to nothing?

"Mother, didn't you know that people would start to question why you weren't at the funeral; why not one Evers came to the funeral? You and the Evers family left the three of us, Ruby Grace, Robert Joseph, and me, to bend in over the casket to see where the bullet went in. It would have subjected Elda Kate, too, if she'd been at the funeral. At least by admitting you had a part in it, shows you have a spine. Is it possible you didn't know what the uncles would do to him? Yes, that's it, isn't it? They kept you stupid to protect you. God knows they've never been afraid of the law. Everybody knows there's no law in Morley except maybe the law of accusation or gossip or being shamed out of your own family."

"Show some guts, Mother, instead of hiding behind your brothers. My question to you is what took you so long? Why didn't you do it sooner?"

She slowly lifted her head and looked straight at me. She wasn't crying.

"When Carl told me your daddy killed for money, I knew he wouldn't have any problem killing me when I made him mad enough or came too close to discovering the truth. All the times when I tried to follow him, when I thought it was another woman, it was killing that was taking him away."

"Well, halleluiah! Finally, you have the courage to admit it—the backbone to do it."

"In all your daddy did and was, he loved me. We loved each other," she cried.

"Listen to what you're saying, Mother—that on that night in Oneonta, it was more important for you to discover he wasn't having an affair than to discover that he killed. My God."

"Was proof of his love the only thing that mattered? For God's sake, he never loved anyone except himself. And it is doubtful that he even loved himself. He was a Halverston. Can you name one Halverston who ever loved himself or anyone else? He tried to kill you! He did kill little parts of you. When I was little, you giggled and played. You laughed out loud. You had dreams. Tell me one dream that is alive today. Name one thing he didn't destroy or damage in this family. Tell me one thing that you wanted to do in your life that he permitted. He broke everyone in his path. Even though he didn't kill you before someone killed him, he did kill little parts of you. Look at me square on and tell me what kept you with him for twenty-three years and four babies, when you feared every day of those twenty-three years that he would kill you? When will you face the truth? The raw truth? Or is it that the truth—admitting it to yourself—would interfere with your misery? Or maybe your guilt will be all you need to sustain you. Do you feel any guilt, Mother?"

"No."

*   *   *

Grandmother pulled the snuff pouch from the bosom of her dress and insisted that I take a little extra money. "It's for emergencies, you see," she whispered. "You may have to stay in a hotel until you find a place. Why, you never know what you might run into. You'll need a quilt, too."

"It's the southern part of Texas, for Pity's sake! I won't need a quilt."

"Oh, it can get fiercely cold in Texas. And what about the bus ride there? You'll get cold, Darlin'. Now go on. Take it."

Once again, in the early hours of the morning, I sat in the Greyhound terminal in the café section, where I knew the sound and swivel of every stool and the feel of running my fingers across the wooden counter.

Cratis Bolinger tended the one-person ticket booth and lowered his head to look over his glasses at me. "You plan on coming back, Lunda Rose?" he asked when I said I wanted a one-way ticket.

"Maybe, someday." He didn't look up as he slid my ticket through the tiny window, and I slowly counted $34.26 onto the counter.

"Your bus leaves for Knoxville at 5:25 a.m.," he said. "It'll roll in from Corbin and stop here only long enough to discharge or board passengers. Its destination sign will say 'ST PETERSBURG', but you'll change buses in Knoxville, Memphis, and Dallas."

Grandmother was still and silent, clutching the quilt and her black vinyl pocketbook as tightly as a child holding a security blanket. She insisted on staying until I boarded, although I was certain her vigilance was to make sure I took the quilt.

Willene poured coffee into Grandmother's cup, but she didn't drink it. Said her hands were shaky. At 5:15 we went outside to wait, and just a few minutes later, the Greyhound displaying "ST PETERSBURG" rounded the corner from Central Avenue. She turned to me, careful not to say so many words that I would detect the small sound struggling at the back of her throat, and said, "Promise that you will come back to me before I'm gone. Practice loving the way you practiced speeches to your father. Remember that the most complicated of changes are sometimes the shortest road back to you. And sometimes you have to pull your head in and face knowing that, if you stop trying, the tether is going to jerk you back, but if you pull hard enough, long enough, you'll snap free."

No passengers were discharged at Maynard Bald, and I was the only one to board with Grandmother right behind me to give instructions to the bus driver who listened attentively and assured her that he would direct me to the right track in Knoxville and that we would find a place for the quilt. The first aisle seat behind the door was vacant, so was the window seat next to it. This was the best place to see everything ahead of me. Even with passengers already on the bus from Corbin, Lexington, Indianapolis, and Cincinnati, the bus was only about three-fourths full. The seat next to me was free for my quilt.

At exactly 5:25 a.m. the bus backed slowly from its track. Grandmother was still as close to it as she could be without touching it. We turned west at the Cherokee Theater onto Central, and, strangely, as we picked up speed on the outskirts of town, I didn't feel afraid. My excitement and impatience for daylight grew. We made brief passenger stops in Lake City and Clinton and rolled into Knoxville at 6:30 a.m.

In Knoxville, I boarded a Super Scenicruiser—a through-coach to Memphis. As daylight came, I felt I would burst with excitement. Again, I sat in the front seat with a view that sprawled in front of me like an infinite, moving painting. Soon after leaving Kingston we crossed the Clinch River, and, as I looked to the right, I saw a colossal TVA coal-fired, steam-powered generating plant with mammoth piles of coal and a rail yard filled with railcars that spread over the terrain like a small city.

We'd left the mountains behind us and the road ahead opened up as we crossed the Cumberland Plateau, once the largest hardwood-forested plateau in the world. Its rocky ridges and deep ravines rose above the Tennessee River Valley making it appear, even in January, as mysterious and beautiful as the mountains.

After passenger stops in Rockwood and Crossville, we had a fifteen-minute rest stop in Sparta at a small Greyhound station called the Rebel Cafeteria. The bus driver pointed out the rock facing on the small station, telling us it was mined from a quarry in nearby Crab Orchard. I spread the quilt across my lap and waited for the others to come back. The driver smiled and said, "You're sure holding onto that quilt. Are you cold or just missin' home already?"

"Neither," I said.

We stopped in Nashville for lunch and a driver change. As the driver collected his things to leave, he pointed and said, "Now that's east, and that building you see about half-way down the block is the Ryman

Auditorium and the Grand Ole Opry. Maybe you'll have time to hear them play on your return trip."

It seemed only minutes had passed before a new driver was backing out of track one and we were leaving Nashville, passing by Vanderbilt University and crossing Nine-Mile Hill. This wasn't the Tennessee I knew. From Sparta to Nashville to the western branch of the Tennessee River, the hills were fewer and smaller, and, after crossing the river, the terrain suddenly became nearly flat.

Daylight started to wane shortly after our stop in Jackson and just before Cobbs, darkness was complete. I thought of my grandmother. I could smell her on the quilt. I hadn't slept or even closed my eyes for a single mile of the 485 miles from Maynard Bald to Memphis, almost the entire length of Tennessee. I was still on fire with excitement. "How can these people be so quiet, so still? Some even sleeping like they were in comas. An outrage," I thought.

We passed a sign that said "LOOSAHATCHIE RIVER," and I knew we must be getting close to Memphis. Two Army boys behind me discussed whether they would use their short time in Memphis to have something to eat or walk two blocks south to the blues district on Beale Street. "You can eat anytime," one said. The decision was made.

Although it was dark now, and I could see only lights that seemed to stretch across Memphis and all the way up to the night sky, it didn't matter. For the first time in my life, I was not straining to see something too far away or too much out of the light. I was not hungry for unknown and unnamed things. I looked out at the lights along the Mississippi River as we crossed the bridge from Tennessee to Arkansas.

Tethered to Wanting

The relentless, uncontrollable yearning slowly faded, dwindled away, disappearing into the night as quietly as rolling fog.

ABOUT THE AUTHOR

Constance Huddleston Anderson was born and raised in LaFollette, Tennessee. She holds a Bachelor of Arts Degree from the University of Alabama, Huntsville. She earned a Master of Arts Degree from Chapman University, Orange, California, and a Doctorate from The George Washington University, Washington, D.C. She currently lives in the Blue Grass Valley of Virginia's Allegheny Highlands. *Tethered to Wanting* is her first novel.

Contact me at: drconsande@gmail.com
http://www.abednigohoggepress.com

Cover photo by Emma McCarty

30499201R00209

Made in the USA
Middletown, DE
27 March 2016